REDLANDS

VOLUME ONE: SISTERS BY BLOOD

JORDIE BELLAIRE writer & color artist

VANESA R. DEL REY artist

CLAYTON COWLES letterer & production

HEATHER ANTOS story consultant

Logo by FONOGRAFIKS

IMAGE COMICS, INC. • Robert Kirkman: Chief Operating Officer • Erik Larsen: Chief Financial Officer • Todd McFarlane: President • Marc Silvestri: Chief Executive Officer • Jim Valentino: Vice President • Eric Stephenson: Publisher / Chief Creative Officer • Corey Hart: Director of Sales • Jeff Boison: Director of Publishing Planning & Book Trade Sales • Chris Ross: Director of Digital Sales • Jeff Stang: Director of Specialty Sales • Kat Salazar: Director of PR & Marketing • Drew Gill: Art Director • Heather Doornink: Production Director • Nicole Lapalme: Controller • **IMAGECOMICS.COM**

ISBN: 978-1-5343-0500-7
ISBN FP/BB Exclusive: 978-1-5343-0909-8
ISBN Independent Bookstore Day Exclusive: 978-5343-0821-3

"To my mother and father who never thought twice about showing me rated-R movies when I was child, this is all because of you."
-Jordie

"To the readers."
-Vanesa

"To all of the witches I know. There are at least two. Jordie is one of them."
-Clayton

This book you've got in your hands - This beautiful, mysterious, bloody tale - I really, seriously want to hate it.

I should explain.

See, REDLANDS is written by Jordie Bellaire. Now, I've had the honor to work with Ms. Bellaire on various projects for the last 5 years or so. She colored the first comic I ever did, a small anthology story. She colored the last comic I did before I wrote this sentence, a rather large Batman story. And undoubtedly, which is to say, hopefully, she'll color the next comic I'm going to do after I write this sentence. Fact is, I've won a lot of awards and some fame and a bit of money by writing comics that Ms. Bellaire colored.

The reason I enjoy teaming with Ms. Bellaire is, simply enough, because she is one of the best storytellers in the history of the comics medium. She does with colors what Alan Moore did with words. She does with colors what Jack Kirby did with pencils. She sets the bar for what comics can do within the confines of panels and balloons. She does what the greatest do: through the manipulations of shades of this and that, she grabs the readers tight, takes them on the journey, and sets them down again.

So, when someone that talented at something tries to do something else, there's a natural tendency to be wary. This is for a variety of reasons, some that make sense and most that don't. For me, obviously, the most essential of these reasons is the selfish one: if she's as good at writing as she is at coloring, she might just quit coloring. And I don't think I could tell the stories I want to tell without her.

Which brings us back to the book in your hands and how much I want to despise it. I want it to be amateur as hell. I want it to be filled with those clichés that hack writers love. I want the dialogue to be stilted, the panels to be confusing, the plot to be either wishy-washy or entirely predetermined. Dammit, if nothing else, I want it to be boring!

I want Ms. Bellaire to realize she can't both be a great colorist and a great writer!

But you don't get everything you want in life, I guess.

REDLANDS is a stunning story stunningly well told. It's a comic that cuts into the heart of America, exposing the rot beneath the endless spurts of blood.

As she does in her colors, Ms. Bellaire constructs characters layer by layer, surprising us with her choices but making it clear that such choices were in retrospect the only choices that could be made. As she does with her colors, Ms. Bellaire builds a world that is at once magical and grounded, that inspires fantasy and fear. And as she does with colors, Ms. Bellaire works in perfect sync with her brilliant artist Vanesa Del Rey to create unforgettable images of horror and occasionally, but maybe not, hope.

Fact is, Ms. Bellaire is going to win a lot of awards and some fame and a bit of money by writing comics this well. And, I'm (reluctantly) happy for her success, mostly 'cause I get to read them.

So this book you have in your hands - this brutal, haunting scream of a book - I really, seriously love it.

And probably so will you.

-Tom King
February 2018

Tom King is the Eisner-winning writer of BATMAN, MISTER MIRACLE, THE SHERIFF OF BABYLON, and THE VISION.

CHAPTER ONE

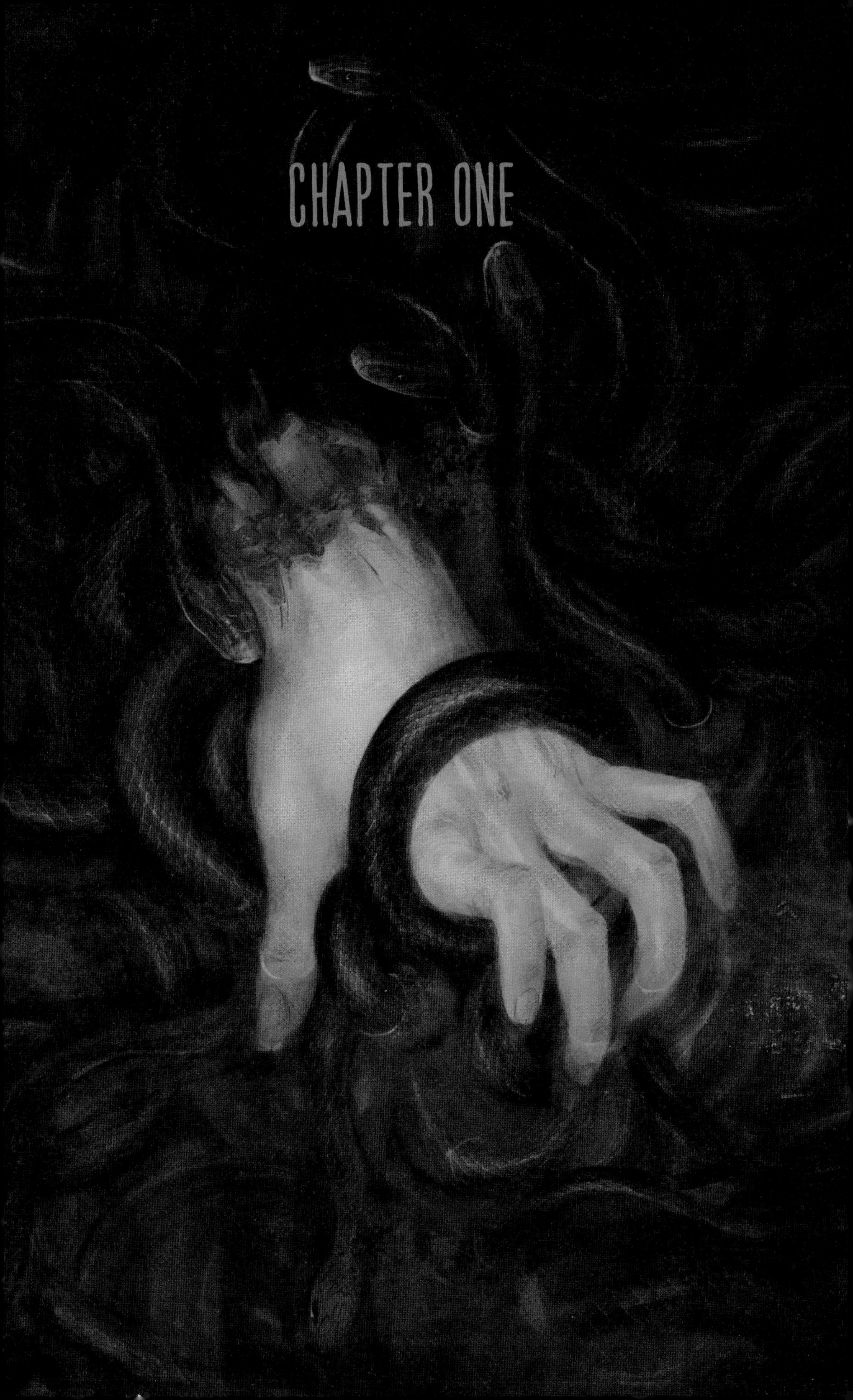

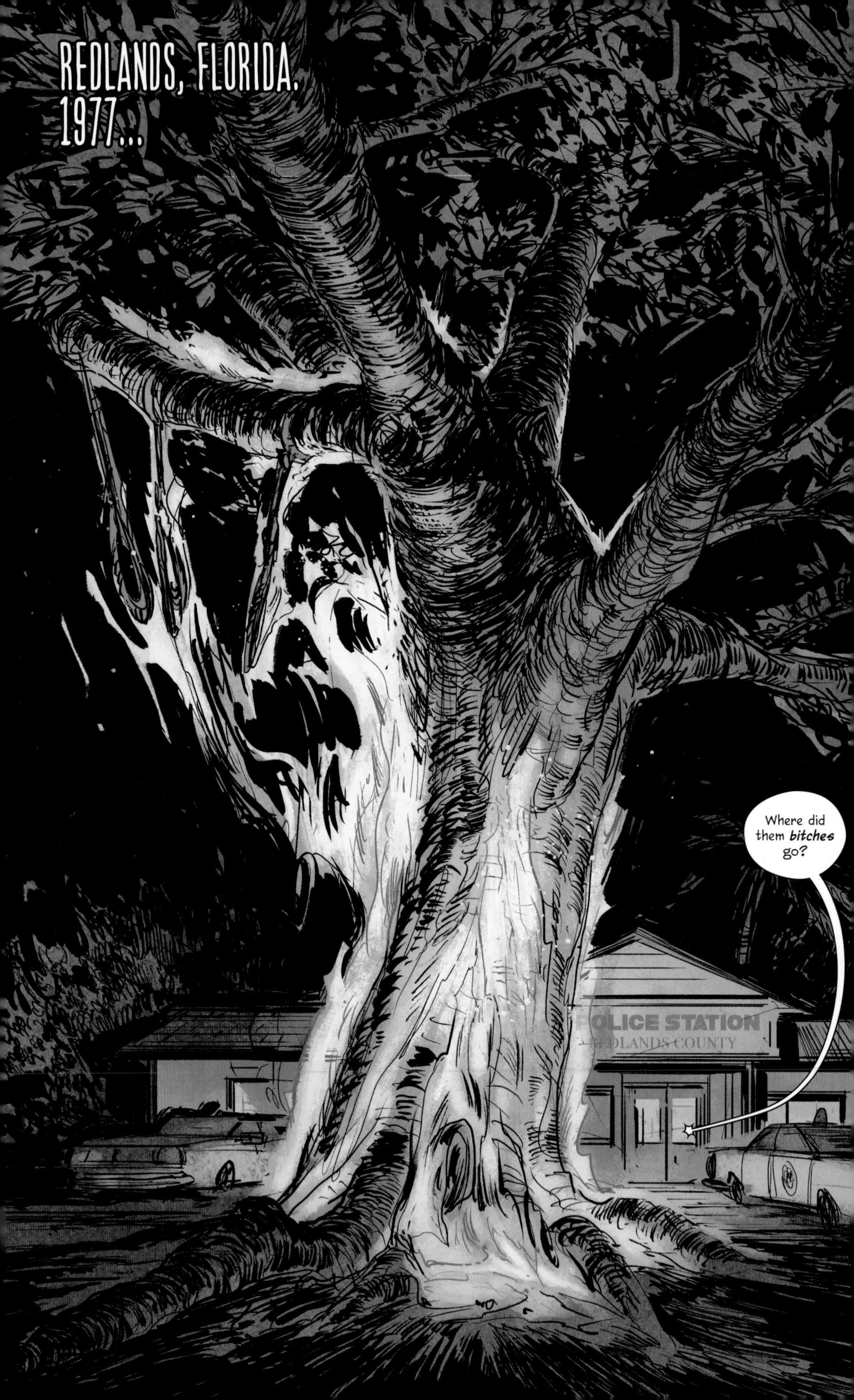
REDLANDS, FLORIDA. 1977...
Where did them *bitches* go?
POLICE STATION
REDLANDS COUNTY

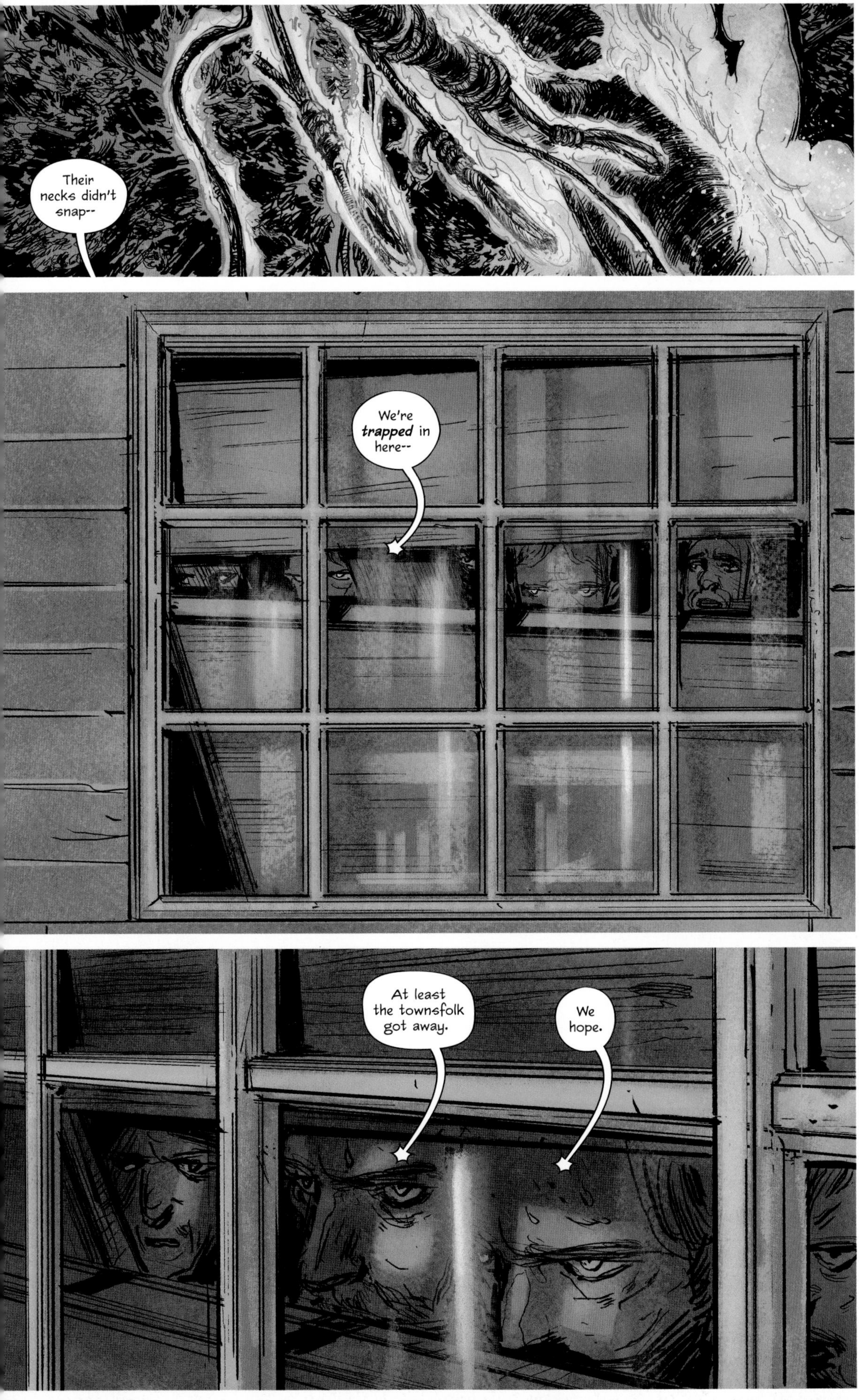
Their necks didn't snap--
We're *trapped* in here--
At least the townsfolk got away.
We hope.

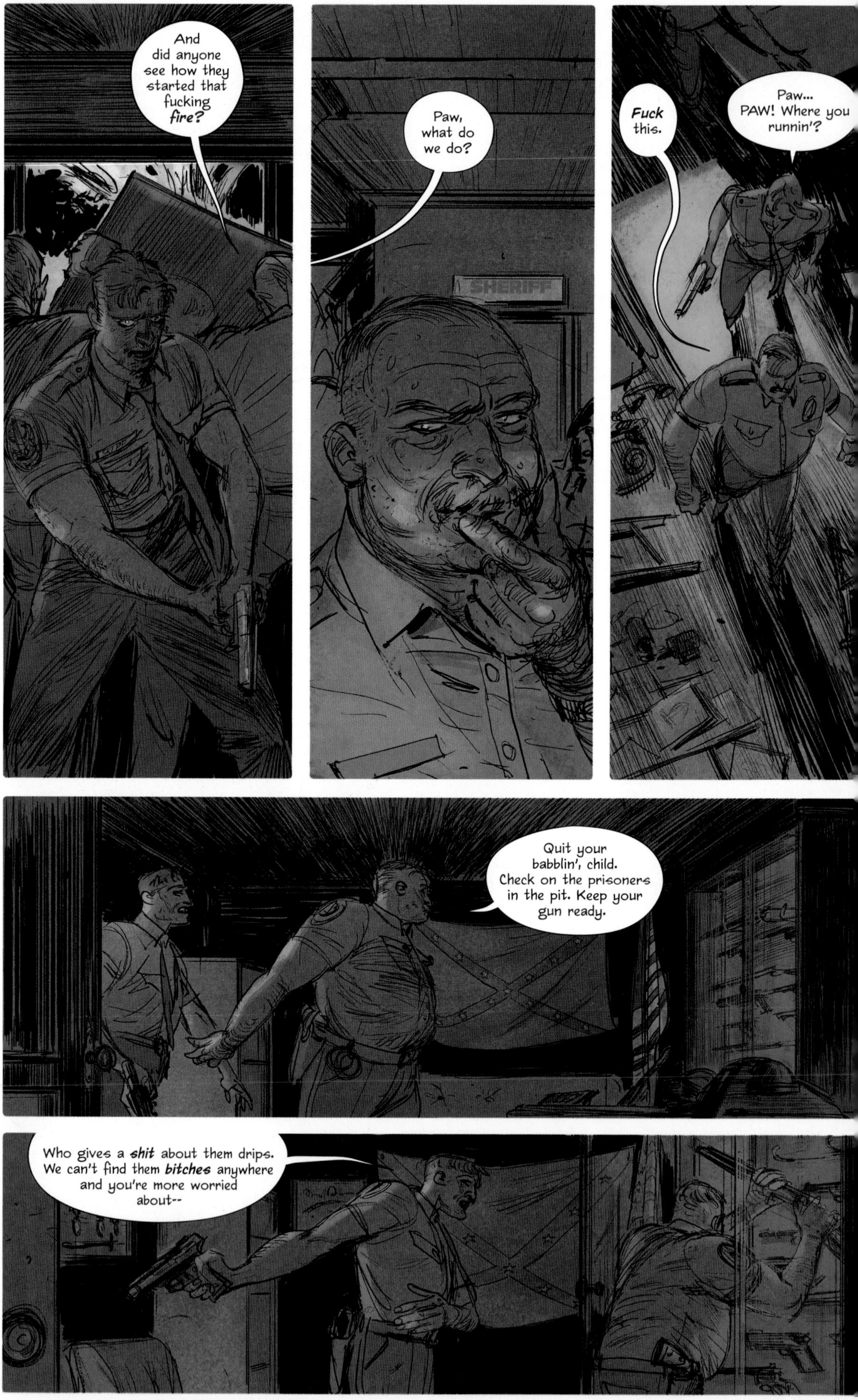
And did anyone see how they started that fucking **fire?**
Paw, what do we do?
Fuck this.
Paw... PAW! Where you runnin'?
Quit your babblin', child. Check on the prisoners in the pit. Keep your gun ready.
SHERIFF
Who gives a **shit** about them drips. We can't find them **bitches** anywhere and you're more worried about--

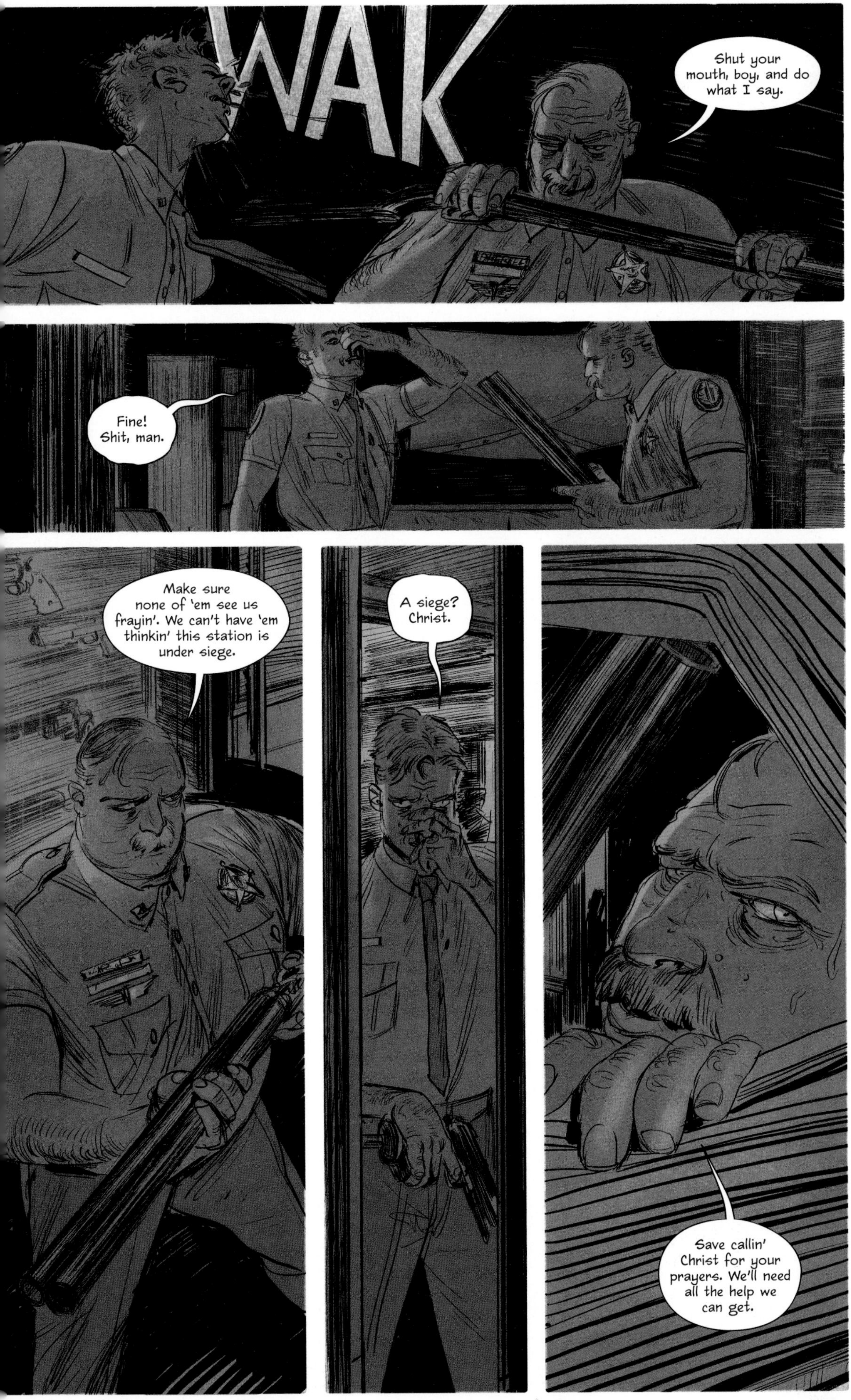
WAK
Shut your mouth, boy, and do what I say.
Fine! Shit, man.
Make sure none of 'em see us frayin'. We can't have 'em thinkin' this station is under siege.
A siege? Christ.
Save callin' Christ for your prayers. We'll need all the help we can get.

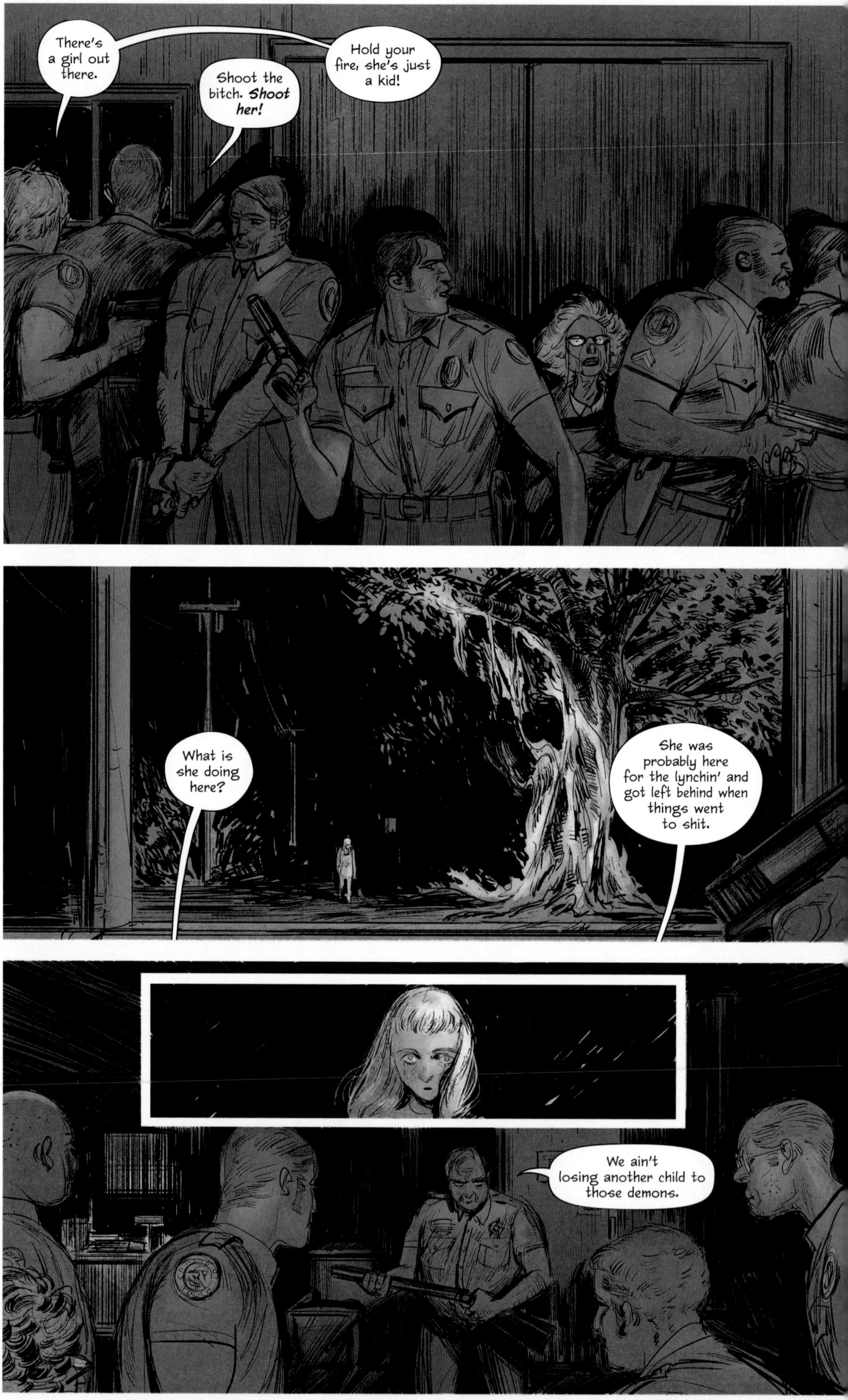
There's a girl out there.
Hold your fire, she's just a kid!
Shoot the bitch. Shoot her!
What is she doing here?
She was probably here for the lynchin' and got left behind when things went to shit.
We ain't losing another child to those demons.

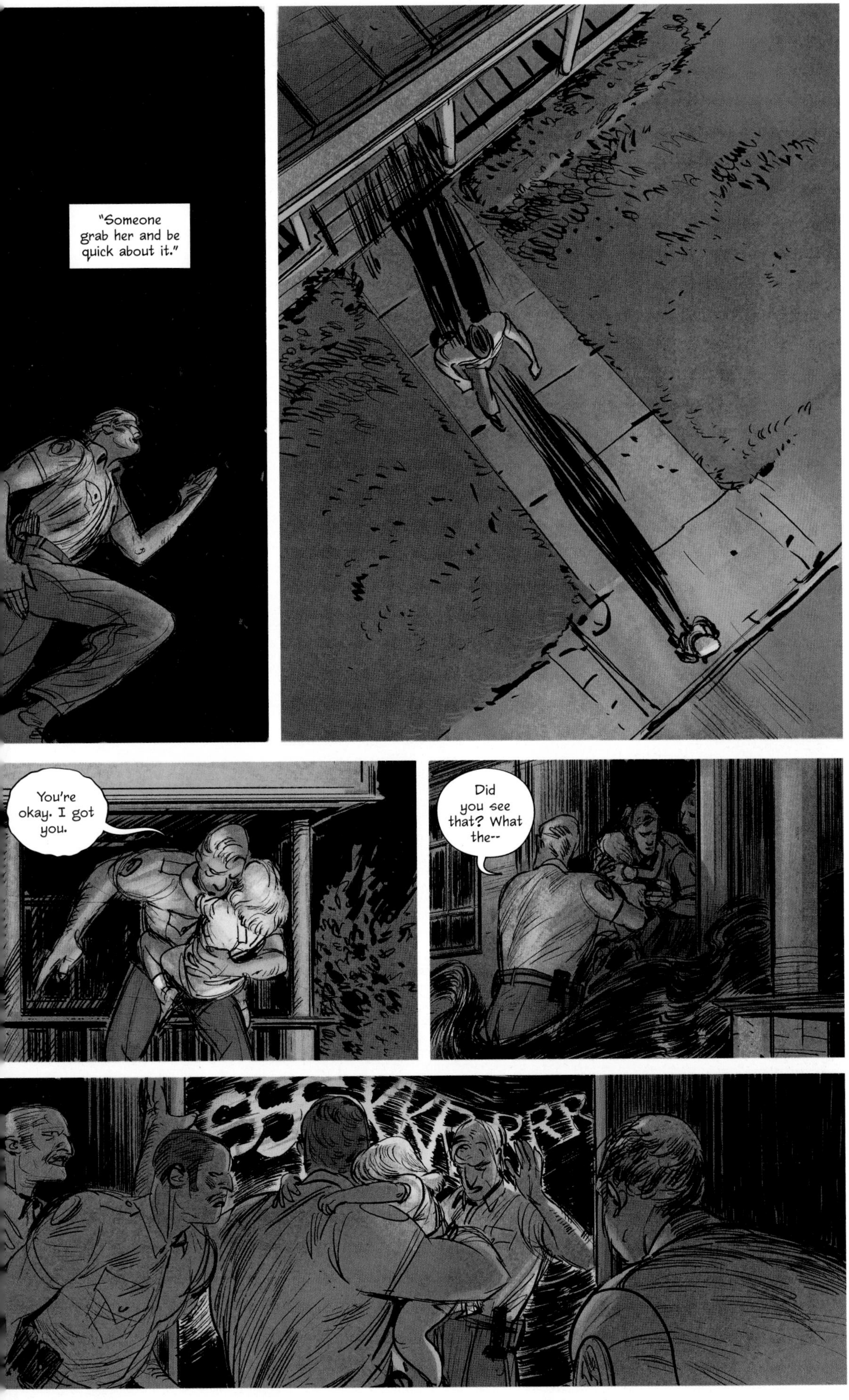
"Someone grab her and be quick about it."
You're okay. I got you.
Did you see that? What the--

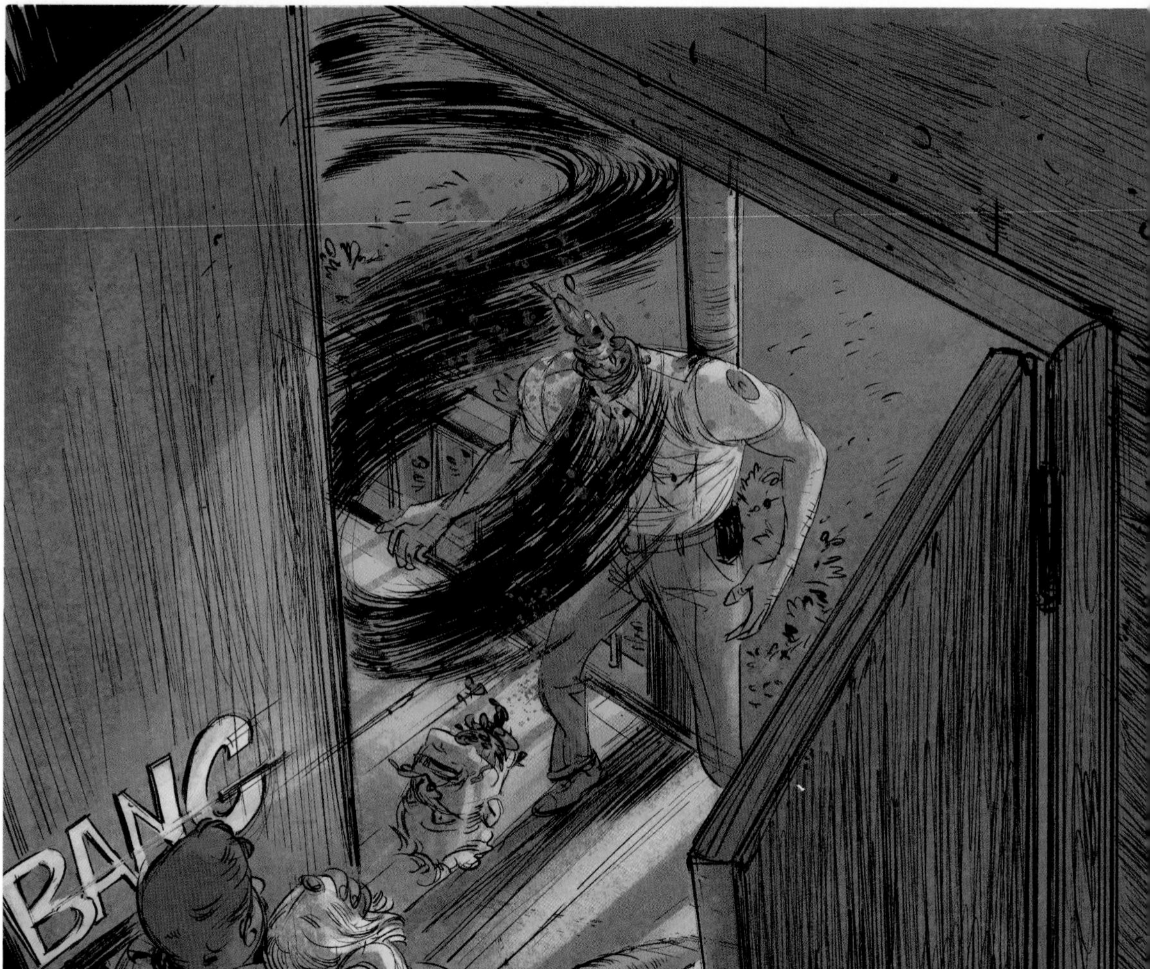
BANG

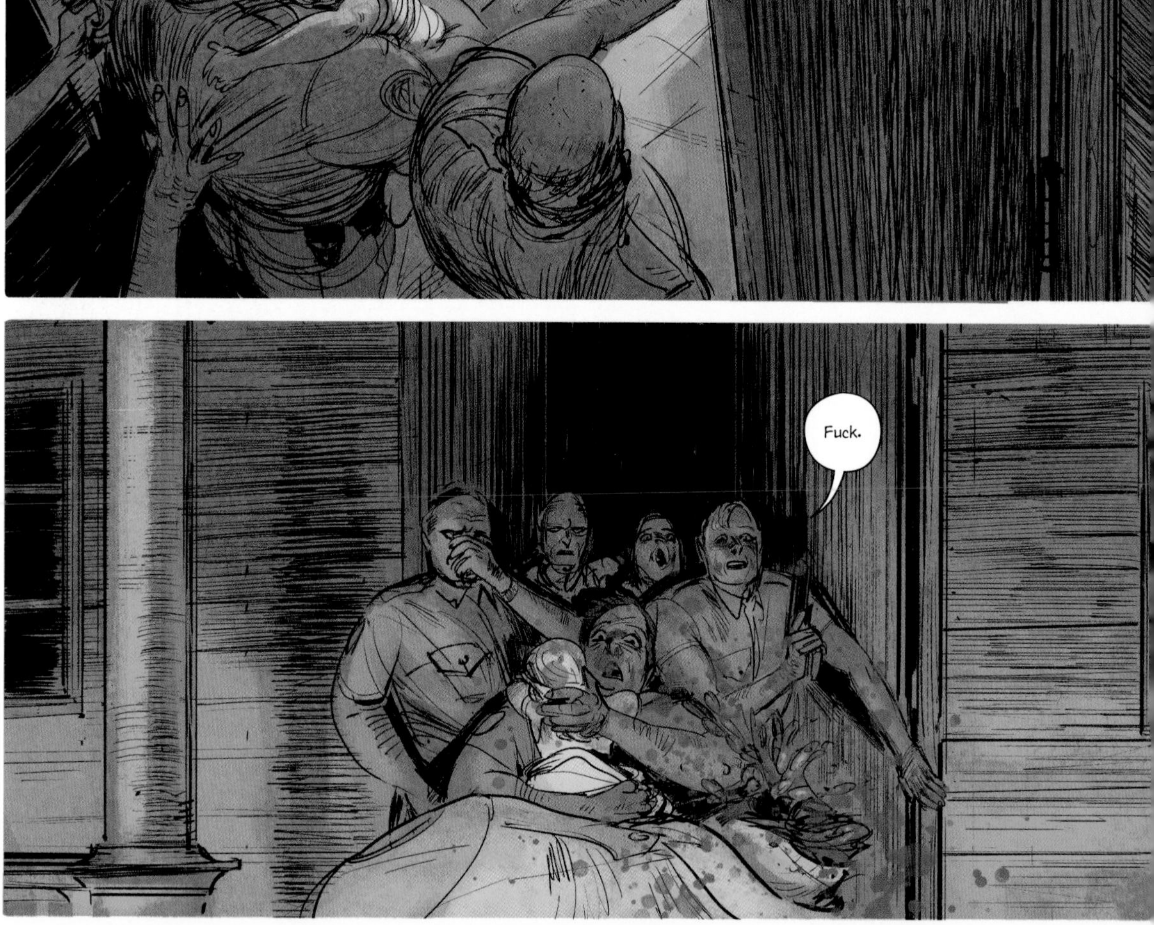
Fuck.

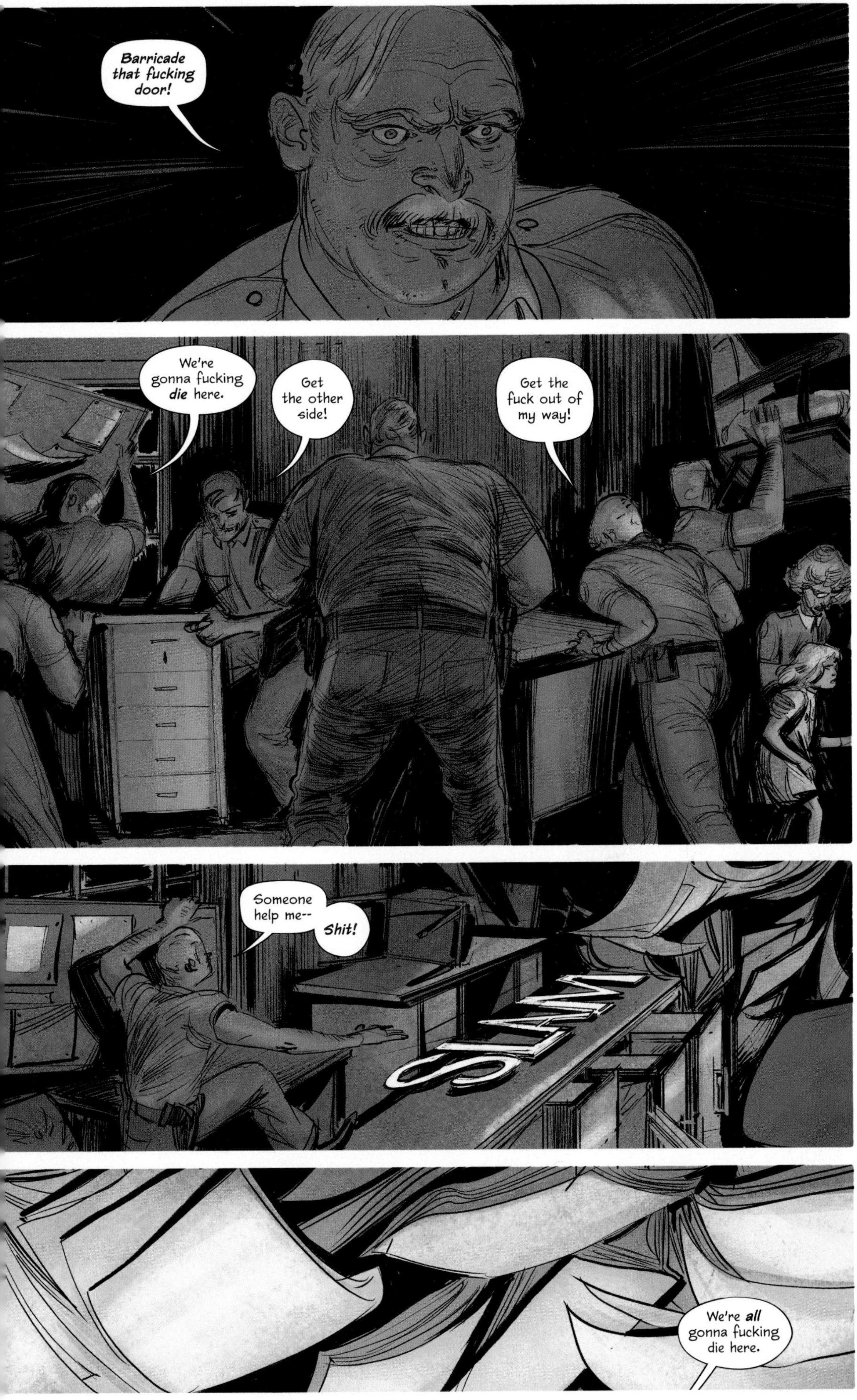
Barricade that fucking door!
We're gonna fucking *die* here.
Get the other side!
Get the fuck out of my way!
Someone help me--
Shit!
SLAM
We're *all* gonna fucking die here.

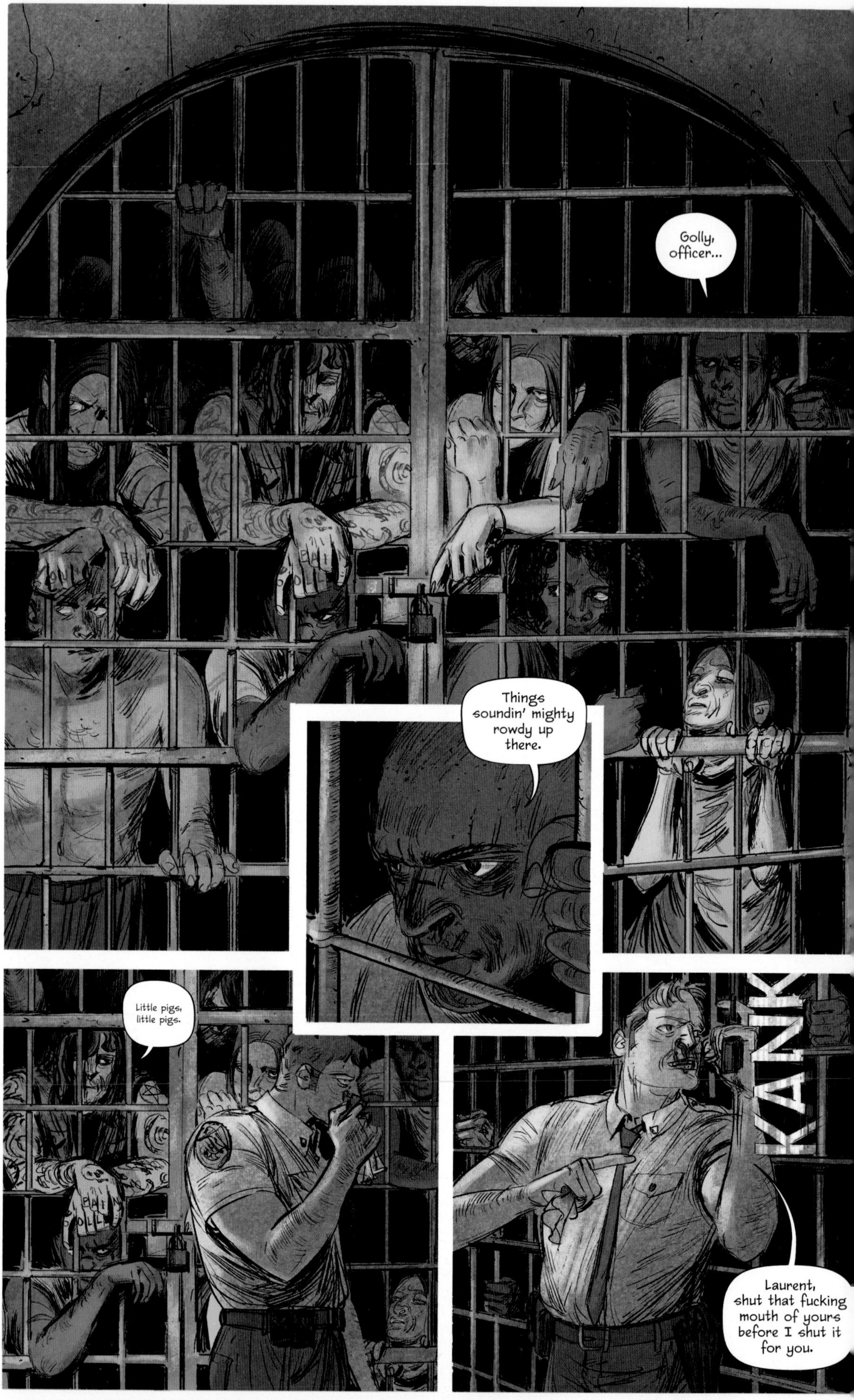
Golly, officer...
Things soundin' mighty rowdy up there.
Little pigs, little pigs.
KANK
Laurent, shut that fucking mouth of yours before I shut it for you.

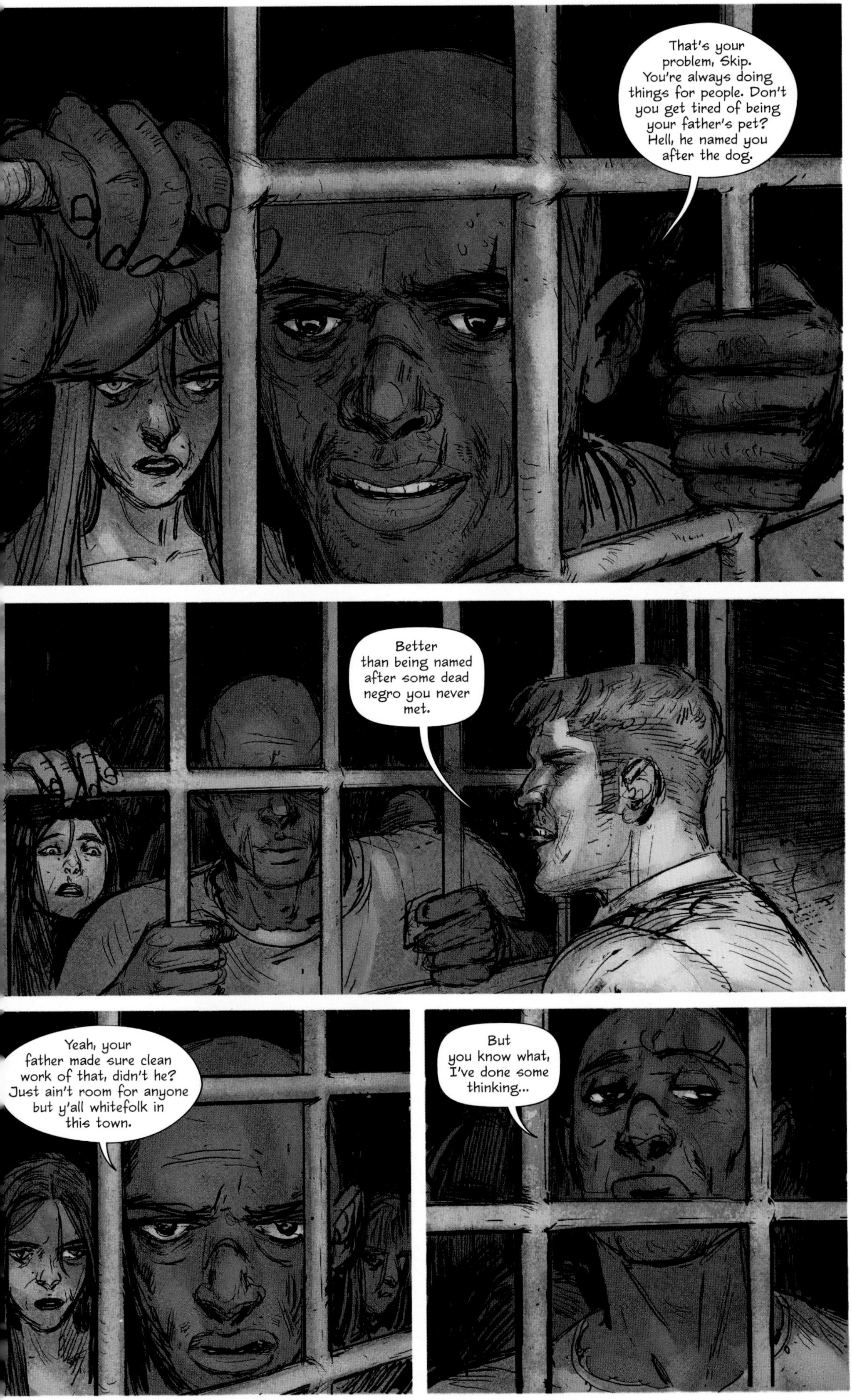
That's your problem, Skip. You're always doing things for people. Don't you get tired of being your father's pet? Hell, he named you after the dog.
Better than being named after some dead negro you never met.
Yeah, your father made sure clean work of that, didn't he? Just ain't room for anyone but y'all whitefolk in this town.
But you know what, I've done some thinking...

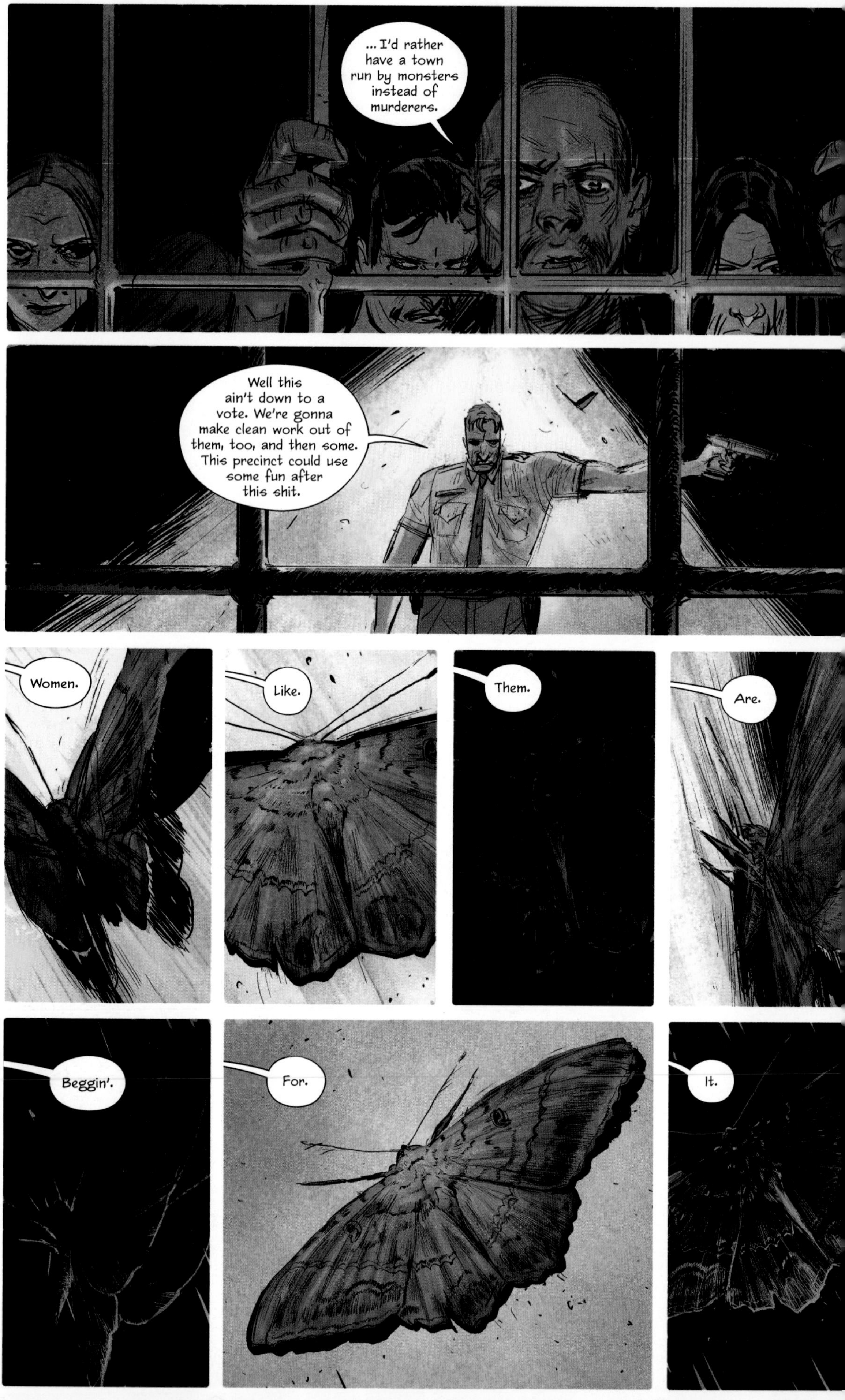
...I'd rather have a town run by monsters instead of murderers.
Well this ain't down to a vote. We're gonna make clean work out of them, too, and then some. This precinct could use some fun after this shit.
Women.
Like.
Them.
Are.
Beggin'.
For.
It.

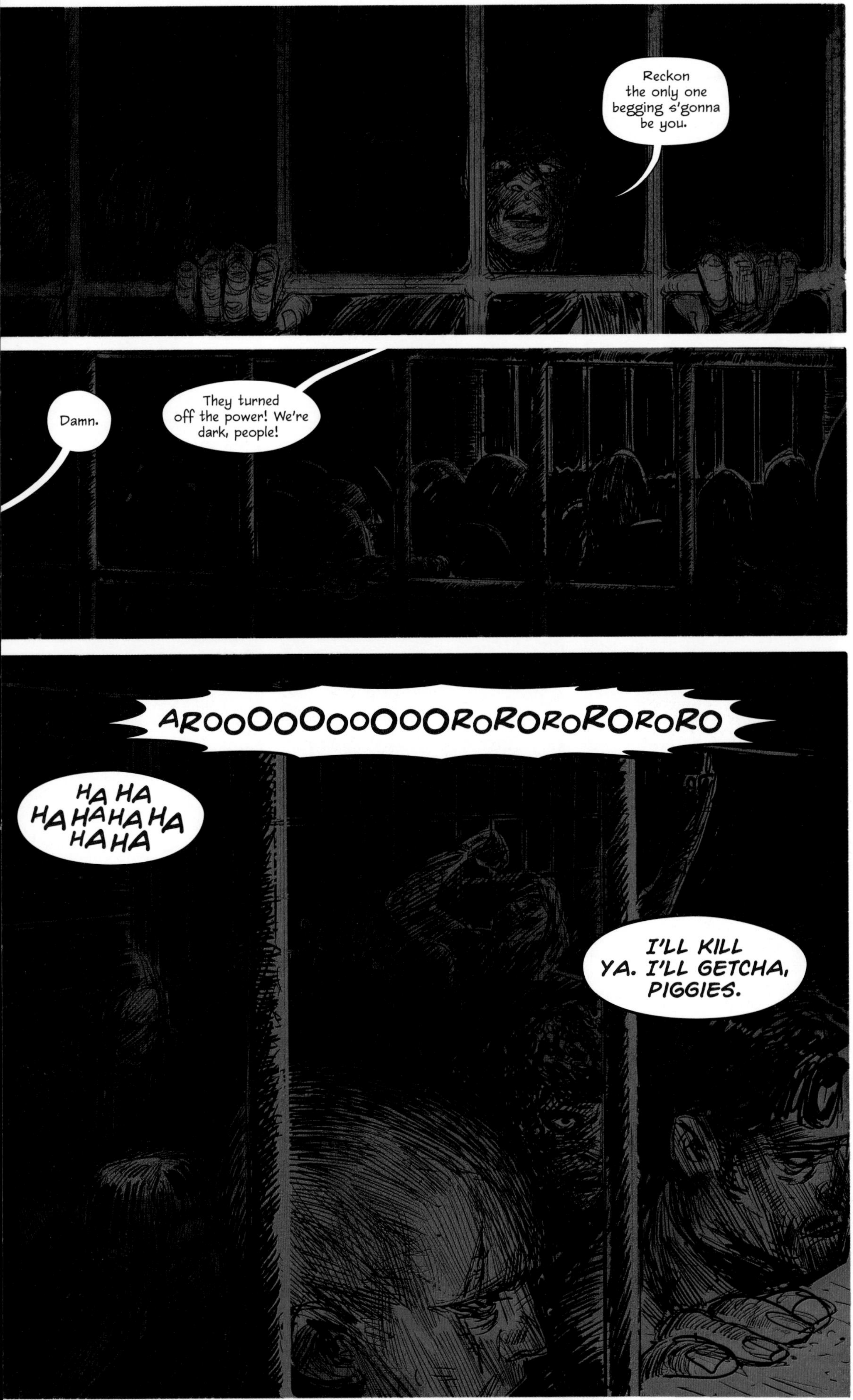
Reckon the only one begging s'gonna be you.
Damn.
They turned off the power! We're dark, people!
AROOOOOOOOOOOOROROROROROROR
HA HA HA HAHAHA HA HA HA
I'LL KILL YA. I'LL GETCHA, PIGGIES.

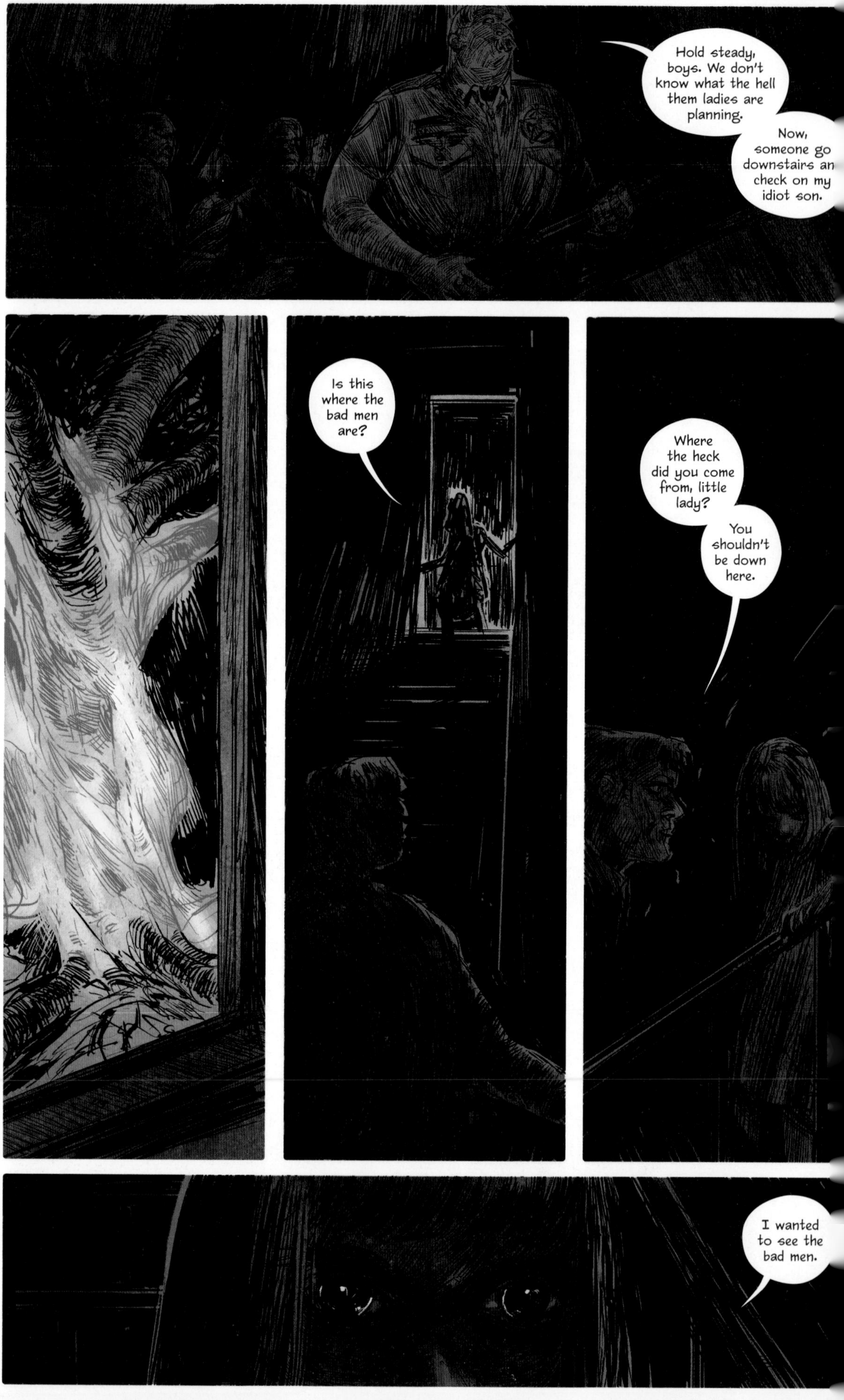
Hold steady, boys. We don't know what the hell them ladies are planning.
Now, someone go downstairs an check on my idiot son.
Is this where the bad men are?
Where the heck did you come from, little lady?
You shouldn't be down here.
I wanted to see the bad men.

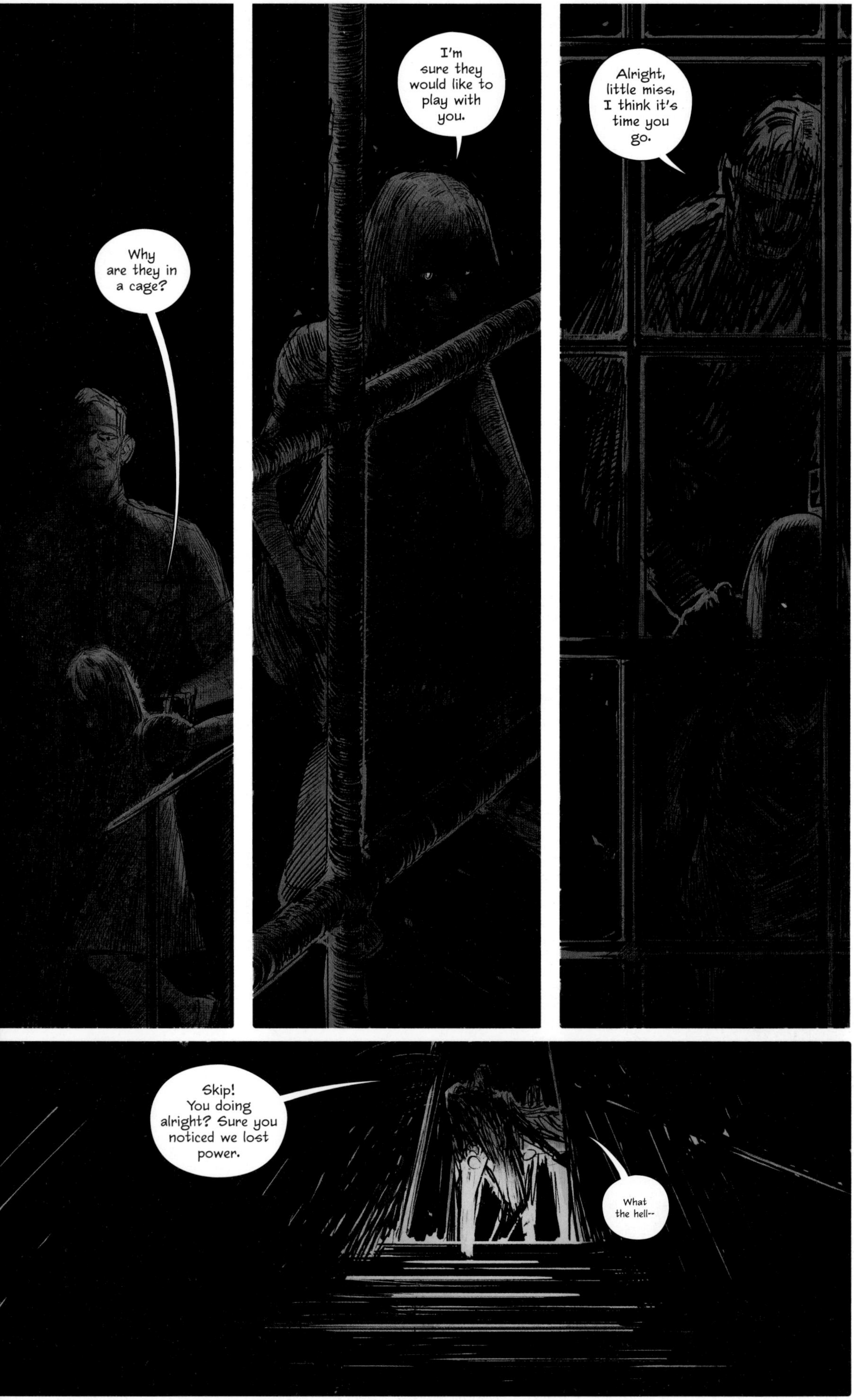
Why are they in a cage?
I'm sure they would like to play with you.
Alright, little miss, I think it's time you go.
Skip! You doing alright? Sure you noticed we lost power.
What the hell--

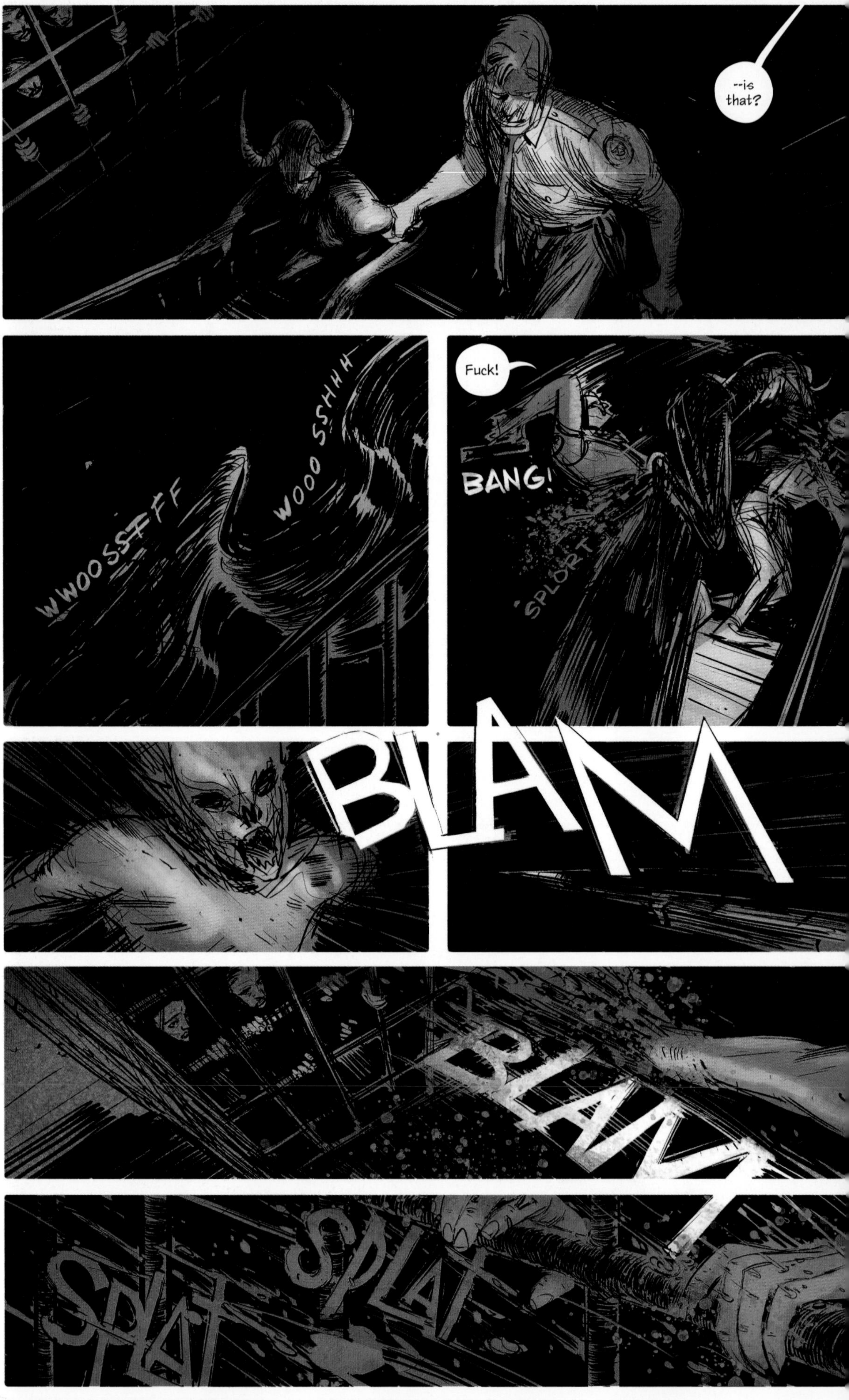
--is that?
WWOOSSFFF
WOOO SSHHH
Fuck!
BANG!
SPLORT
BLAM
BLAM
SPLAT
SPLAT

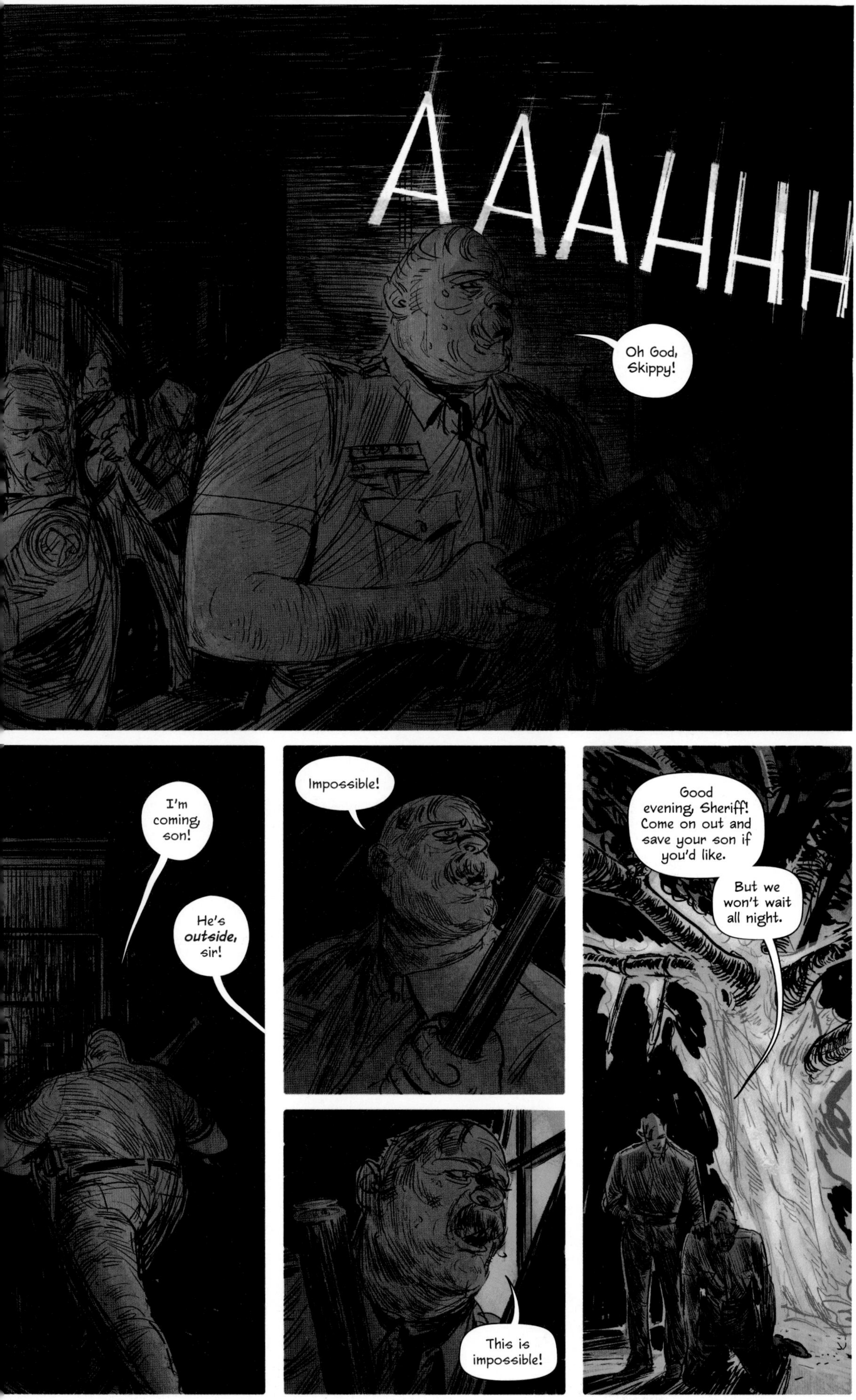
AAAHHHH
Oh God, Skippy!
I'm coming, son!
He's *outside,* sir!
Impossible!
This is impossible!
Good evening, Sheriff! Come on out and save your son if you'd like.
But we won't wait all night.

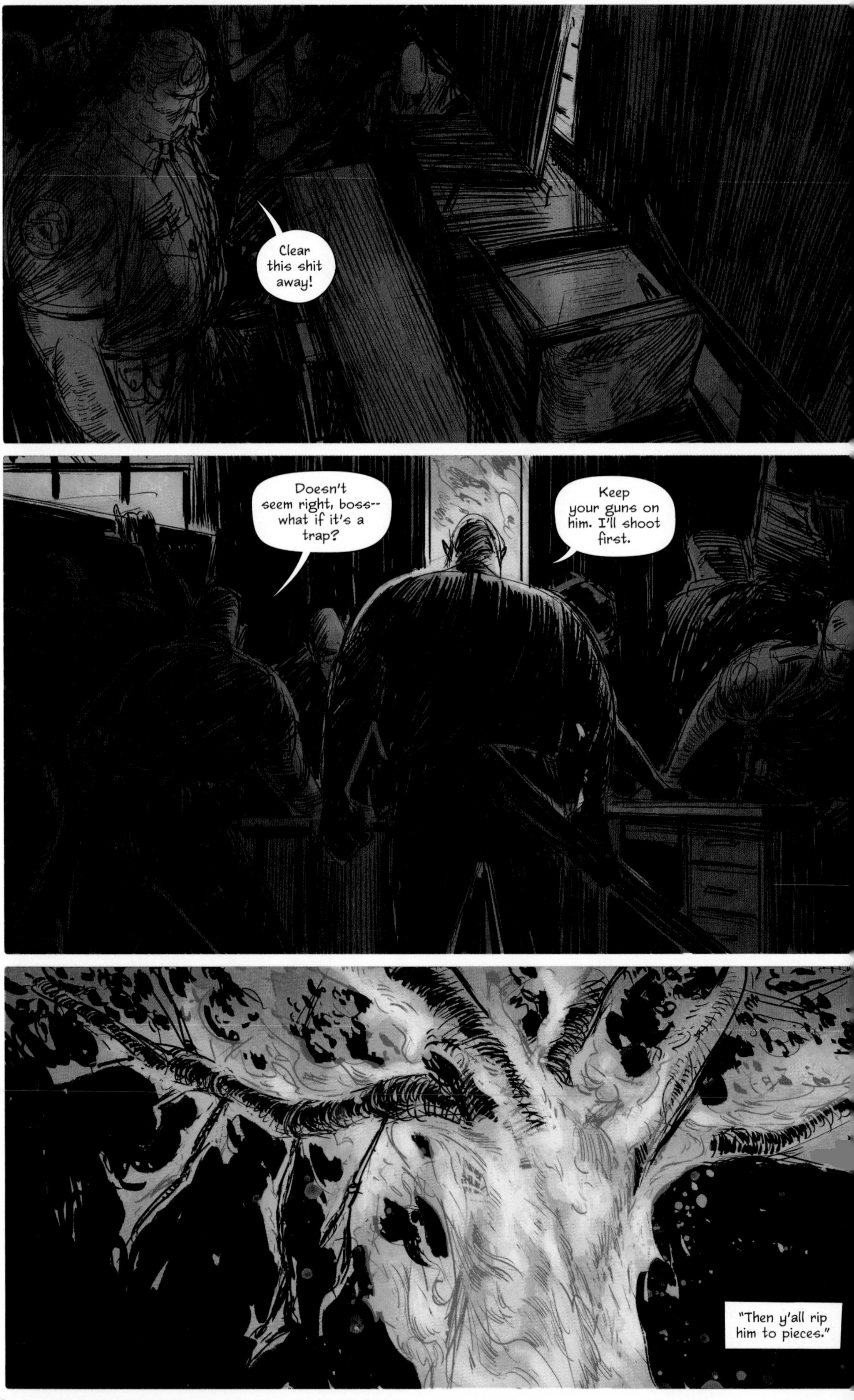
Clear this shit away!
Doesn't seem right, boss-- what if it's a trap?
Keep your guns on him. I'll shoot first.
"Then y'all rip him to pieces."

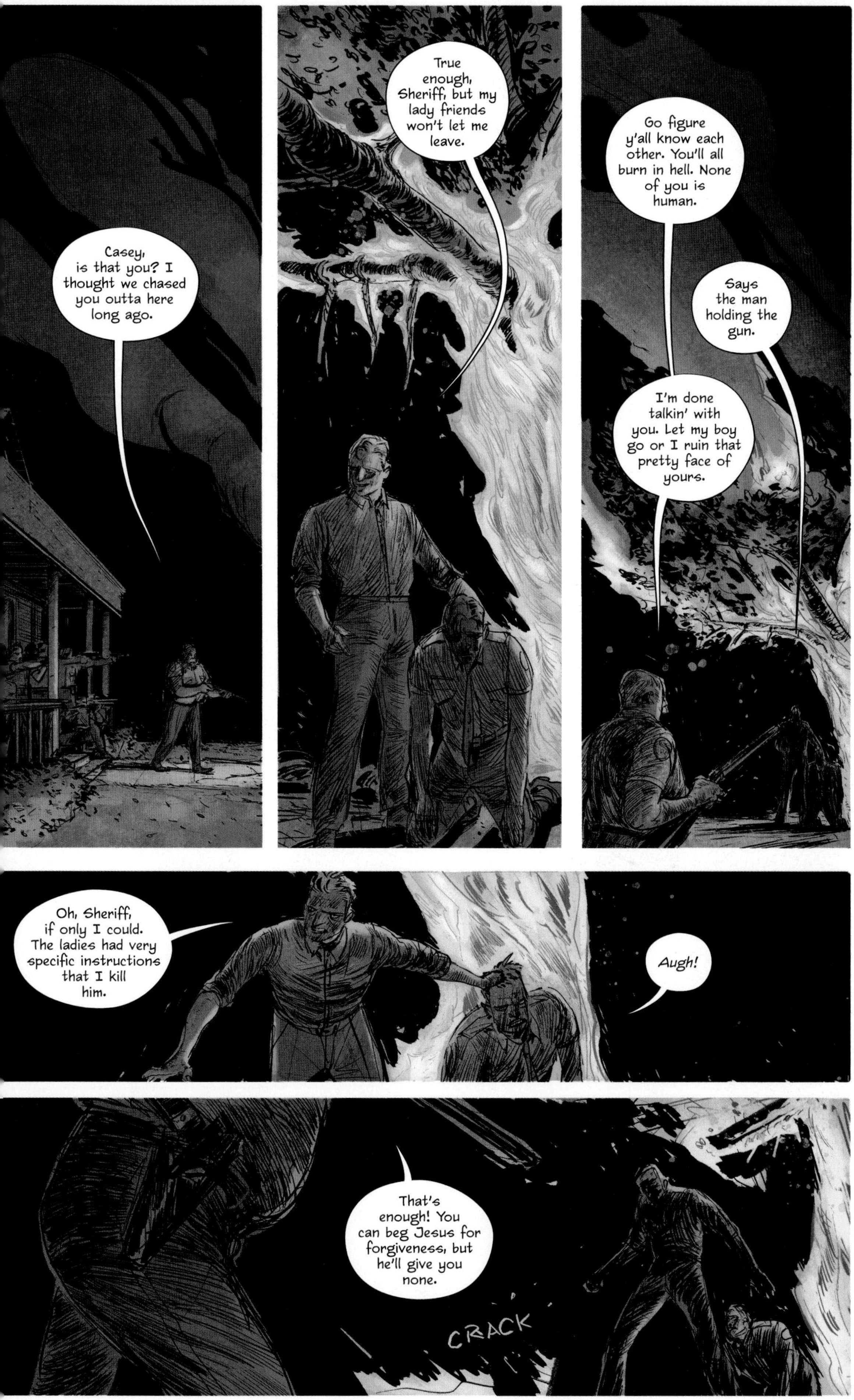
Casey, is that you? I thought we chased you outta here long ago.
True enough, Sheriff, but my lady friends won't let me leave.
Go figure y'all know each other. You'll all burn in hell. None of you is human.
Says the man holding the gun.
I'm done talkin' with you. Let my boy go or I ruin that pretty face of yours.
Oh, Sheriff, if only I could. The ladies had very specific instructions that I kill him.
Augh!
That's enough! You can beg Jesus for forgiveness, but he'll give you none.
CRACK

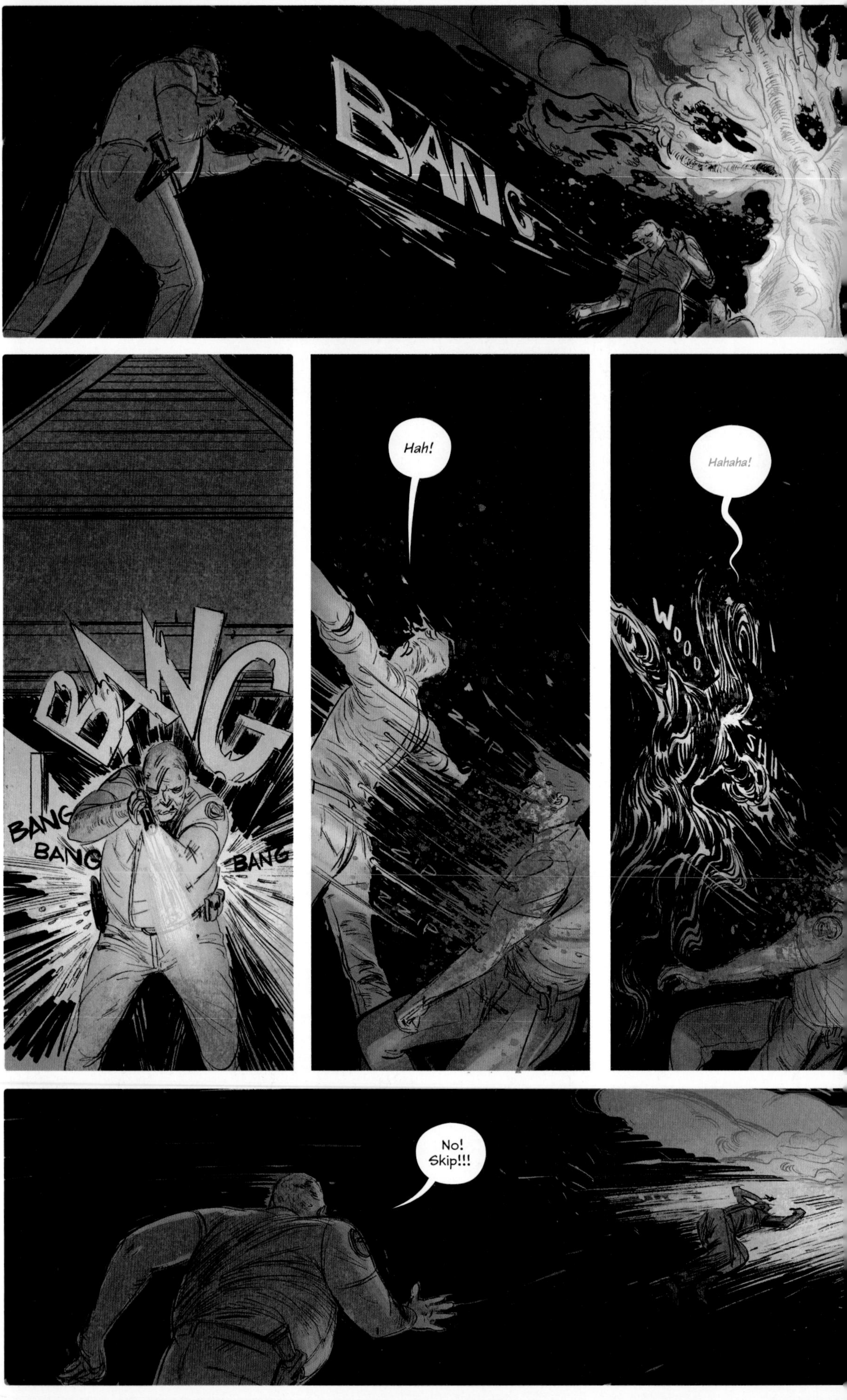
BANG
BANG
BANG
BANG
BANG
Hah!
Hahaha!
WOOOOSH!!
No! Skip!!!

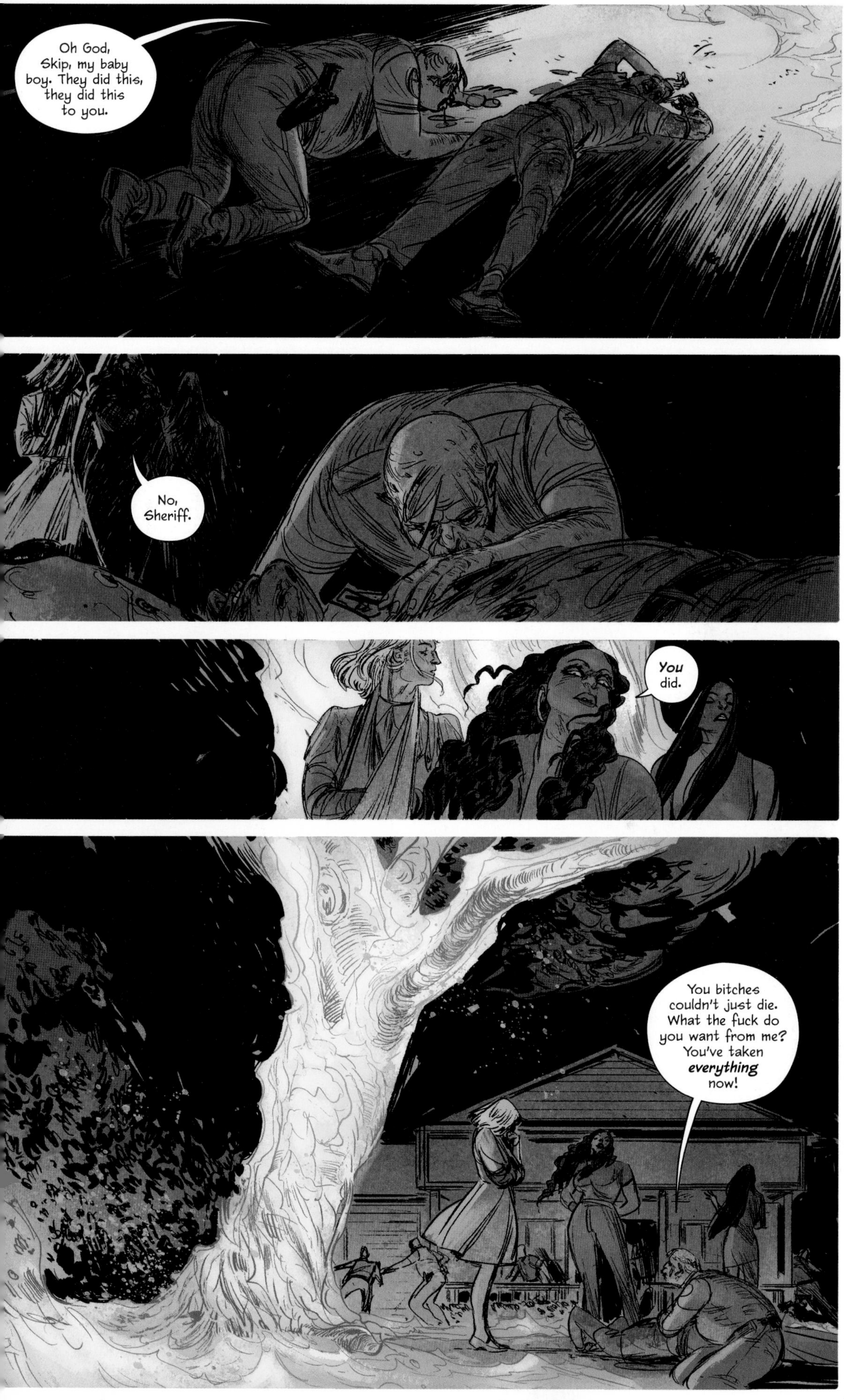
Oh God, Skip, my baby boy. They did this, they did this to you.
No, Sheriff.
You did.
You bitches couldn't just die. What the fuck do you want from me? You've taken everything now!

We chose this town because we saw it needed the most. Your soil is rot. Your people are vacant. We needed a place to make *new...*

"... through *sacrifice...*

WAK   BANG   UMFF

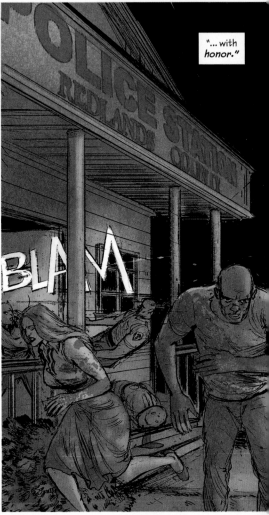

"... with *honor.*"

BLAM

We've seen it for centuries. Kings like you take all you want and never give back. Your dynasty has come to an end. No one is left to take your throne. You're already forgotten.

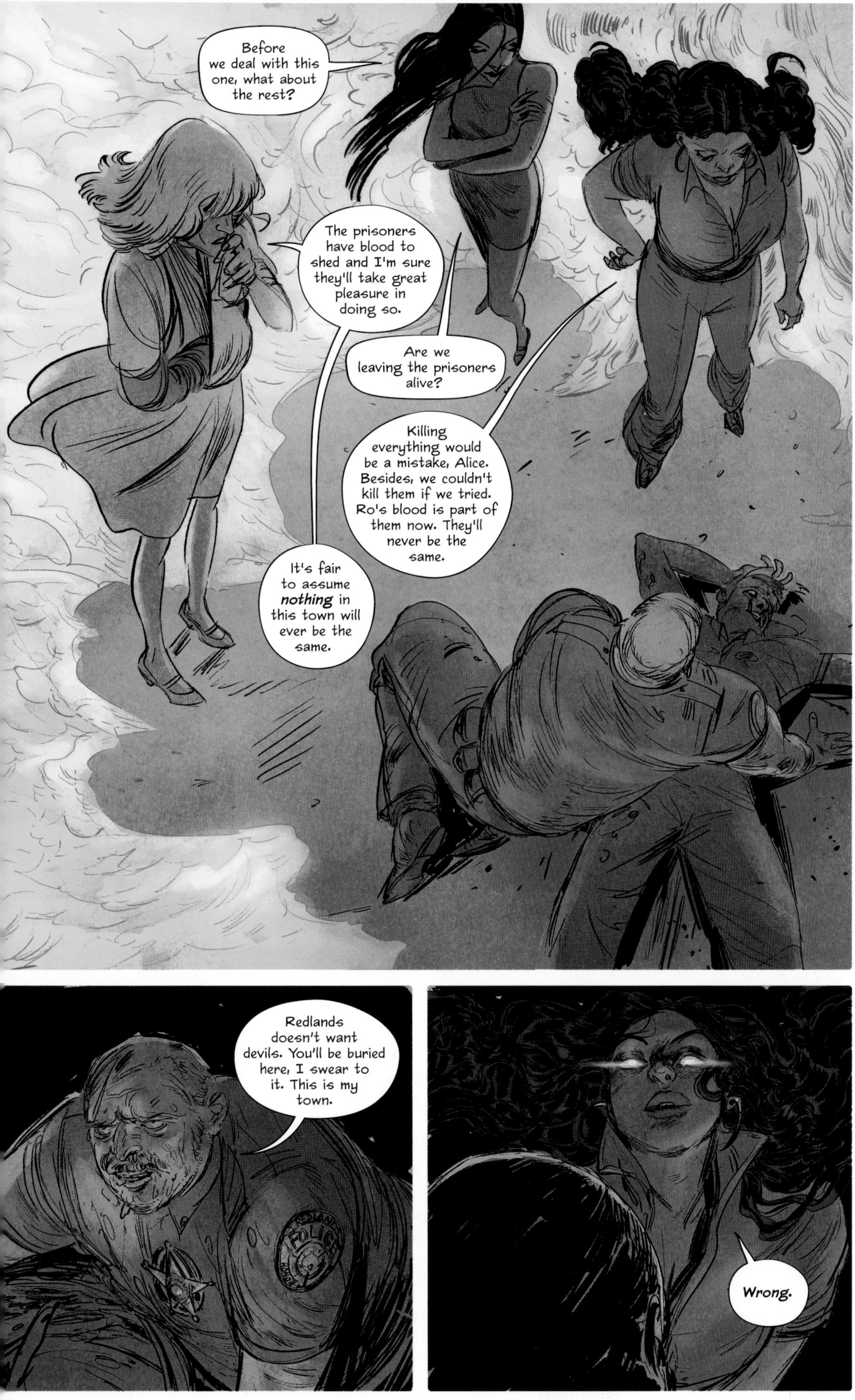
Before we deal with this one, what about the rest?
The prisoners have blood to shed and I'm sure they'll take great pleasure in doing so.
Are we leaving the prisoners alive?
Killing everything would be a mistake, Alice. Besides, we couldn't kill them if we tried. Ro's blood is part of them now. They'll never be the same.
It's fair to assume *nothing* in this town will ever be the same.
Redlands doesn't want devils. You'll be buried here, I swear to it. This is my town.
Wrong.

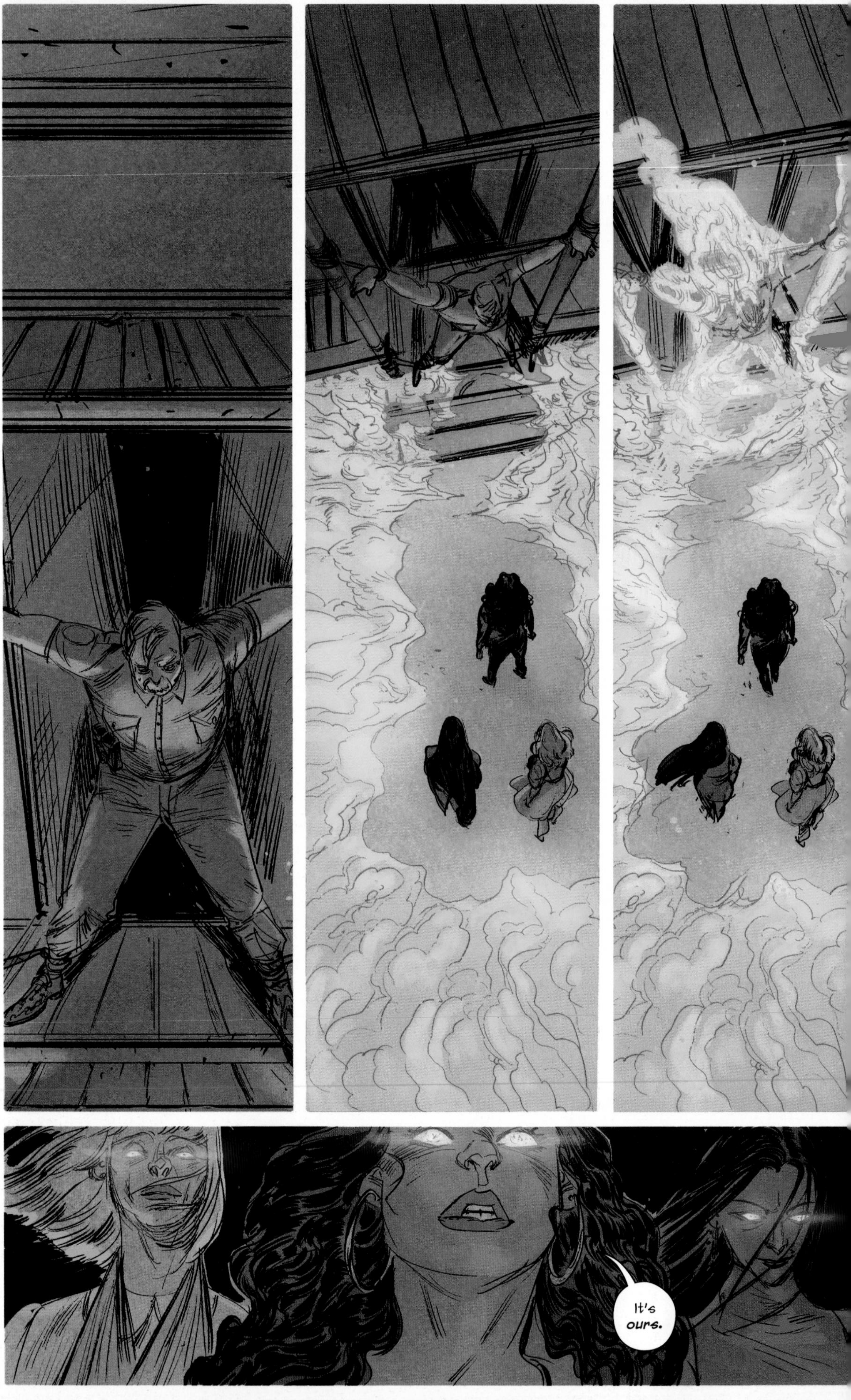
It's ours.

CHAPTER TWO

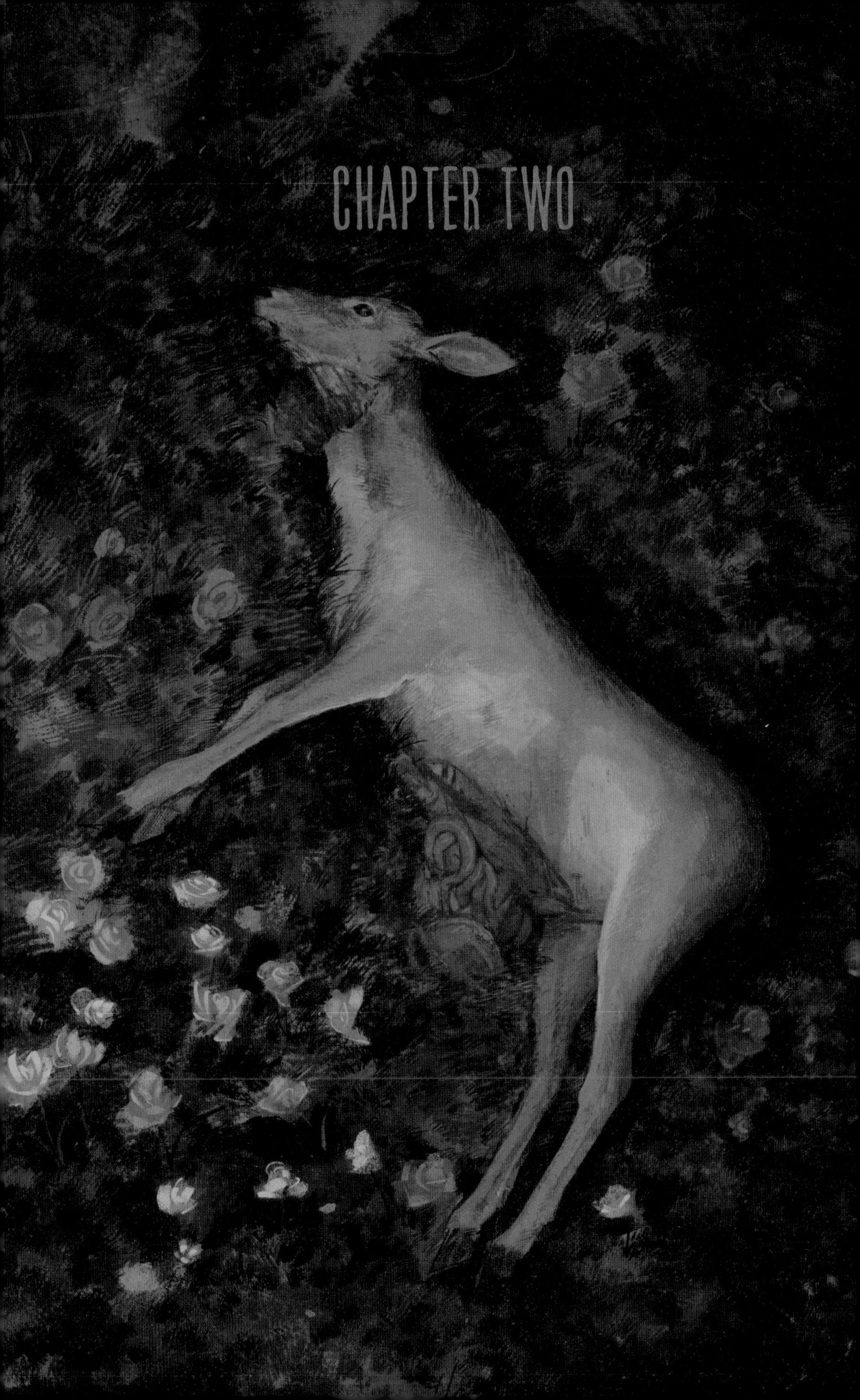

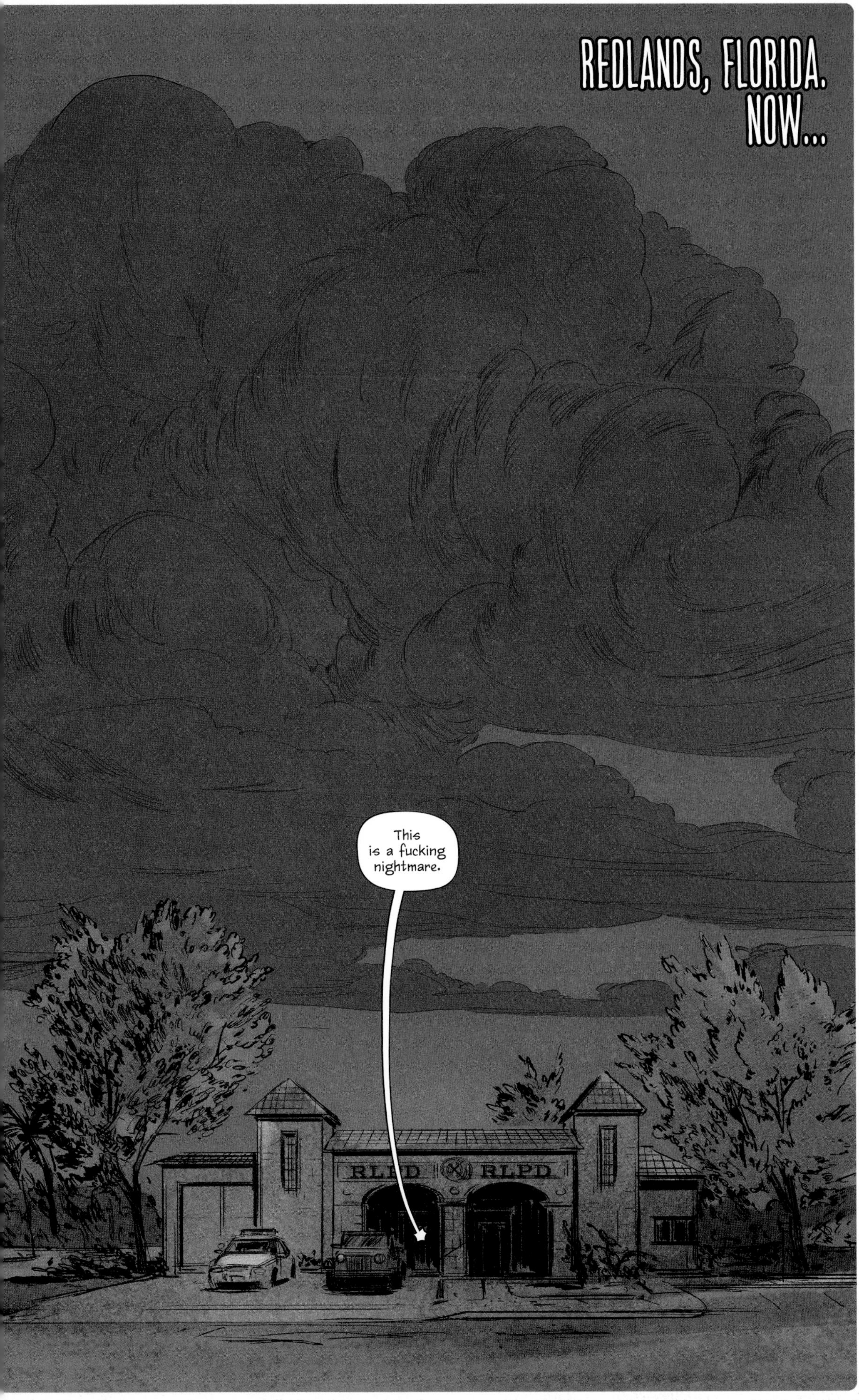
REDLANDS, FLORIDA. NOW...
This is a fucking nightmare.
RLPD RLPD

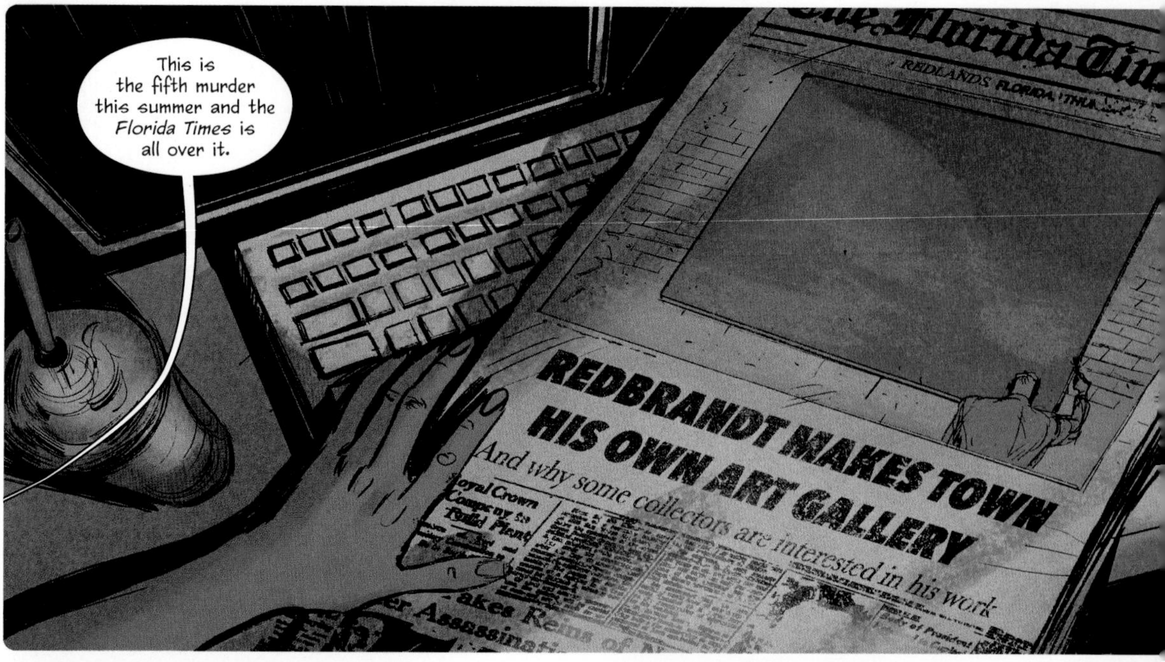
This is the fifth murder this summer and the *Florida Times* is all over it.
REDBRANDT MAKES TOWN HIS OWN ART GALLERY
And why some collectors are interested in his work

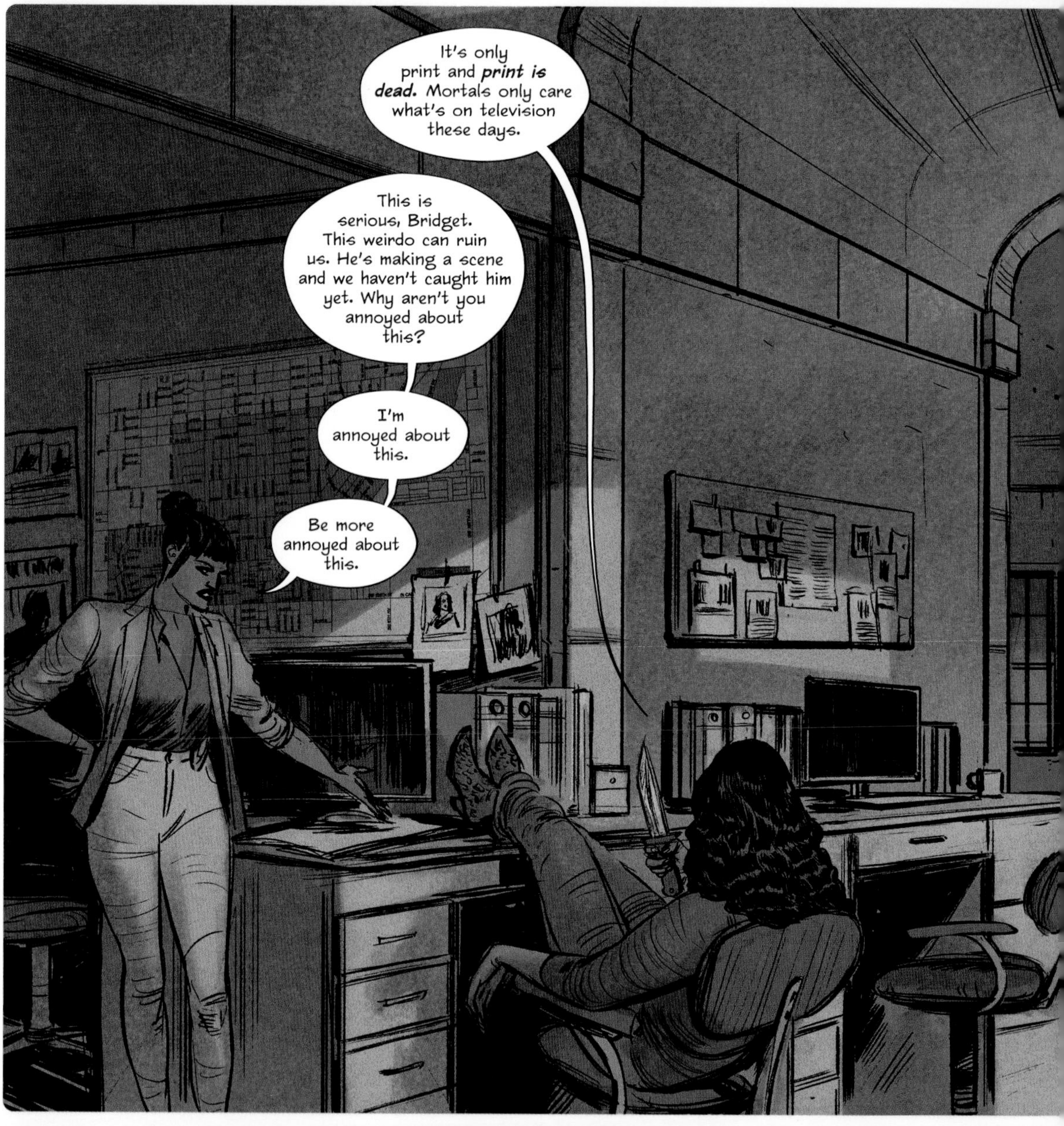
It's only print and ***print is dead.*** Mortals only care what's on television these days.
This is serious, Bridget. This weirdo can ruin us. He's making a scene and we haven't caught him yet. Why aren't you annoyed about this?
I'm annoyed about this.
Be more annoyed about this.

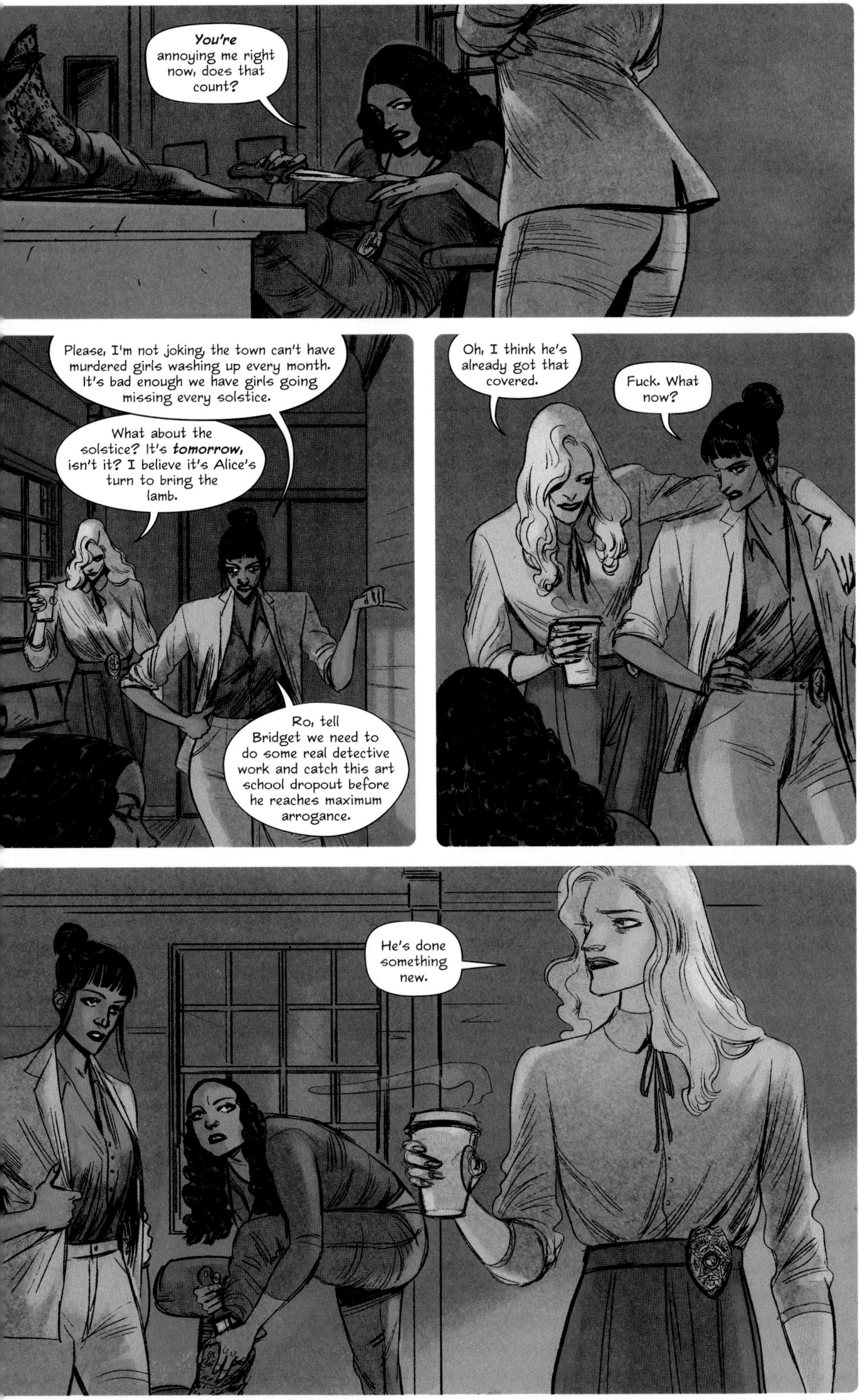
You're annoying me right now, does that count?
Please, I'm not joking, the town can't have murdered girls washing up every month. It's bad enough we have girls going missing every solstice.
What about the solstice? It's *tomorrow,* isn't it? I believe it's Alice's turn to bring the lamb.
Ro, tell Bridget we need to do some real detective work and catch this art school dropout before he reaches maximum arrogance.
Oh, I think he's already got that covered.
Fuck. What now?
He's done something new.

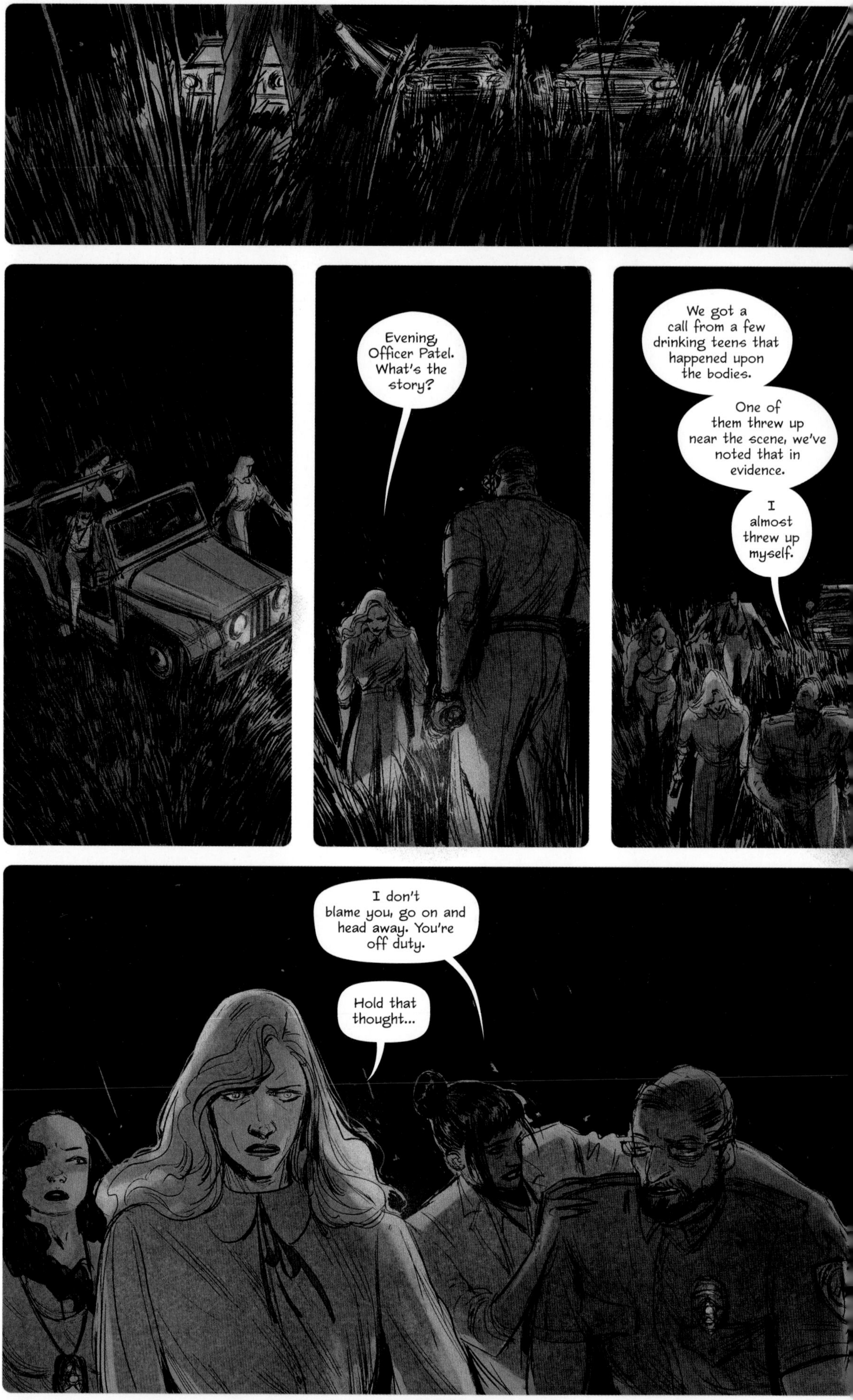
Evening, Officer Patel. What's the story?
We got a call from a few drinking teens that happened upon the bodies.
One of them threw up near the scene, we've noted that in evidence.
I almost threw up myself.
I don't blame you, go on and head away. You're off duty.
Hold that thought...

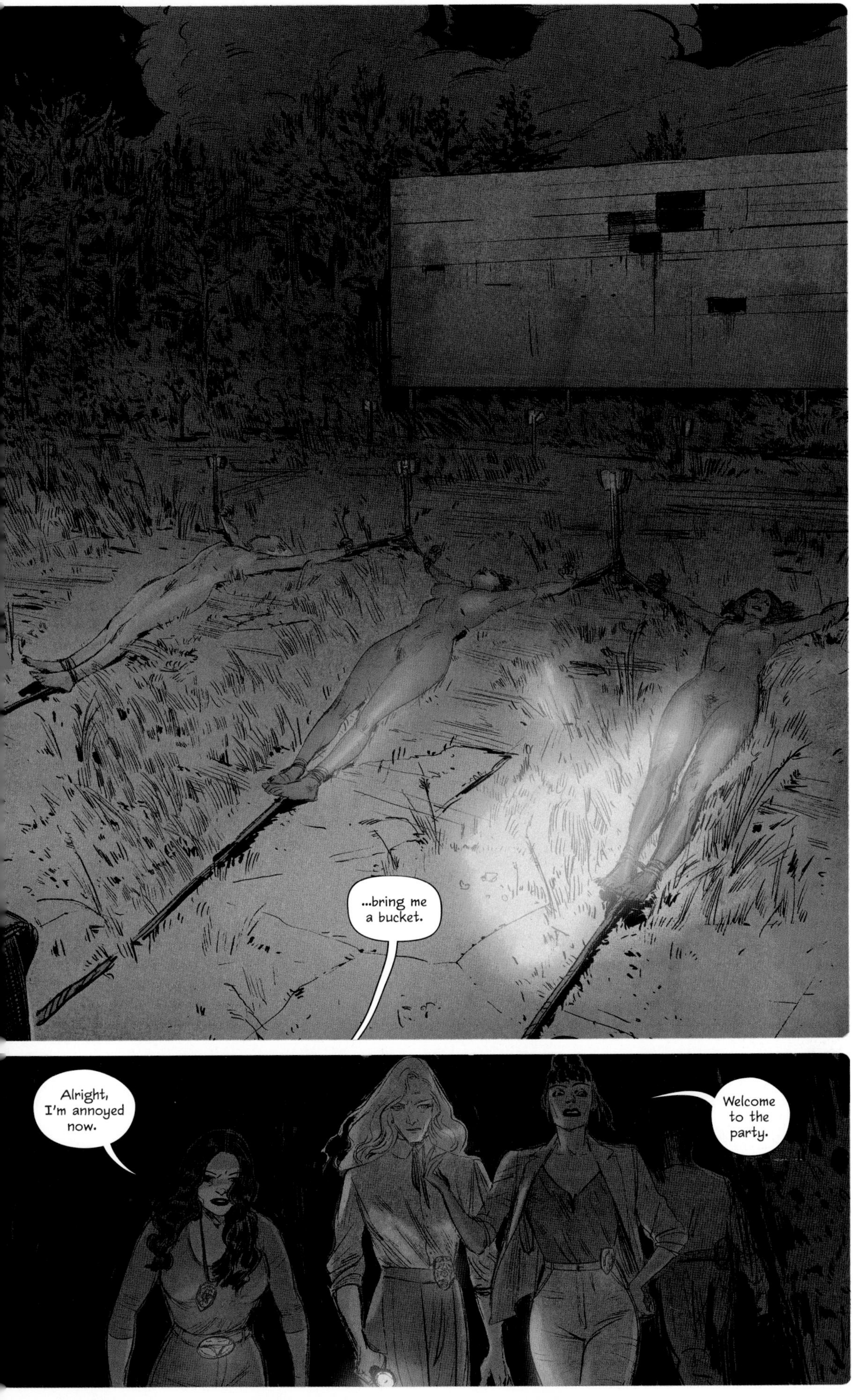
...bring me a bucket.
Alright, I'm annoyed now.
Welcome to the party.

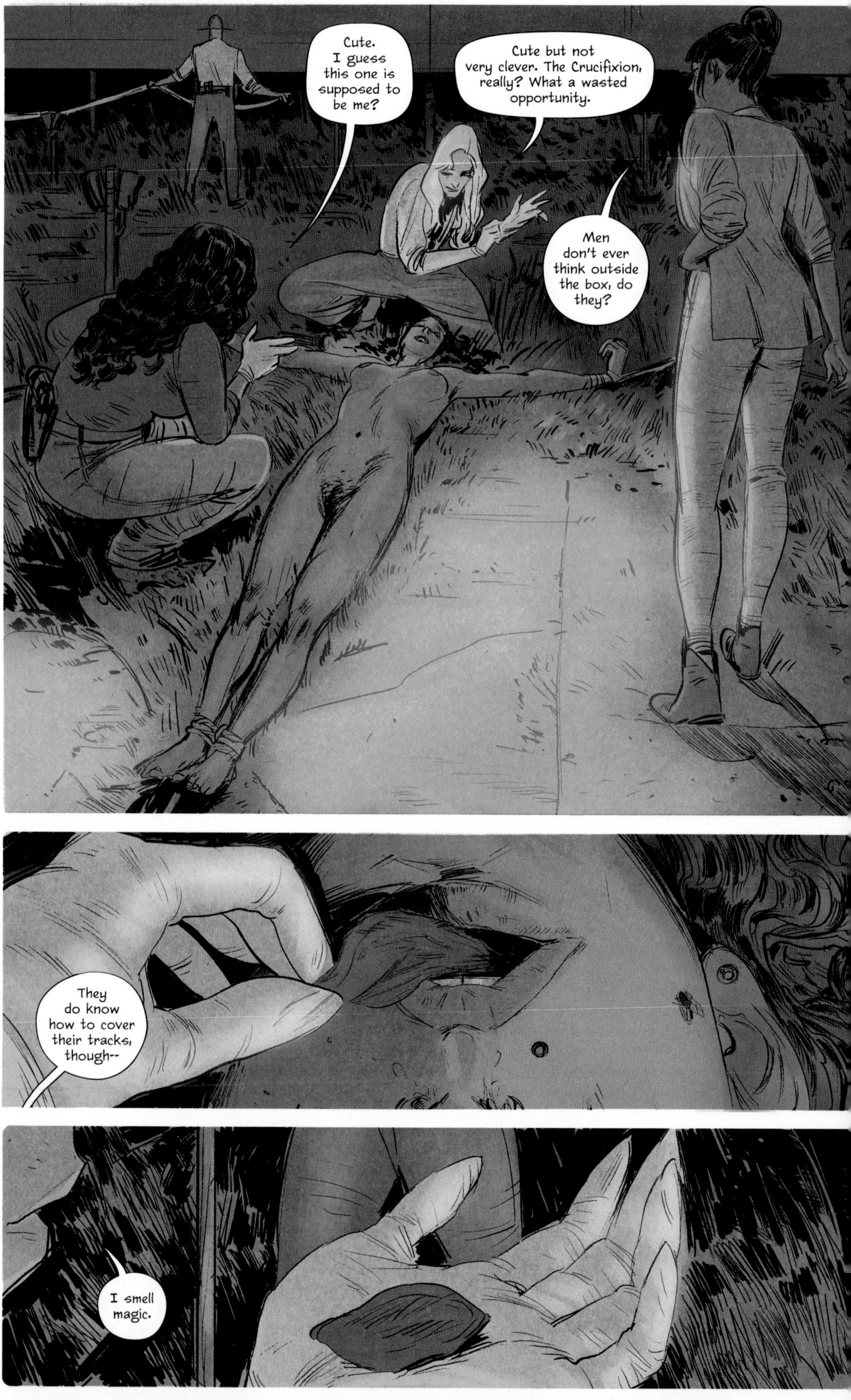
Cute. I guess this one is supposed to be me?
Cute but not very clever. The Crucifixion, really? What a wasted opportunity.
Men don't ever think outside the box, do they?
They do know how to cover their tracks, though--
I smell magic.

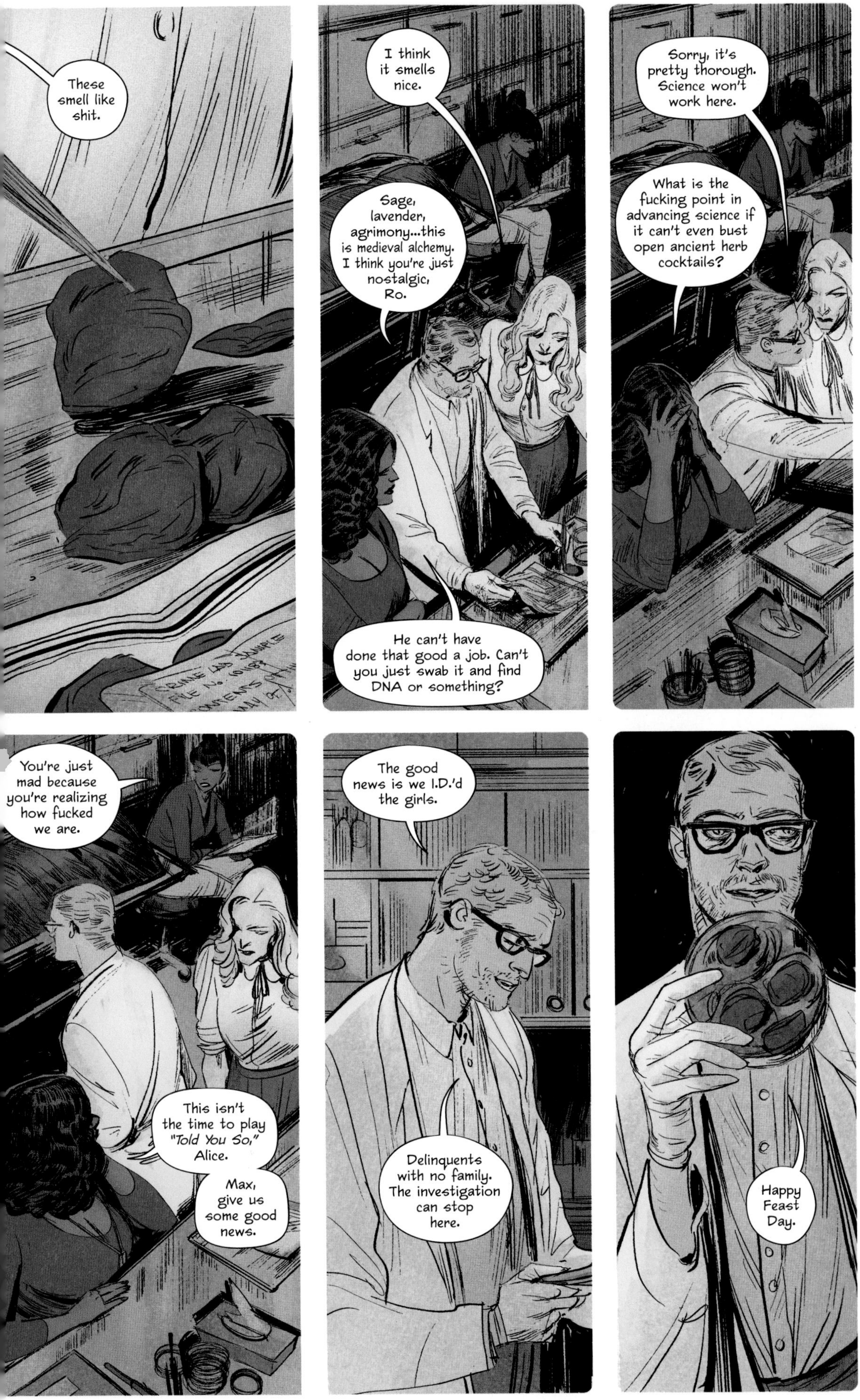
These smell like shit.
I think it smells nice.
Sage, lavender, agrimony...this is medieval alchemy. I think you're just nostalgic, Ro.
He can't have done that good a job. Can't you just swab it and find DNA or something?
Sorry, it's pretty thorough. Science won't work here.
What is the fucking point in advancing science if it can't even bust open ancient herb cocktails?
You're just mad because you're realizing how fucked we are.
This isn't the time to play *"Told You So,"* Alice.
Max, give us some good news.
The good news is we I.D.'d the girls.
Delinquents with no family. The investigation can stop here.
Happy Feast Day.

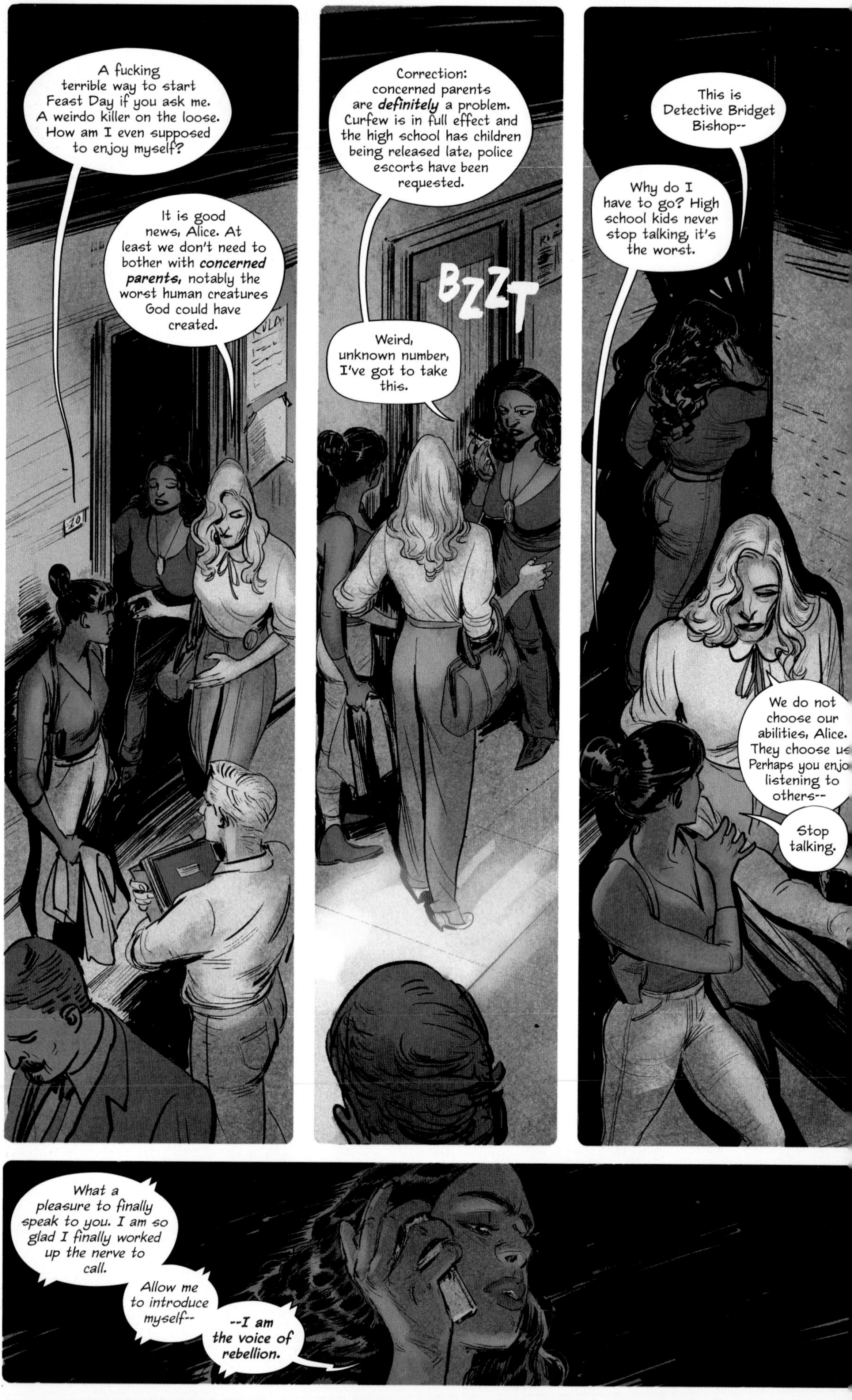
A fucking terrible way to start Feast Day if you ask me. A weirdo killer on the loose. How am I even supposed to enjoy myself?
It is good news, Alice. At least we don't need to bother with **concerned parents,** notably the worst human creatures God could have created.
Correction: concerned parents are ***definitely*** a problem. Curfew is in full effect and the high school has children being released late, police escorts have been requested.
BZZT
Weird, unknown number, I've got to take this.
This is Detective Bridget Bishop--
Why do I have to go? High school kids never stop talking, it's the worst.
We do not choose our abilities, Alice. They choose us Perhaps you enjo listening to others--
Stop talking.
What a pleasure to finally speak to you. I am so glad I finally worked up the nerve to call.
Allow me to introduce myself--
--I am the voice of rebellion.

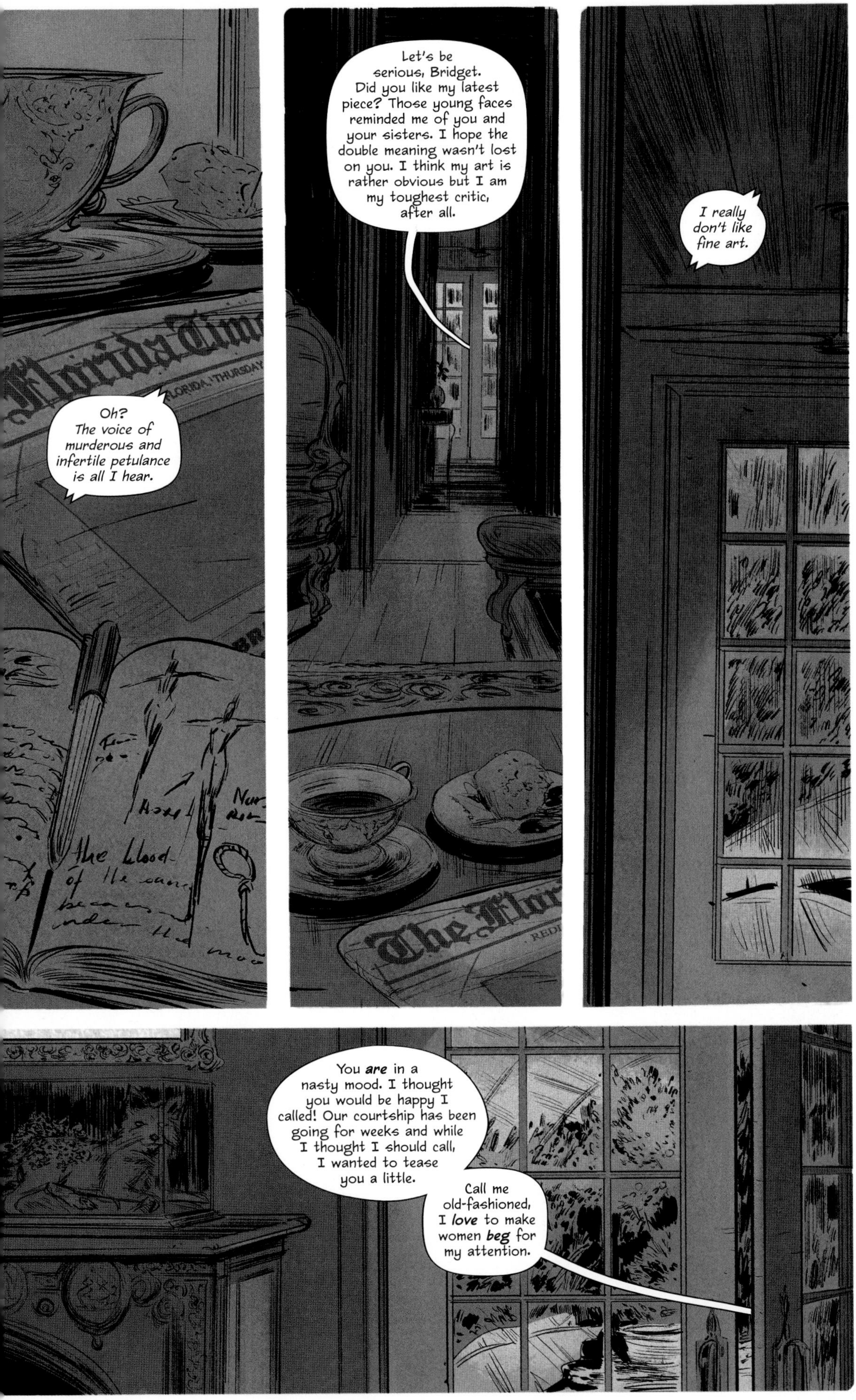
Oh? The voice of murderous and infertile petulance is all I hear.
Let's be serious, Bridget. Did you like my latest piece? Those young faces reminded me of you and your sisters. I hope the double meaning wasn't lost on you. I think my art is rather obvious but I am my toughest critic, after all.
I really don't like fine art.
You **are** in a nasty mood. I thought you would be happy I called! Our courtship has been going for weeks and while I thought I should call, I wanted to tease you a little.
Call me old-fashioned, I **love** to make women **beg** for my attention.

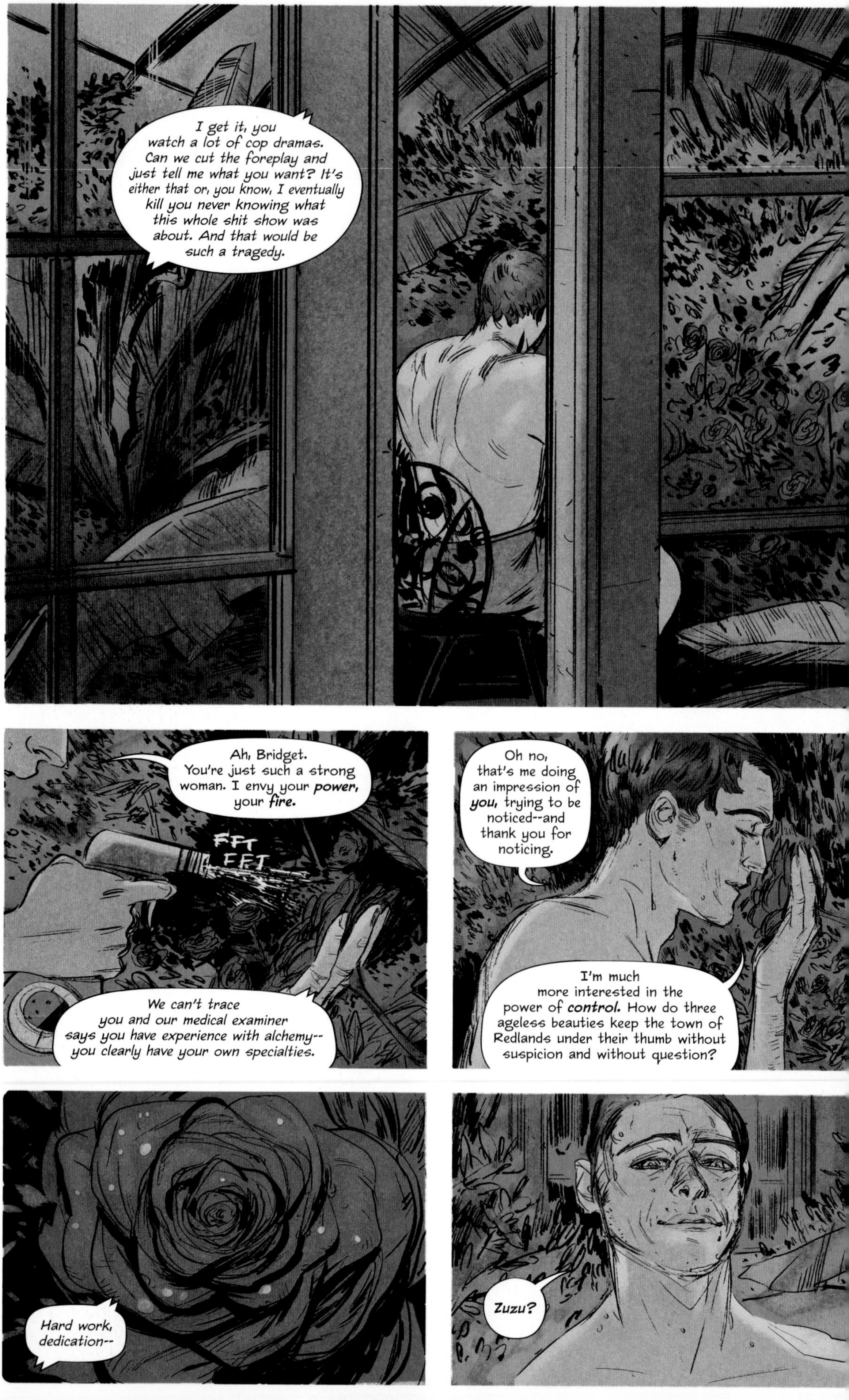
I get it, you watch a lot of cop dramas. Can we cut the foreplay and just tell me what you want? It's either that or, you know, I eventually kill you never knowing what this whole shit show was about. And that would be such a tragedy.
Ah, Bridget. You're just such a strong woman. I envy your **power,** your **fire.**
FFT FFT
We can't trace you and our medical examiner says you have experience with alchemy--you clearly have your own specialties.
Oh no, that's me doing an impression of **you,** trying to be noticed--and thank you for noticing.
I'm much more interested in the power of **control.** How do three ageless beauties keep the town of Redlands under their thumb without suspicion and without question?
Hard work, dedication--
Zuzu?

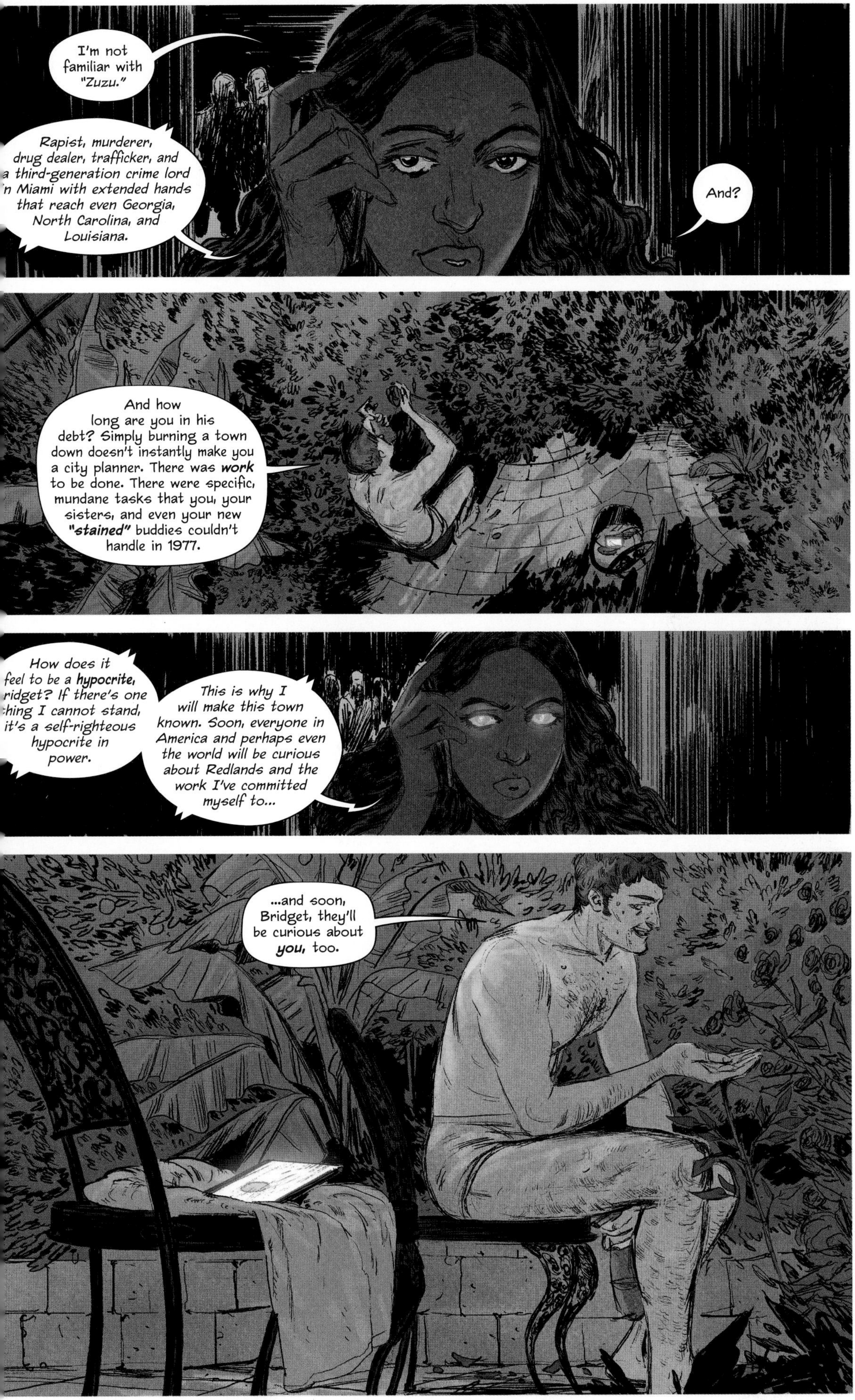

I'm not familiar with "Zuzu."
Rapist, murderer, drug dealer, trafficker, and a third-generation crime lord n Miami with extended hands that reach even Georgia, North Carolina, and Louisiana.
And?
And how long are you in his debt? Simply burning a town down doesn't instantly make you a city planner. There was **work** to be done. There were specific, mundane tasks that you, your sisters, and even your new ***"stained"*** buddies couldn't handle in 1977.
How does it feel to be a **hypocrite,** ridget? If there's one hing I cannot stand, it's a self-righteous hypocrite in power.
This is why I will make this town known. Soon, everyone in America and perhaps even the world will be curious about Redlands and the work I've committed myself to...
...and soon, Bridget, they'll be curious about **you,** too.

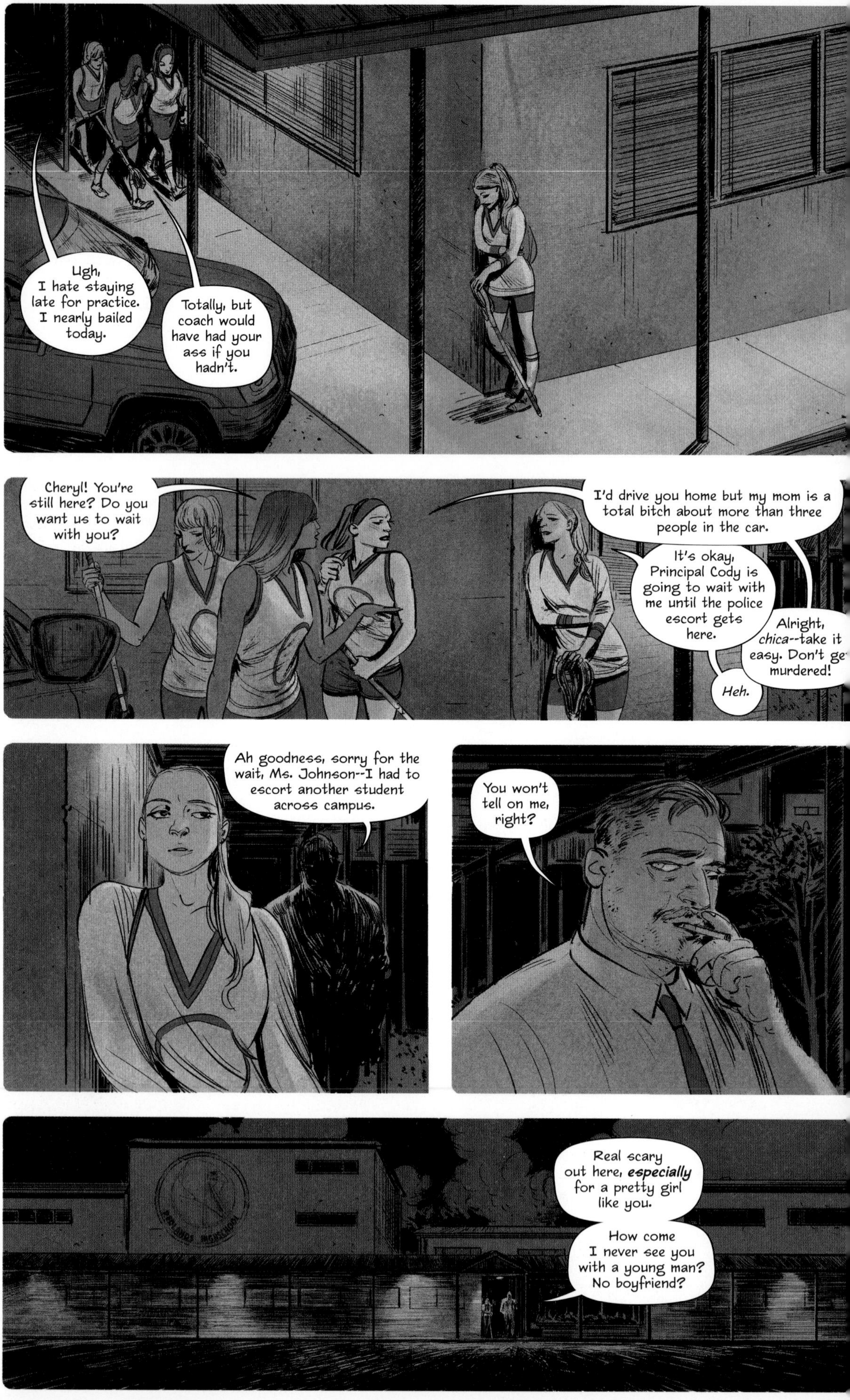
Ugh, I hate staying late for practice. I nearly bailed today.
Totally, but coach would have had your ass if you hadn't.
Cheryl! You're still here? Do you want us to wait with you?
I'd drive you home but my mom is a total bitch about more than three people in the car.
It's okay, Principal Cody is going to wait with me until the police escort gets here.
Alright, *chica*--take it easy. Don't ge murdered!
Heh.
Ah goodness, sorry for the wait, Ms. Johnson--I had to escort another student across campus.
You won't tell on me, right?
Real scary out here, ***especially*** for a pretty girl like you.
How come I never see you with a young man? No boyfriend?

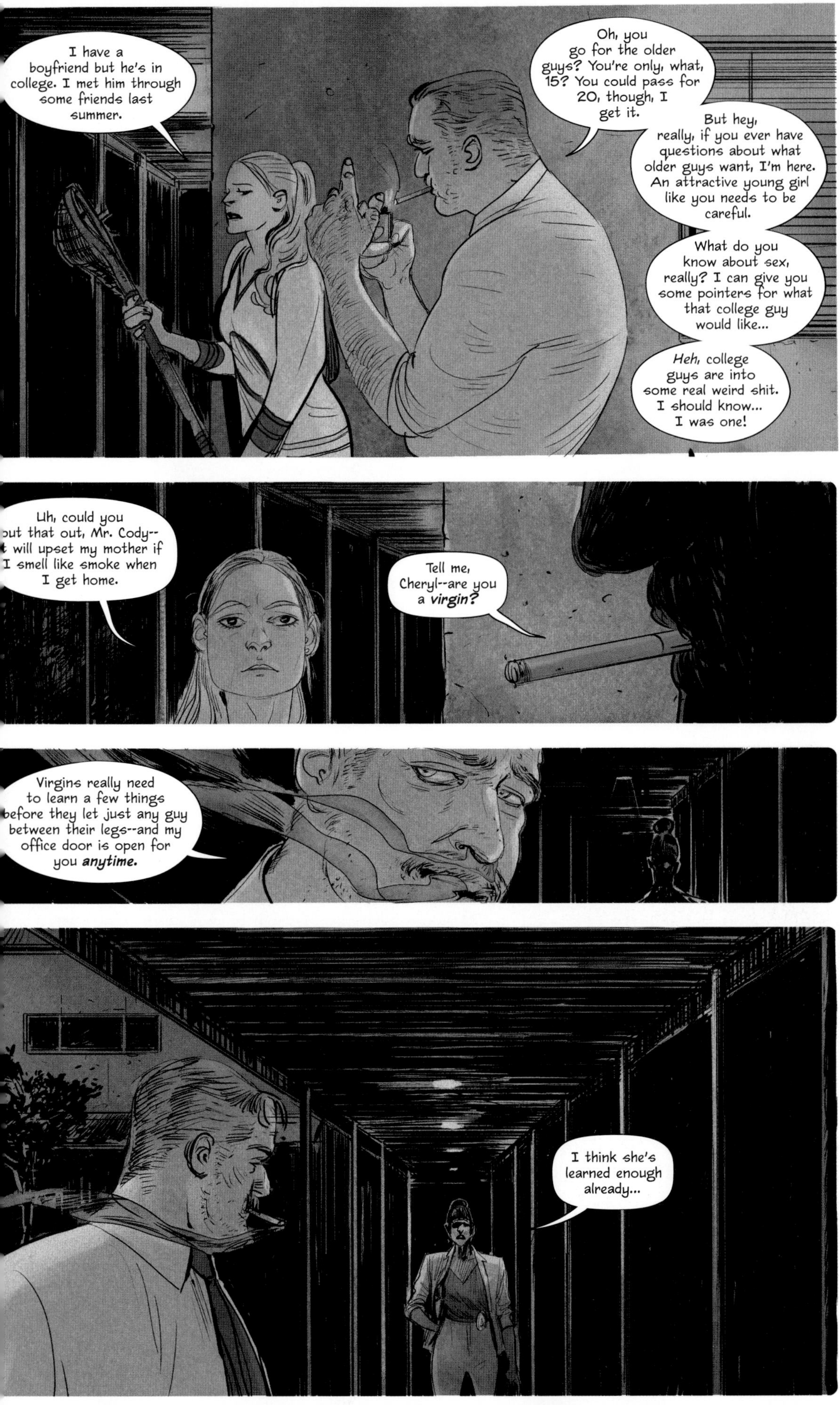

I have a boyfriend but he's in college. I met him through some friends last summer.
Oh, you go for the older guys? You're only, what, 15? You could pass for 20, though, I get it.
But hey, really, if you ever have questions about what older guys want, I'm here. An attractive young girl like you needs to be careful.
What do you know about sex, really? I can give you some pointers for what that college guy would like...
Heh, college guys are into some real weird shit. I should know... I was one!
Uh, could you ut that out, Mr. Cody-- t will upset my mother if I smell like smoke when I get home.
Tell me, Cheryl--are you a ***virgin?***
Virgins really need to learn a few things efore they let just any guy between their legs--and my office door is open for you ***anytime.***
I think she's learned enough already...

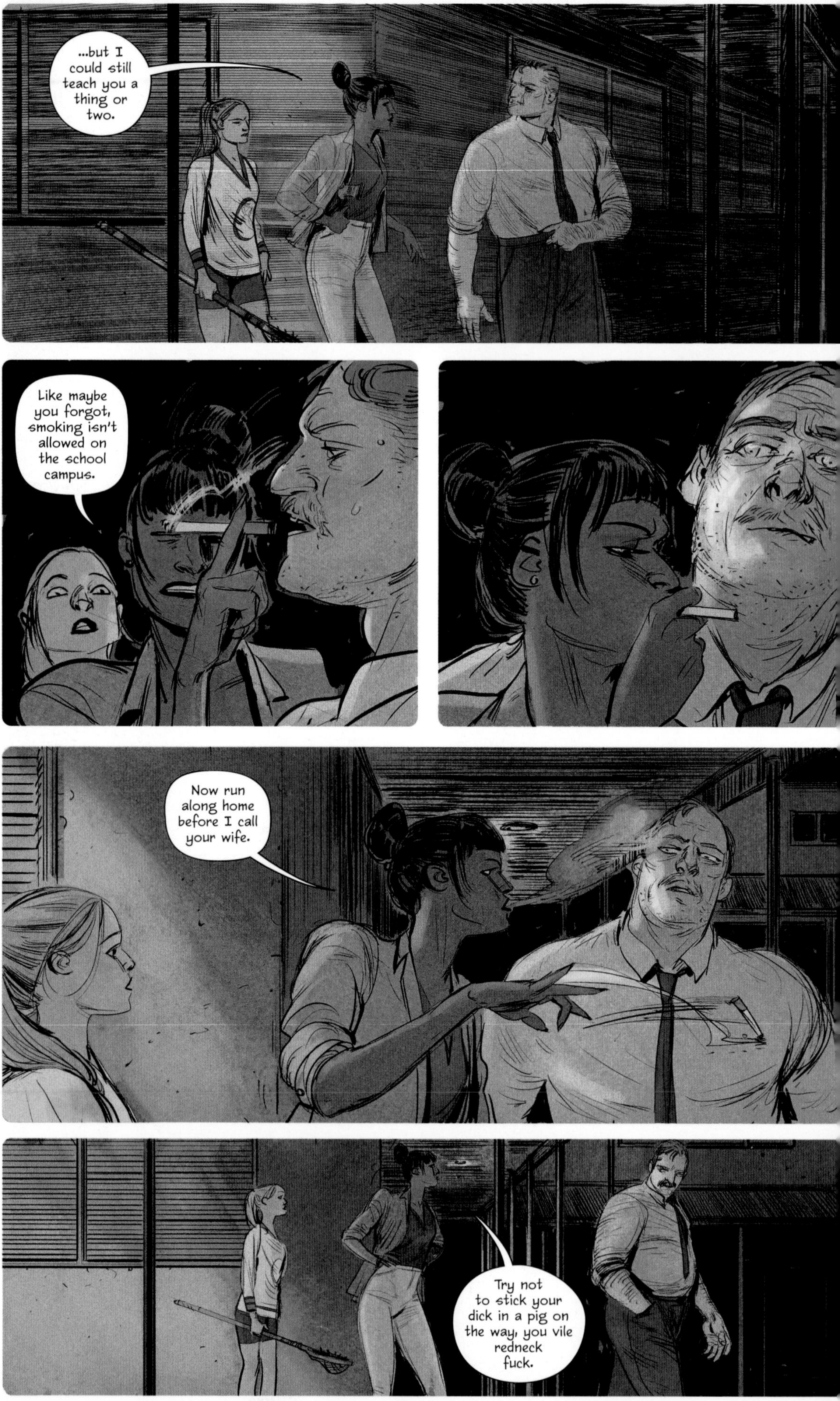
...but I could still teach you a thing or two.
Like maybe you forgot, smoking isn't allowed on the school campus.
Now run along home before I call your wife.
Try not to stick your dick in a pig on the way, you vile redneck fuck.

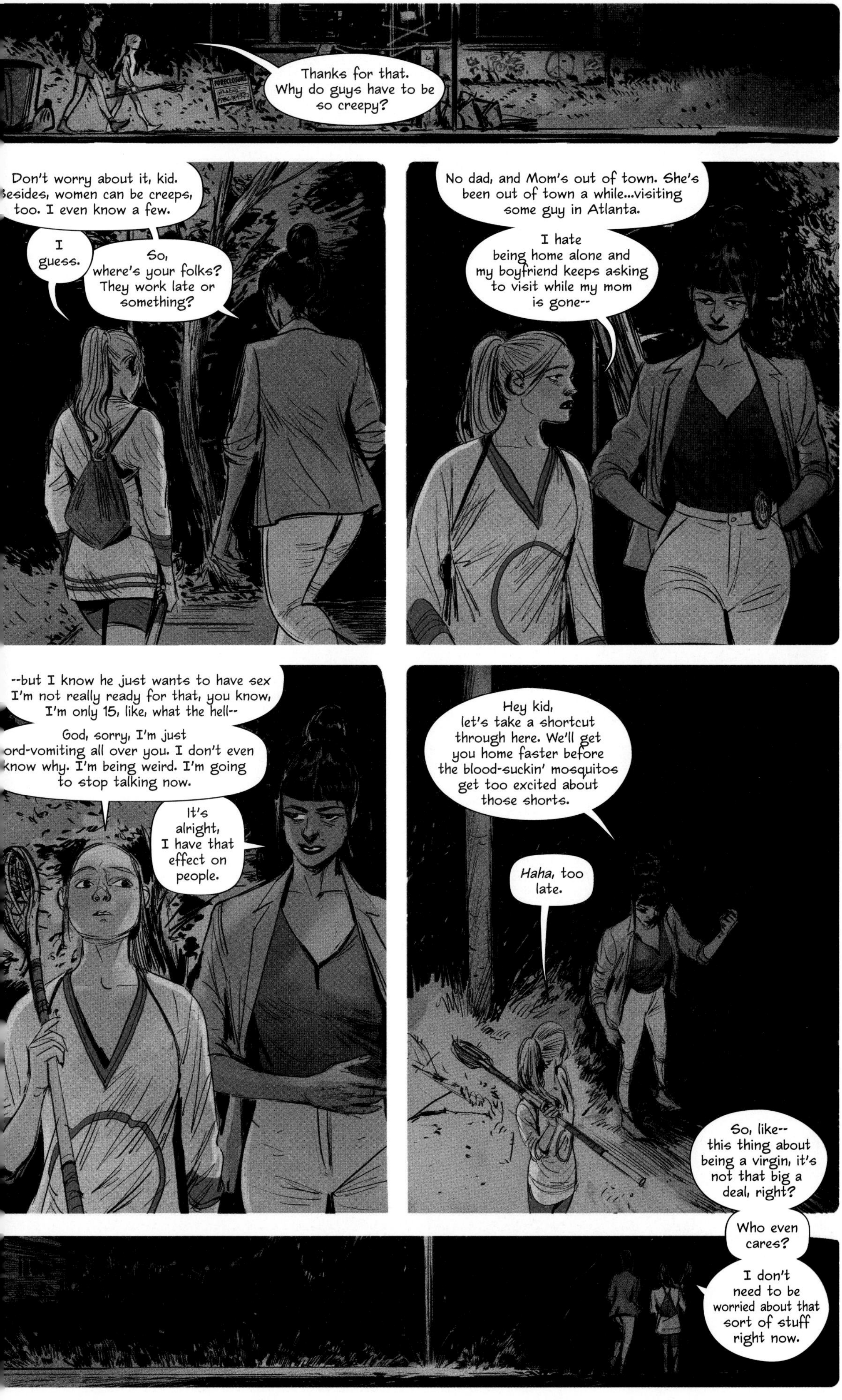
FORECLOSURE
Thanks for that. Why do guys have to be so creepy?
Don't worry about it, kid. esides, women can be creeps, too. I even know a few.
I guess.
So, where's your folks? They work late or something?
No dad, and Mom's out of town. She's been out of town a while...visiting some guy in Atlanta.
I hate being home alone and my boyfriend keeps asking to visit while my mom is gone--
--but I know he just wants to have sex I'm not really ready for that, you know, I'm only 15, like, what the hell--
God, sorry, I'm just ord-vomiting all over you. I don't even now why. I'm being weird. I'm going to stop talking now.
It's alright, I have that effect on people.
Hey kid, let's take a shortcut through here. We'll get you home faster before the blood-suckin' mosquitos get too excited about those shorts.
Haha, too late.
So, like-- this thing about being a virgin, it's not that big a deal, right?
Who even cares?
I don't need to be worried about that sort of stuff right now.

TFFFF
Is the offering clean? Is the offering sacred?

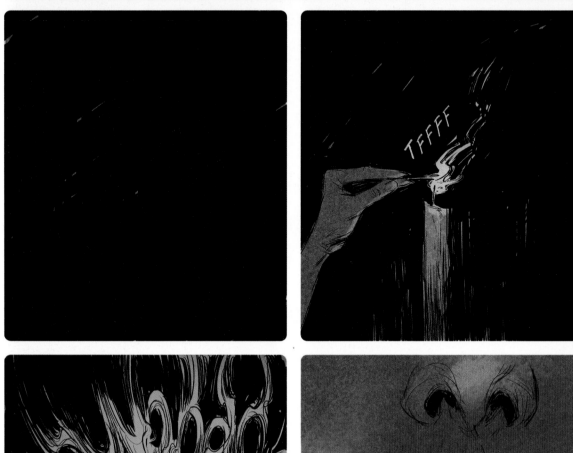

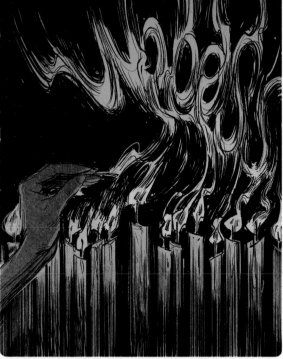

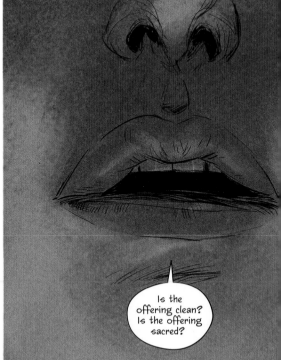

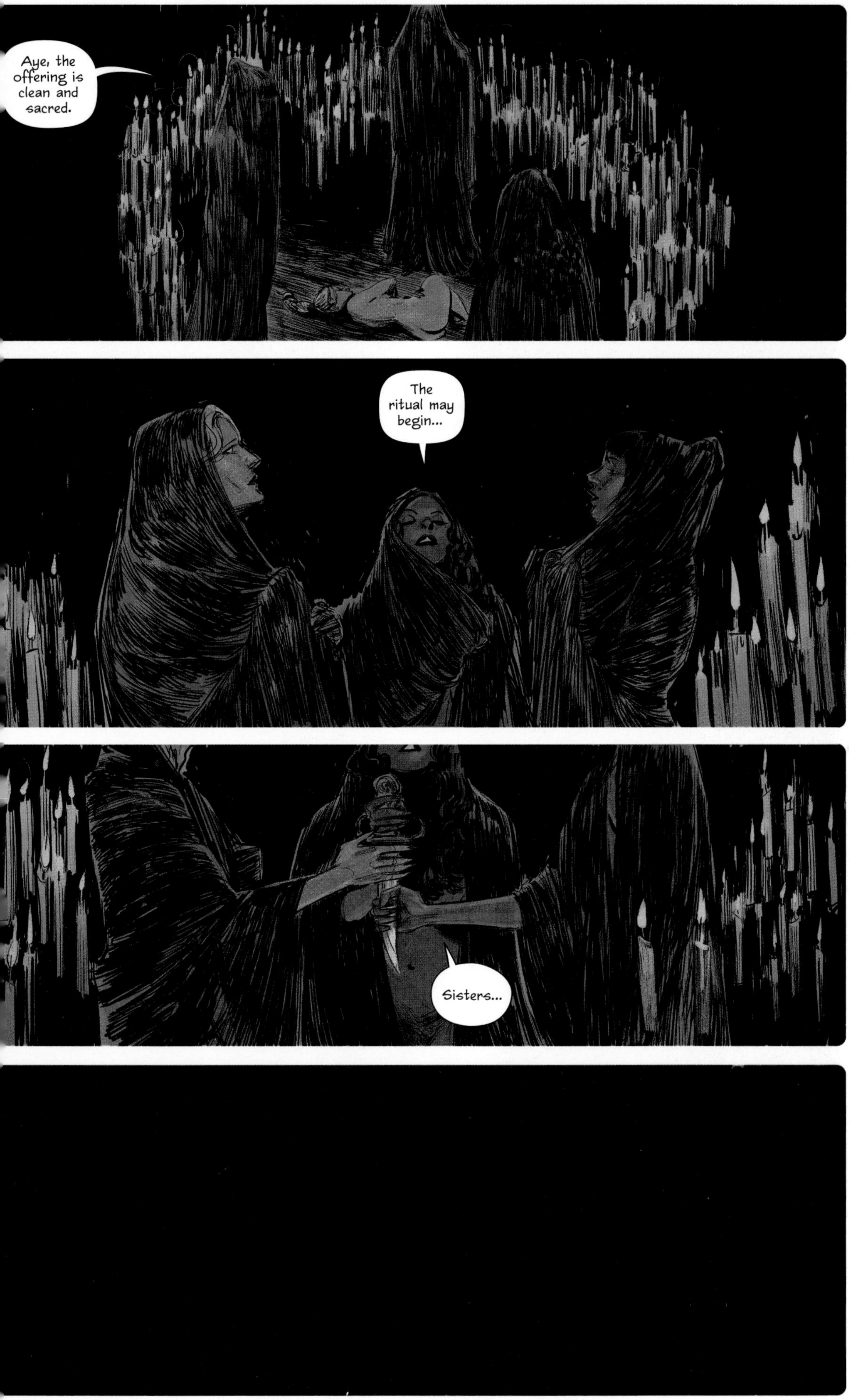
Aye, the offering is clean and sacred.
The ritual may begin...
Sisters...

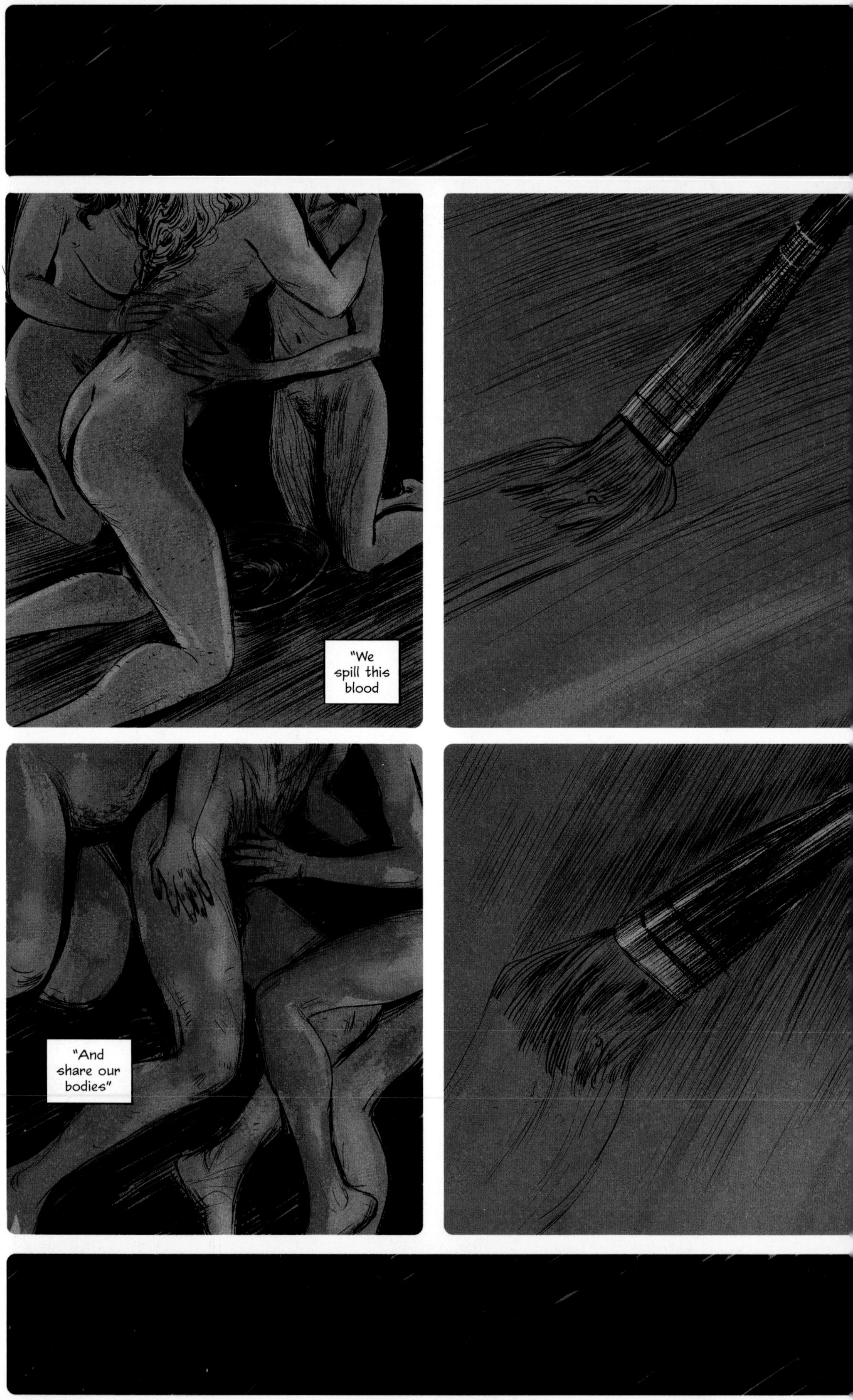
"We spill this blood
"And share our bodies"

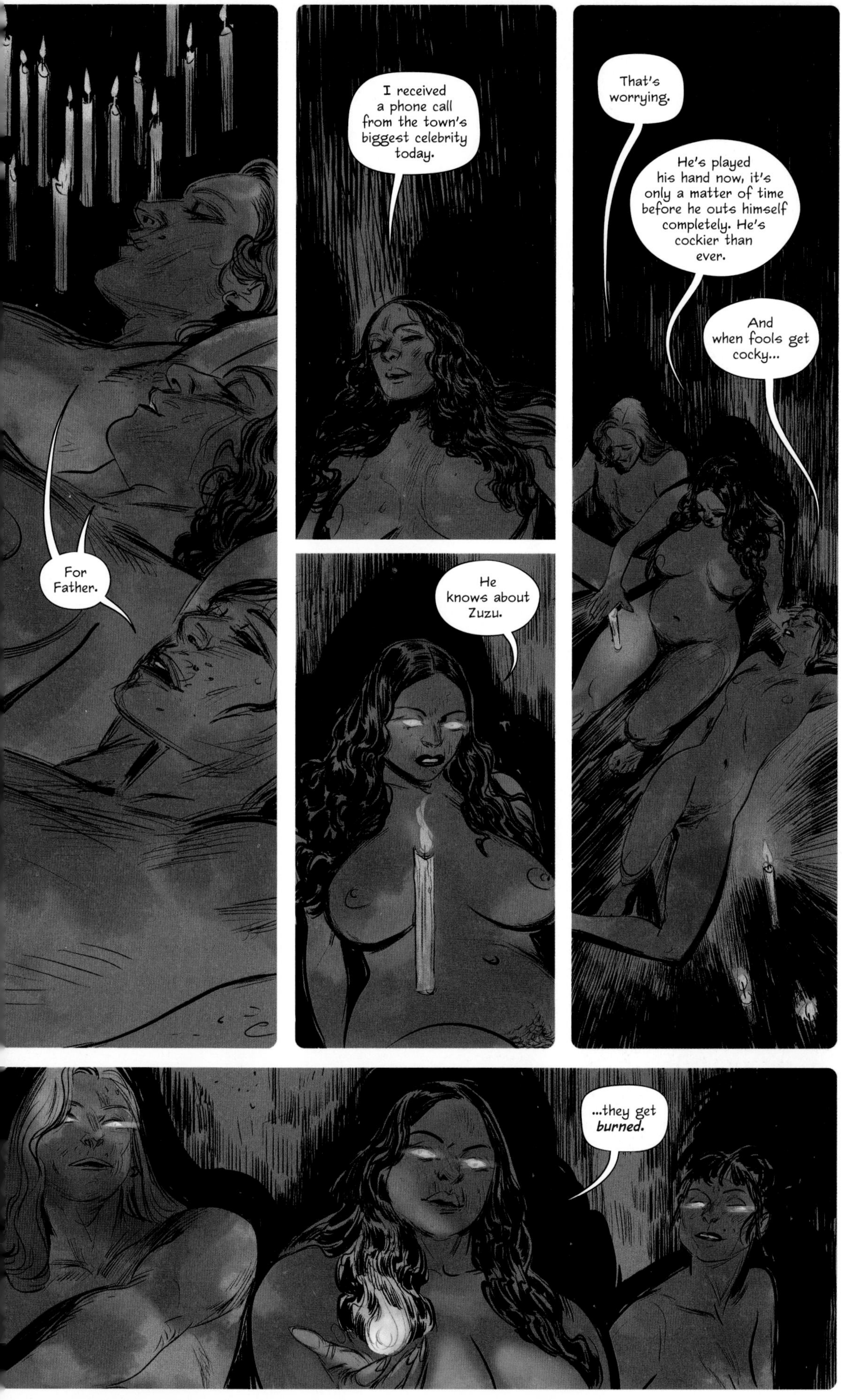
For Father.
I received a phone call from the town's biggest celebrity today.
He knows about Zuzu.
That's worrying.
He's played his hand now, it's only a matter of time before he outs himself completely. He's cockier than ever.
And when fools get cocky...
...they get *burned.*

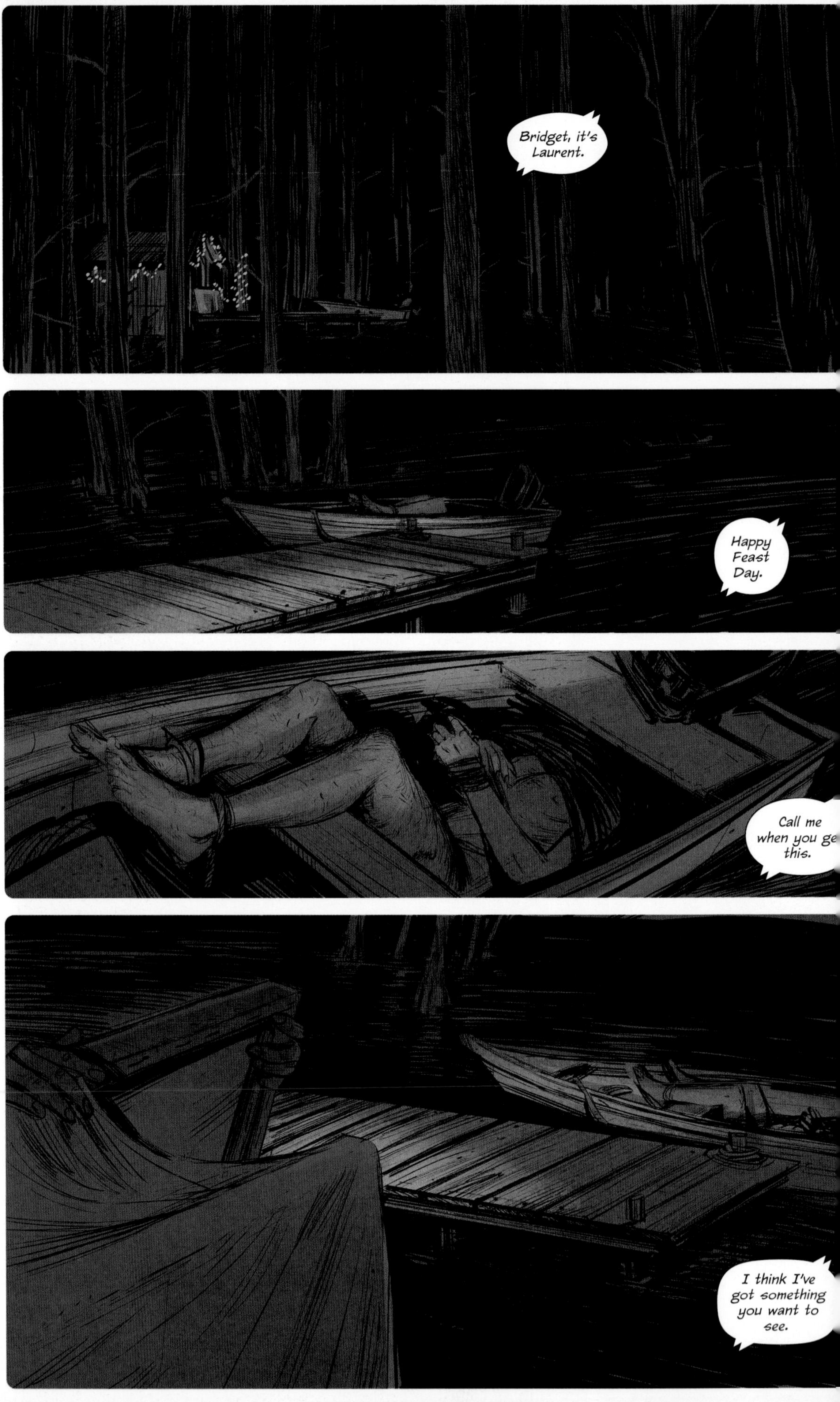
Bridget, it's Laurent.
Happy Feast Day.
Call me when you ge this.
I think I've got something you want to see.

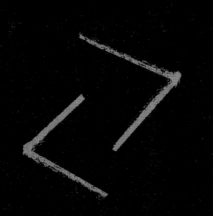

CHAPTER THREE

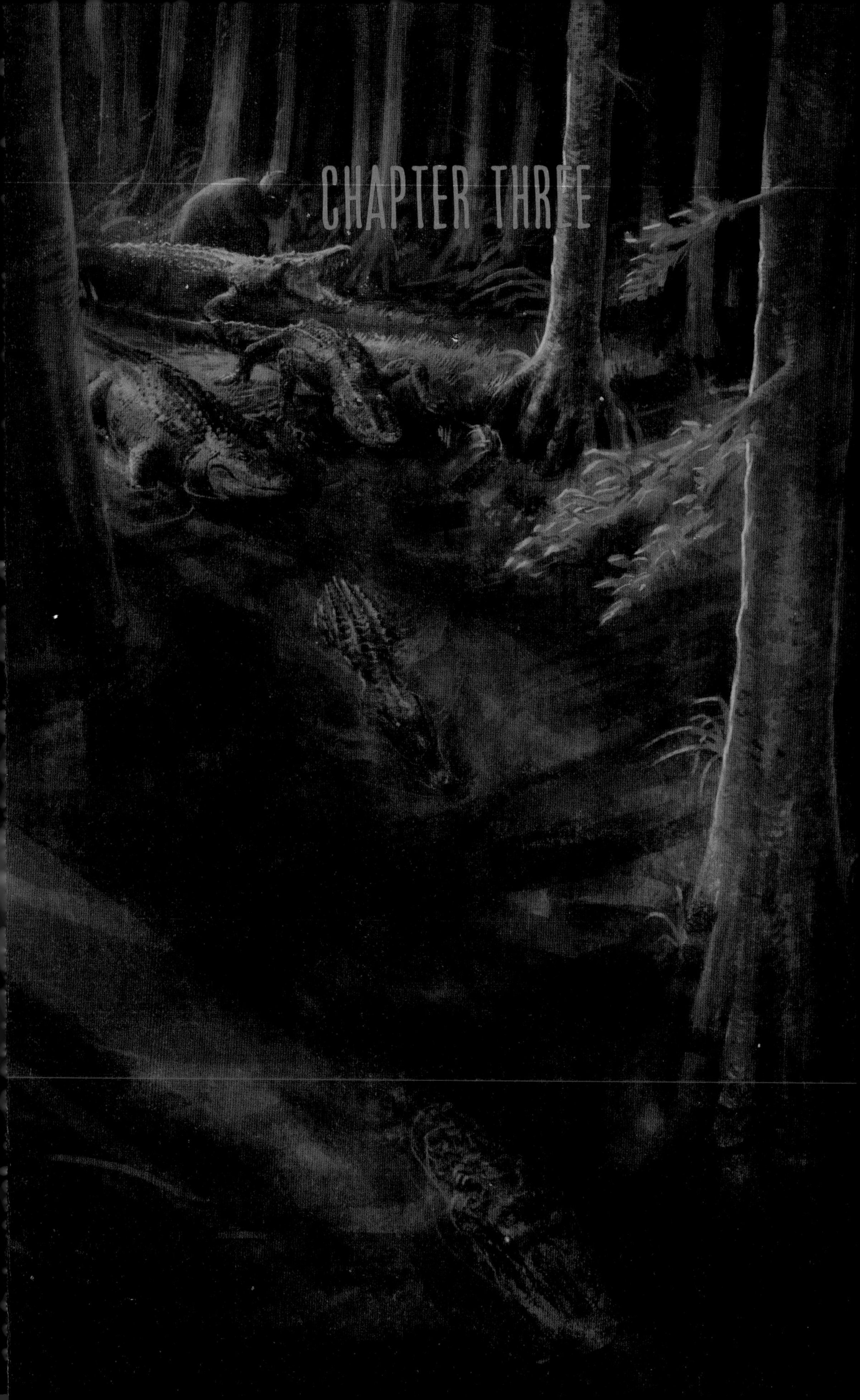

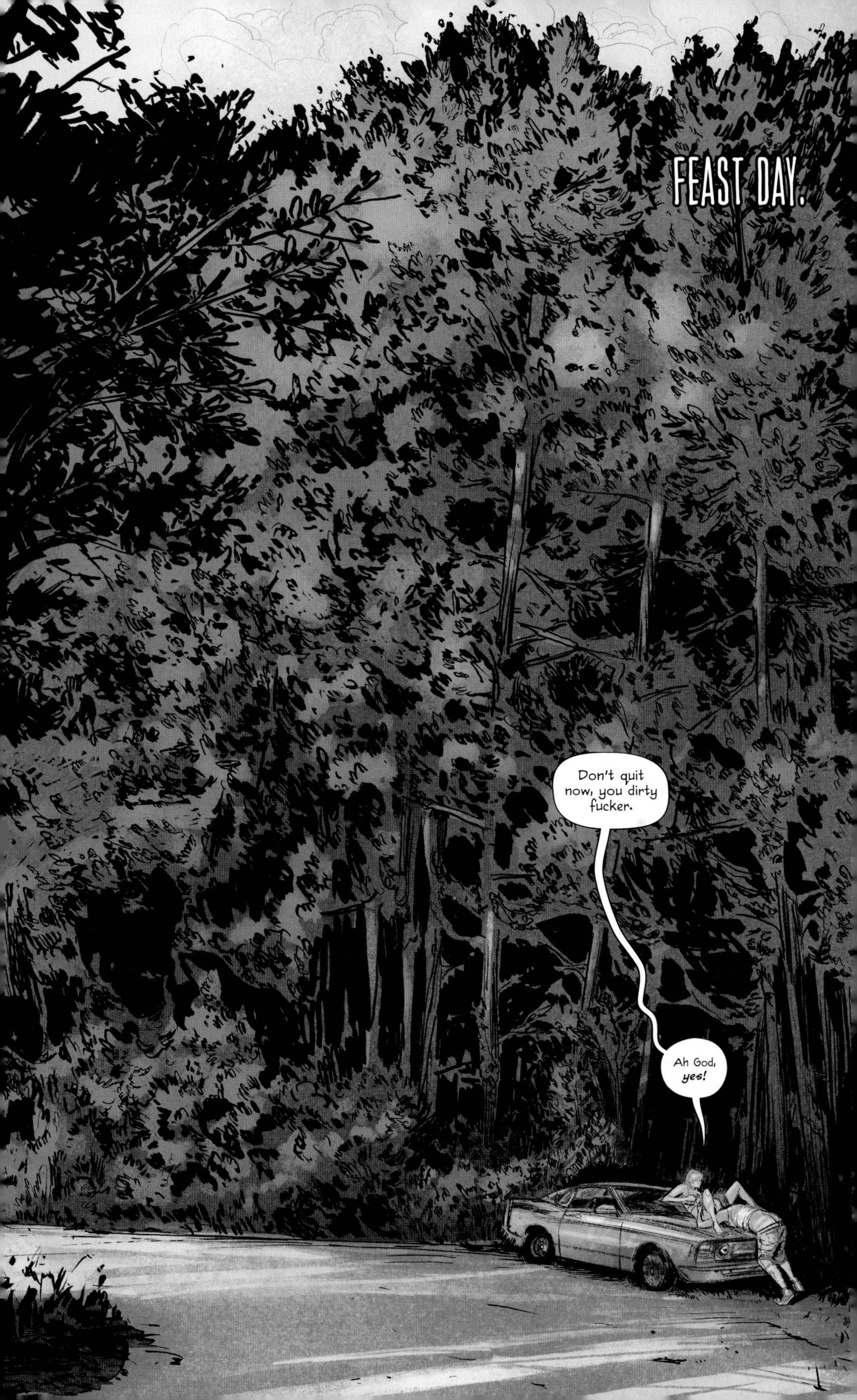
FEAST DAY.
Don't quit now, you dirty fucker.
Ah God, *yes!*

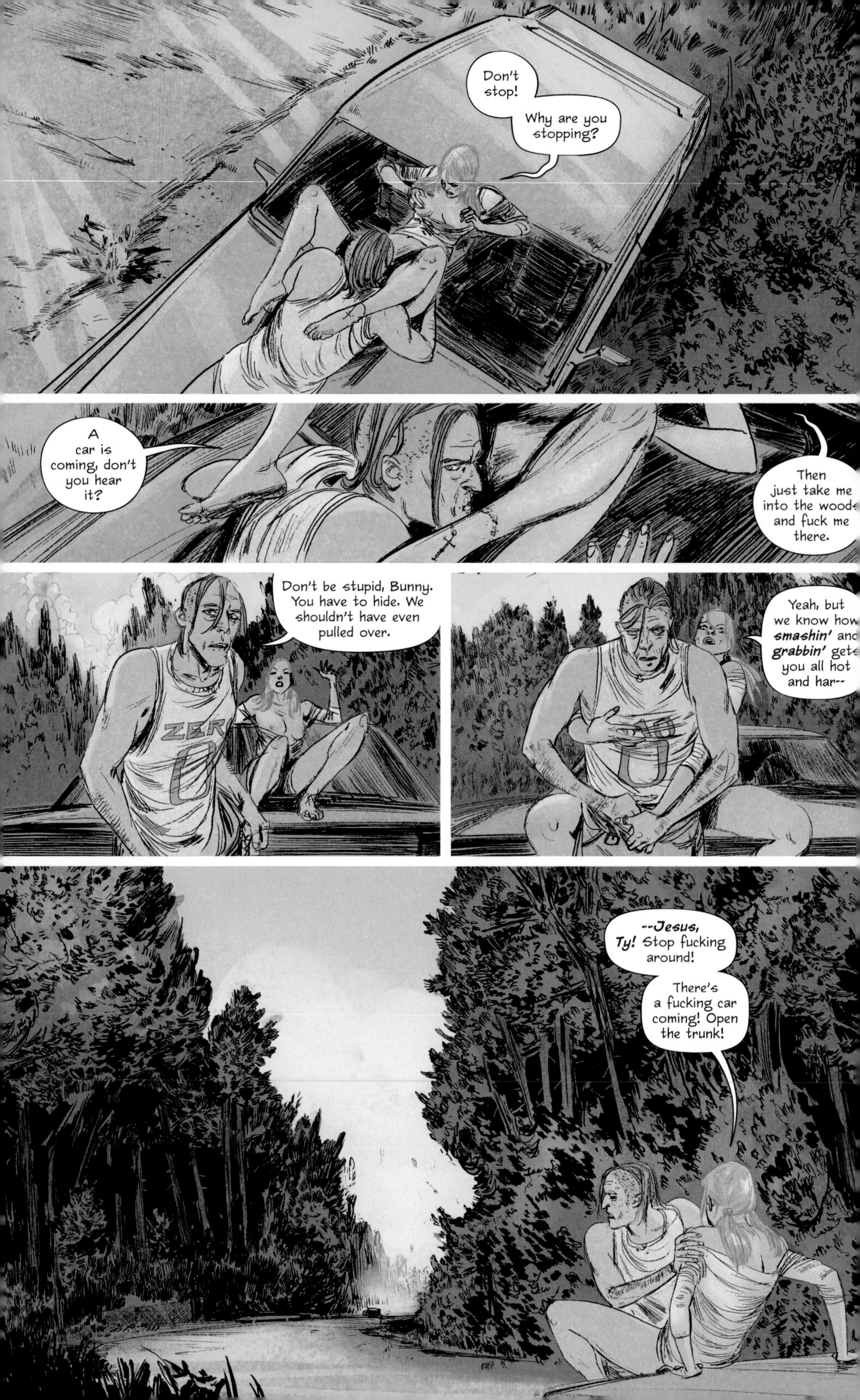
Don't stop!
Why are you stopping?
A car is coming, don't you hear it?
Then just take me into the woods and fuck me there.
Don't be stupid, Bunny. You have to hide. We shouldn't have even pulled over.
Yeah, but we know how *smashin'* and *grabbin'* gets you all hot and har--
--Jesus, Ty! Stop fucking around!
There's a fucking car coming! Open the trunk!

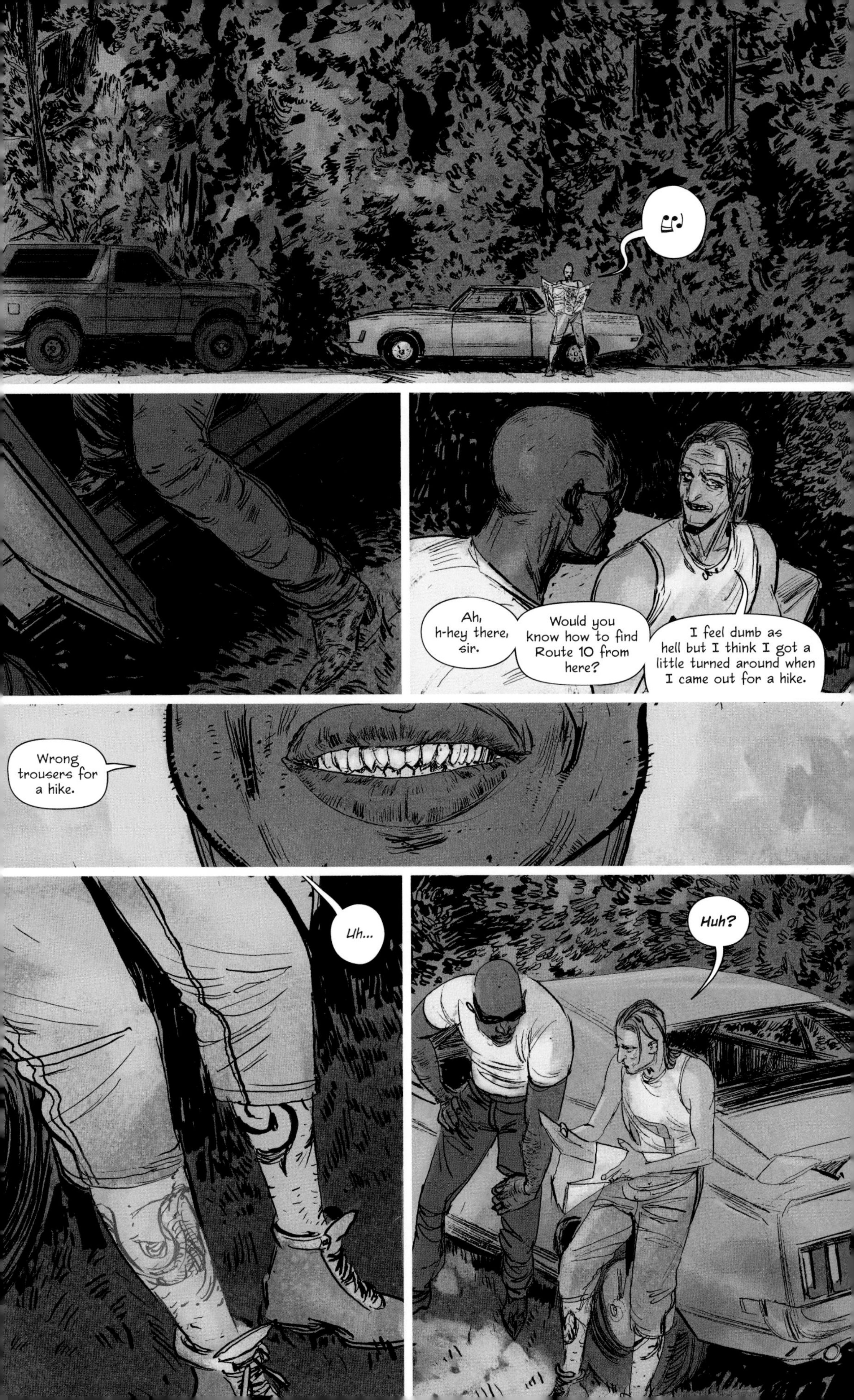
Ah, h-hey there, sir.
Would you know how to find Route 10 from here?
I feel dumb as hell but I think I got a little turned around when I came out for a hike.
Wrong trousers for a hike.
Uh...
Huh?

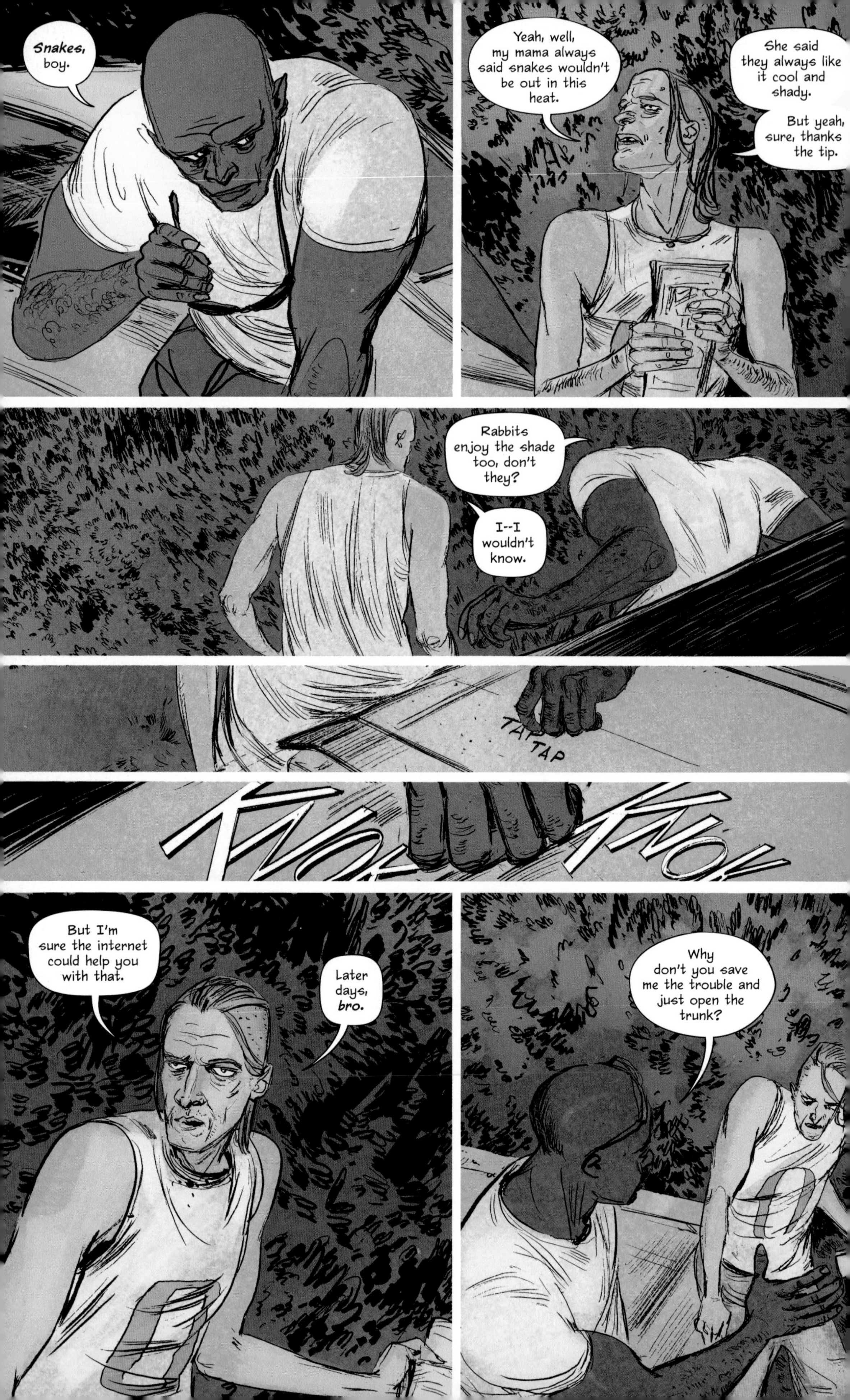
Snakes, boy.
Yeah, well, my mama always said snakes wouldn't be out in this heat.
She said they always like it cool and shady.
But yeah, sure, thanks the tip.
Rabbits enjoy the shade too, don't they?
I--I wouldn't know.
TAP TAP
KNOK KNOK
But I'm sure the internet could help you with that.
Later days, bro.
Why don't you save me the trouble and just open the trunk?

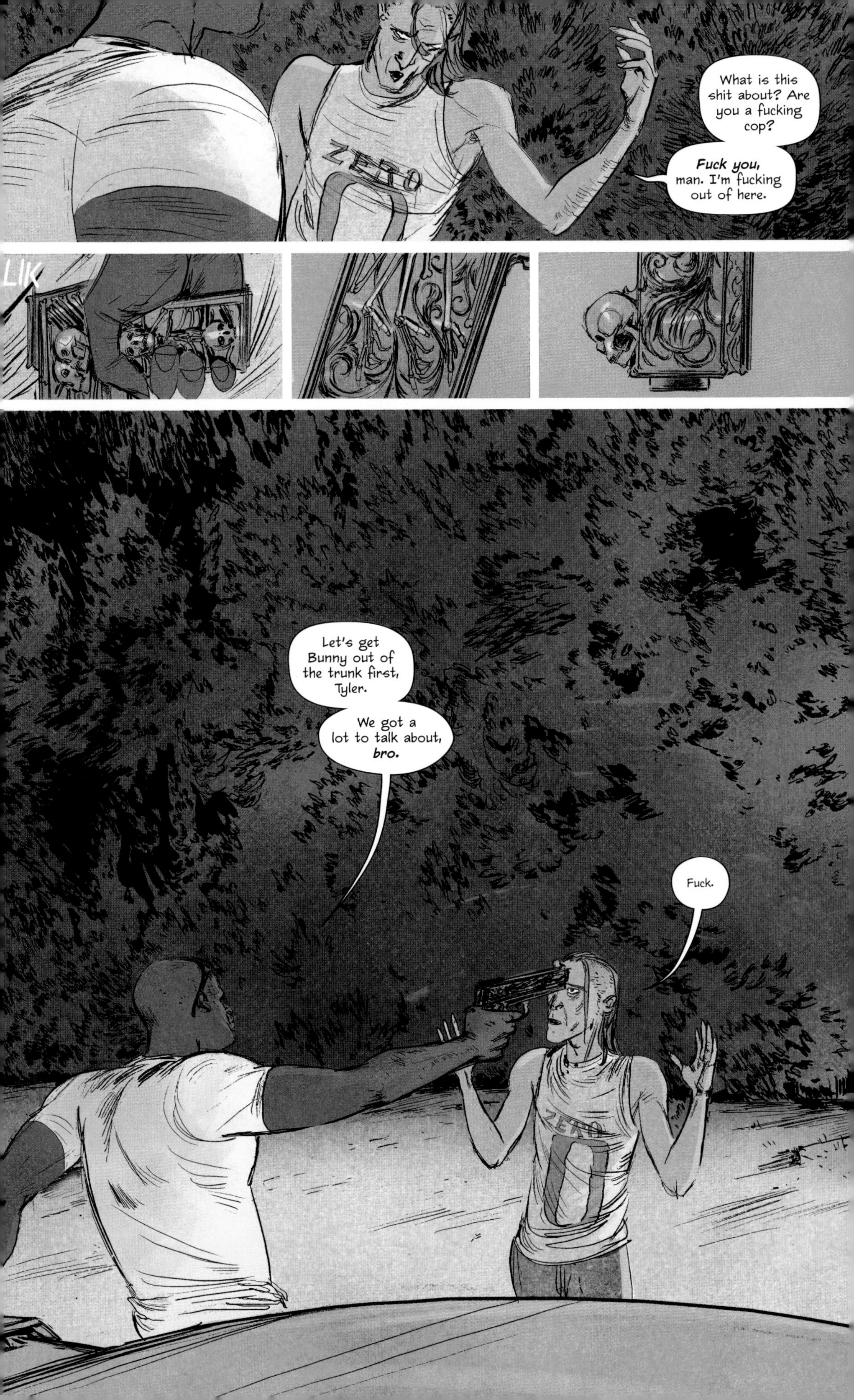
What is this shit about? Are you a fucking cop?
Fuck you, man. I'm fucking out of here.
LIK
ZERO
Let's get Bunny out of the trunk first, Tyler.
We got a lot to talk about, ***bro.***
Fuck.
ZERO

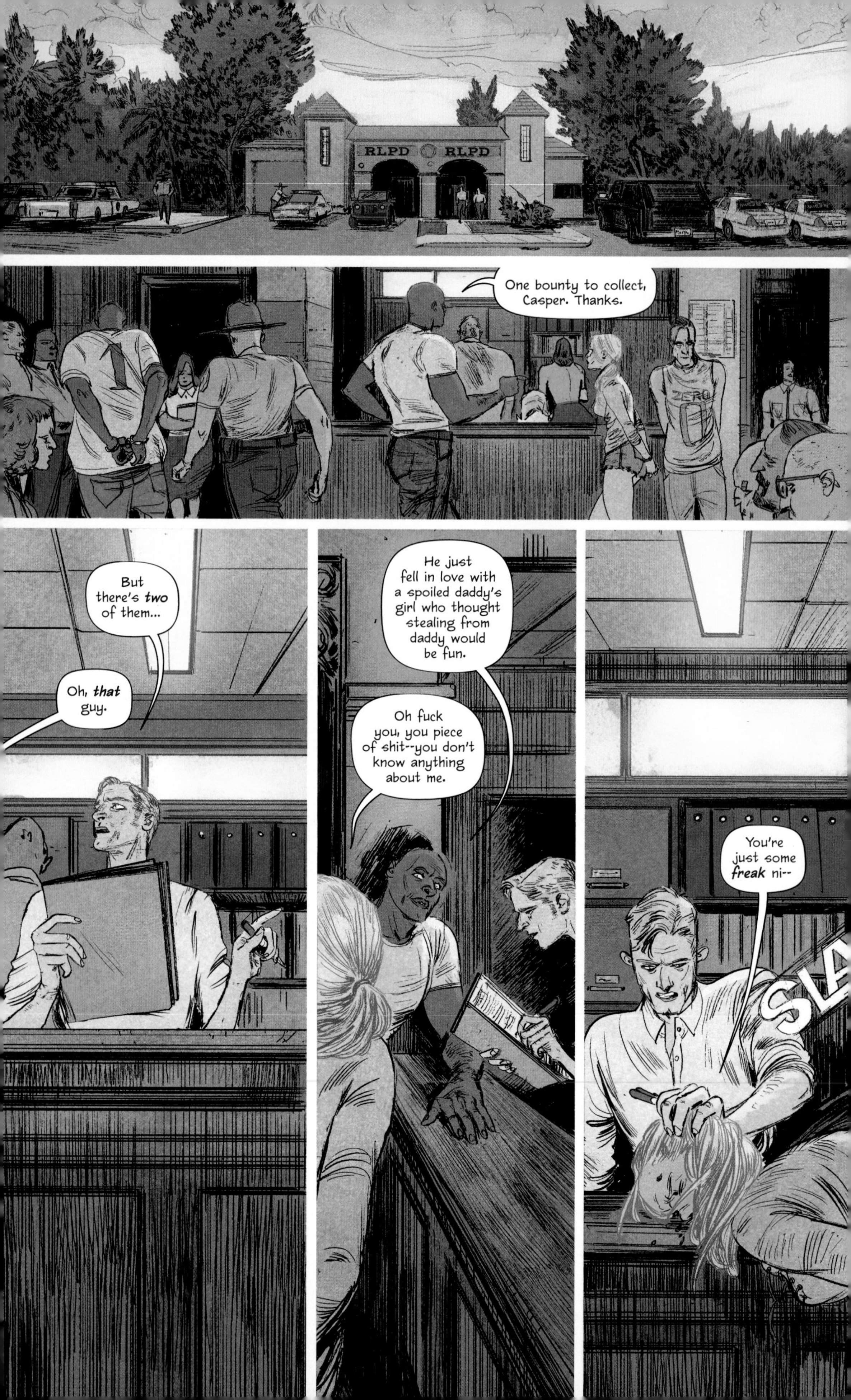
RLPD RLPD
One bounty to collect, Casper. Thanks.
ZERO
But there's **two** of them...
Oh, **that** guy.
He just fell in love with a spoiled daddy's girl who thought stealing from daddy would be fun.
Oh fuck you, you piece of shit--you don't know anything about me.
You're just some **freak** ni--
SLA

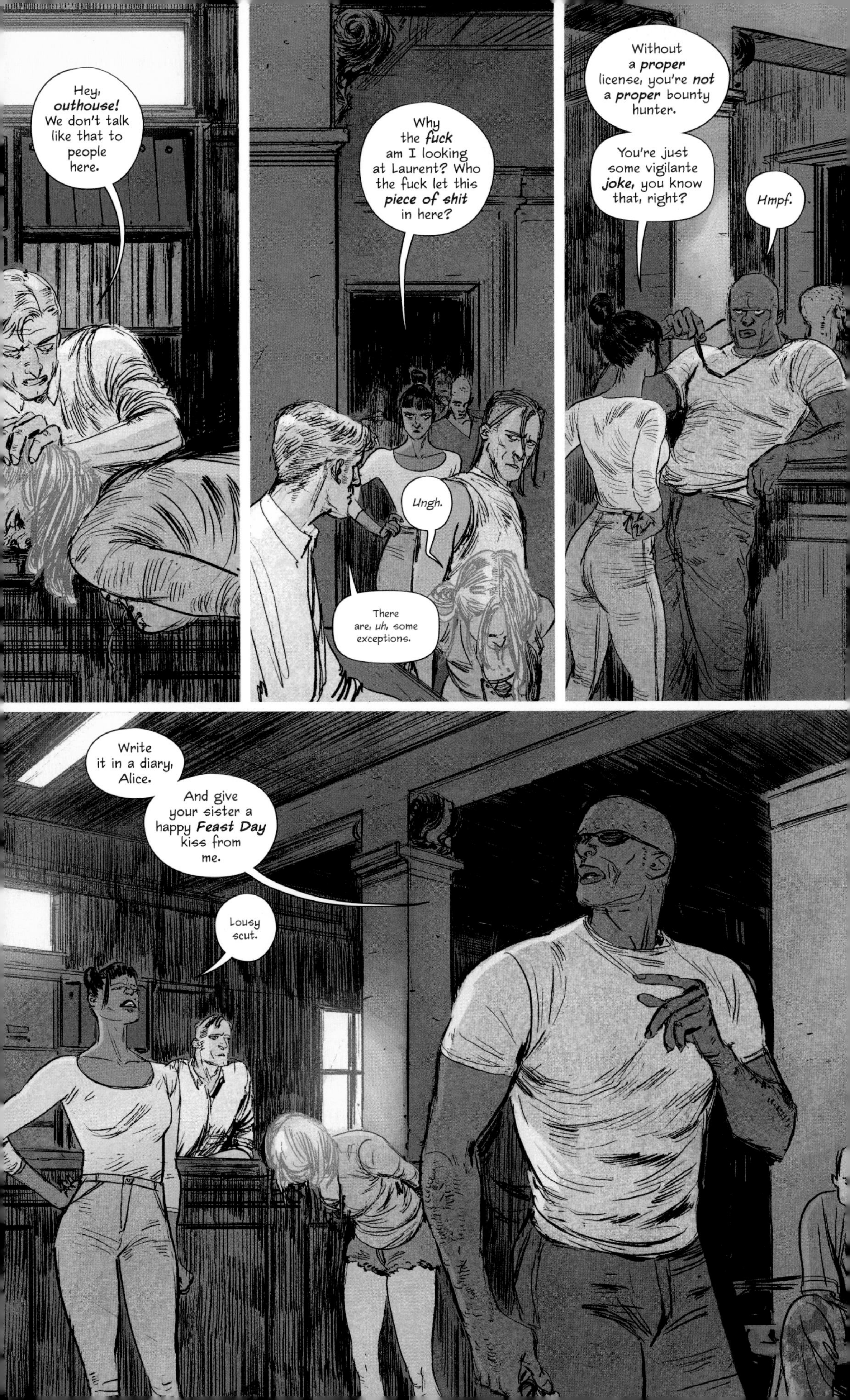
Hey, outhouse! We don't talk like that to people here.
Why the fuck am I looking at Laurent? Who the fuck let this piece of shit in here?
Ungh.
There are, uh, some exceptions.
Without a proper license, you're not a proper bounty hunter.
You're just some vigilante joke, you know that, right?
Hmpf.
Write it in a diary, Alice.
And give your sister a happy Feast Day kiss from me.
Lousy scut.

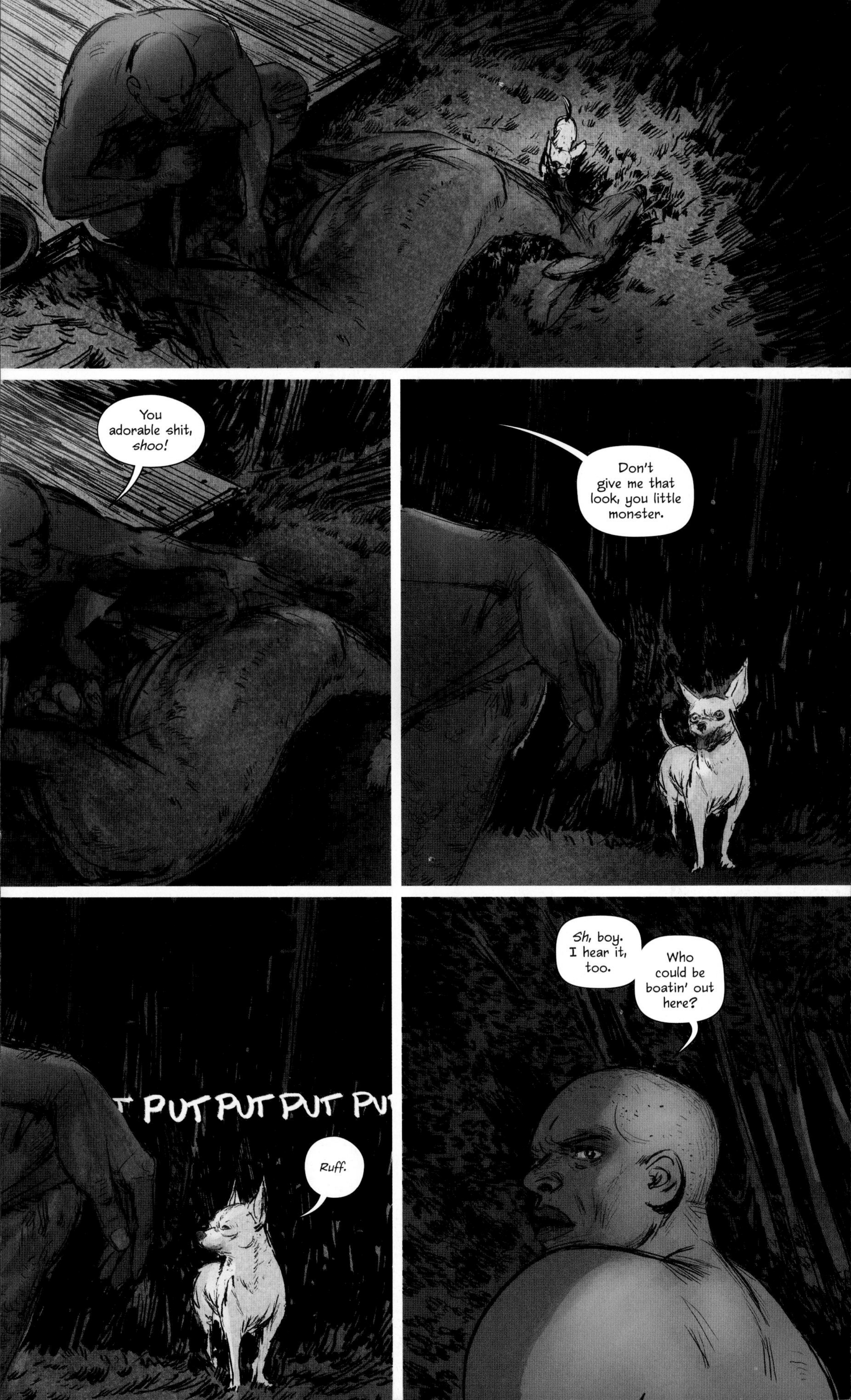

You adorable shit, *shoo!*
Don't give me that look, you little monster.
PUT PUT PUT PUT
Ruff.
Sh, boy. I hear it, too.
Who could be boatin' out here?

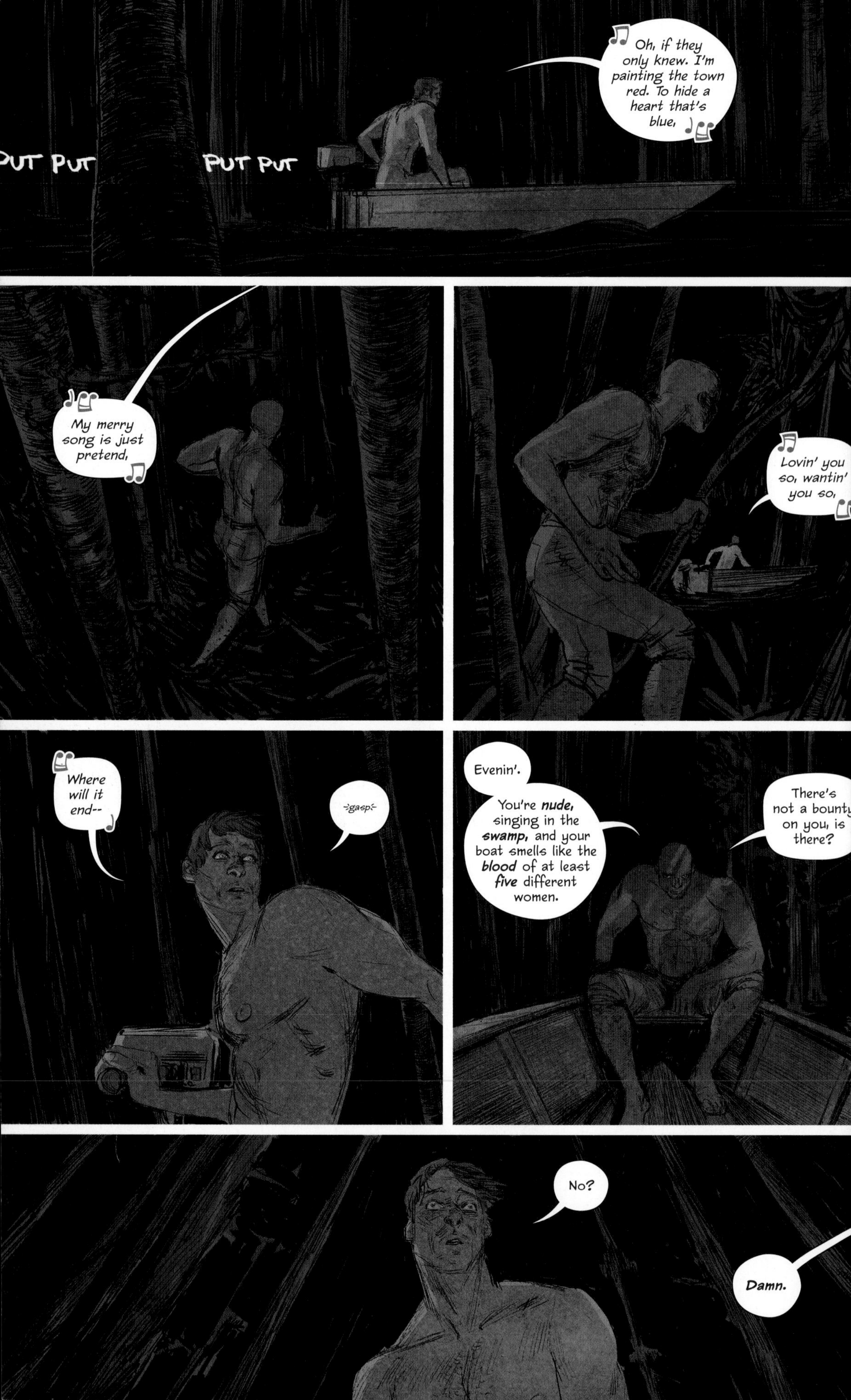
PUT PUT
PUT PUT
Oh, if they only knew. I'm painting the town red. To hide a heart that's blue,
My merry song is just pretend,
Lovin' you so, wantin' you so,
Where will it end--
-gasp-
Evenin'.
You're *nude,* singing in the *swamp,* and your boat smells like the *blood* of at least *five* different women.
There's not a bounty on you, is there?
No?
Damn.

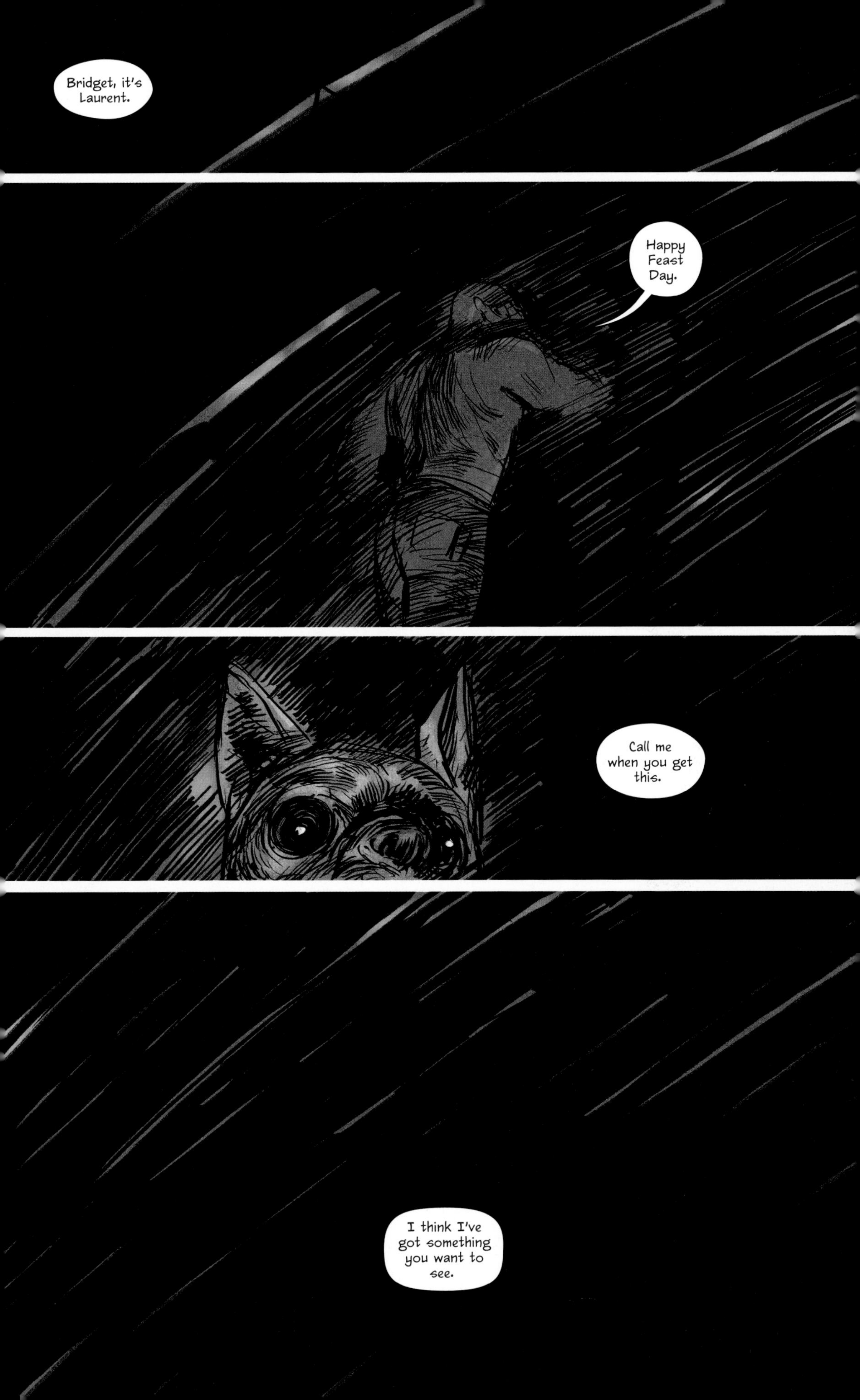
Bridget, it's Laurent.
Happy Feast Day.
Call me when you get this.
I think I've got something you want to see.

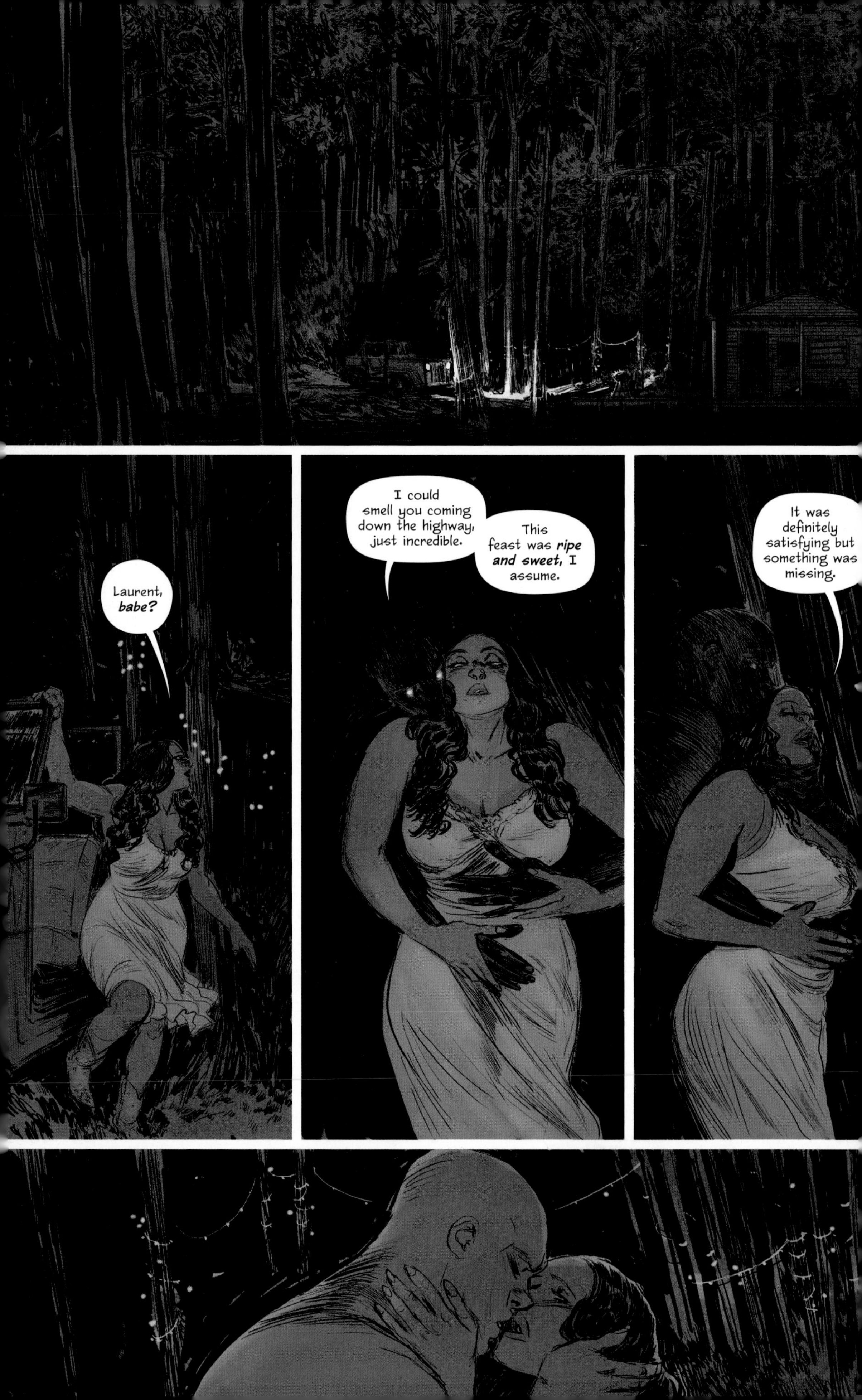
Laurent, *babe?*
I could smell you coming down the highway, just incredible.
This feast was ***ripe and sweet,*** I assume.
It was definitely satisfying but something was missing.

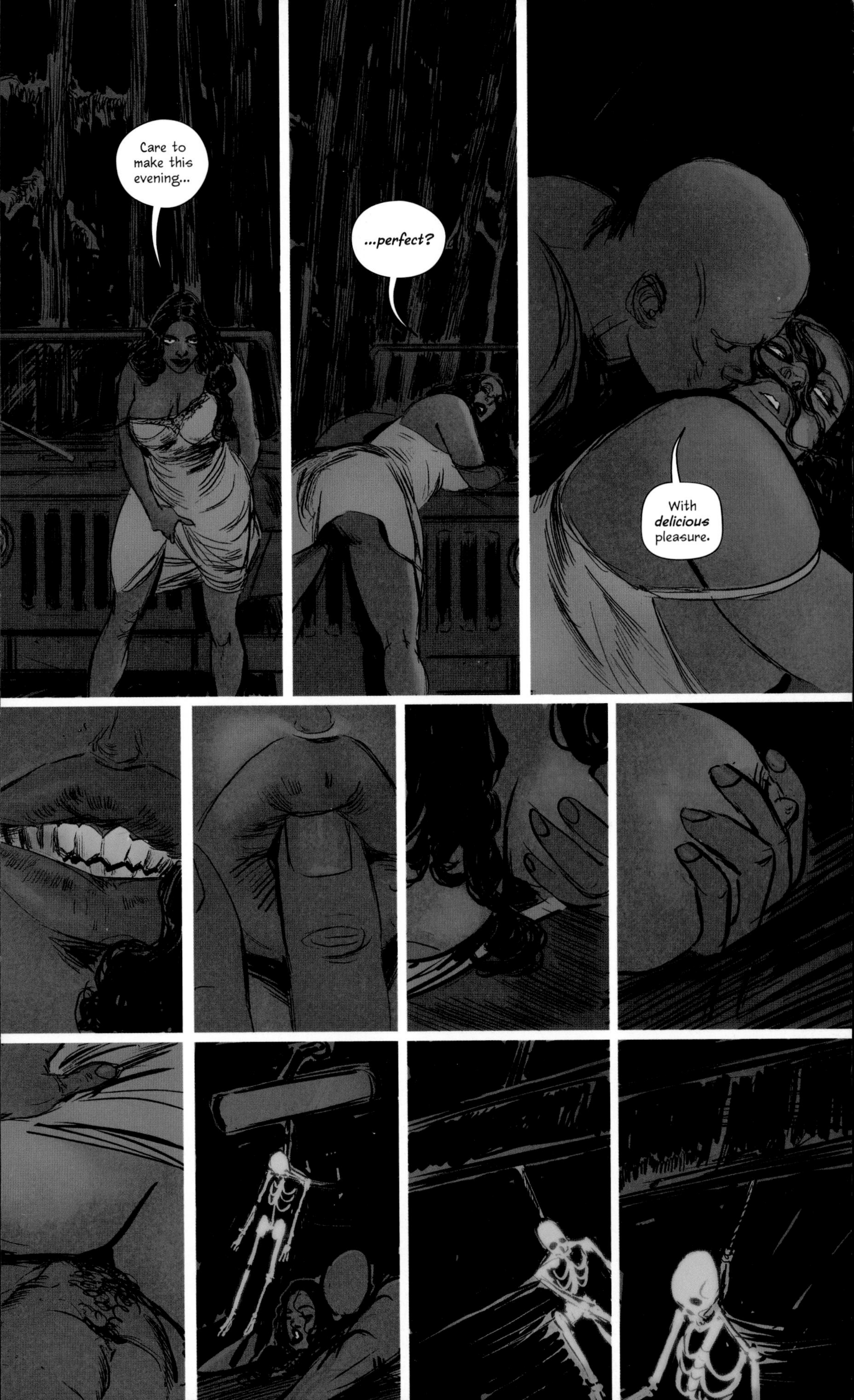
Care to make this evening...
...perfect?
With delicious pleasure.

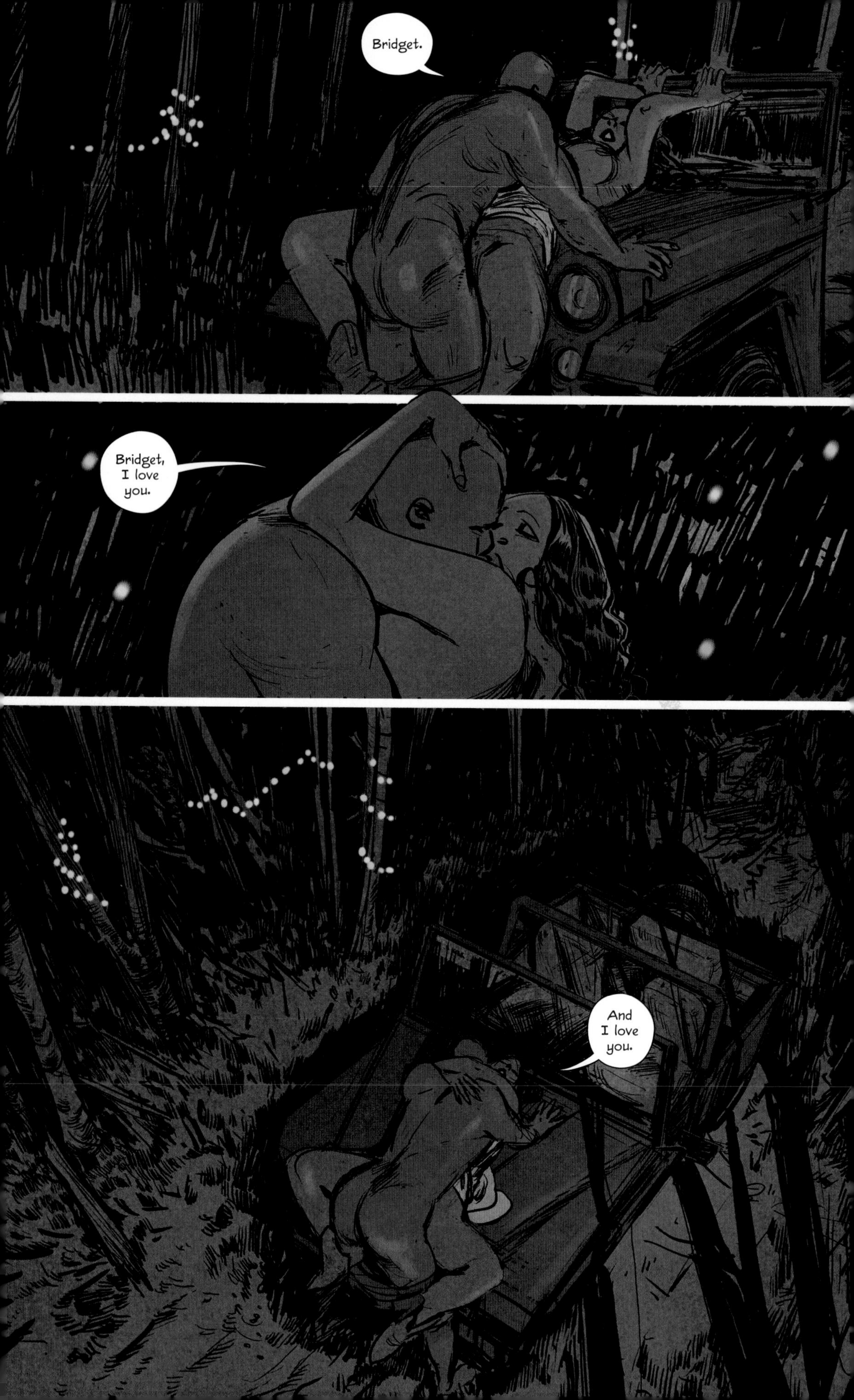
Bridget.
Bridget, I love you.
And I love you.

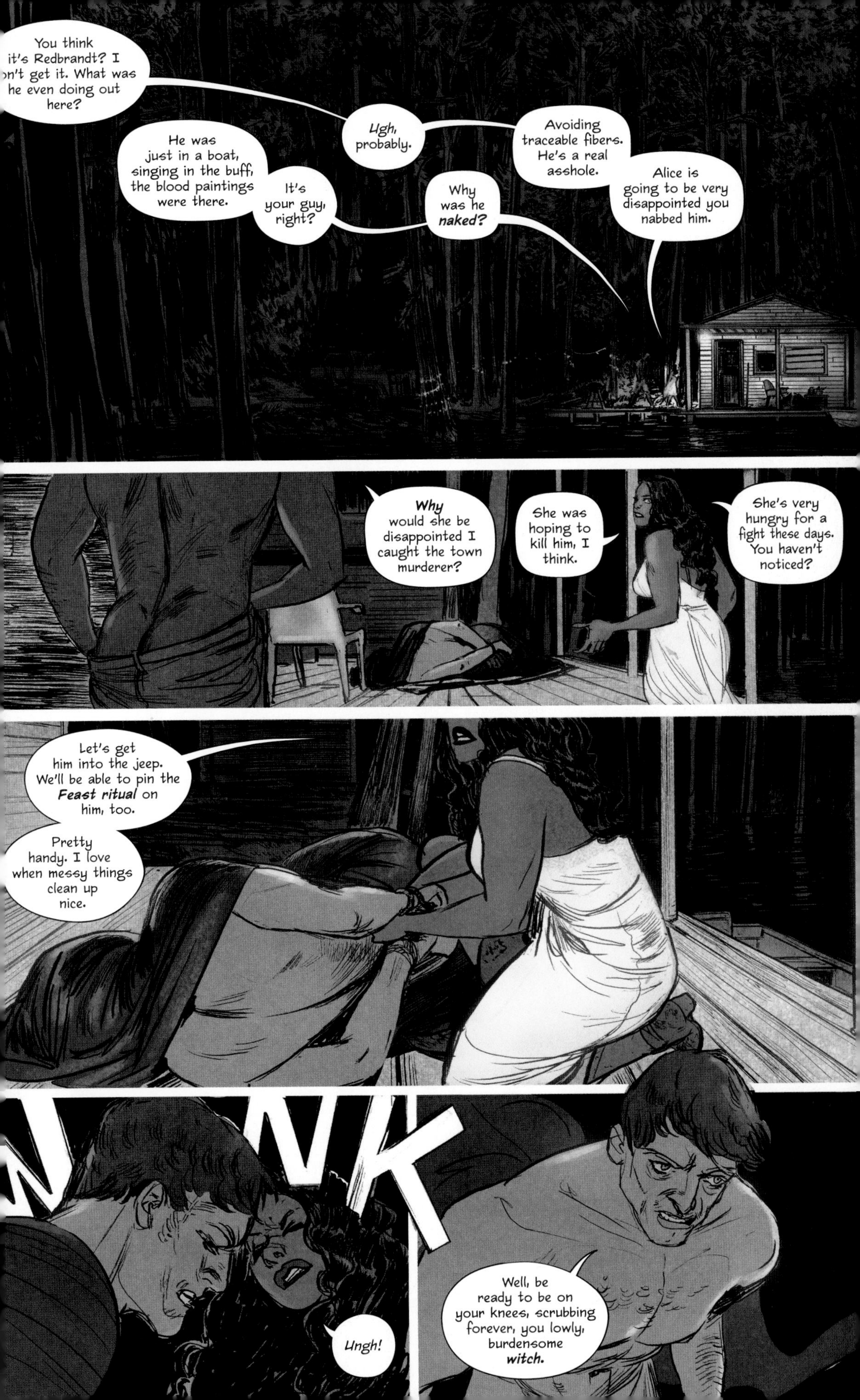

You think it's Redbrandt? I n't get it. What was he even doing out here?
He was just in a boat, singing in the buff, the blood paintings were there.
It's your guy, right?
Ugh, probably.
Why was he *naked?*
Avoiding traceable fibers. He's a real asshole.
Alice is going to be very disappointed you nabbed him.
Why would she be disappointed I caught the town murderer?
She was hoping to kill him, I think.
She's very hungry for a fight these days. You haven't noticed?
Let's get him into the jeep. We'll be able to pin the *Feast ritual* on him, too.
Pretty handy. I love when messy things clean up nice.
Ungh!
Well, be ready to be on your knees, scrubbing forever, you lowly, burdensome *witch.*

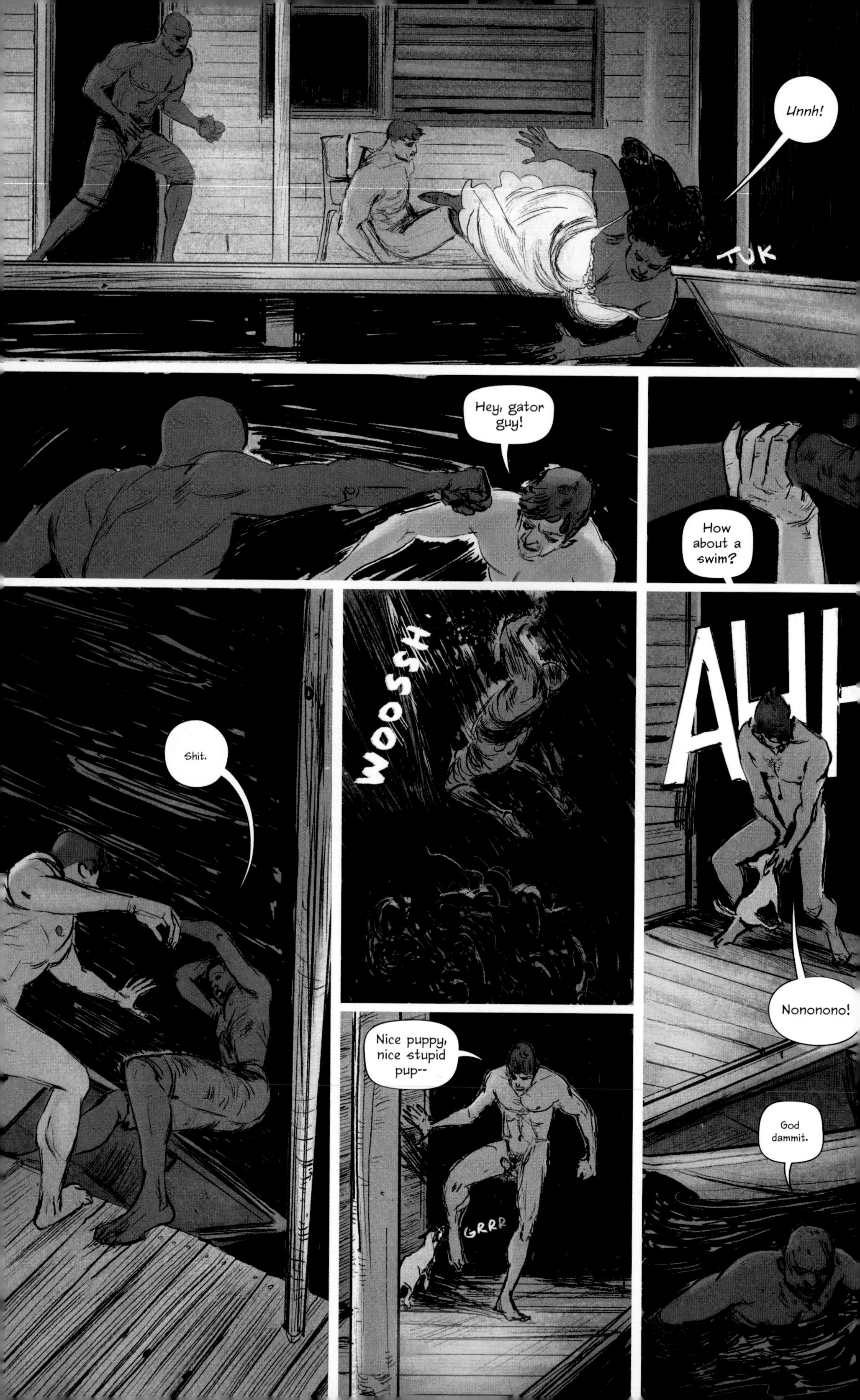
Unnh!
TUK
Hey, gator guy!
How about a swim?
Shit.
WOOSH
AHH
Nononono!
Nice puppy, nice stupid pup--
GRRR
God dammit.

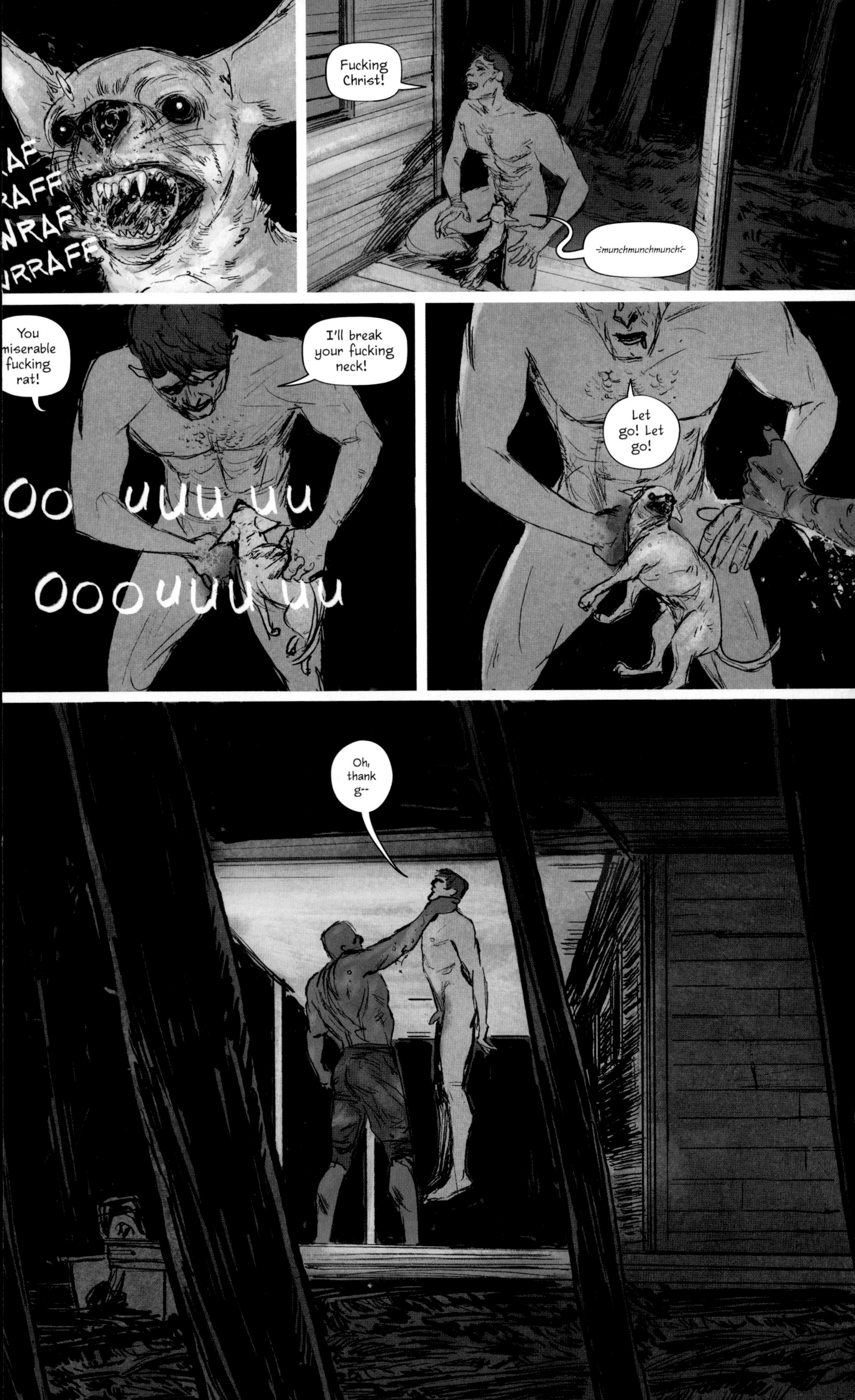
RAF
RAFF
WRAF
WRRAFF
Fucking Christ!
munchmunchmunch
You miserable fucking rat!
I'll break your fucking neck!
OO UUU UU
OOOUUU UU
Let go! Let go!
Oh, thank g--

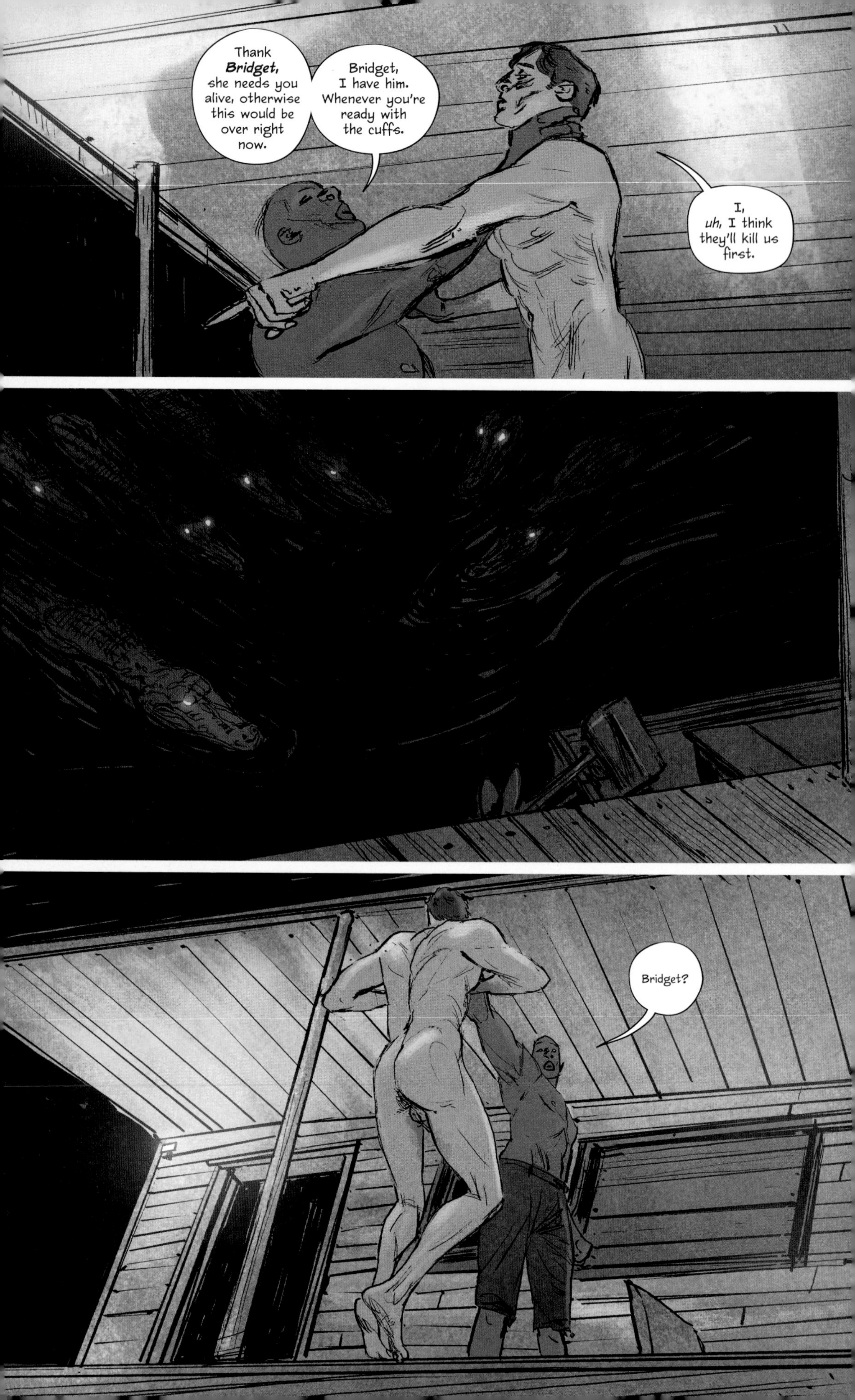
Thank **Bridget,** she needs you alive, otherwise this would be over right now.
Bridget, I have him. Whenever you're ready with the cuffs.
I, *uh,* I think they'll kill us first.
Bridget?

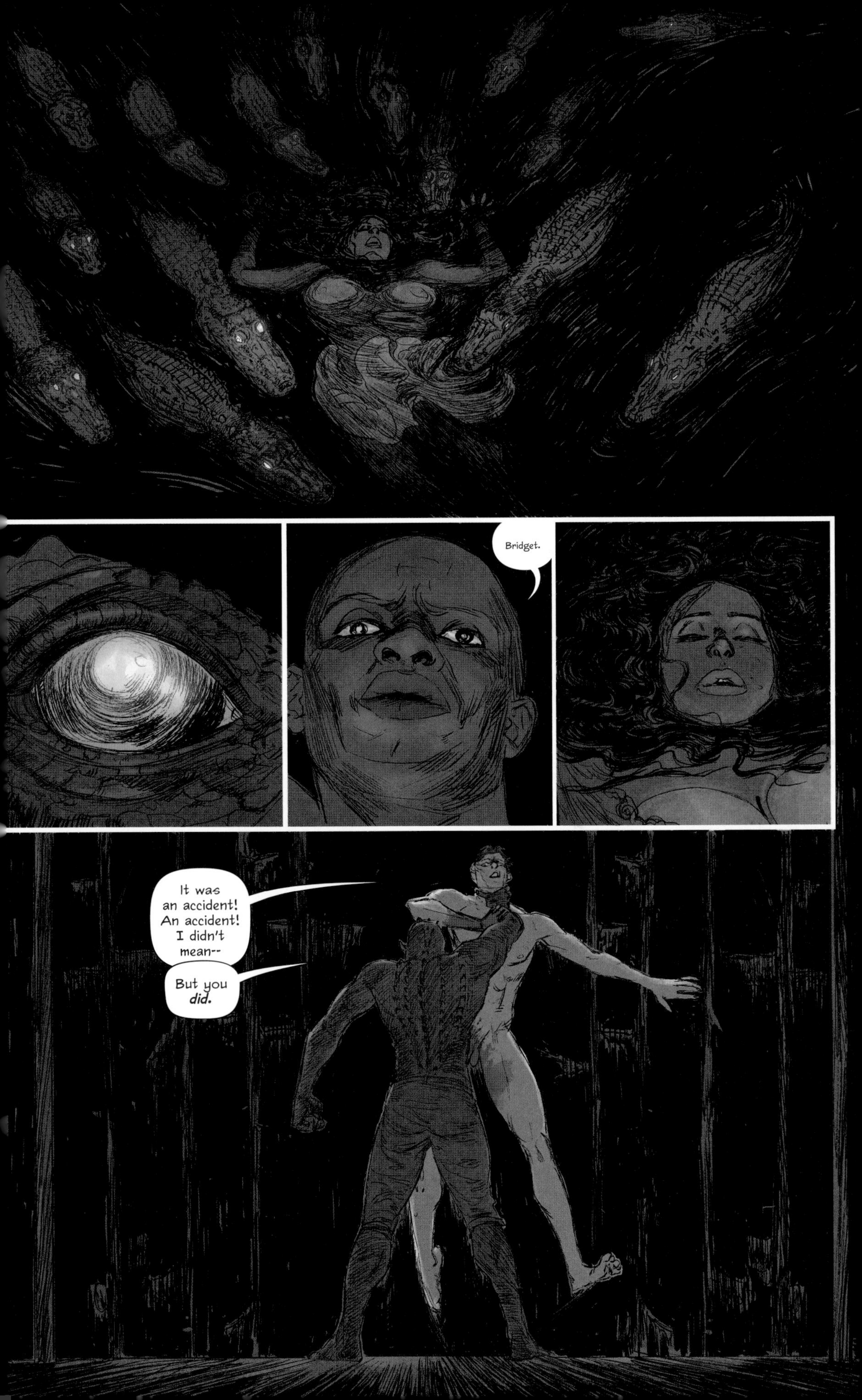

Bridget.
It was an accident! An accident! I didn't mean--
But you did.

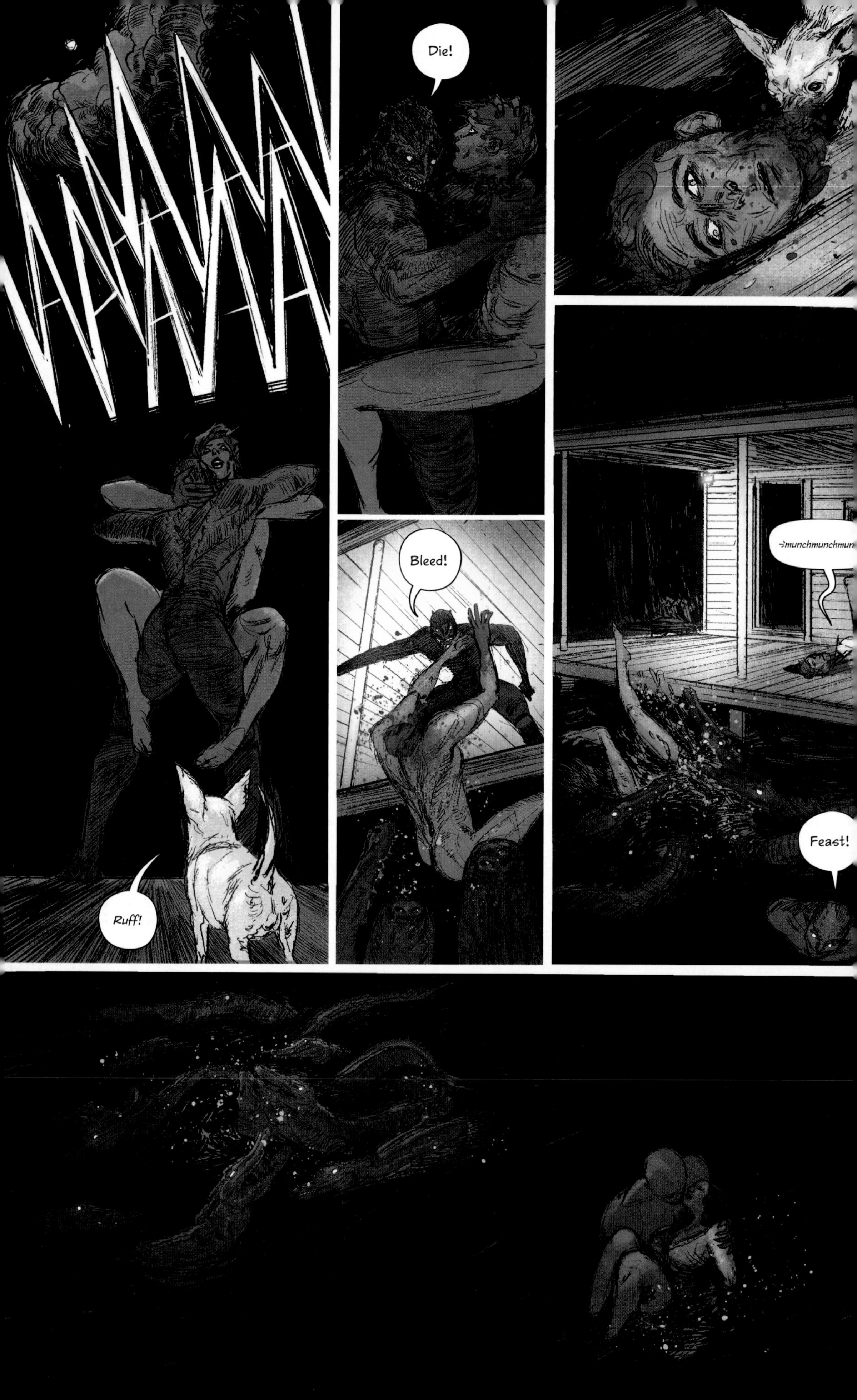
Ruff!
Die!
Bleed!
munchmunchmun
Feast!

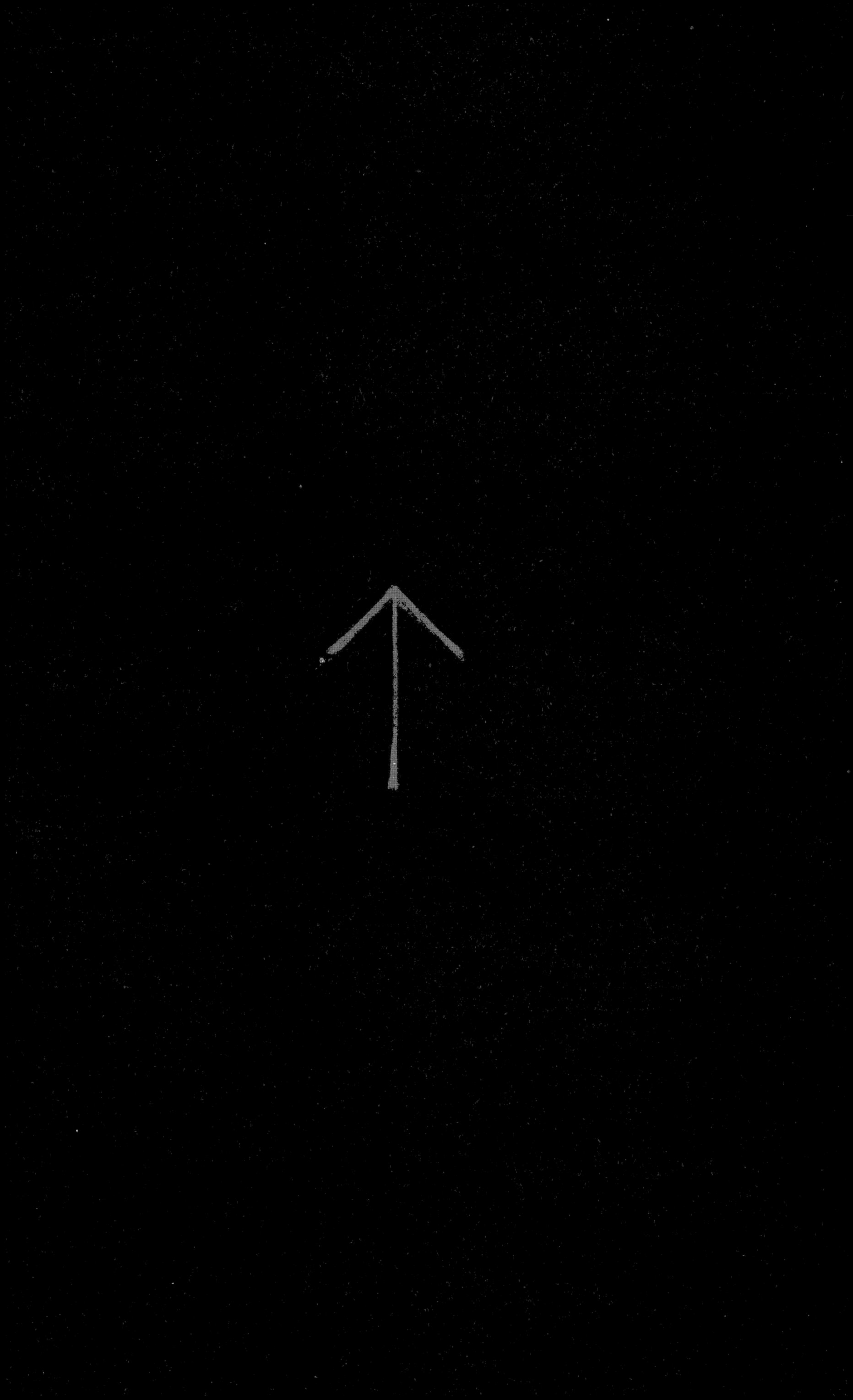

CHAPTER FOUR

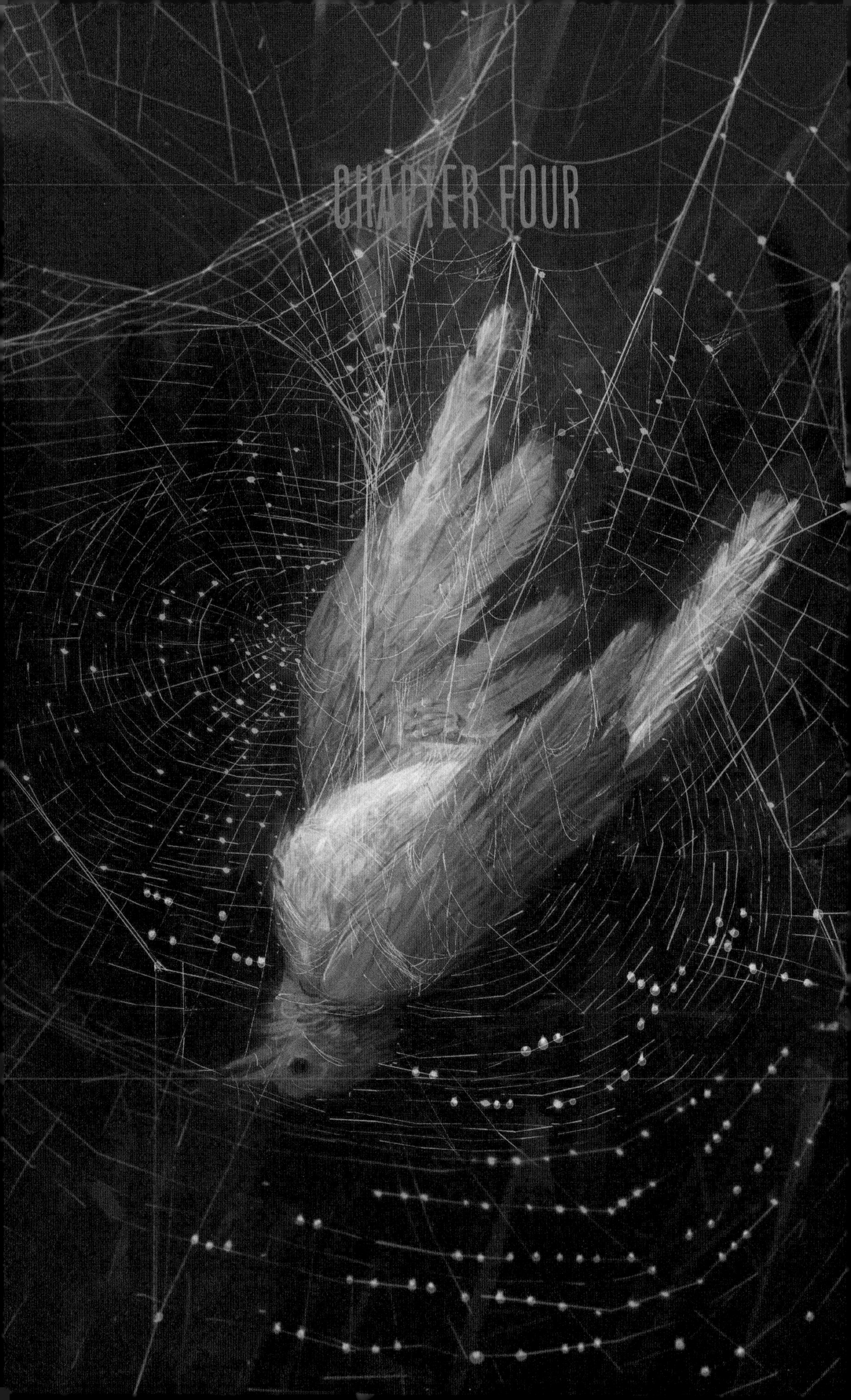

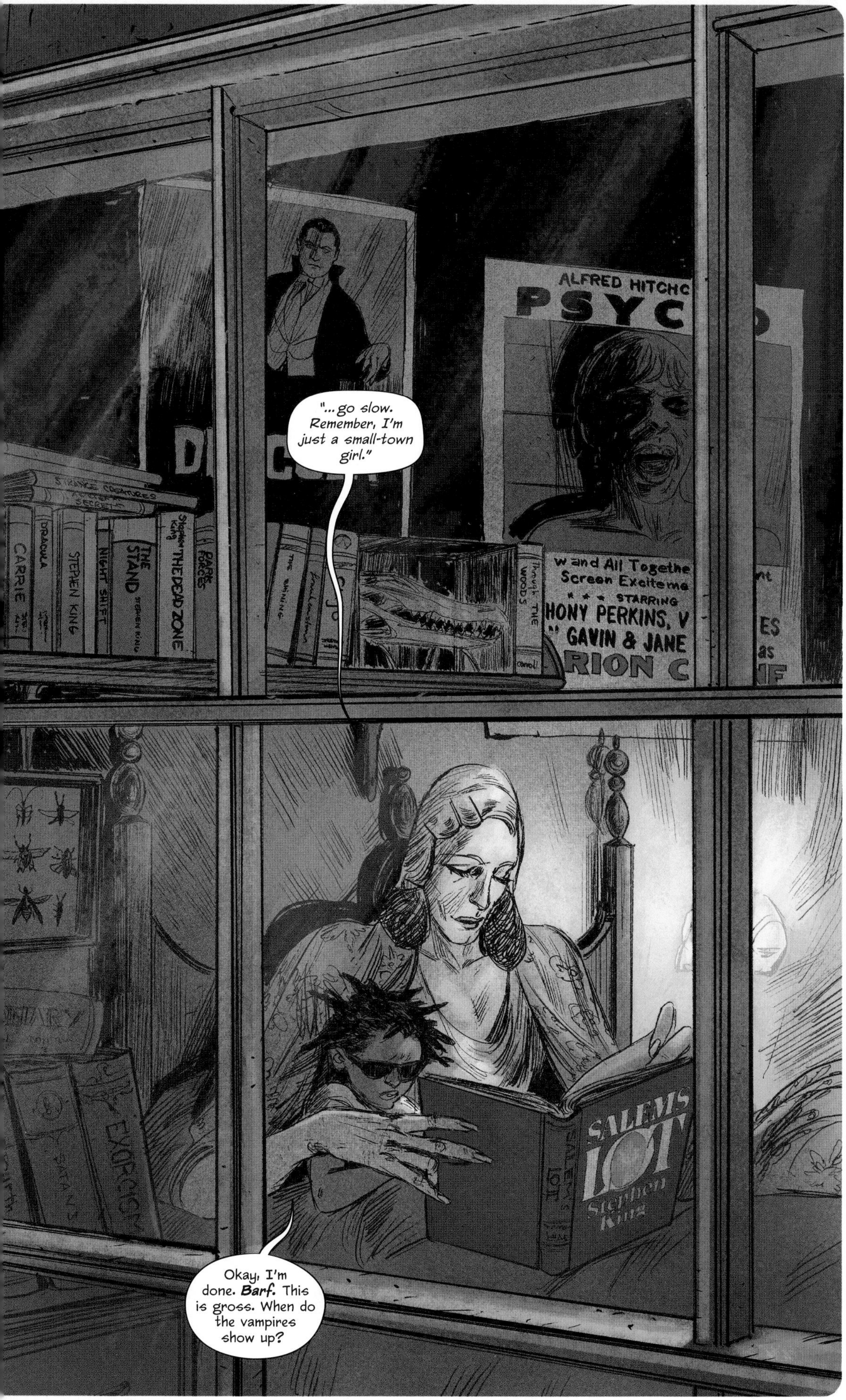

ALFRED HITCHC
PSYC
CARRIE
DRACULA
STEPHEN KING
NIGHT SHIFT
THE STAND
THE DEAD ZONE
"...go slow. Remember, I'm just a small-town girl."
w and All Togethe
Screen Exciteme
STARRING
HONY PERKINS, V
GAVIN & JANE
RION C
SALEMS LOT
Stephen King
Okay, I'm done. **Barf.** This is gross. When do the vampires show up?

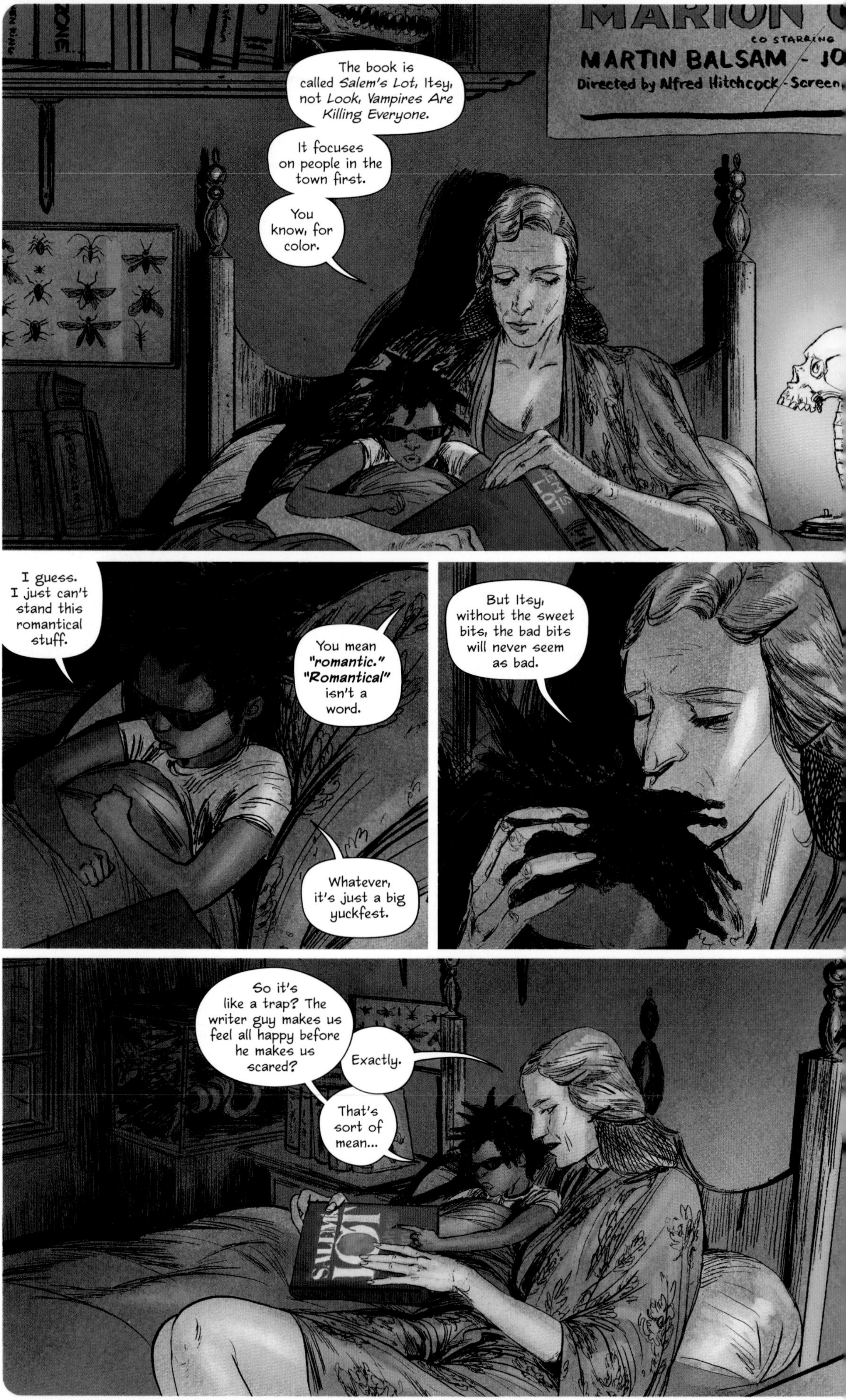
CO STARRING
MARTIN BALSAM
Directed by Alfred Hitchcock
The book is called *Salem's Lot*, Itsy, not *Look, Vampires Are Killing Everyone*.
It focuses on people in the town first.
You know, for color.
I guess. I just can't stand this romantical stuff.
You mean ***"romantic." "Romantical"*** isn't a word.
Whatever, it's just a big yuckfest.
But Itsy, without the sweet bits, the bad bits will never seem as bad.
So it's like a trap? The writer guy makes us feel all happy before he makes us scared?
Exactly.
That's sort of mean...

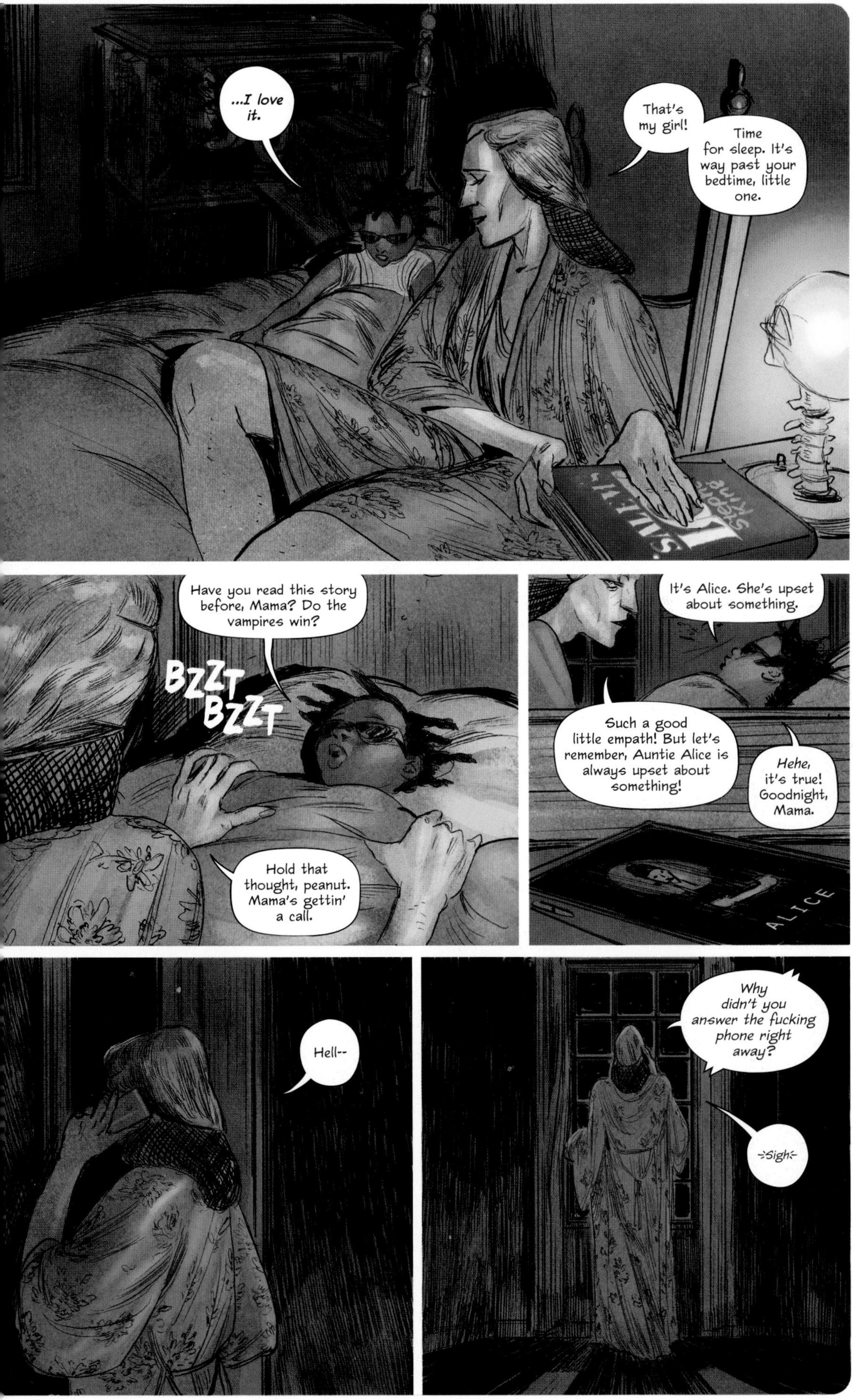
...I love it.
That's my girl!
Time for sleep. It's way past your bedtime, little one.
Have you read this story before, Mama? Do the vampires win?
BZZT BZZT
Hold that thought, peanut. Mama's gettin' a call.
It's Alice. She's upset about something.
Such a good little empath! But let's remember, Auntie Alice is always upset about something!
Hehe, it's true! Goodnight, Mama.
ALICE
Hell--
Why didn't you answer the fucking phone right away?
-Sigh-

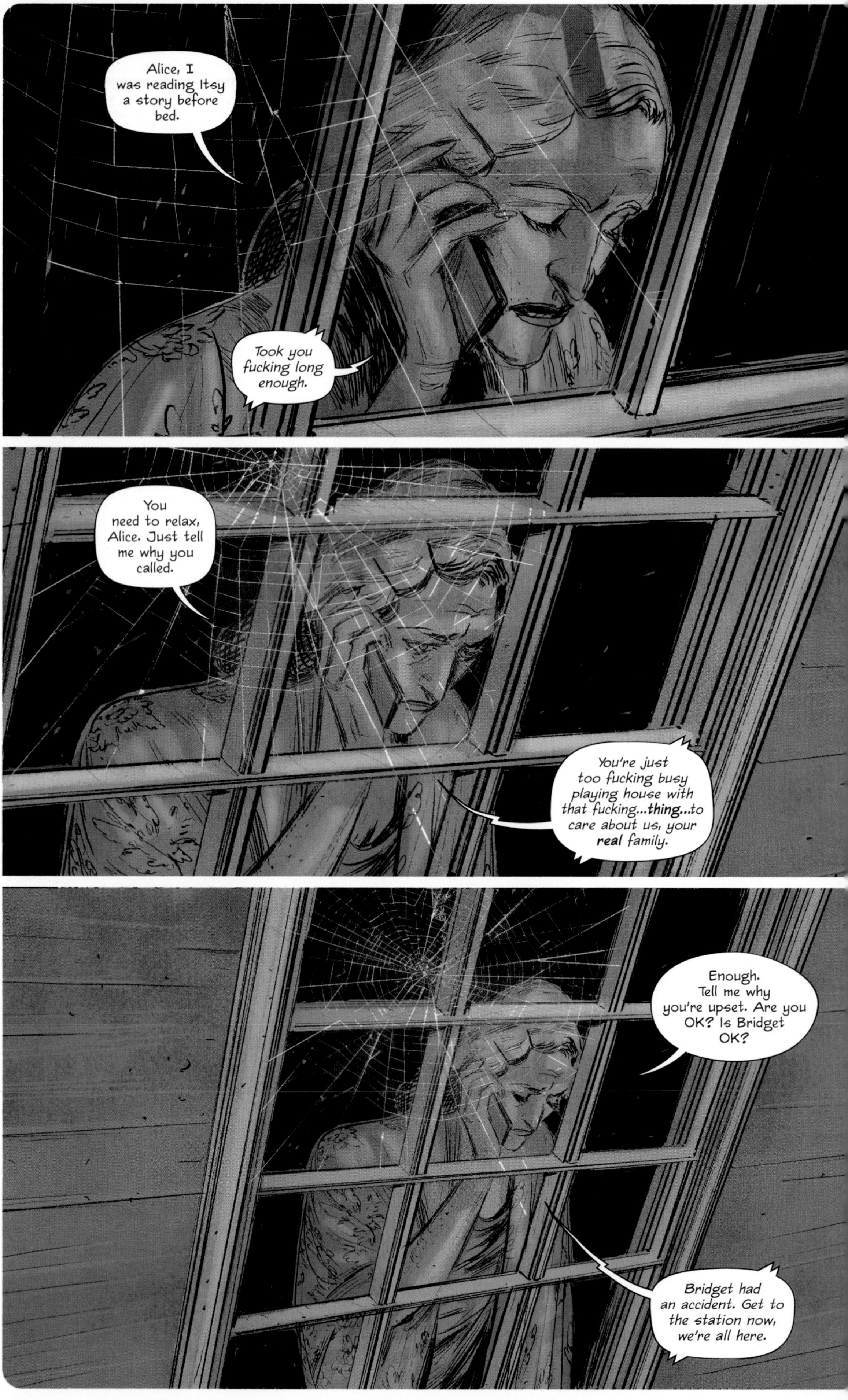
Alice, I was reading Itsy a story before bed.
Took you fucking long enough.
You need to relax, Alice. Just tell me why you called.
You're just too fucking busy playing house with that fucking...**thing**...to care about us, your **real** family.
Enough. Tell me why you're upset. Are you OK? Is Bridget OK?
Bridget had an accident. Get to the station now, we're all here.

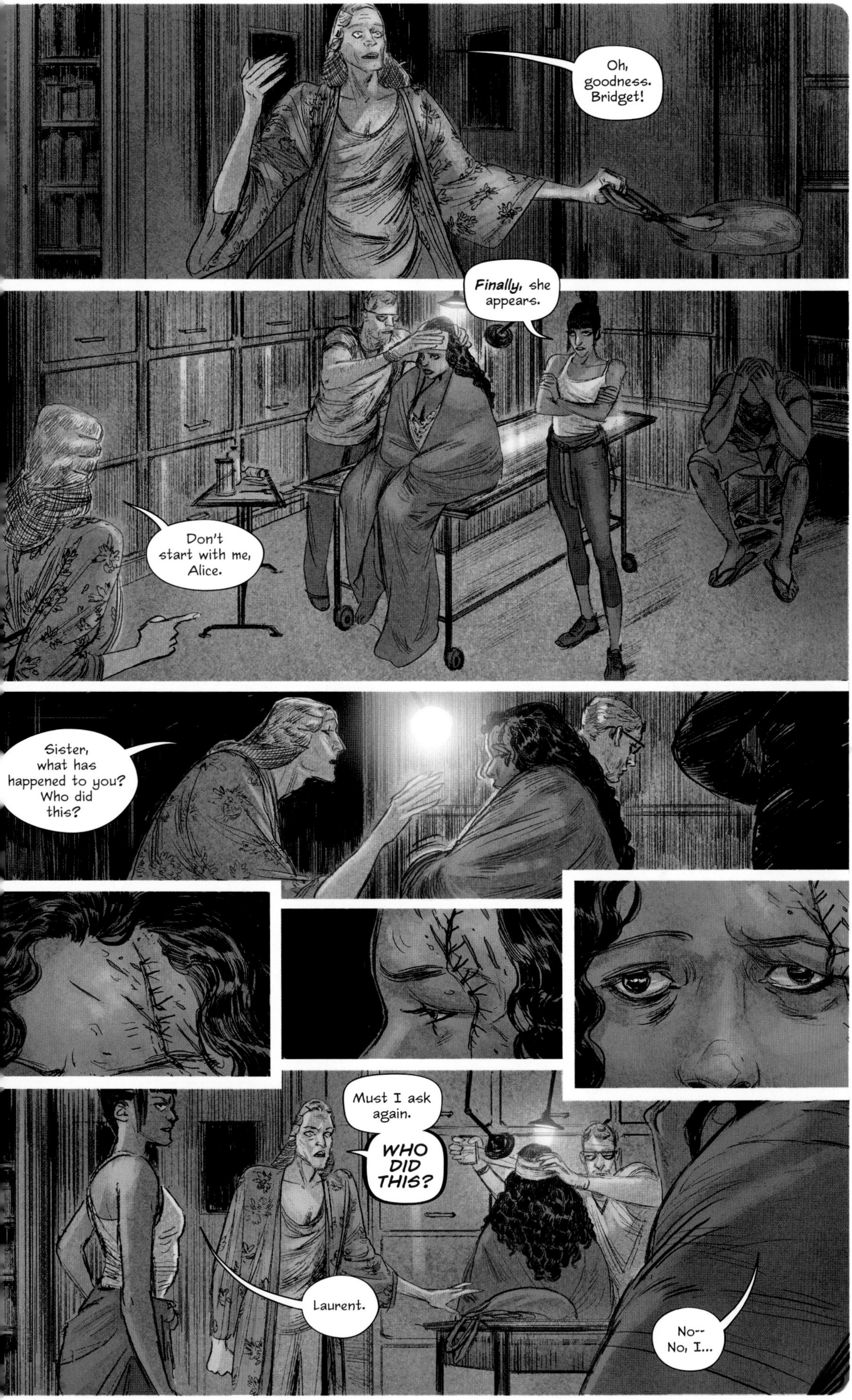
Oh, goodness. Bridget!
Finally, she appears.
Don't start with me, Alice.
Sister, what has happened to you? Who did this?
Must I ask again.
WHO DID THIS?
Laurent.
No-- No, I...

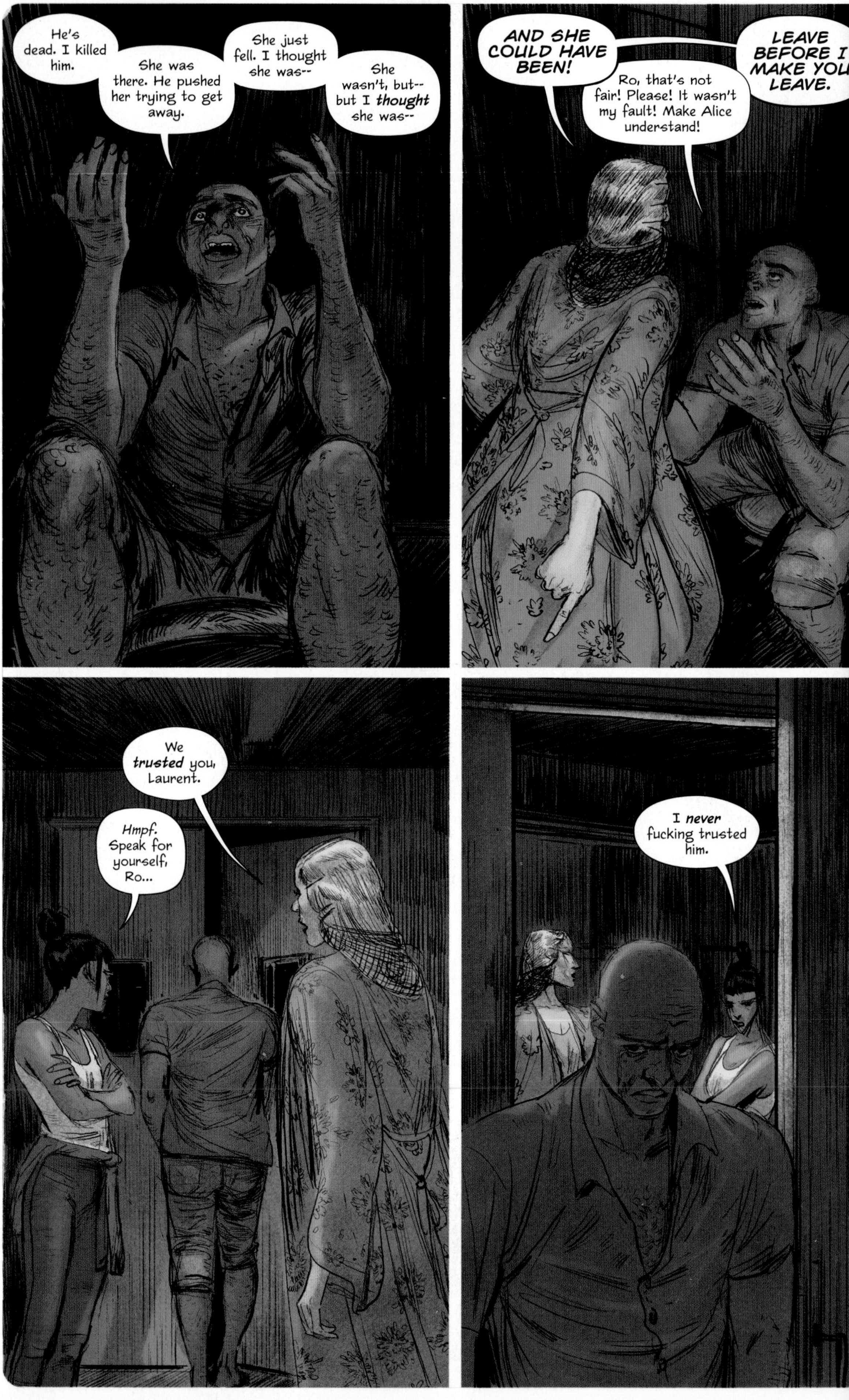
He's dead. I killed him.
She was there. He pushed her trying to get away.
She just fell. I thought she was--
She wasn't, but-- but I *thought* she was--
AND SHE COULD HAVE BEEN!
LEAVE BEFORE I MAKE YOU LEAVE.
Ro, that's not fair! Please! It wasn't my fault! Make Alice understand!
We *trusted* you, Laurent.
Hmpf. Speak for yourself, Ro...
I *never* fucking trusted him.

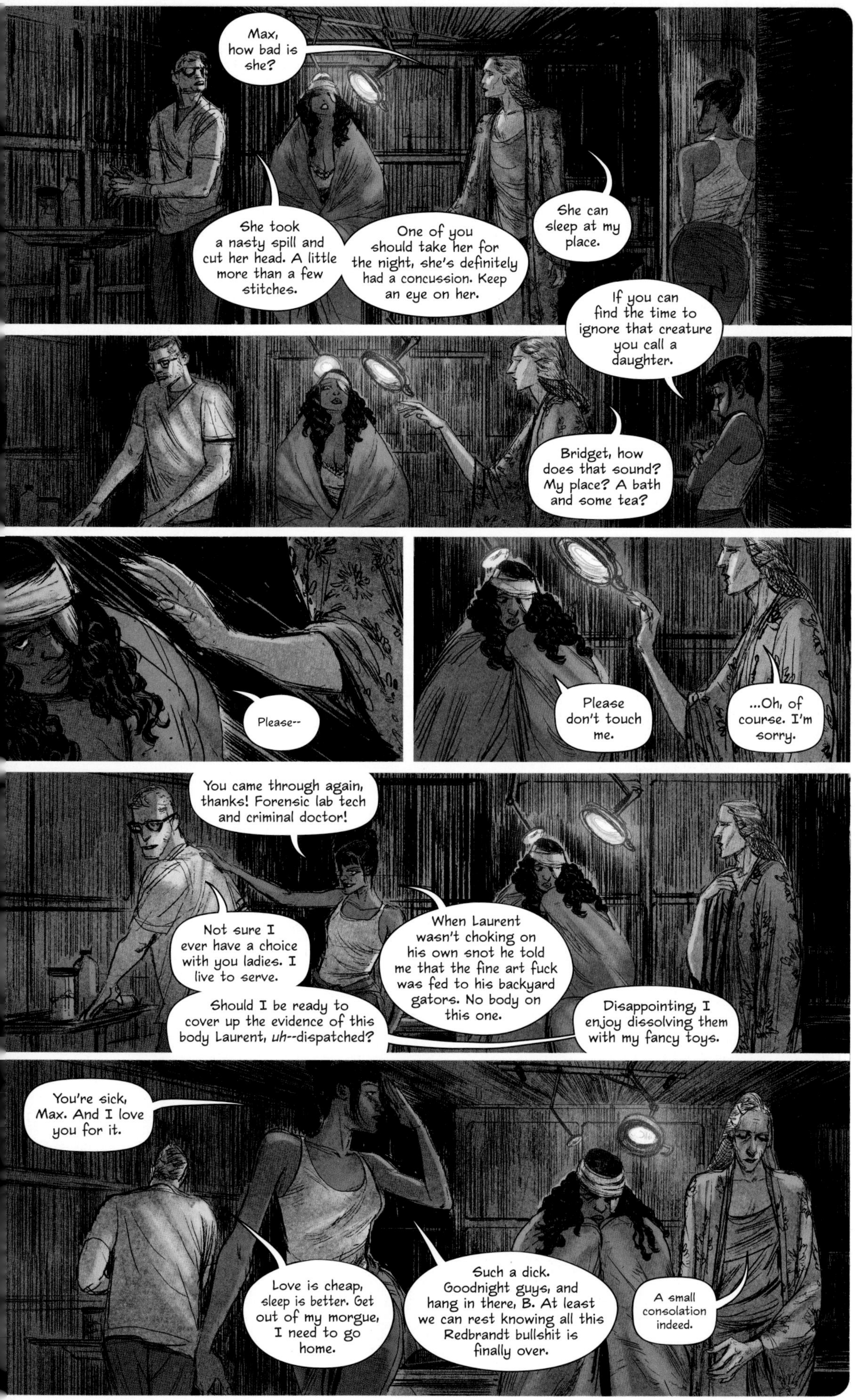
Max, how bad is she?
She took a nasty spill and cut her head. A little more than a few stitches.
One of you should take her for the night, she's definitely had a concussion. Keep an eye on her.
She can sleep at my place.
If you can find the time to ignore that creature you call a daughter.
Bridget, how does that sound? My place? A bath and some tea?
Please--
Please don't touch me.
...Oh, of course. I'm sorry.
You came through again, thanks! Forensic lab tech and criminal doctor!
Not sure I ever have a choice with you ladies. I live to serve.
Should I be ready to cover up the evidence of this body Laurent, *uh*--dispatched?
When Laurent wasn't choking on his own snot he told me that the fine art fuck was fed to his backyard gators. No body on this one.
Disappointing, I enjoy dissolving them with my fancy toys.
You're sick, Max. And I love you for it.
Love is cheap, sleep is better. Get out of my morgue, I need to go home.
Such a dick. Goodnight guys, and hang in there, B. At least we can rest knowing all this Redbrandt bullshit is finally over.
A small consolation indeed.

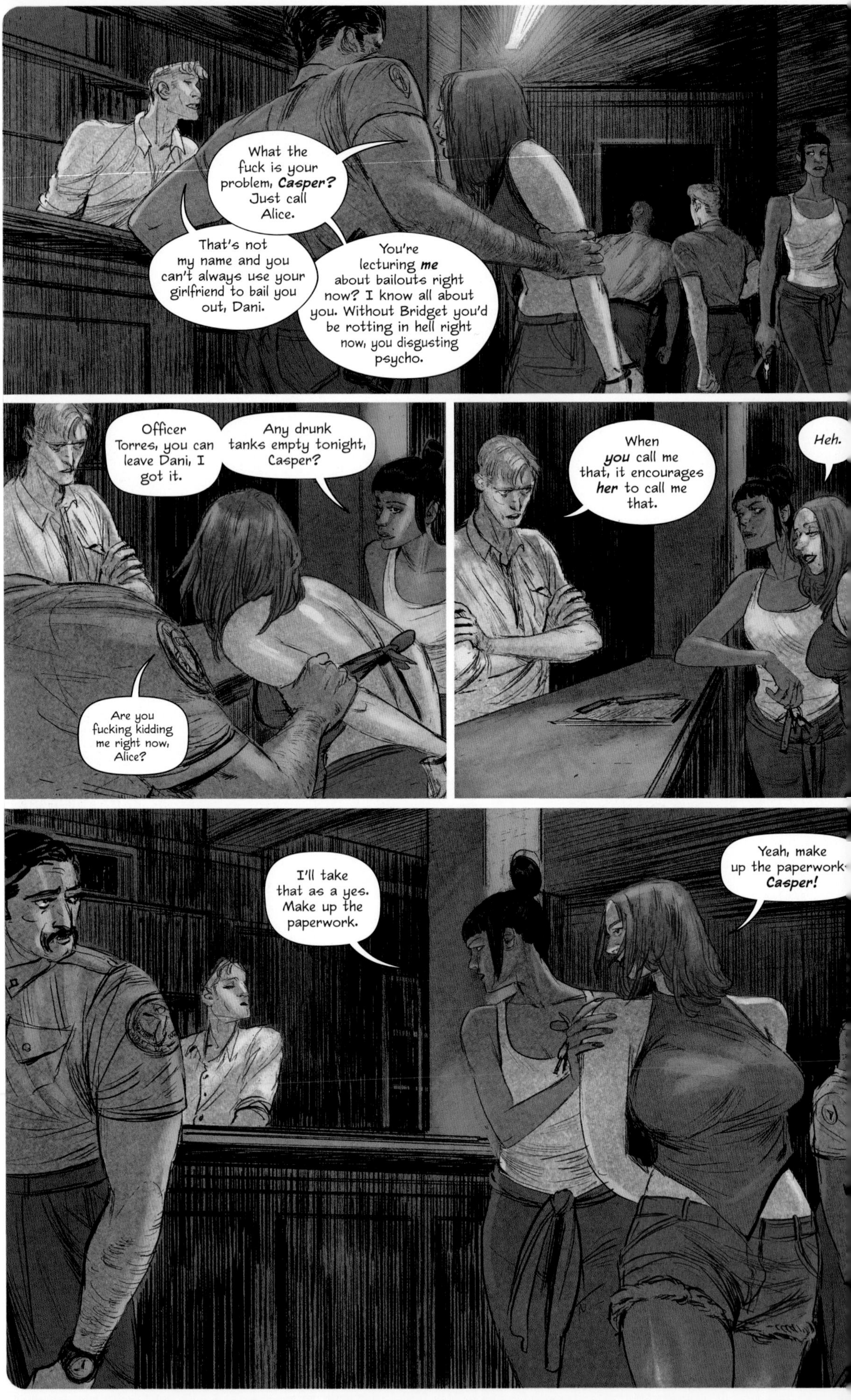
What the fuck is your problem, **Casper?** Just call Alice.
That's not my name and you can't always use your girlfriend to bail you out, Dani.
You're lecturing **me** about bailouts right now? I know all about you. Without Bridget you'd be rotting in hell right now, you disgusting psycho.
Officer Torres, you can leave Dani, I got it.
Any drunk tanks empty tonight, Casper?
Are you fucking kidding me right now, Alice?
When **you** call me that, it encourages **her** to call me that.
Heh.
I'll take that as a yes. Make up the paperwork.
Yeah, make up the paperwork, **Casper!**

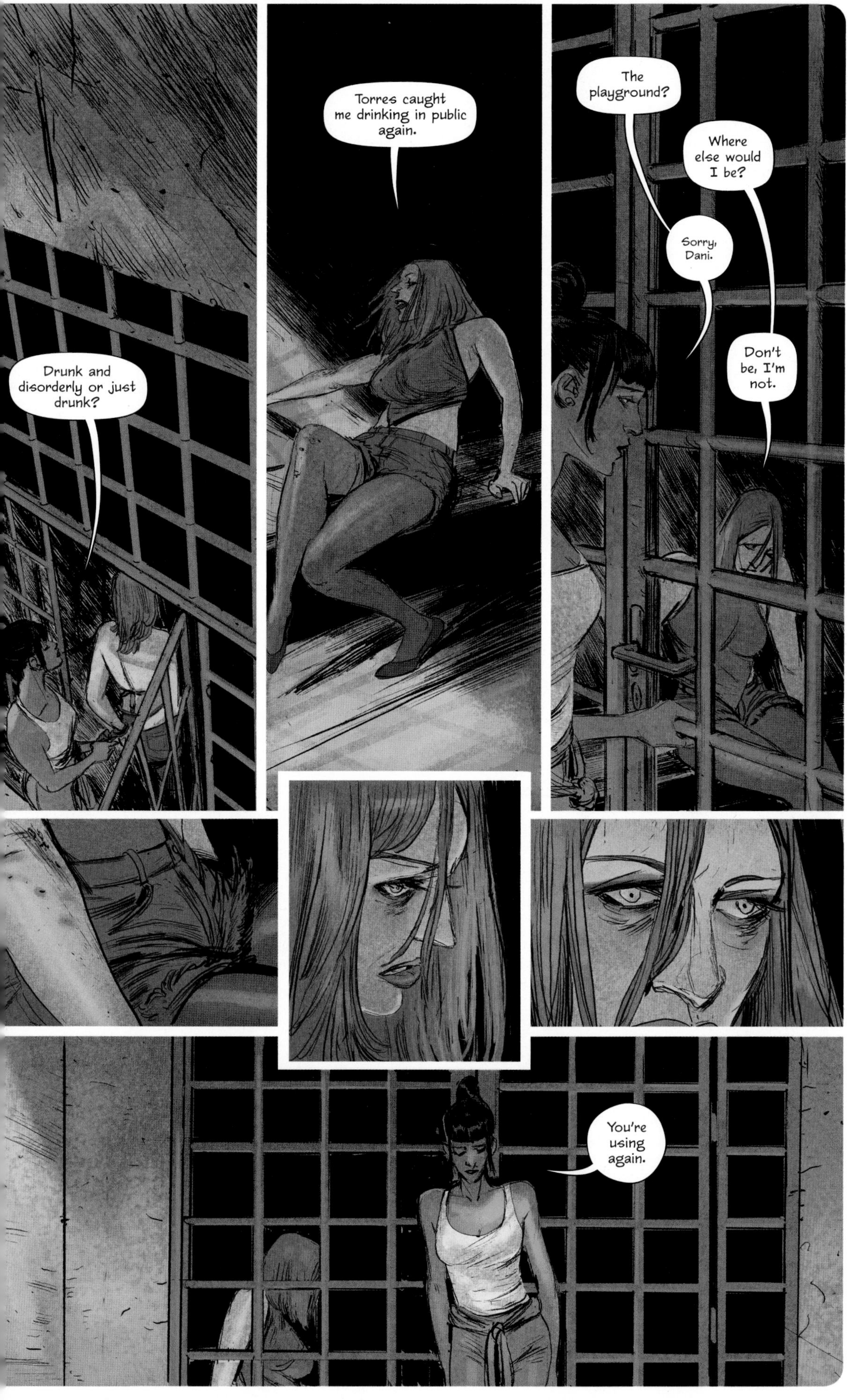
Drunk and disorderly or just drunk?
Torres caught me drinking in public again.
The playground?
Sorry, Dani.
Where else would I be?
Don't be, I'm not.
You're using again.

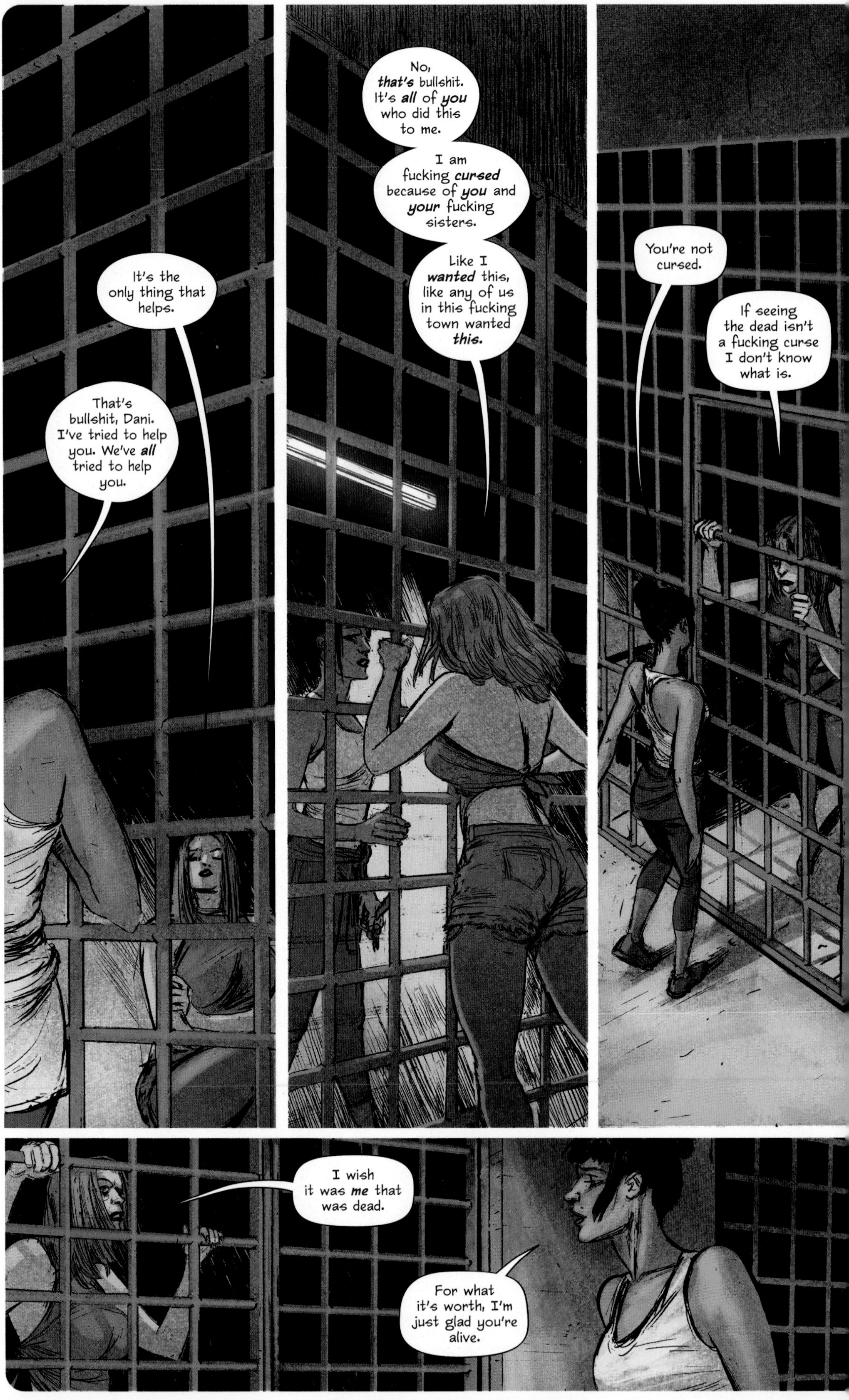
It's the only thing that helps.
That's bullshit, Dani. I've tried to help you. We've *all* tried to help you.
No, *that's* bullshit. It's *all* of *you* who did this to me.
I am fucking *cursed* because of *you* and *your* fucking sisters.
Like I *wanted* this, like any of us in this fucking town wanted *this.*
You're not cursed.
If seeing the dead isn't a fucking curse I don't know what is.
I wish it was *me* that was dead.
For what it's worth, I'm just glad you're alive.

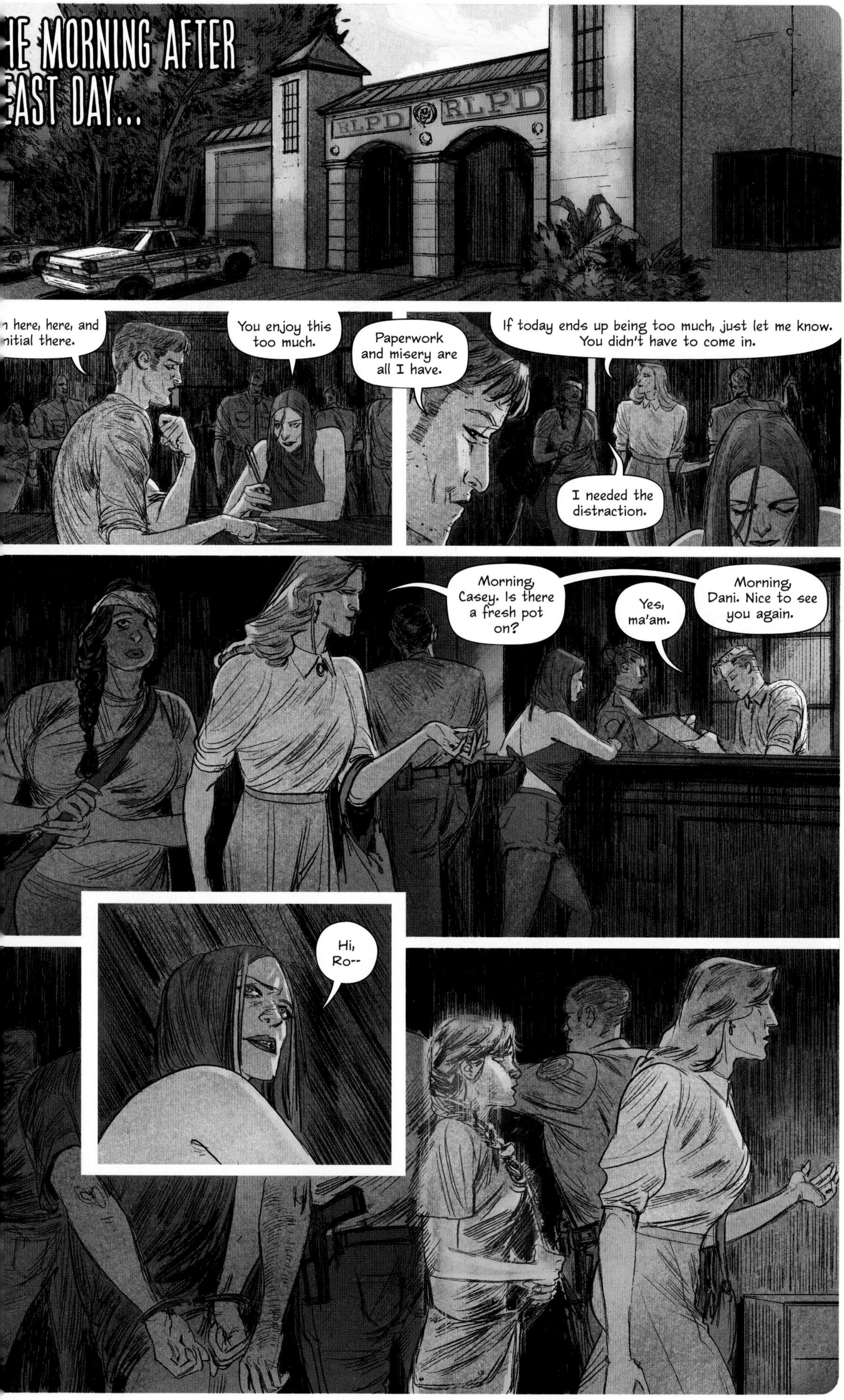
HE MORNING AFTER
EAST DAY...
RLPD
RLPD
n here, here, and
nitial there.
You enjoy this too much.
Paperwork and misery are all I have.
If today ends up being too much, just let me know. You didn't have to come in.
I needed the distraction.
Morning, Casey. Is there a fresh pot on?
Yes, ma'am.
Morning, Dani. Nice to see you again.
Hi, Ro--

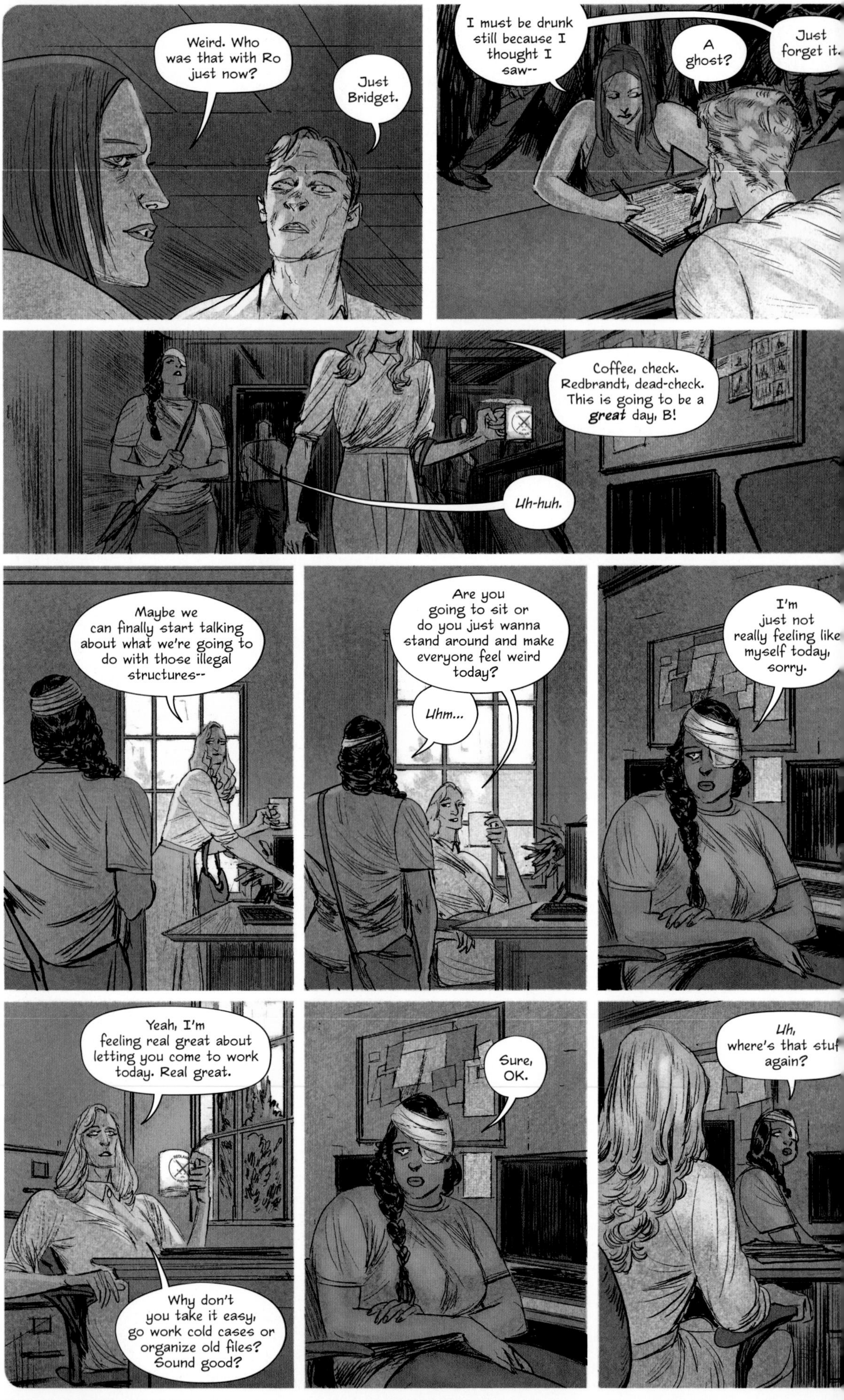
Weird. Who was that with Ro just now?
Just Bridget.
I must be drunk still because I thought I saw--
A ghost?
Just forget it.
Coffee, check. Redbrandt, dead-check. This is going to be a **great** day, B!
Uh-huh.
Maybe we can finally start talking about what we're going to do with those illegal structures--
Are you going to sit or do you just wanna stand around and make everyone feel weird today?
Uhm...
I'm just not really feeling like myself today, sorry.
Yeah, I'm feeling real great about letting you come to work today. Real great.
Why don't you take it easy, go work cold cases or organize old files? Sound good?
Sure, OK.
Uh, where's that stuf again?

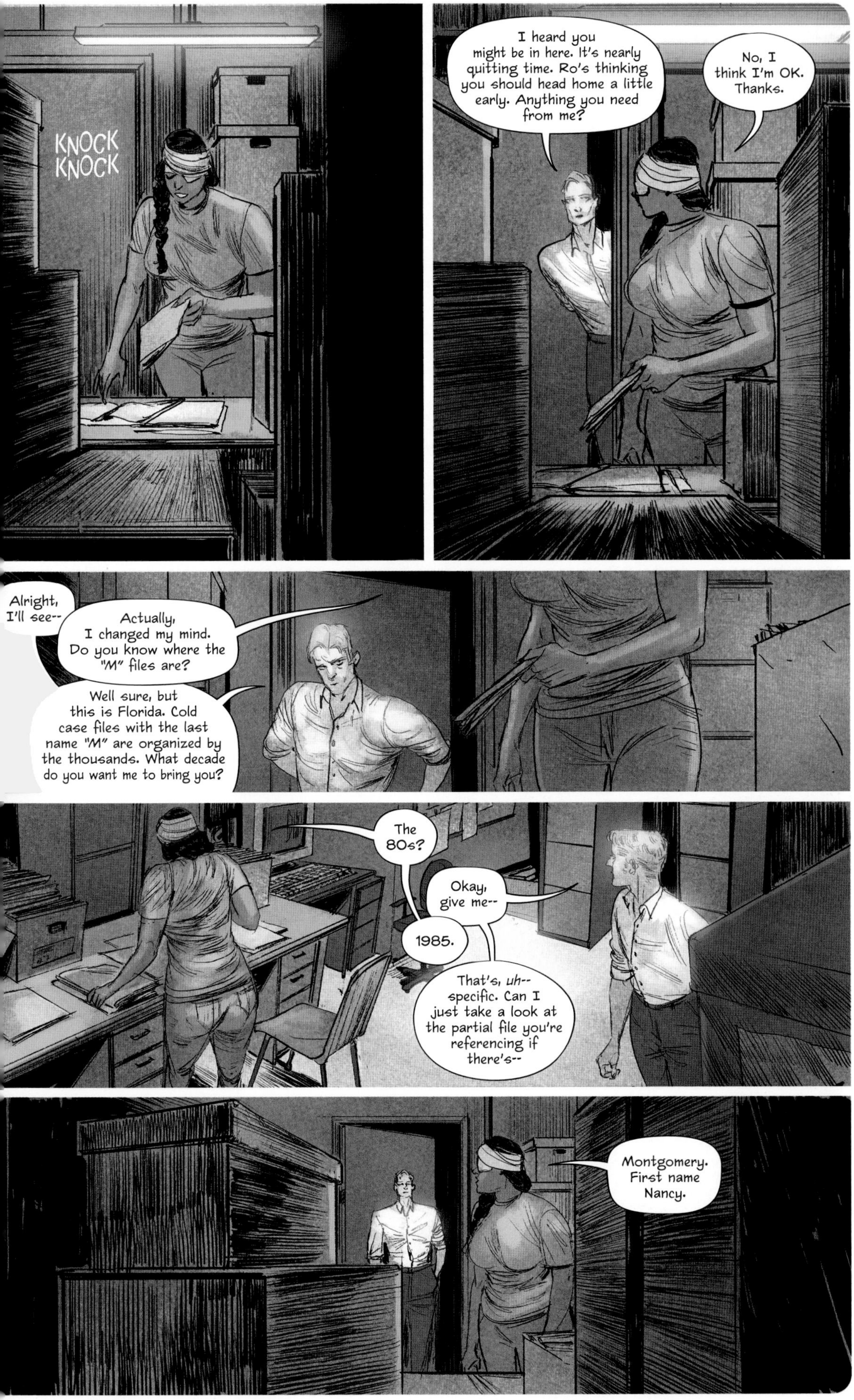
KNOCK KNOCK
I heard you might be in here. It's nearly quitting time. Ro's thinking you should head home a little early. Anything you need from me?
No, I think I'm OK. Thanks.
Alright, I'll see--
Actually, I changed my mind. Do you know where the "M" files are?
Well sure, but this is Florida. Cold case files with the last name "M" are organized by the thousands. What decade do you want me to bring you?
The 80s?
Okay, give me--
1985.
That's, *uh*-- specific. Can I just take a look at the partial file you're referencing if there's--
Montgomery. First name Nancy.

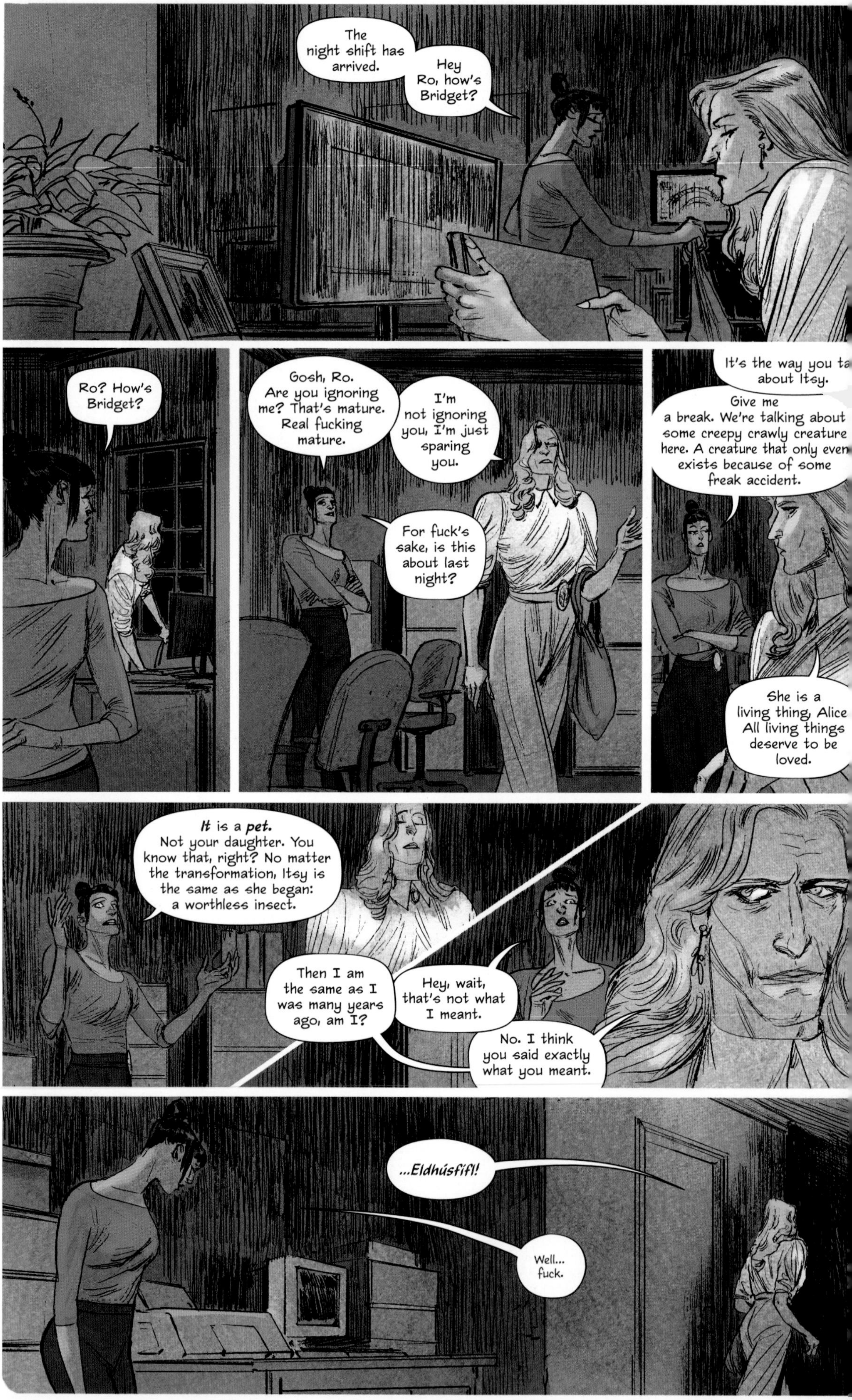
The night shift has arrived.
Hey Ro, how's Bridget?
Ro? How's Bridget?
Gosh, Ro. Are you ignoring me? That's mature. Real fucking mature.
I'm not ignoring you, I'm just sparing you.
For fuck's sake, is this about last night?
It's the way you ta about Itsy.
Give me a break. We're talking about some creepy crawly creature here. A creature that only even exists because of some freak accident.
She is a living thing, Alice All living things deserve to be loved.
It is a ***pet.*** Not your daughter. You know that, right? No matter the transformation, Itsy is the same as she began: a worthless insect.
Then I am the same as I was many years ago, am I?
Hey, wait, that's not what I meant.
No. I think you said exactly what you meant.
...Eldhúsfífl!
Well... fuck.

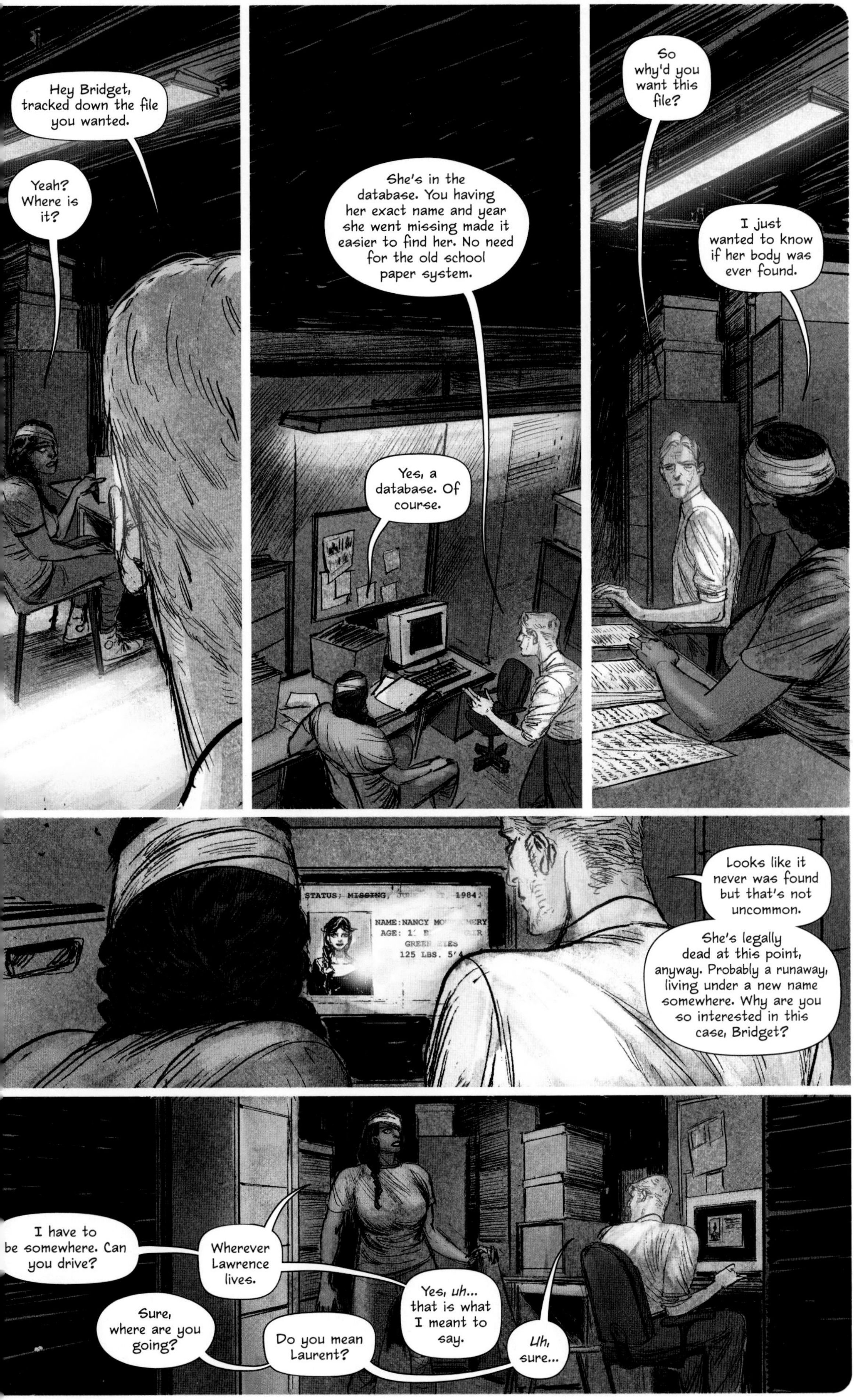
Hey Bridget, tracked down the file you wanted.
Yeah? Where is it?
She's in the database. You having her exact name and year she went missing made it easier to find her. No need for the old school paper system.
Yes, a database. Of course.
So why'd you want this file?
I just wanted to know if her body was ever found.
STATUS; MISSING,
1984.
NAME:NANCY
125 LBS.
Looks like it never was found but that's not uncommon.
She's legally dead at this point, anyway. Probably a runaway, living under a new name somewhere. Why are you so interested in this case, Bridget?
I have to be somewhere. Can you drive?
Sure, where are you going?
Wherever Lawrence lives.
Do you mean Laurent?
Yes, uh... that is what I meant to say.
Uh, sure...

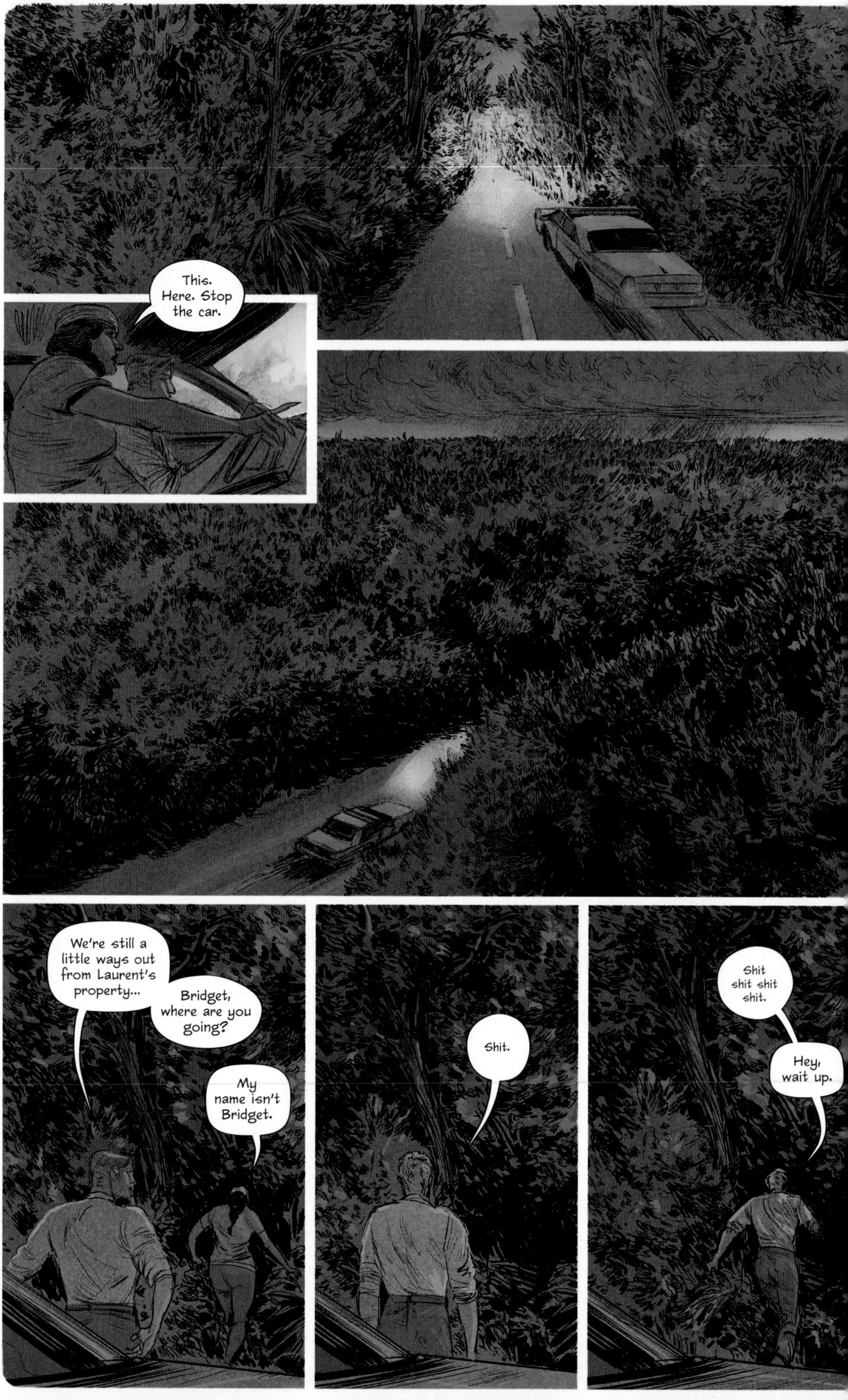
This. Here. Stop the car.
We're still a little ways out from Laurent's property...
Bridget, where are you going?
My name isn't Bridget.
Shit.
Shit shit shit shit.
Hey, wait up.

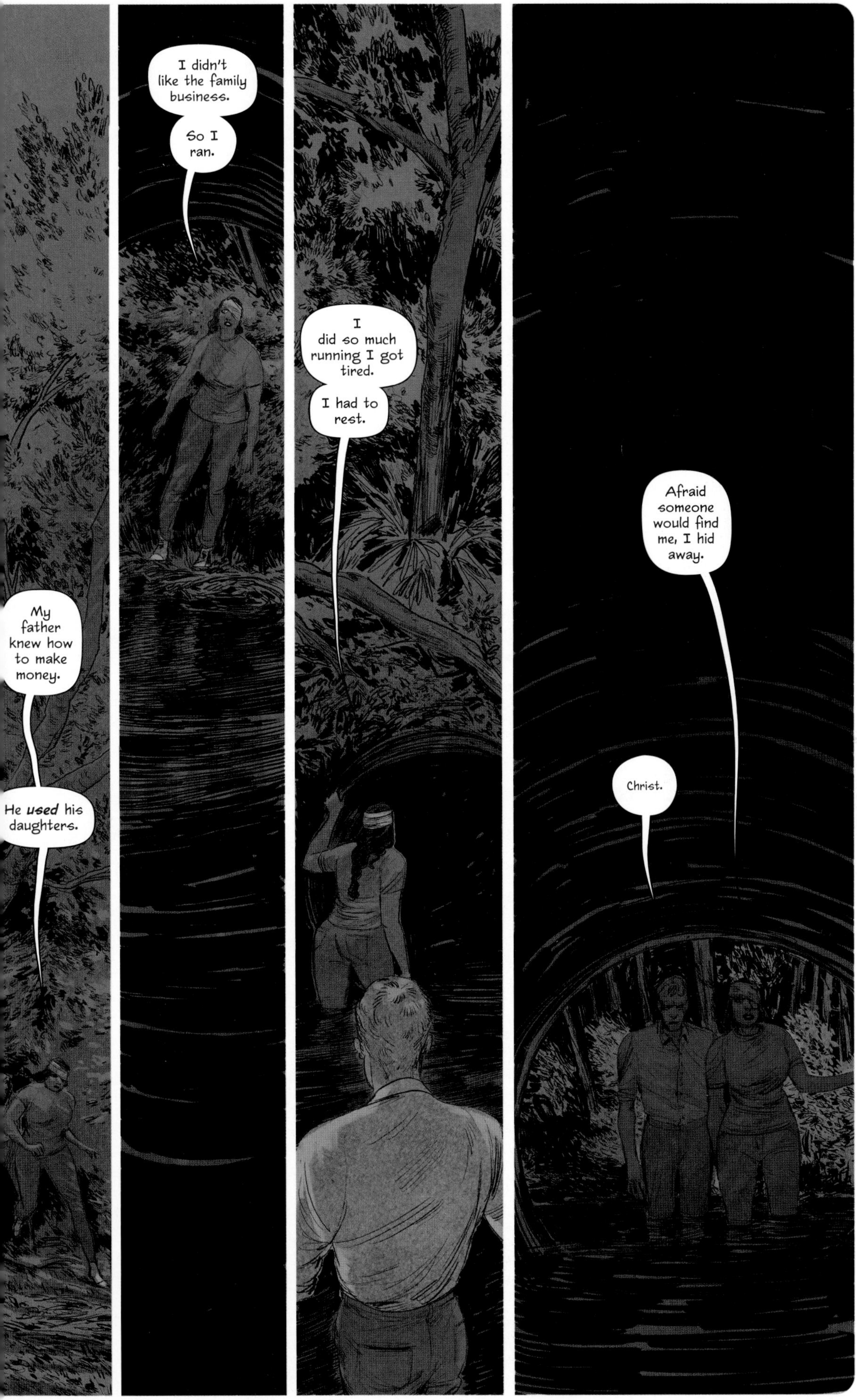
My father knew how to make money.
He *used* his daughters.
I didn't like the family business.
So I ran.
I did so much running I got tired.
I had to rest.
Afraid someone would find me, I hid away.
Christ.

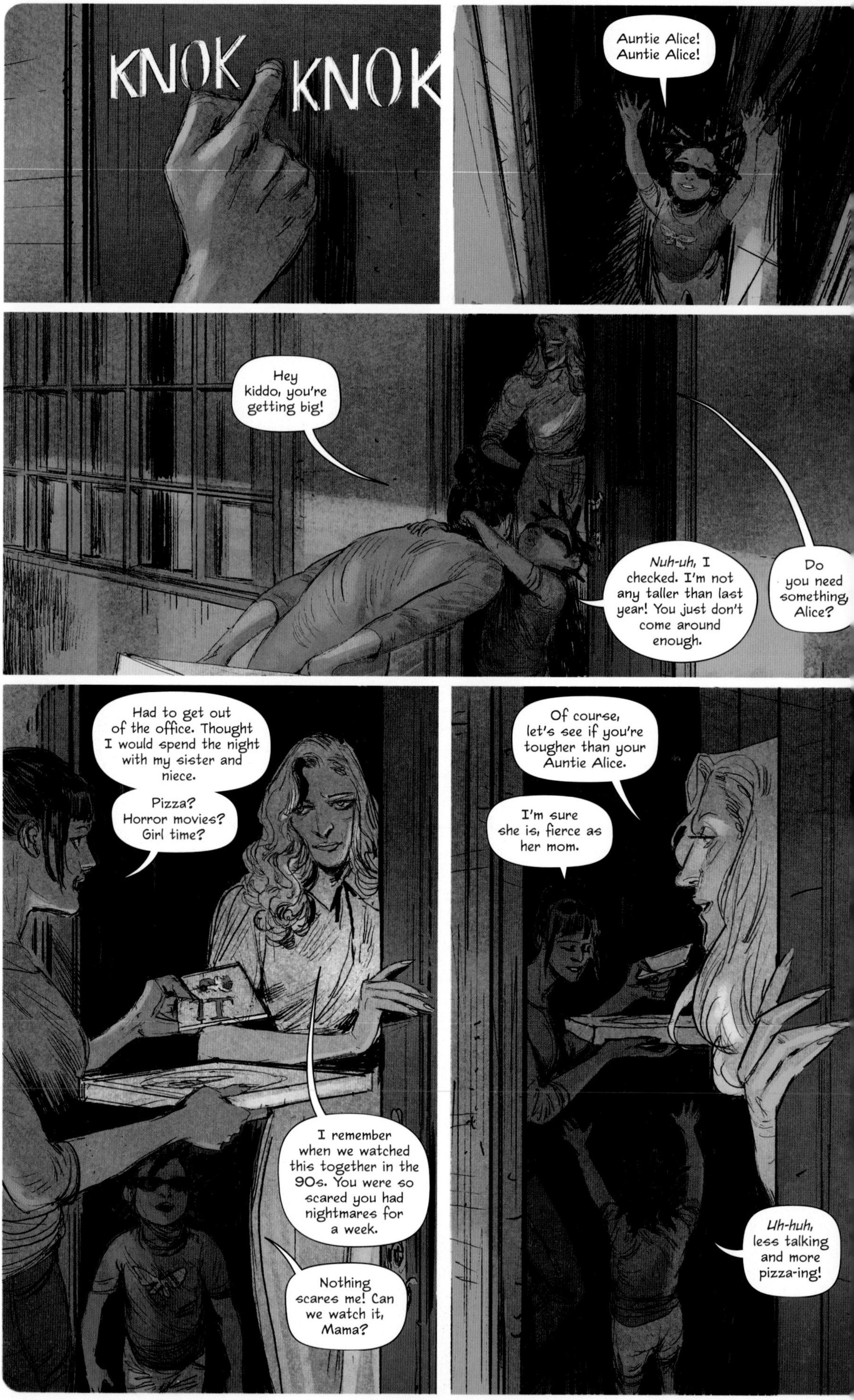
KNOK KNOK
Auntie Alice! Auntie Alice!
Hey kiddo, you're getting big!
Nuh-uh, I checked. I'm not any taller than last year! You just don't come around enough.
Do you need something, Alice?
Had to get out of the office. Thought I would spend the night with my sister and niece.
Pizza? Horror movies? Girl time?
I remember when we watched this together in the 90s. You were so scared you had nightmares for a week.
Nothing scares me! Can we watch it, Mama?
Of course, let's see if you're tougher than your Auntie Alice.
I'm sure she is, fierce as her mom.
Uh-huh, less talking and more pizza-ing!

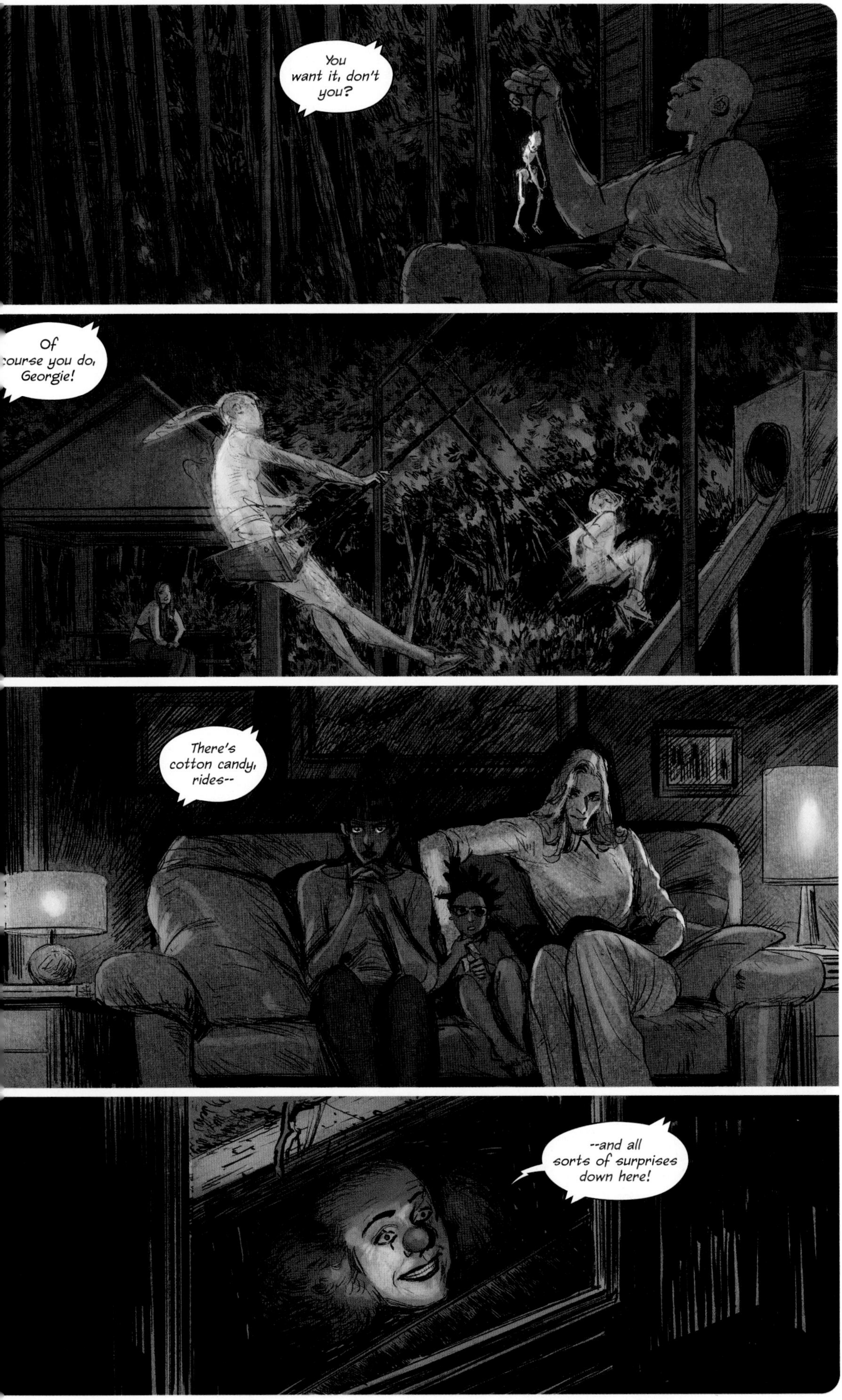
You want it, don't you?
Of course you do, Georgie!
There's cotton candy, rides--
--and all sorts of surprises down here!

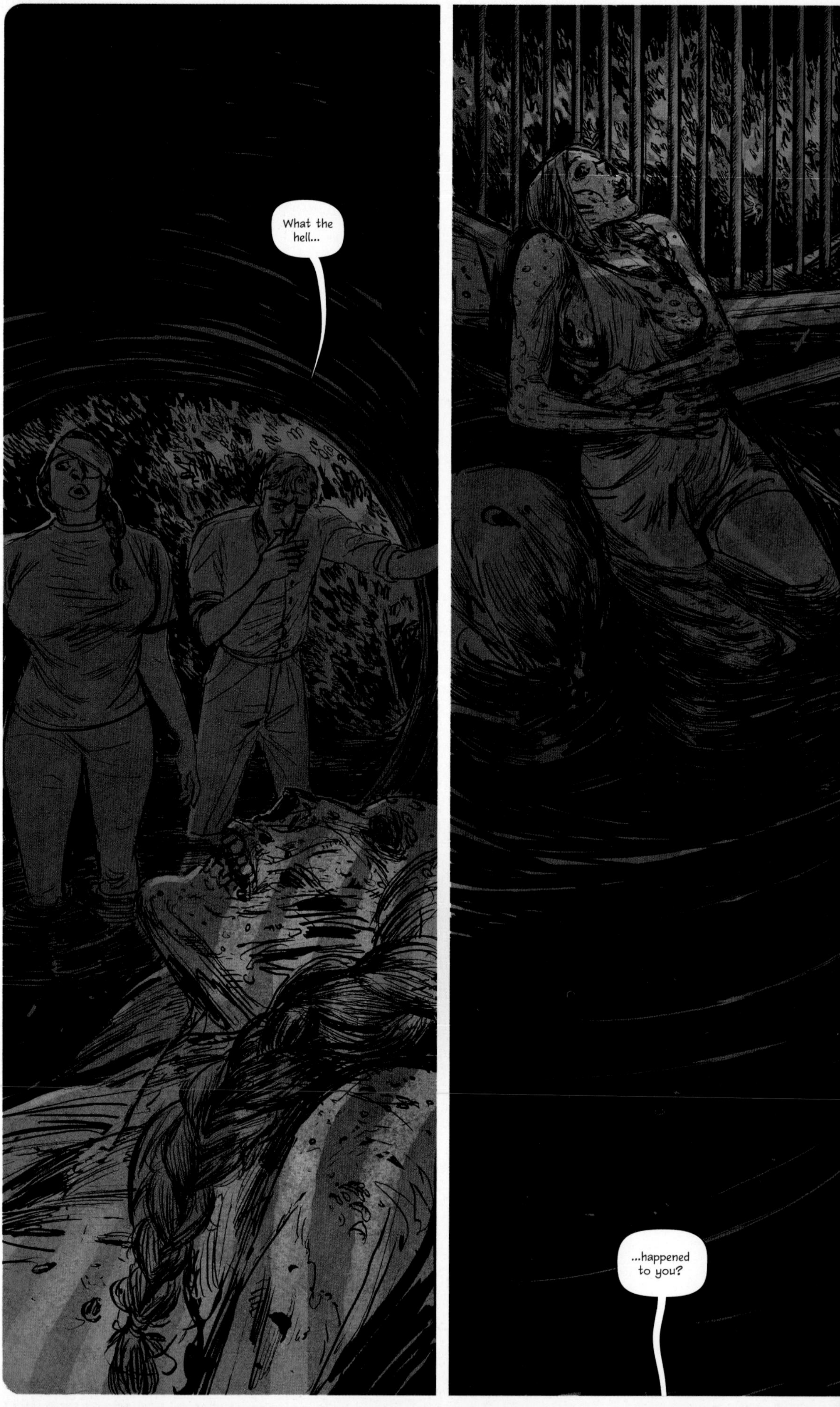
What the hell...
...happened to you?

ᚠ

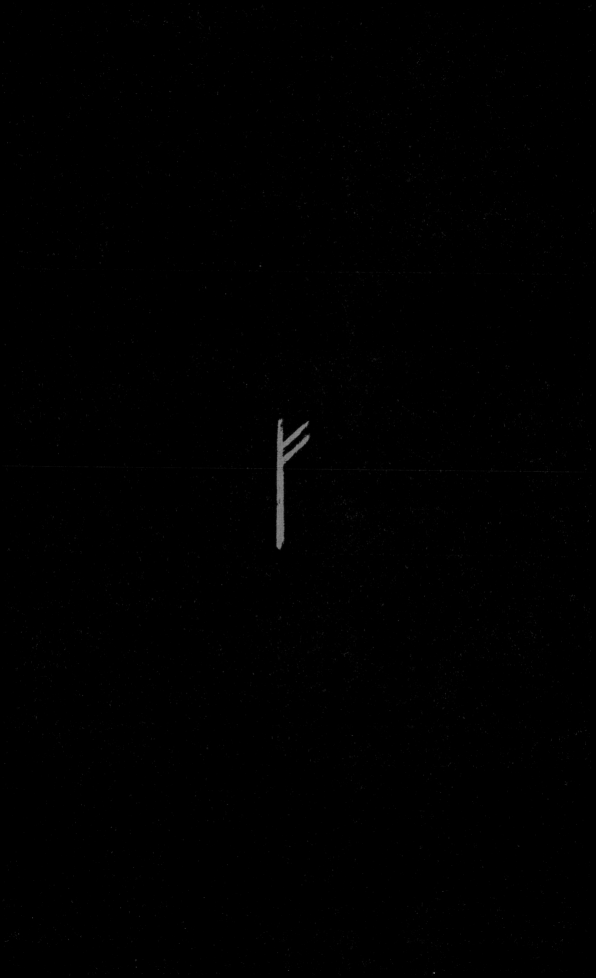

CHAPTER FIVE

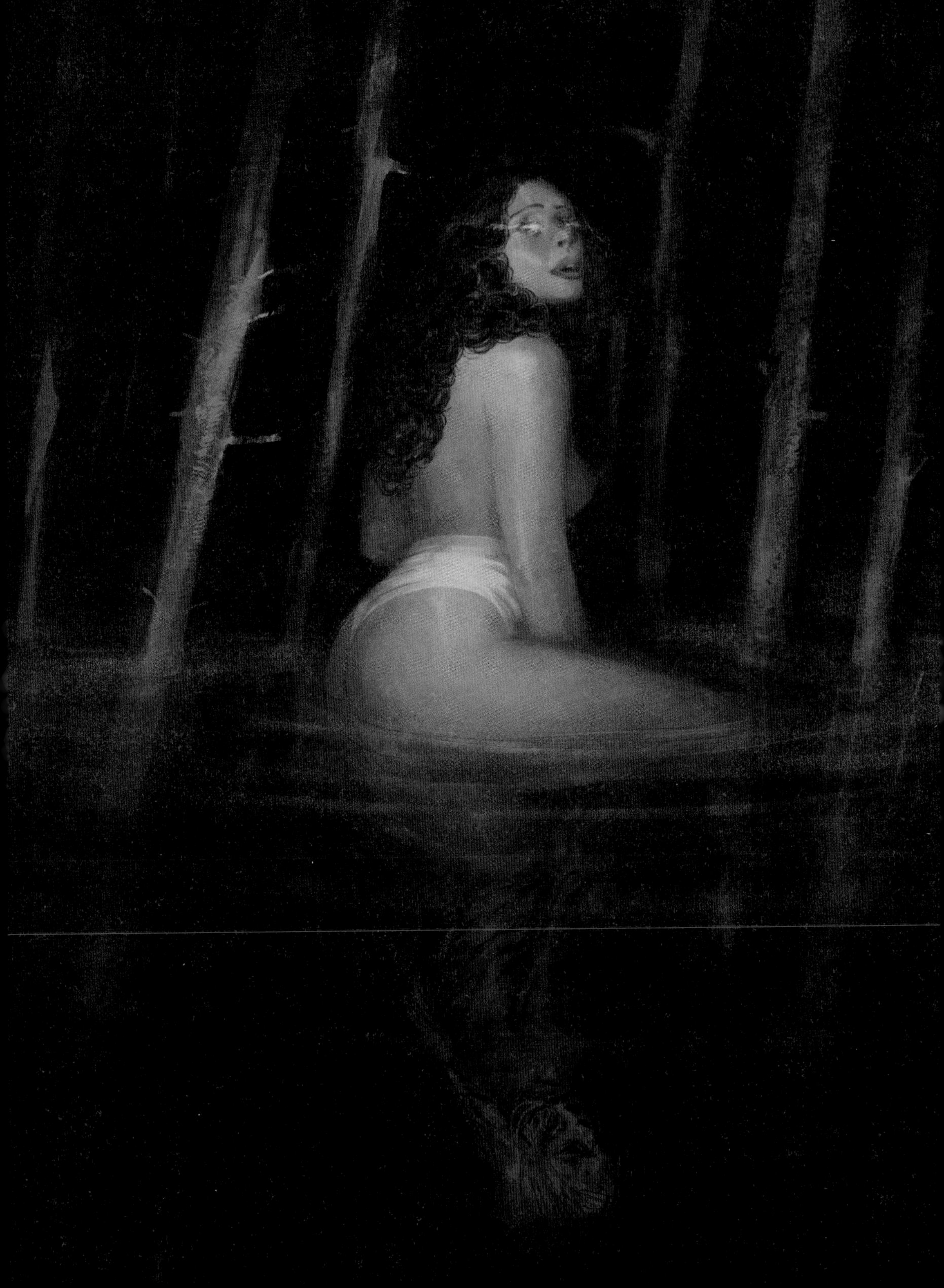

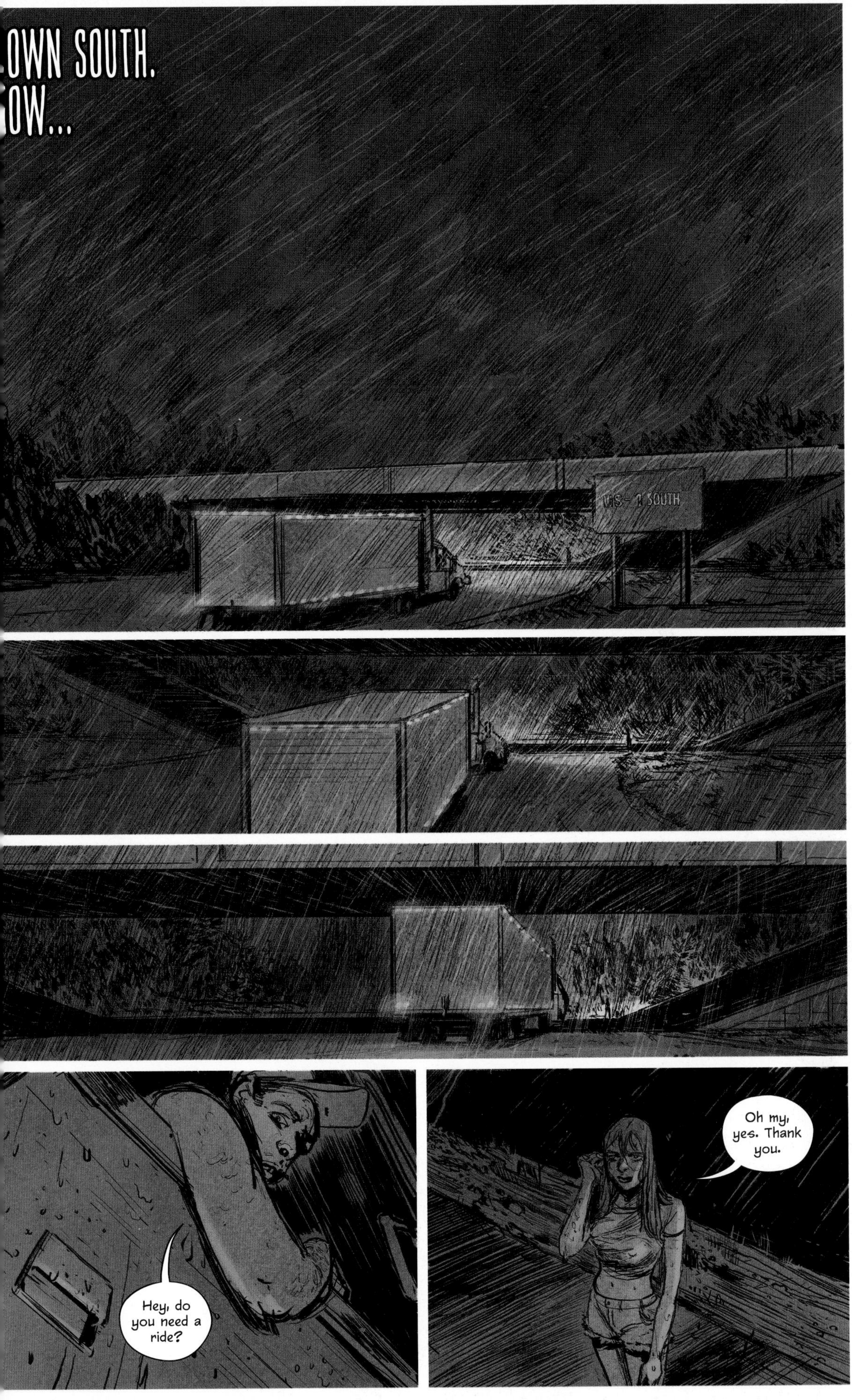
OWN SOUTH.
OW...
US-1 SOUTH
Hey, do you need a ride?
Oh my, yes. Thank you.

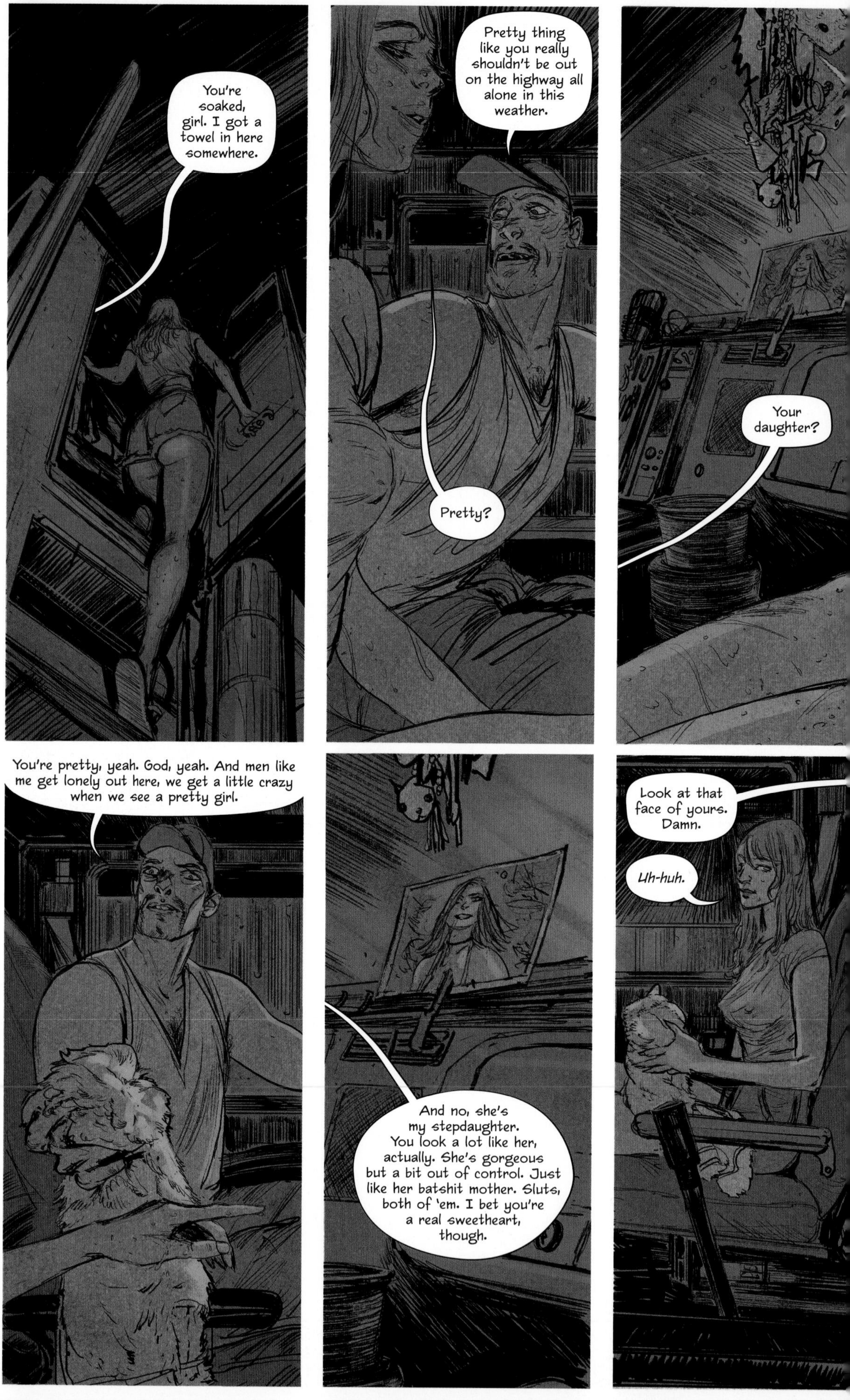
You're soaked, girl. I got a towel in here somewhere.
Pretty thing like you really shouldn't be out on the highway all alone in this weather.
Pretty?
Your daughter?
You're pretty, yeah. God, yeah. And men like me get lonely out here, we get a little crazy when we see a pretty girl.
And no, she's my stepdaughter. You look a lot like her, actually. She's gorgeous but a bit out of control. Just like her batshit mother. Sluts, both of 'em. I bet you're a real sweetheart, though.
Look at that face of yours. Damn.
Uh-huh.

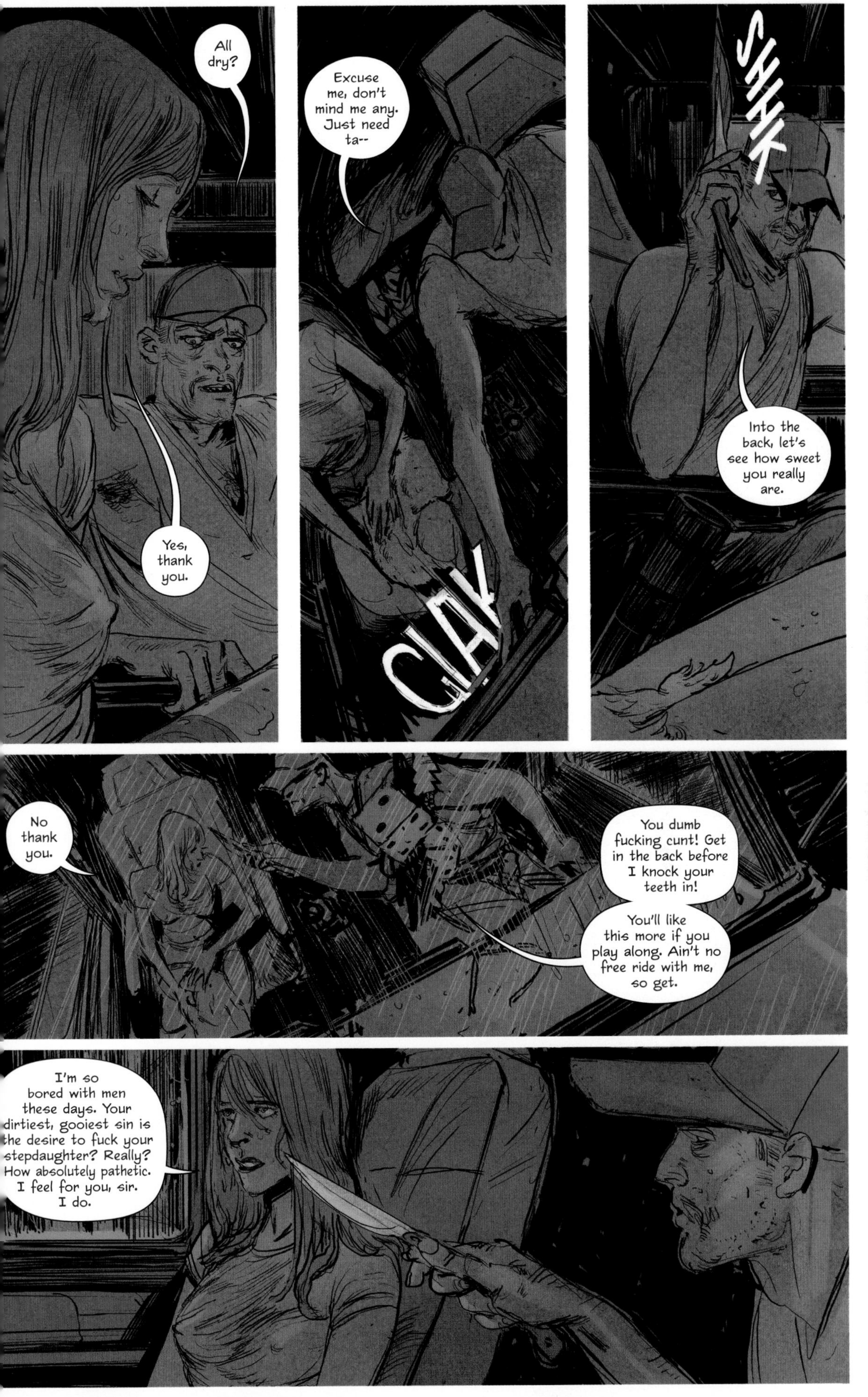
All dry?
Yes, thank you.
Excuse me, don't mind me any. Just need ta--
CLAK
SHHK
Into the back, let's see how sweet you really are.
No thank you.
You dumb fucking cunt! Get in the back before I knock your teeth in!
You'll like this more if you play along. Ain't no free ride with me, so get.
I'm so bored with men these days. Your dirtiest, gooiest sin is the desire to fuck your stepdaughter? Really? How absolutely pathetic. I feel for you, sir. I do.

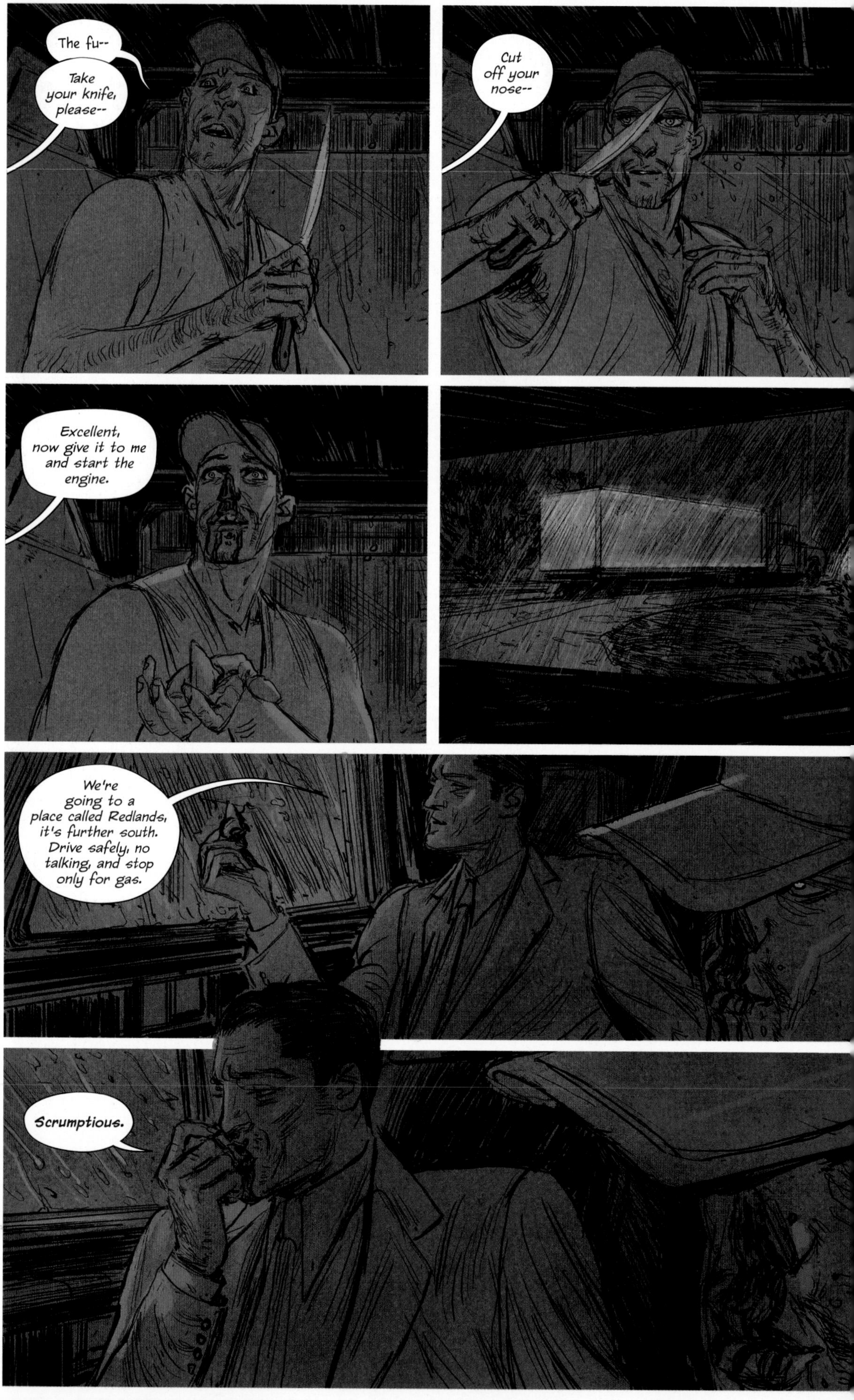
The fu--
Take your knife, please--
Cut off your nose--
Excellent, now give it to me and start the engine.
We're going to a place called Redlands, it's further south. Drive safely, no talking, and stop only for gas.
Scrumptious.

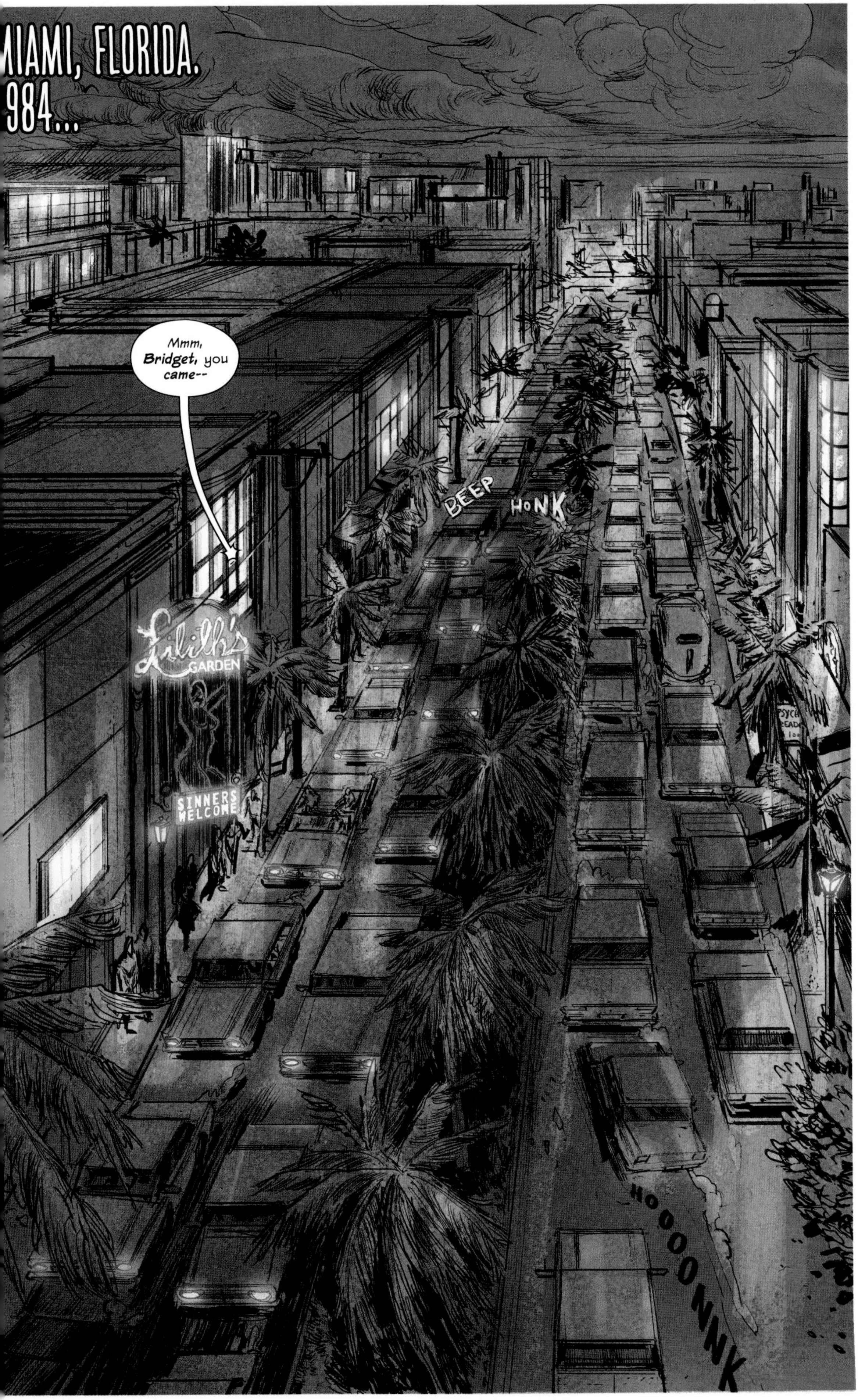
MIAMI, FLORIDA. 1984...
Mmm, Bridget, you came--
Lilith's GARDEN
SINNERS WELCOME
BEEP
HONK
HOOOONNK

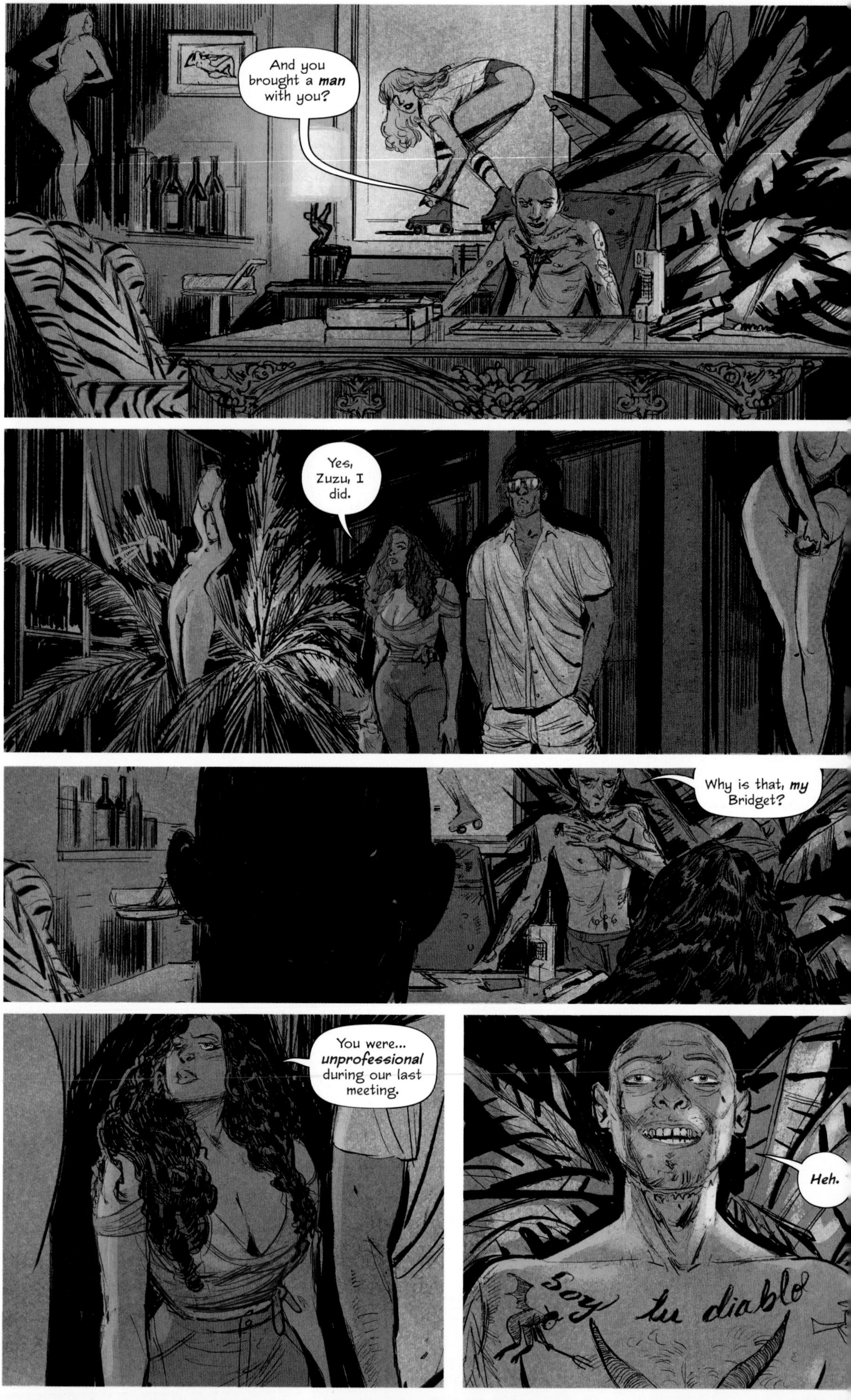
And you brought a *man* with you?
Yes, Zuzu, I did.
Why is that, *my* Bridget?
You were... *unprofessional* during our last meeting.
Heh.
Soy tu diablo

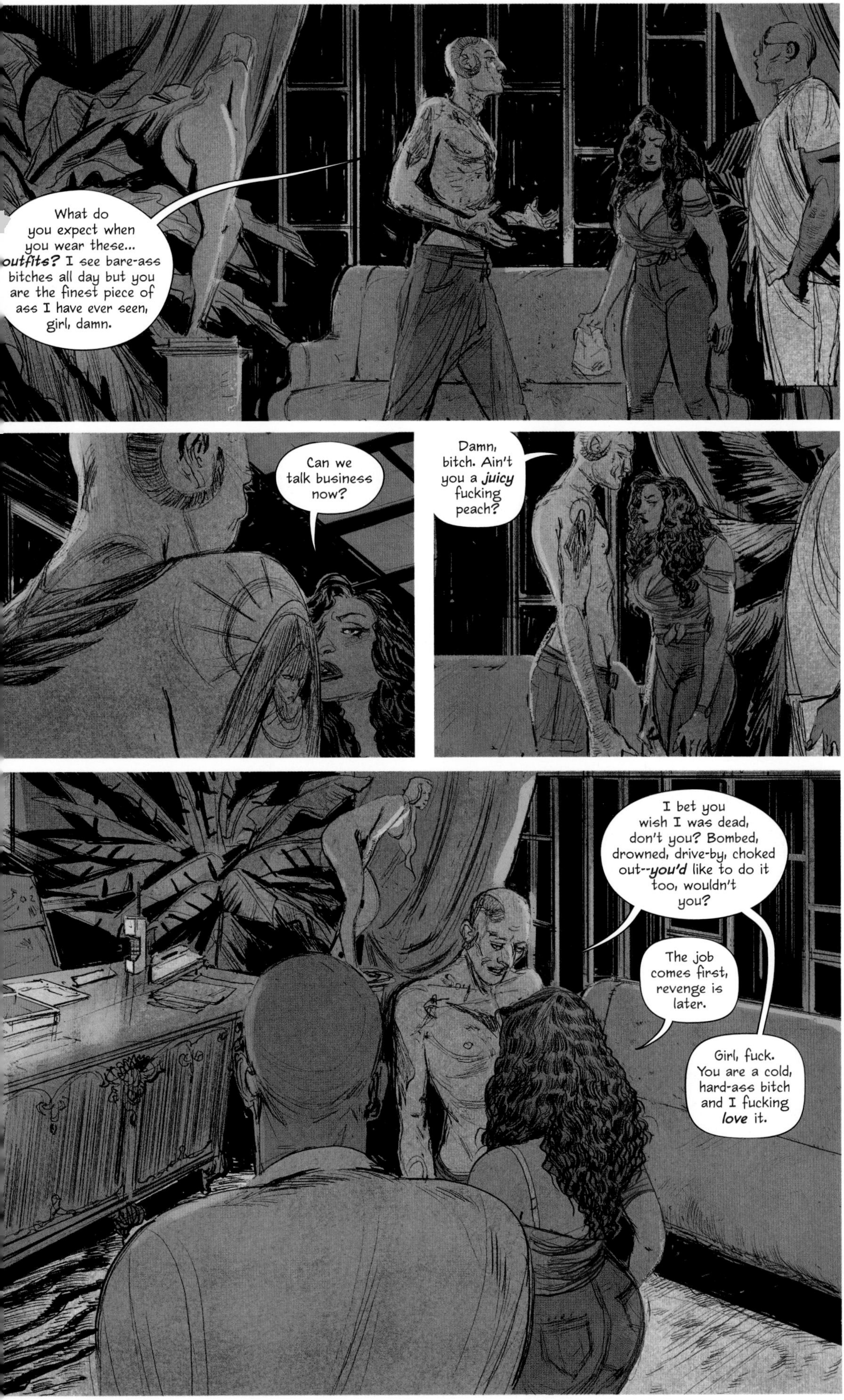
What do you expect when you wear these... outfits? I see bare-ass bitches all day but you are the finest piece of ass I have ever seen, girl, damn.
Can we talk business now?
Damn, bitch. Ain't you a juicy fucking peach?
I bet you wish I was dead, don't you? Bombed, drowned, drive-by, choked out--you'd like to do it too, wouldn't you?
The job comes first, revenge is later.
Girl, fuck. You are a cold, hard-ass bitch and I fucking love it.

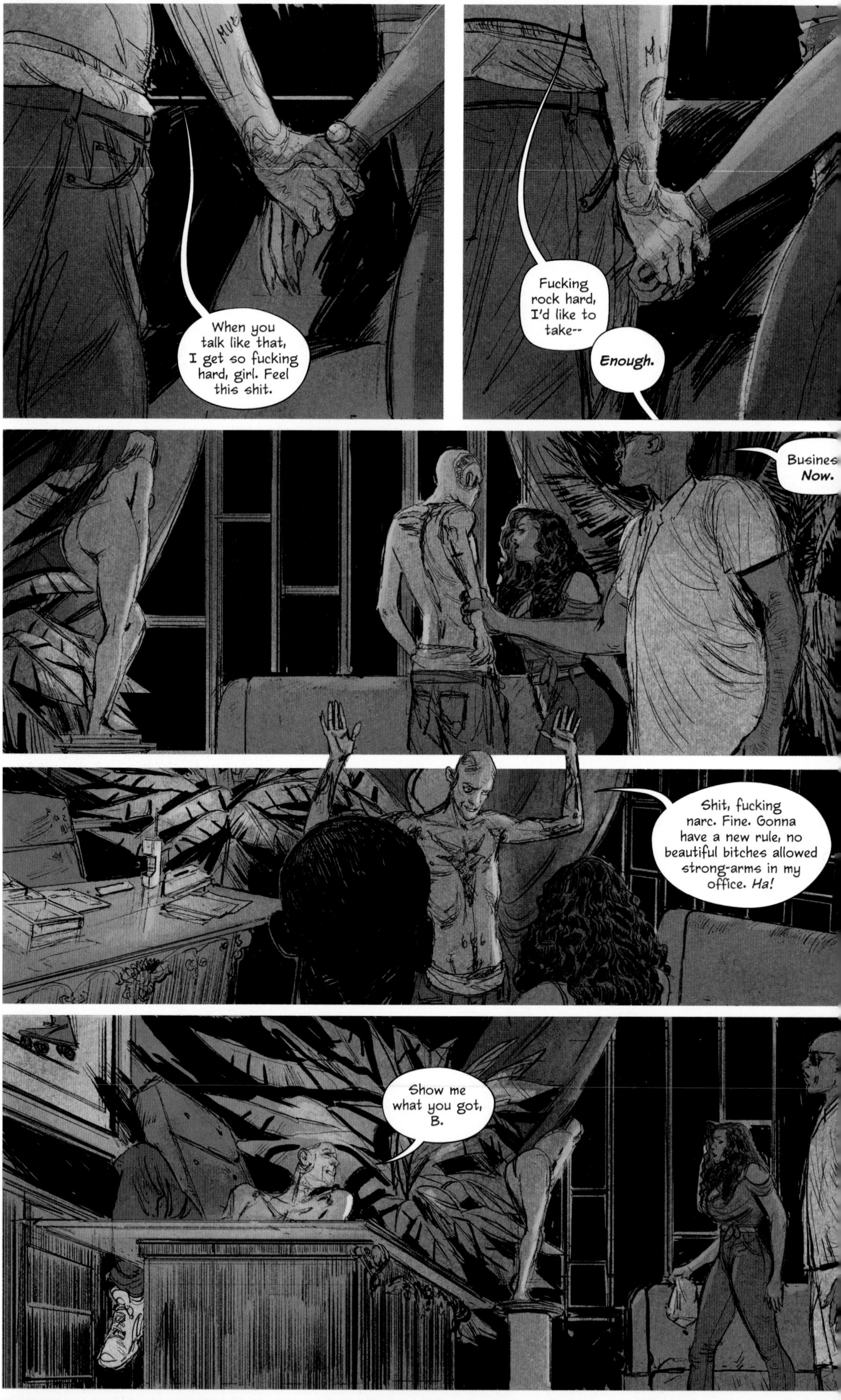
When you talk like that, I get so fucking hard, girl. Feel this shit.
Fucking rock hard, I'd like to take--
Enough.
Busines
Now.
Shit, fucking narc. Fine. Gonna have a new rule, no beautiful bitches allowed strong-arms in my office. *Ha!*
Show me what you got, B.

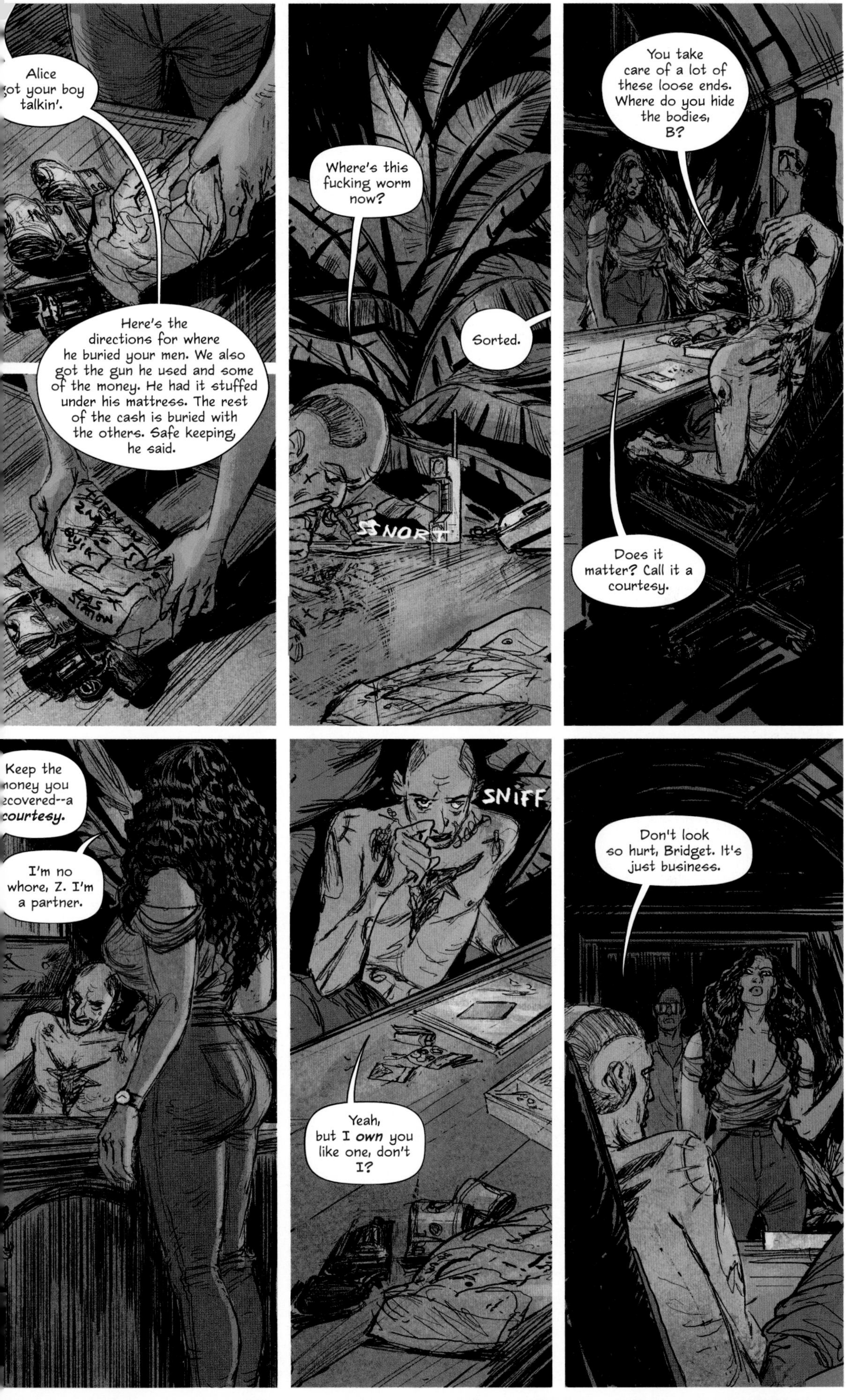
Alice
got your boy
talkin'.
Here's the directions for where he buried your men. We also got the gun he used and some of the money. He had it stuffed under his mattress. The rest of the cash is buried with the others. Safe keeping, he said.
Where's this fucking worm now?
Sorted.
SSNORT
You take care of a lot of these loose ends. Where do you hide the bodies, B?
Does it matter? Call it a courtesy.
Keep the
money you
recovered--a
courtesy.
I'm no whore, Z. I'm a partner.
SNIFF
Yeah, but I *own* you like one, don't I?
Don't look so hurt, Bridget. It's just business.

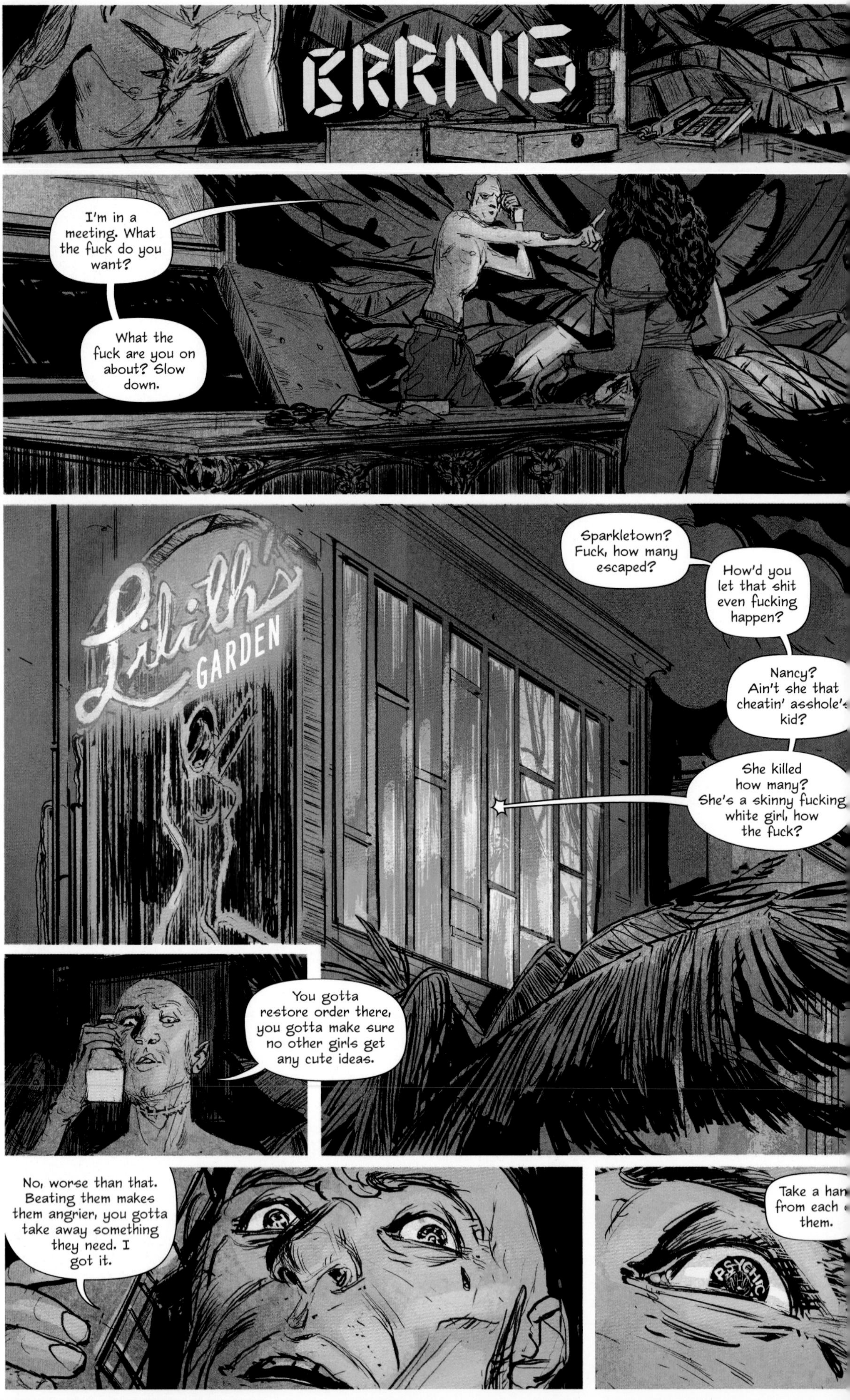
BRRNG
I'm in a meeting. What the fuck do you want?
What the fuck are you on about? Slow down.
Lilith's GARDEN
Sparkletown? Fuck, how many escaped?
How'd you let that shit even fucking happen?
Nancy? Ain't she that cheatin' asshole's kid?
She killed how many? She's a skinny fucking white girl, how the fuck?
You gotta restore order there, you gotta make sure no other girls get any cute ideas.
No, worse than that. Beating them makes them angrier, you gotta take away something they need. I got it.
Take a han from each them.
PSYCHIC

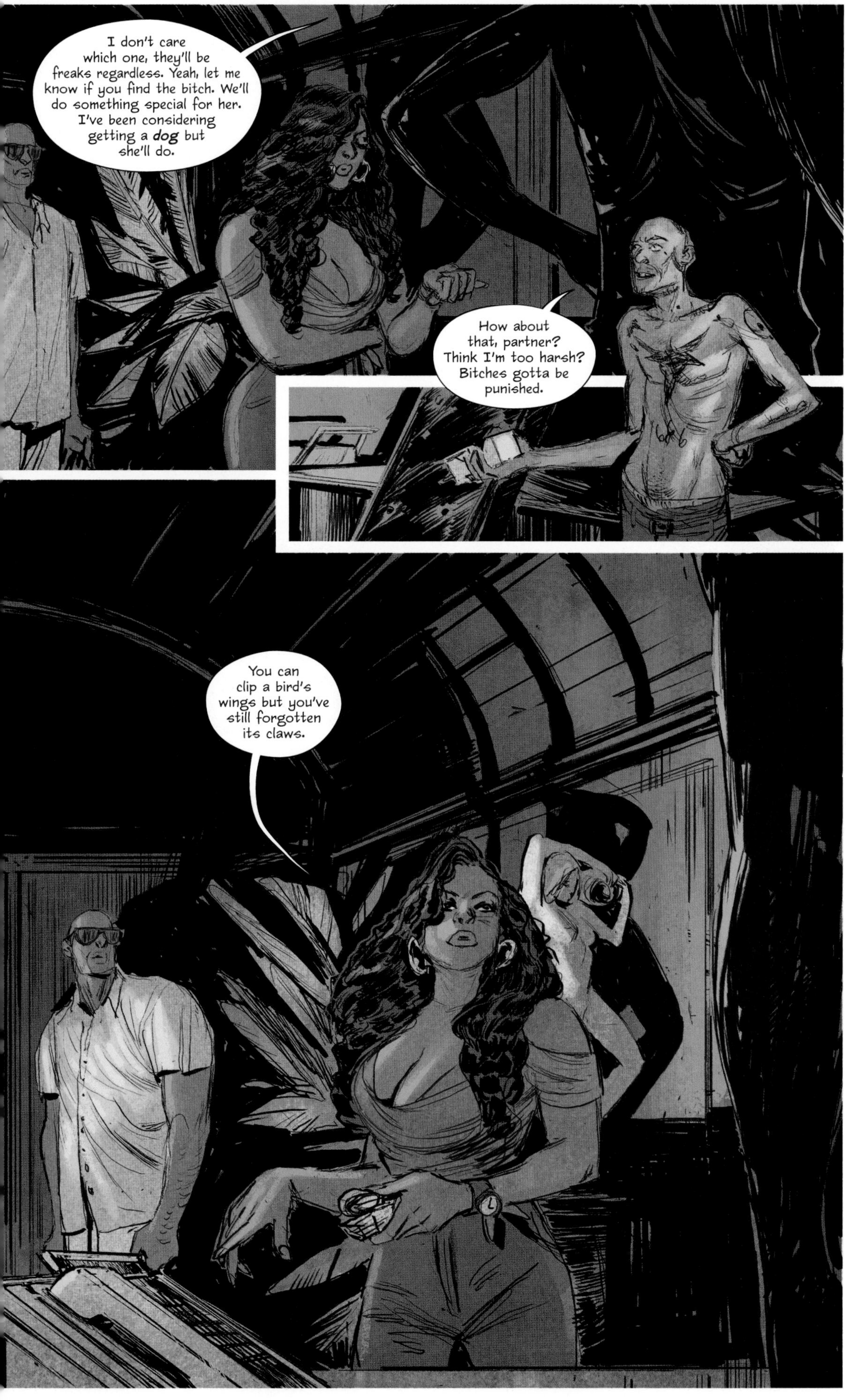
I don't care which one, they'll be freaks regardless. Yeah, let me know if you find the bitch. We'll do something special for her. I've been considering getting a *dog* but she'll do.
How about that, partner? Think I'm too harsh? Bitches gotta be punished.
You can clip a bird's wings but you've still forgotten its claws.

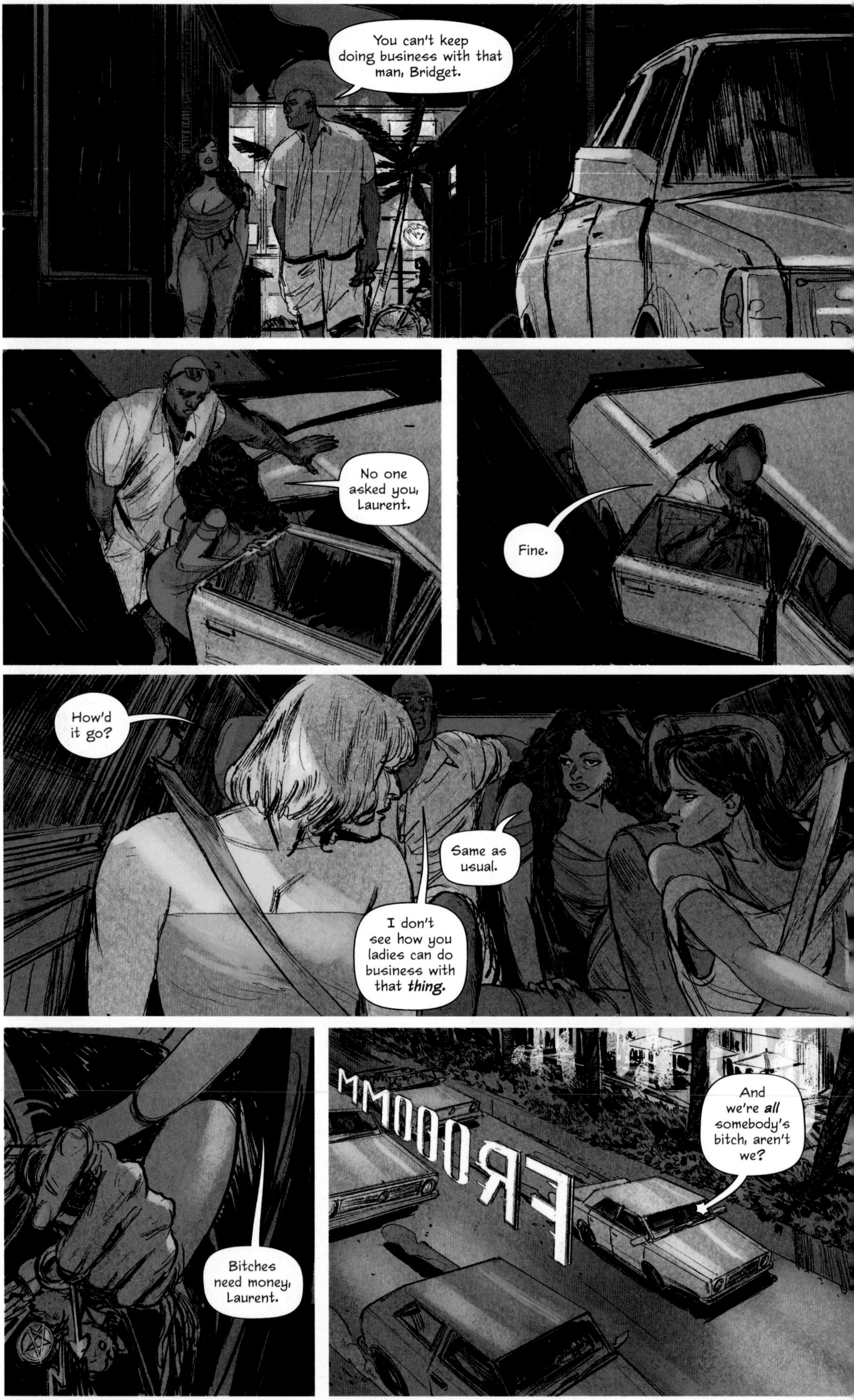
You can't keep doing business with that man, Bridget.
No one asked you, Laurent.
Fine.
How'd it go?
Same as usual.
I don't see how you ladies can do business with that *thing.*
Bitches need money, Laurent.
FROOOMM
And we're *all* somebody's bitch, aren't we?

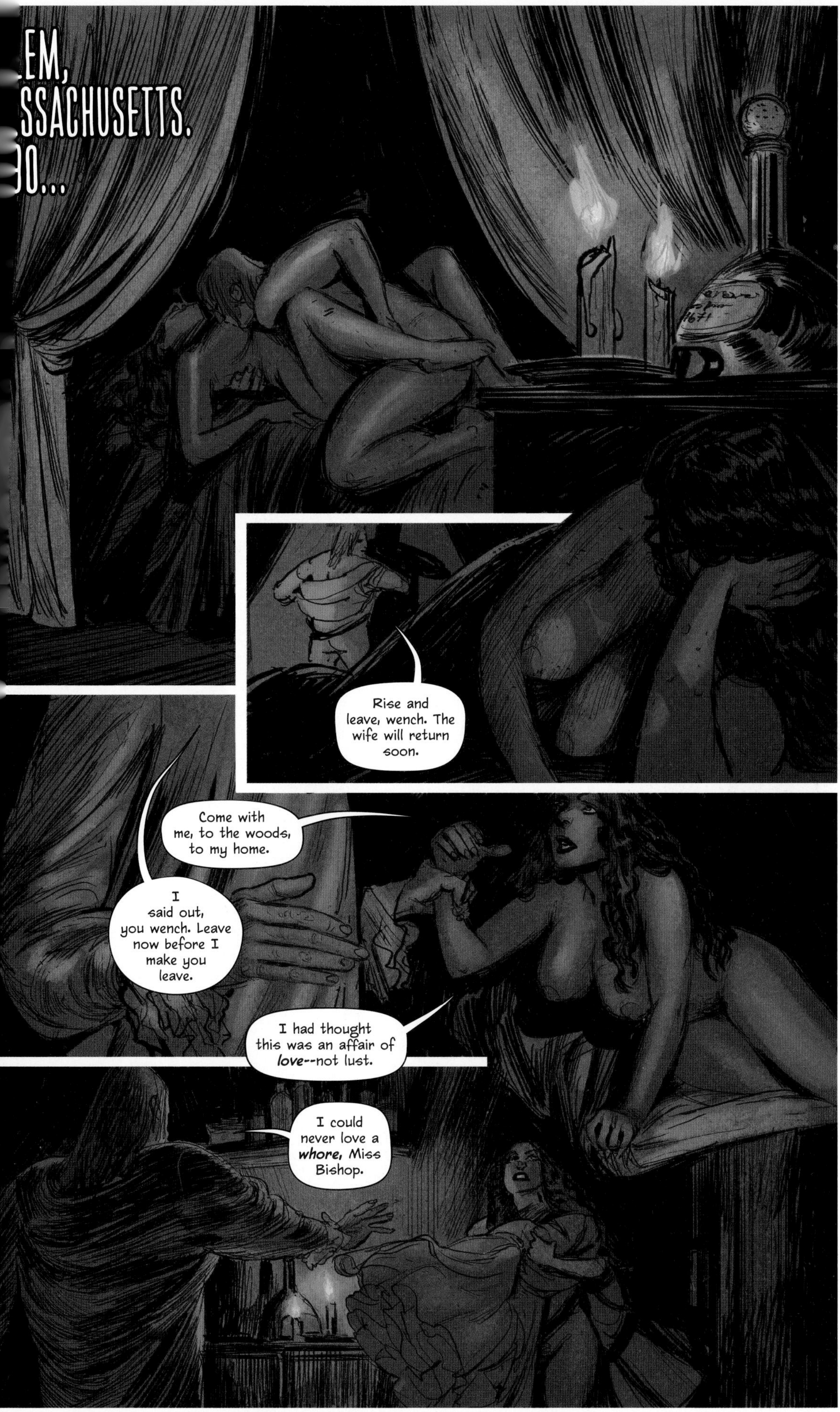
LEM,
SSACHUSETTS.
90...
Rise and leave, wench. The wife will return soon.
Come with me, to the woods, to my home.
I said out, you wench. Leave now before I make you leave.
I had thought this was an affair of *love*--not lust.
I could never love a *whore,* Miss Bishop.

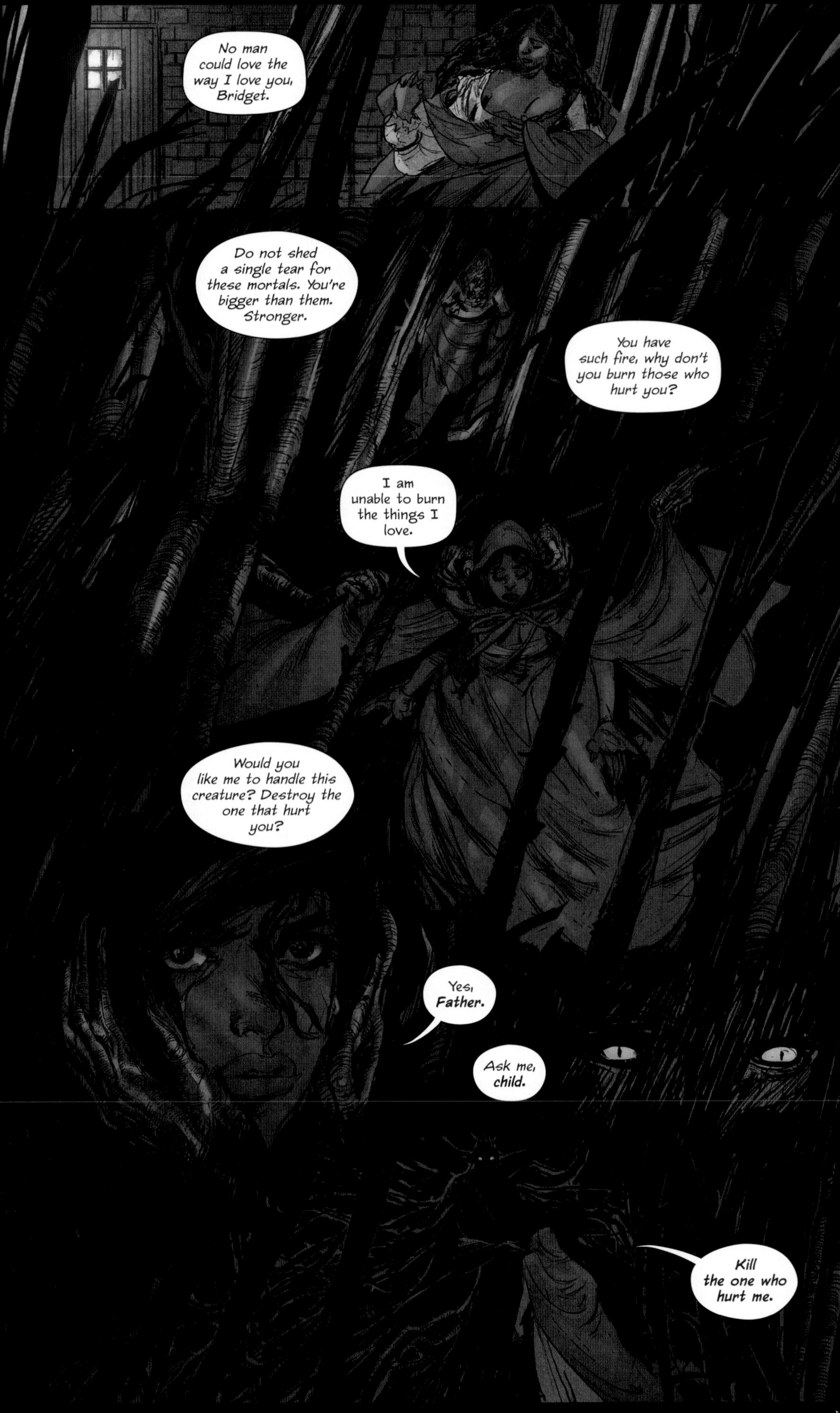
No man could love the way I love you, Bridget.
Do not shed a single tear for these mortals. You're bigger than them. Stronger.
You have such fire, why don't you burn those who hurt you?
I am unable to burn the things I love.
Would you like me to handle this creature? Destroy the one that hurt you?
Yes, **Father.**
Ask me, **child.**
Kill the one who hurt me.

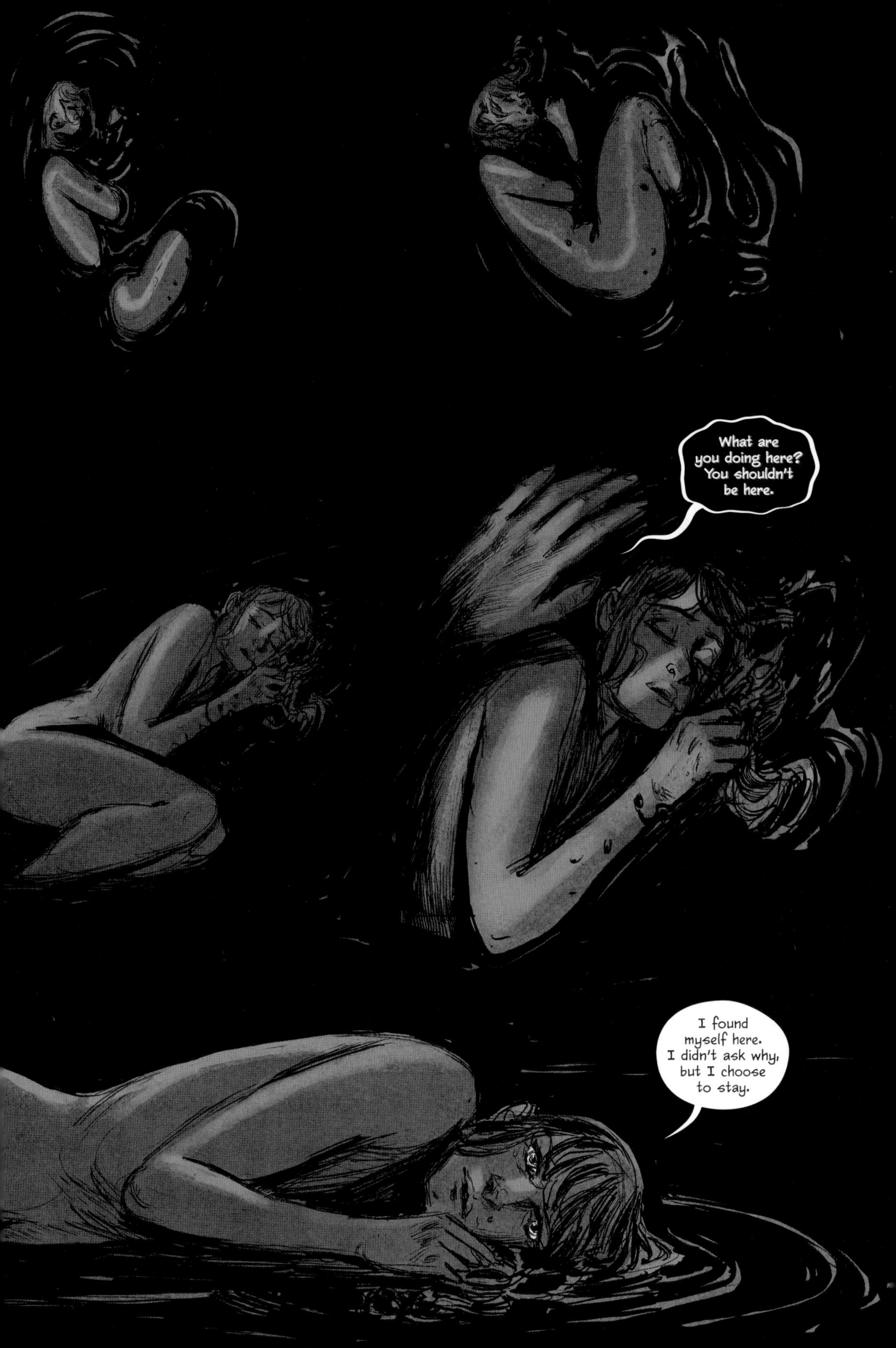
What are you doing here? You shouldn't be here.
I found myself here. I didn't ask why, but I choose to stay.

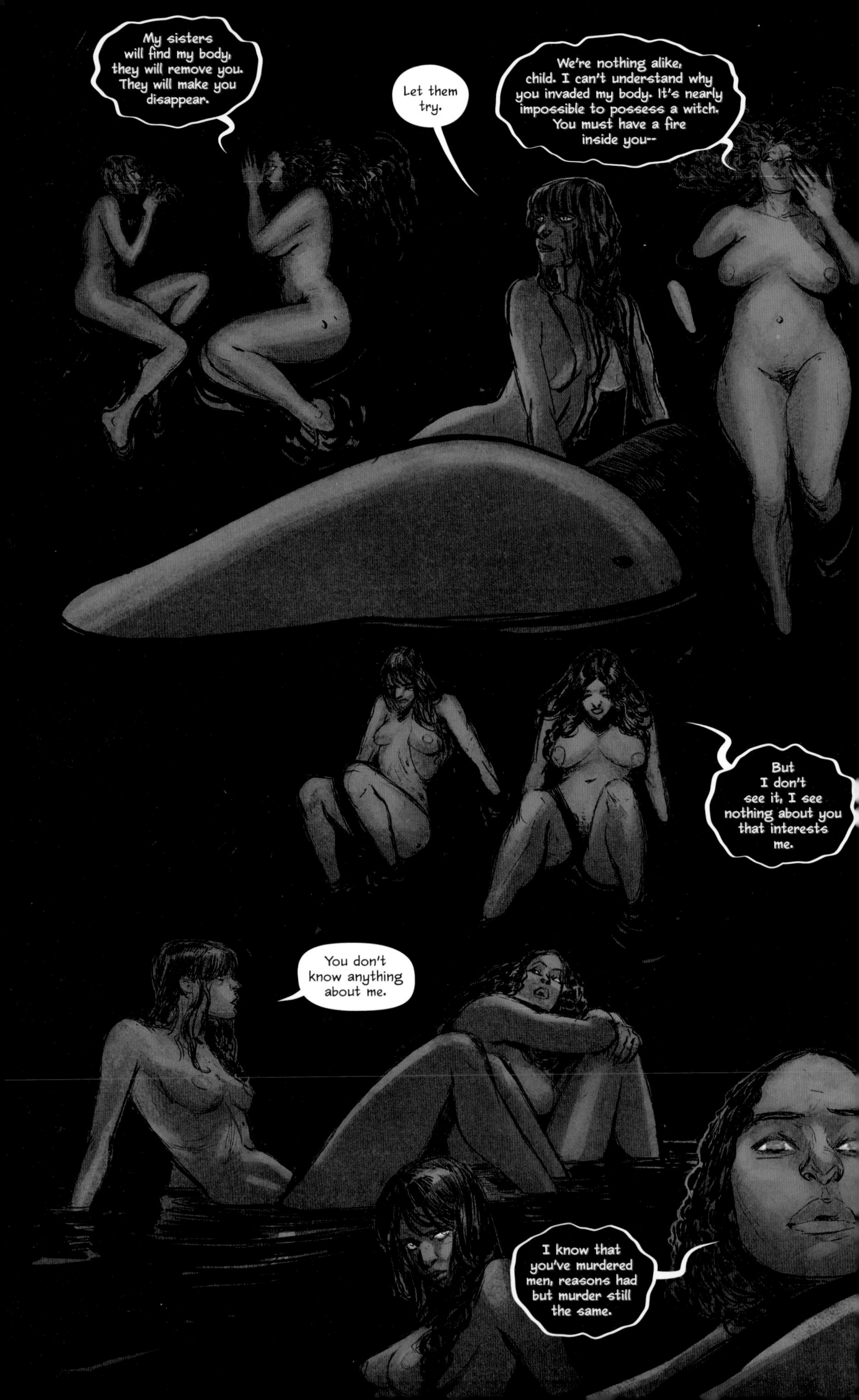
My sisters will find my body, they will remove you. They will make you disappear.
Let them try.
We're nothing alike, child. I can't understand why you invaded my body. It's nearly impossible to possess a witch. You must have a fire inside you--
But I don't see it, I see nothing about you that interests me.
You don't know anything about me.
I know that you've murdered men, reasons had but murder still the same.

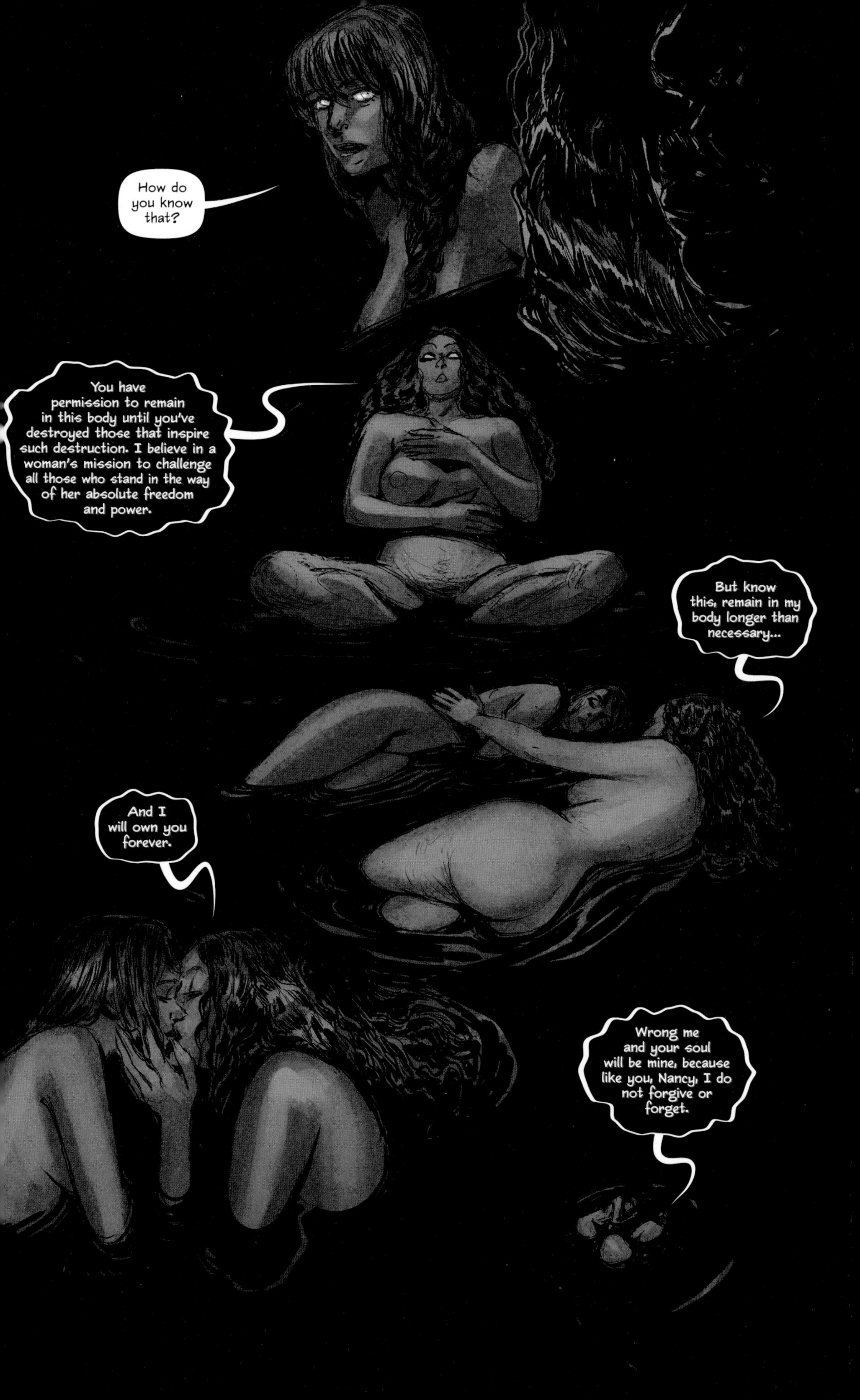
How do you know that?
You have permission to remain in this body until you've destroyed those that inspire such destruction. I believe in a woman's mission to challenge all those who stand in the way of her absolute freedom and power.
But know this, remain in my body longer than necessary...
And I will own you forever.
Wrong me and your soul will be mine, because like you, Nancy, I do not forgive or forget.

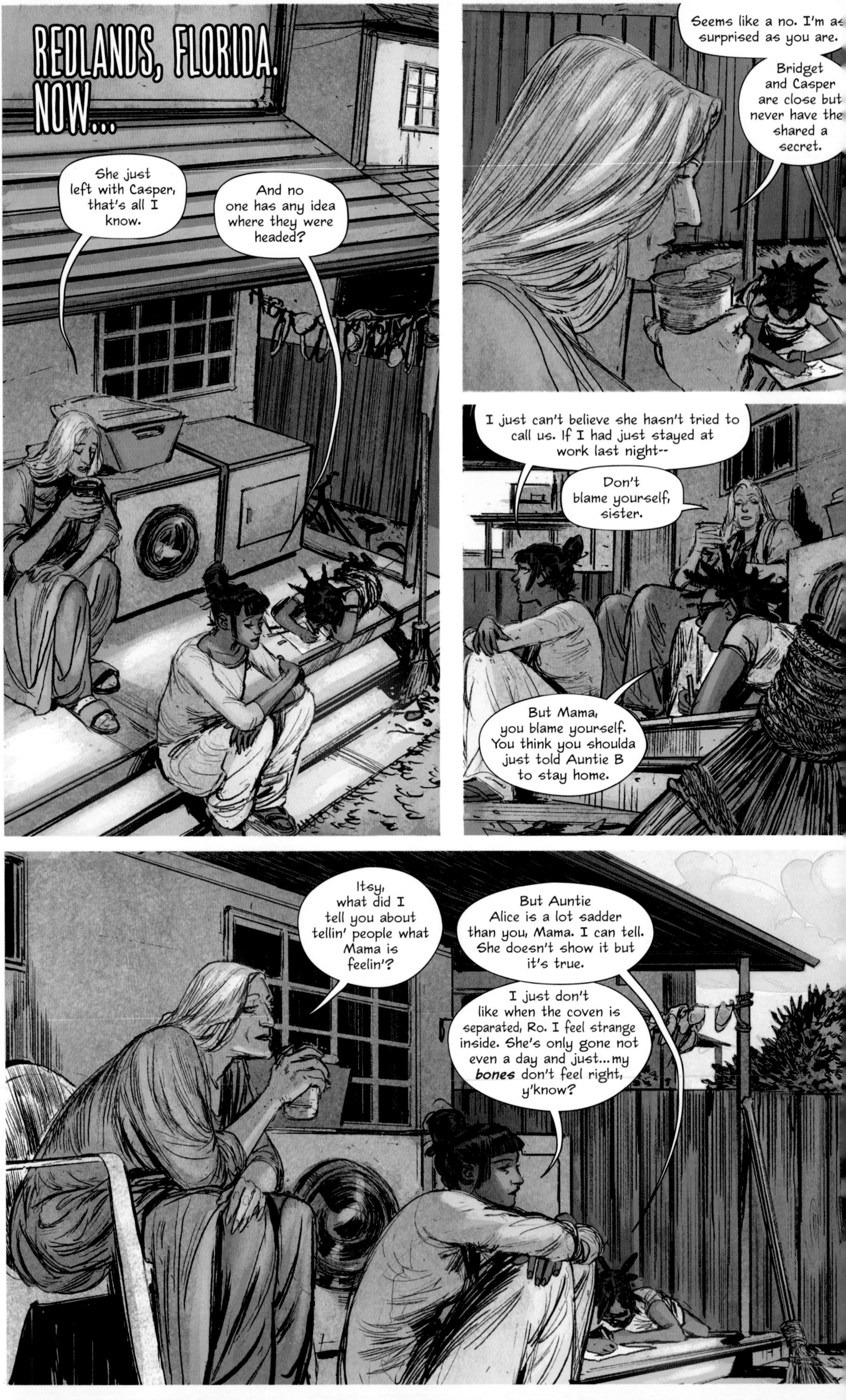
REDLANDS, FLORIDA. NOW...
She just left with Casper, that's all I know.
And no one has any idea where they were headed?
Seems like a no. I'm as surprised as you are.
Bridget and Casper are close but never have they shared a secret.
I just can't believe she hasn't tried to call us. If I had just stayed at work last night--
Don't blame yourself, sister.
But Mama, you blame yourself. You think you shoulda just told Auntie B to stay home.
Itsy, what did I tell you about tellin' people what Mama is feelin'?
But Auntie Alice is a lot sadder than you, Mama. I can tell. She doesn't show it but it's true.
I just don't like when the coven is separated, Ro. I feel strange inside. She's only gone not even a day and just...my *bones* don't feel right, y'know?

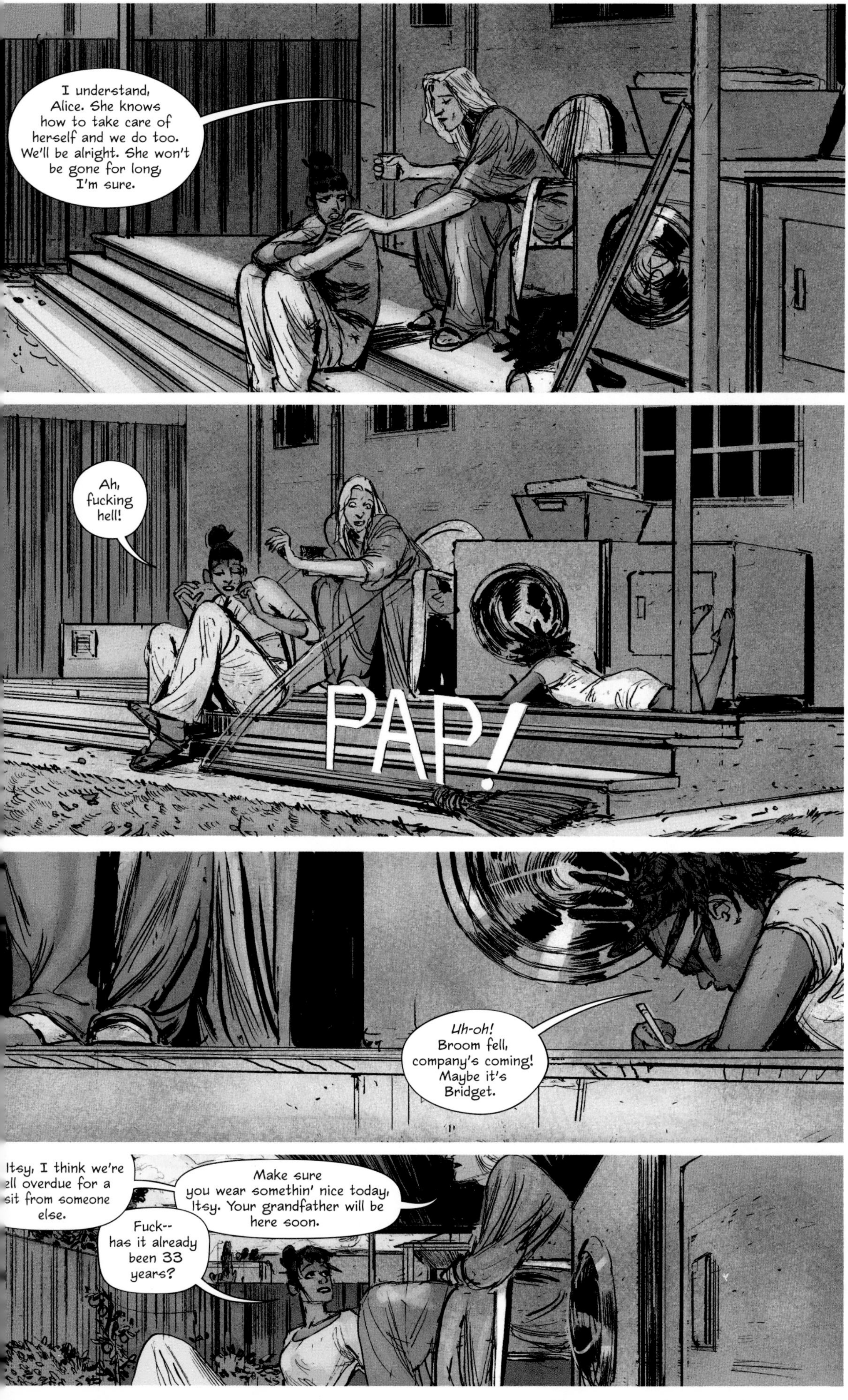
I understand, Alice. She knows how to take care of herself and we do too. We'll be alright. She won't be gone for long, I'm sure.
Ah, fucking hell!
PAP!
Uh-oh! Broom fell, company's coming! Maybe it's Bridget.
Itsy, I think we're ell overdue for a sit from someone else.
Make sure you wear somethin' nice today, Itsy. Your grandfather will be here soon.
Fuck-- has it already been 33 years?

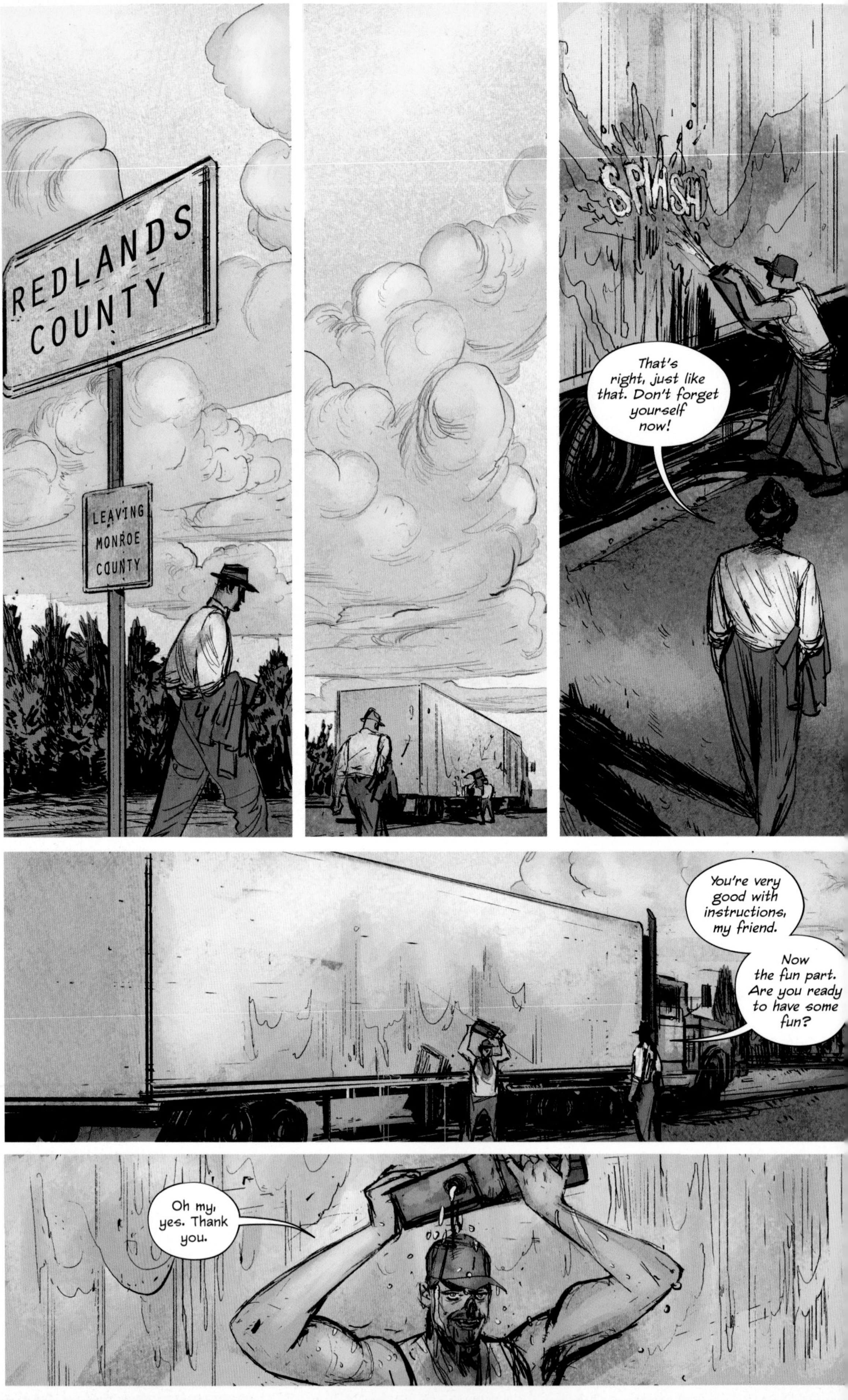
REDLANDS COUNTY
LEAVING MONROE COUNTY
SPLASH
That's right, just like that. Don't forget yourself now!
You're very good with instructions, my friend.
Now the fun part. Are you ready to have some fun?
Oh my, yes. Thank you.

I

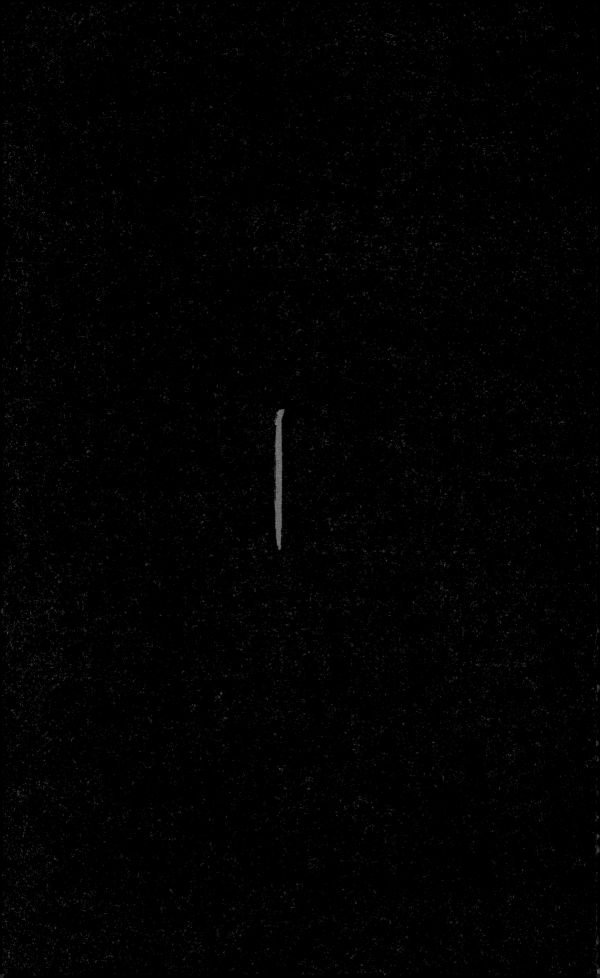

CHAPTER SIX

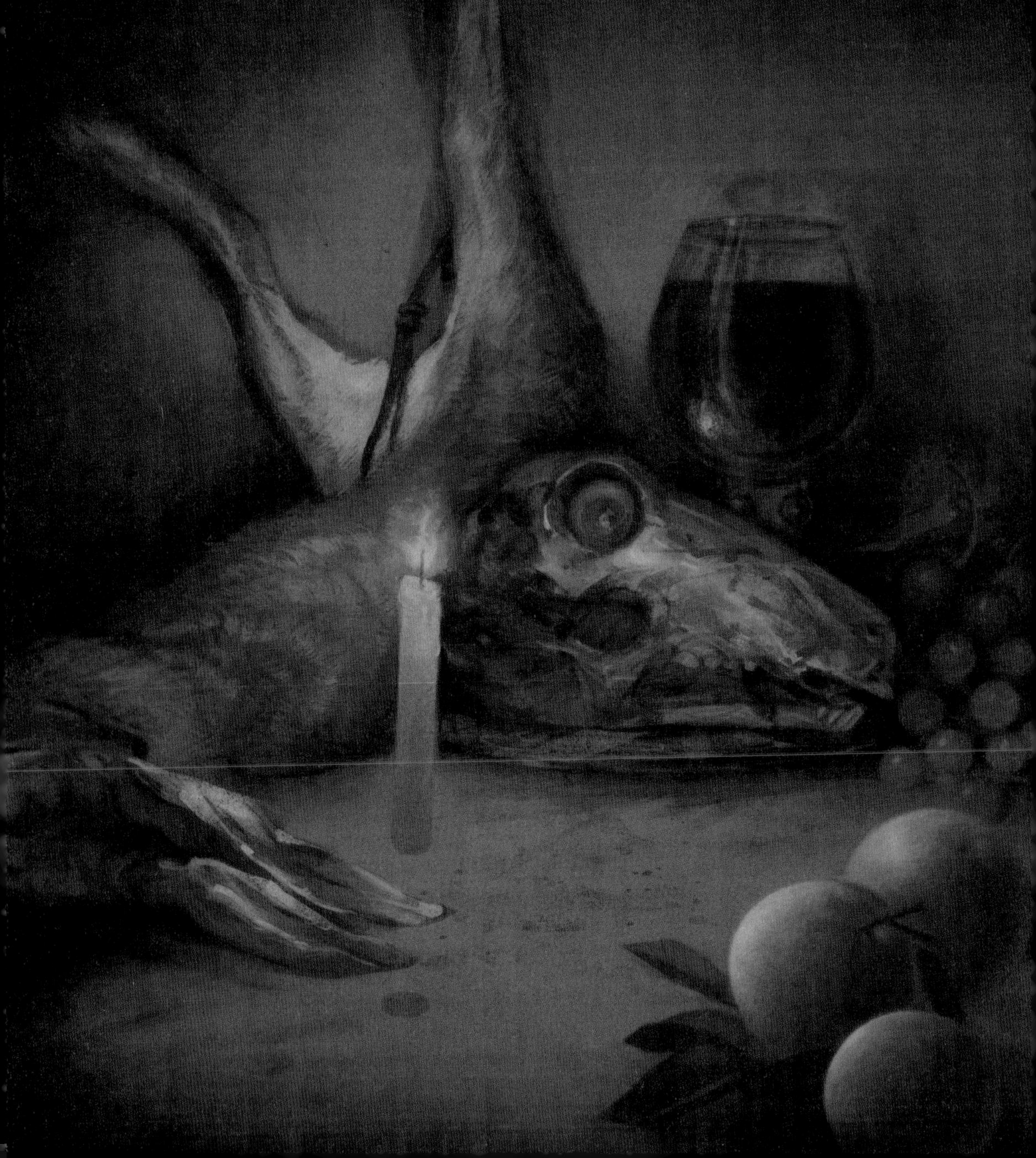

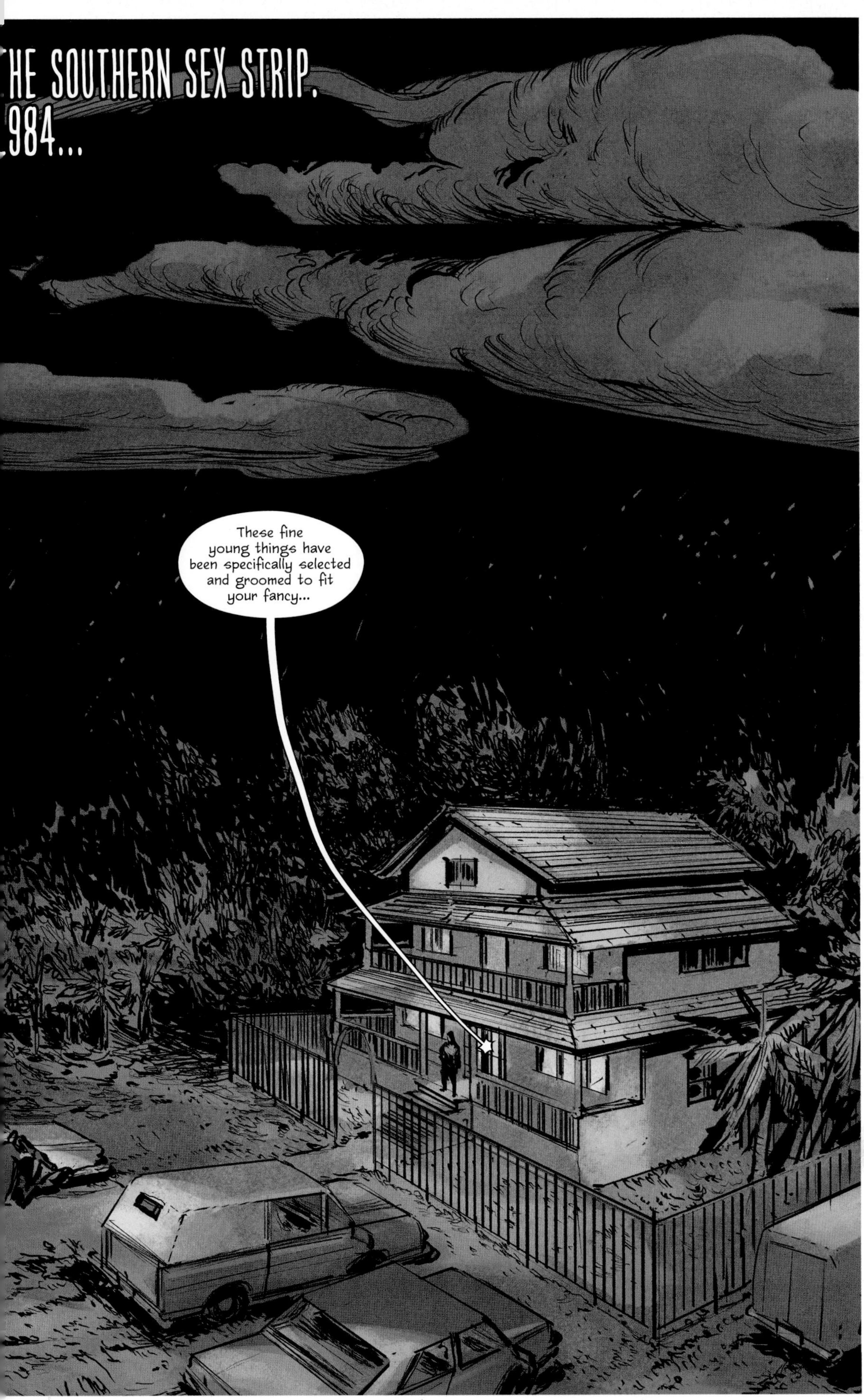
HE SOUTHERN SEX STRIP.
984...
These fine young things have been specifically selected and groomed to fit your fancy...

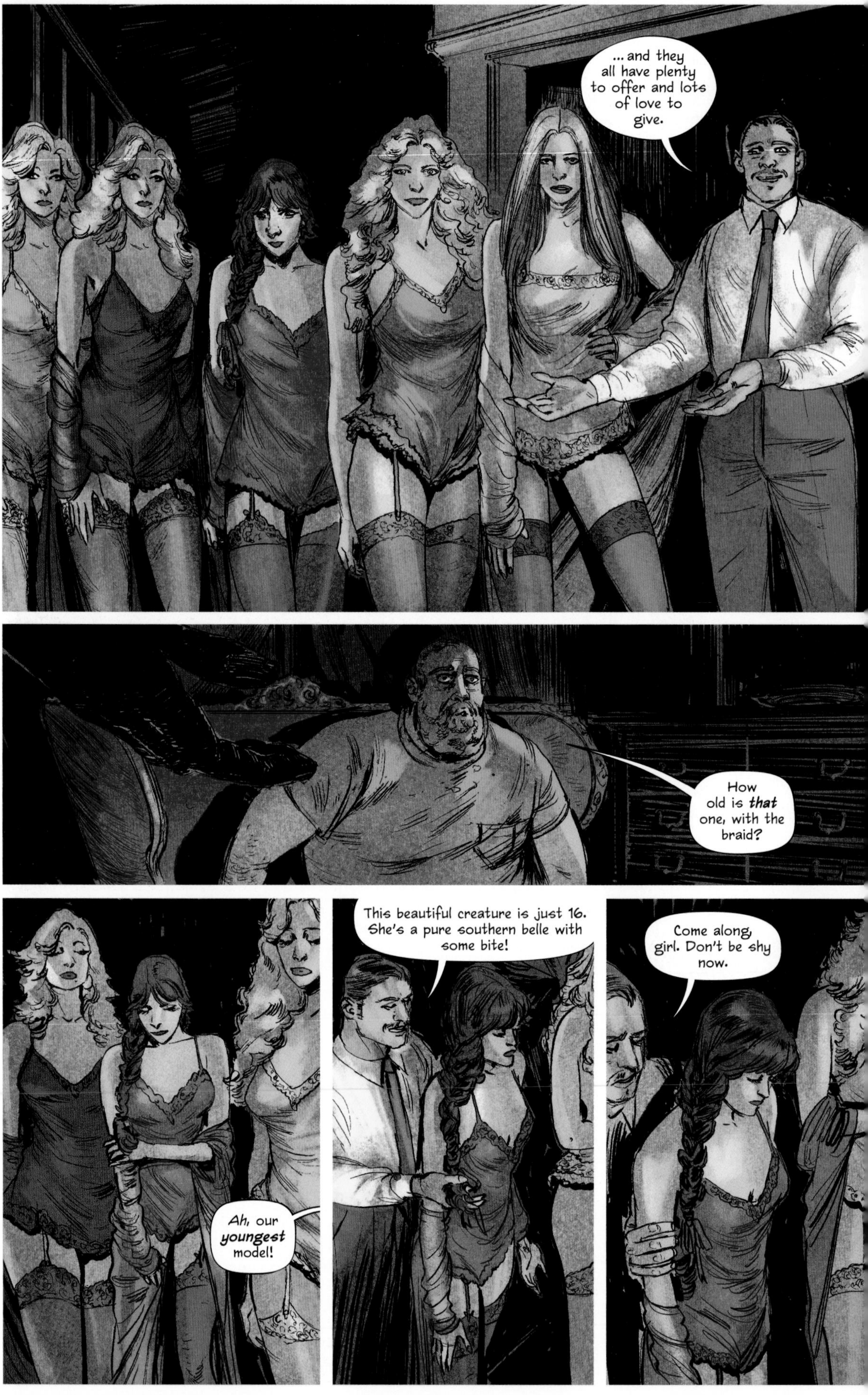
...and they all have plenty to offer and lots of love to give.
How old is *that* one, with the braid?
Ah, our ***youngest*** model!
This beautiful creature is just 16. She's a pure southern belle with some bite!
Come along, girl. Don't be shy now.

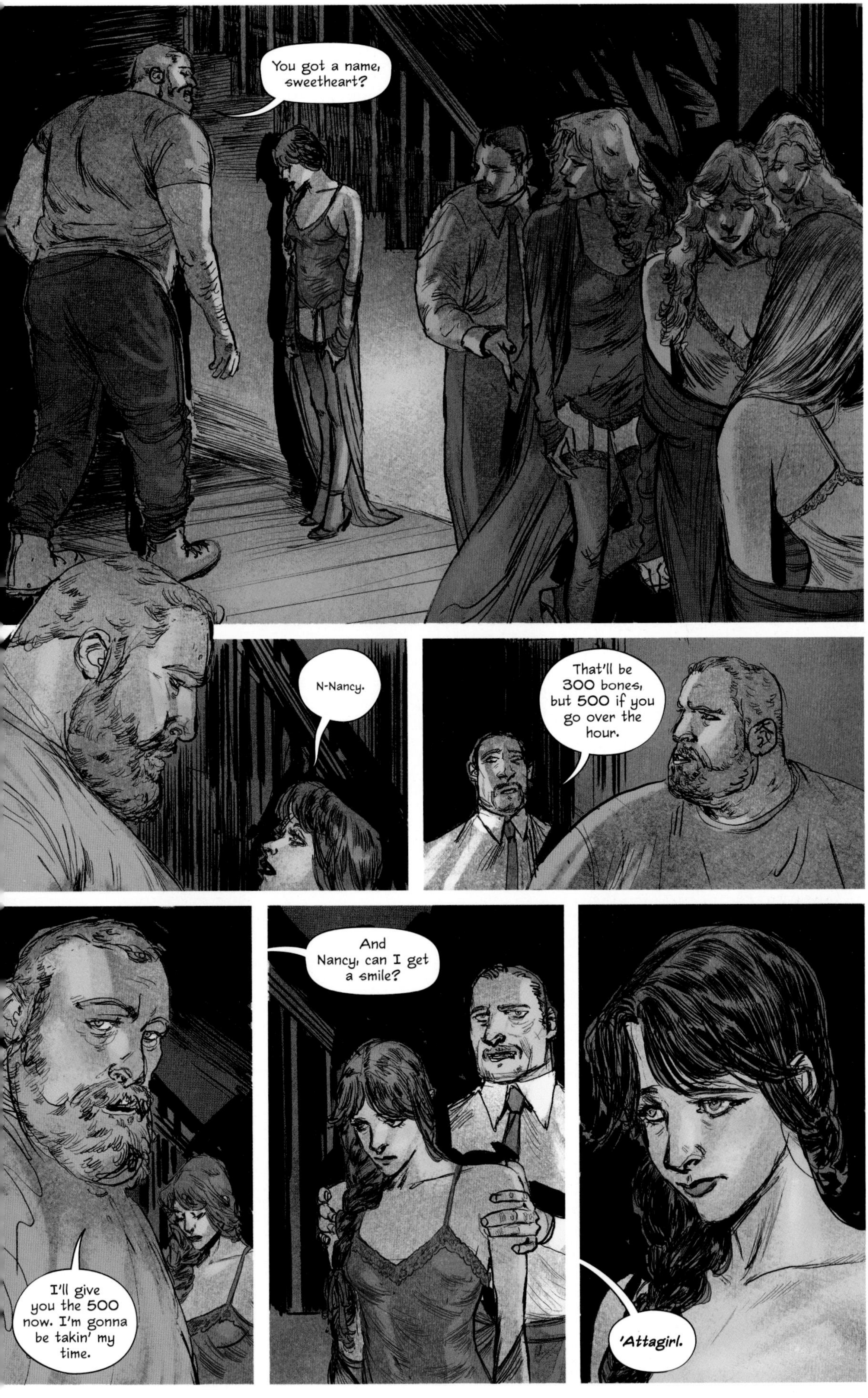
You got a name, sweetheart?
N-Nancy.
That'll be 300 bones, but 500 if you go over the hour.
I'll give you the 500 now. I'm gonna be takin' my time.
And Nancy, can I get a smile?
'Attagirl.

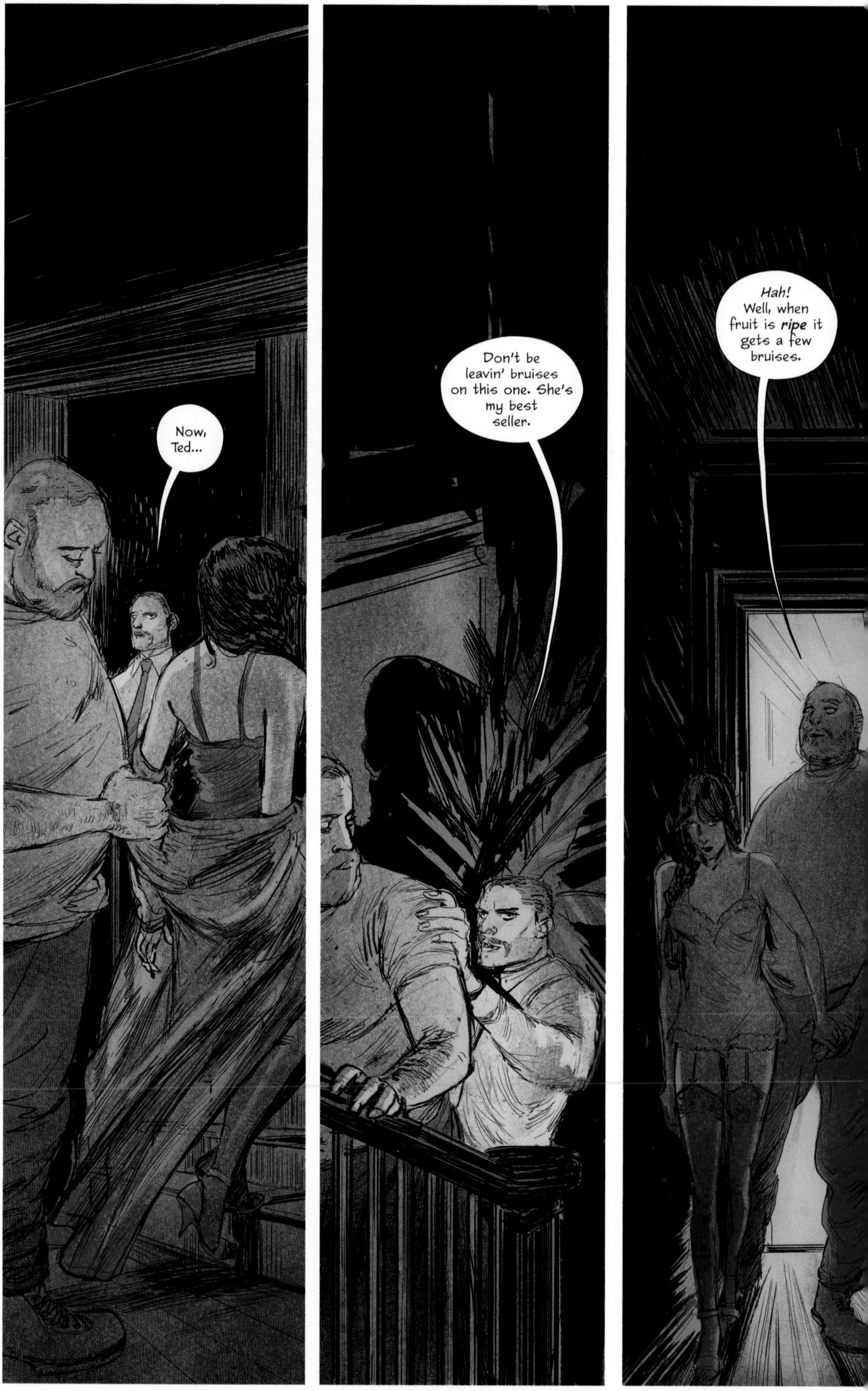
Now, Ted...
Don't be leavin' bruises on this one. She's my best seller.
Hah! Well, when fruit is ***ripe*** it gets a few bruises.

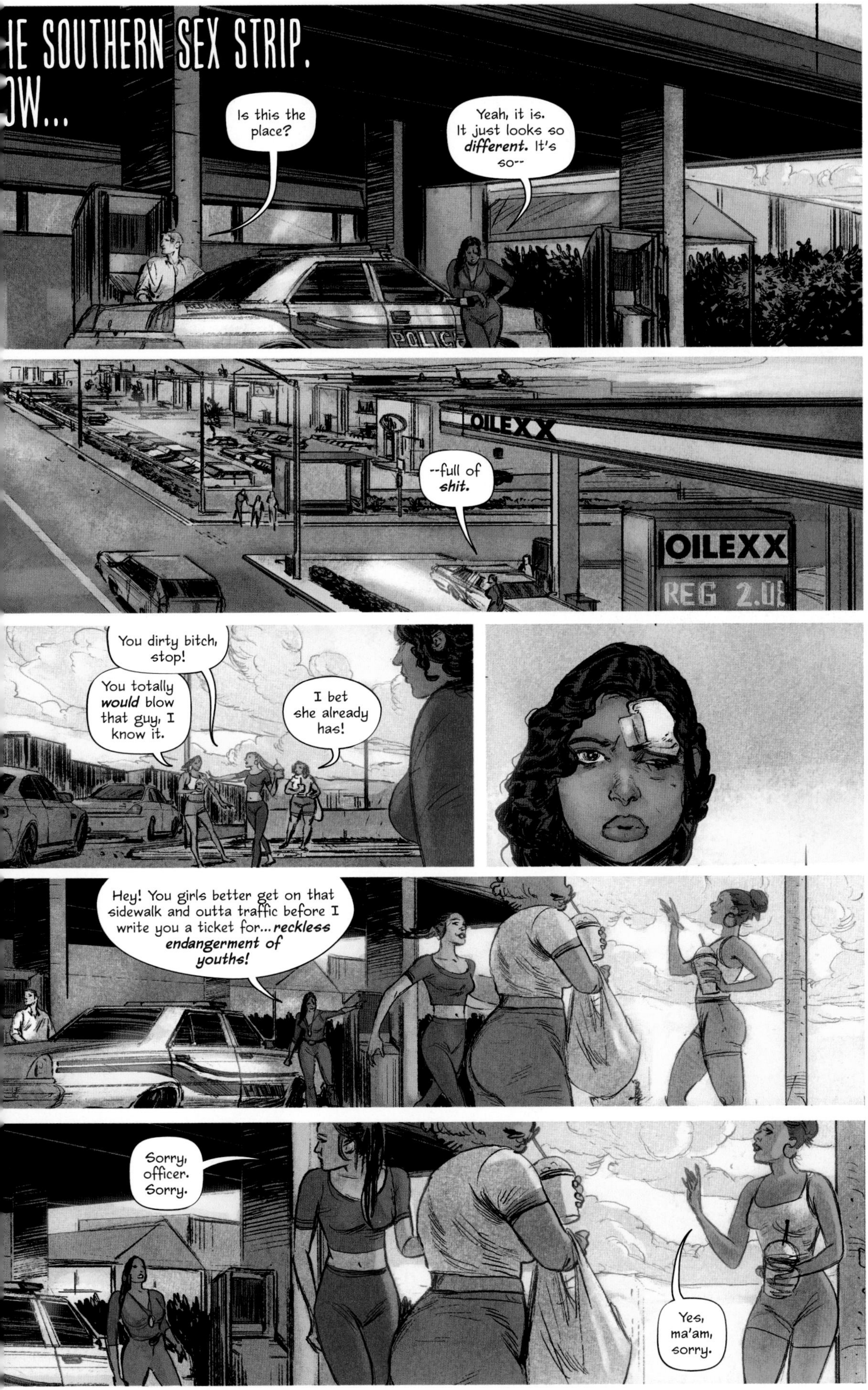
HE SOUTHERN SEX STRIP.
OW...
Is this the place?
Yeah, it is. It just looks so different. It's so--
POLICE
OILEXX
--full of shit.
OILEXX
REG 2.0
You dirty bitch, stop!
You totally would blow that guy, I know it.
I bet she already has!
Hey! You girls better get on that sidewalk and outta traffic before I write you a ticket for... reckless endangerment of youths!
Sorry, officer. Sorry.
Yes, ma'am, sorry.

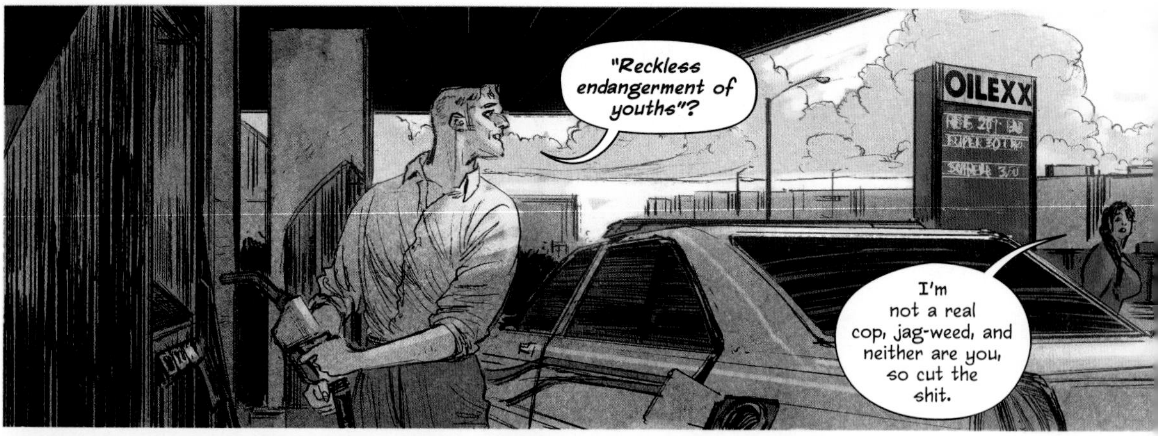
"Reckless endangerment of youths"?
I'm not a real cop, jag-weed, and neither are you, so cut the shit.
OILEXX

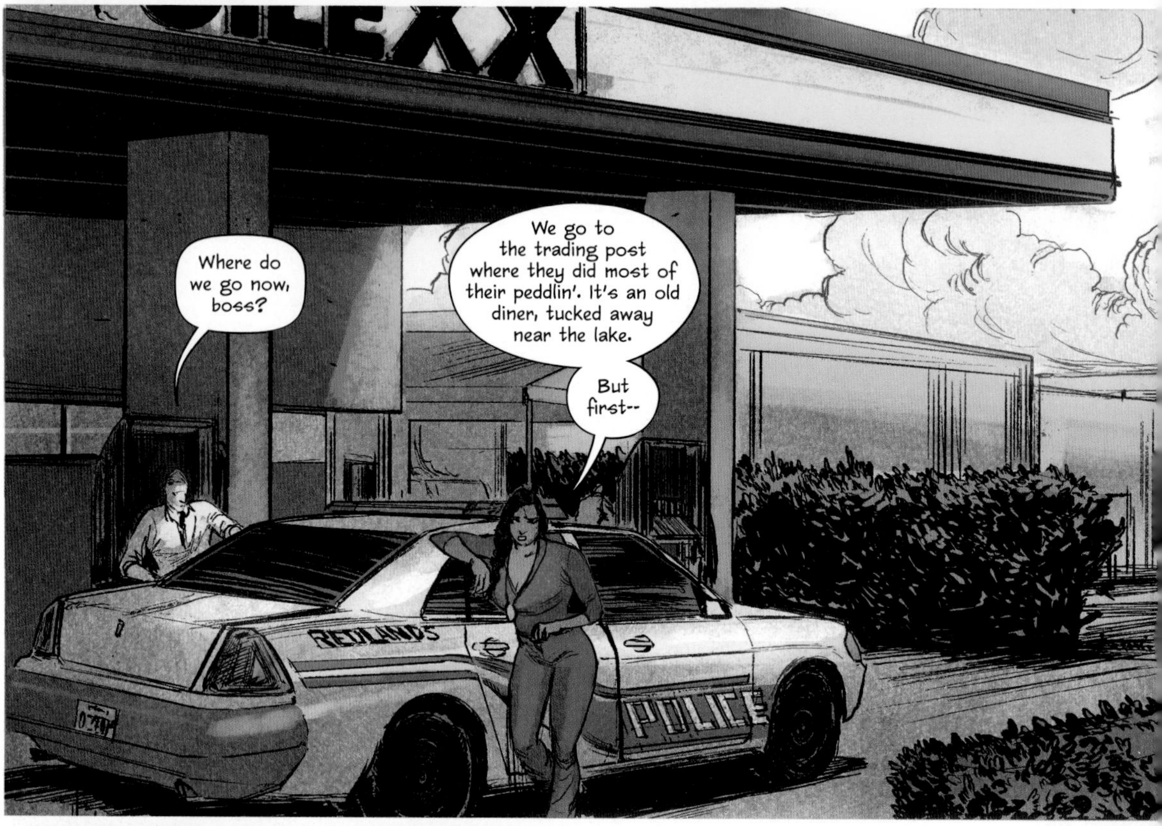
Where do we go now, boss?
We go to the trading post where they did most of their peddlin'. It's an old diner, tucked away near the lake.
But first--
REDLANDS
POLICE

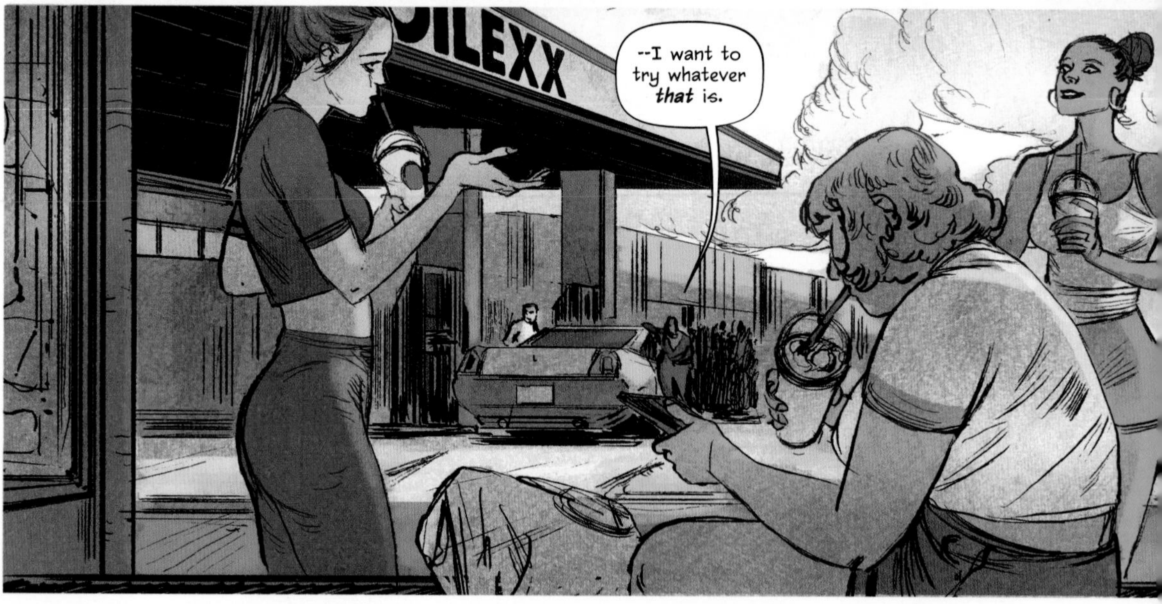
OILEXX
--I want to try whatever *that* is.

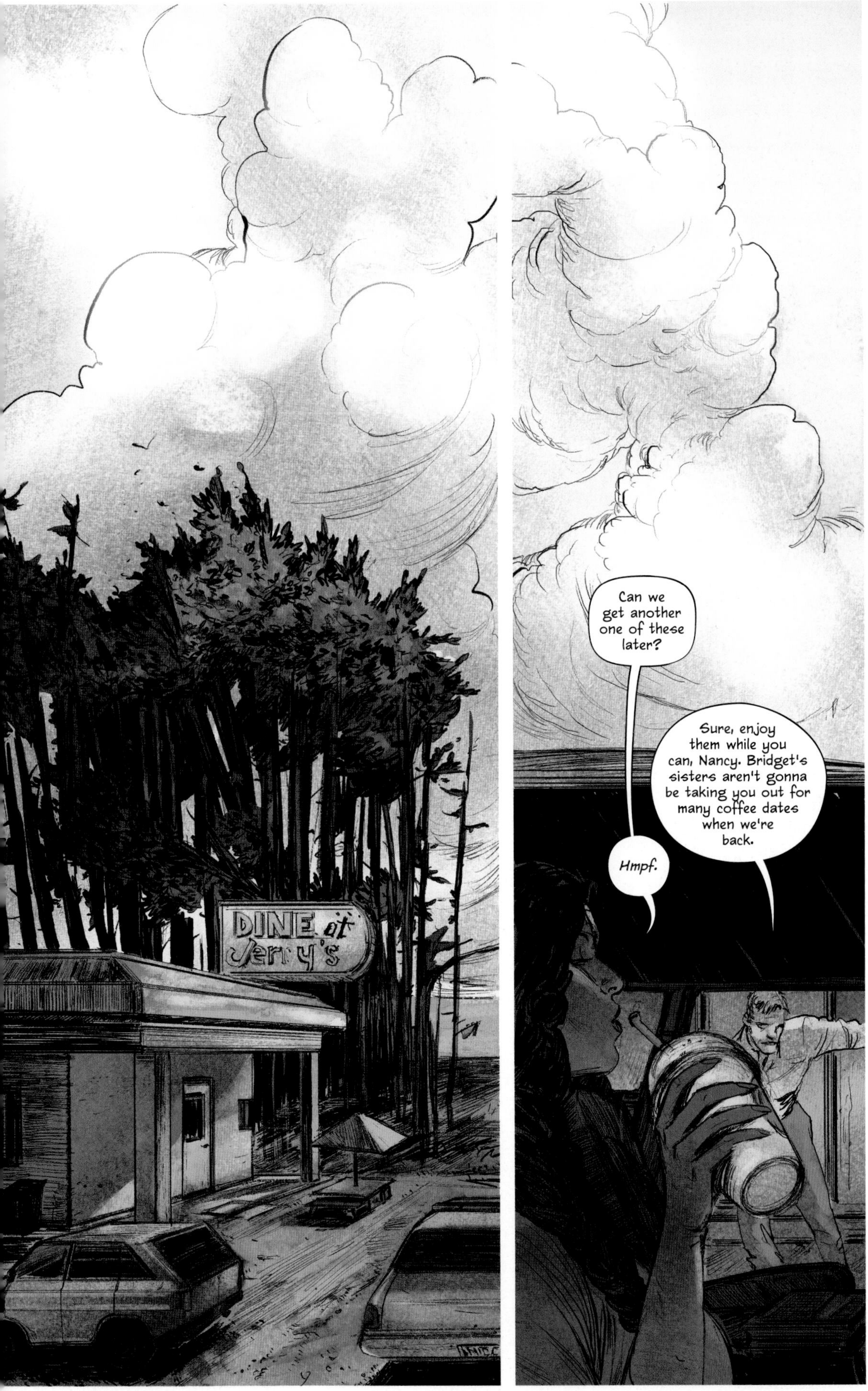
DINE at Jerry's
Can we get another one of these later?
Sure, enjoy them while you can, Nancy. Bridget's sisters aren't gonna be taking you out for many coffee dates when we're back.
Hmpf.

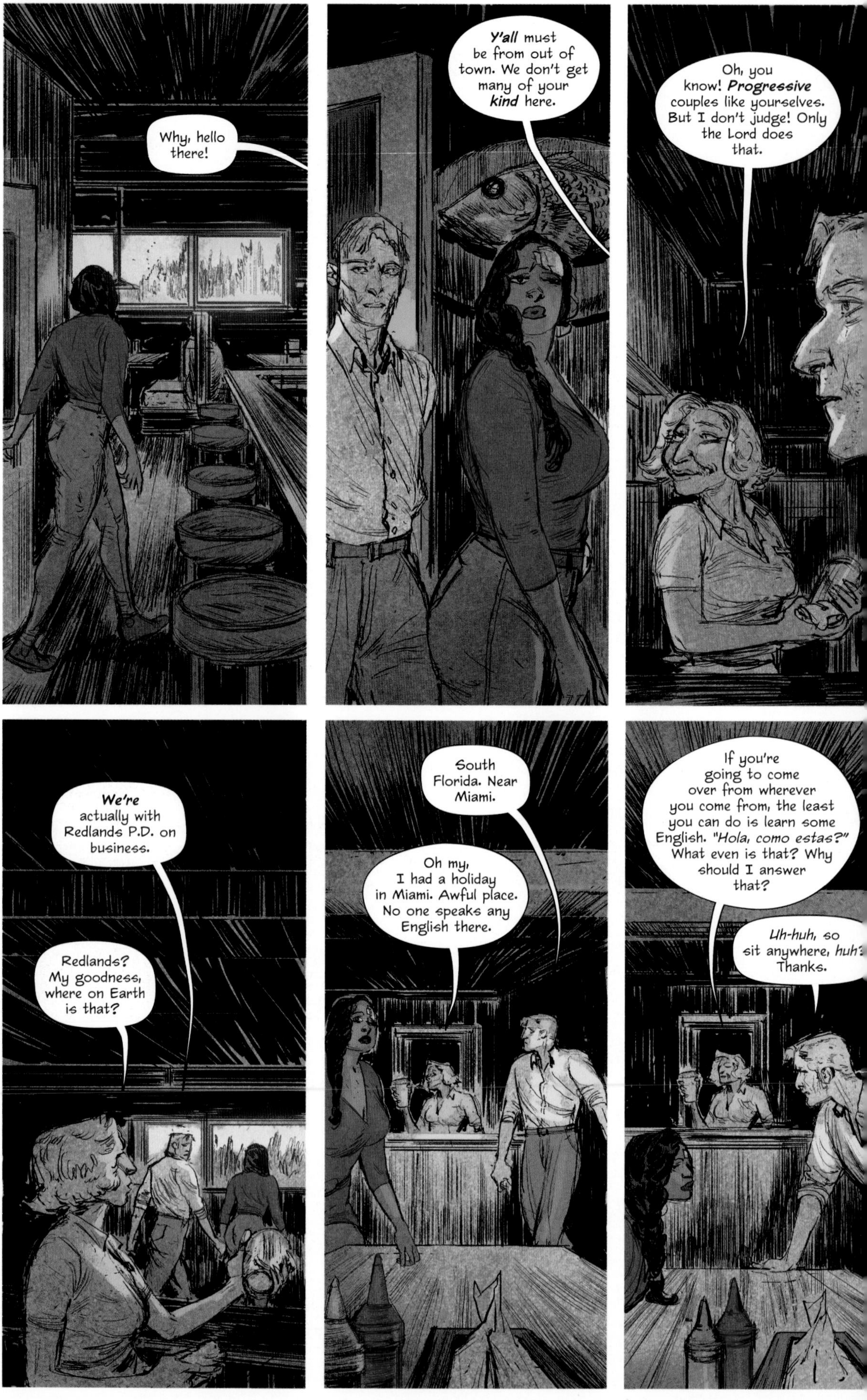

Why, hello there!
Y'all must be from out of town. We don't get many of your *kind* here.
Oh, you know! ***Progressive*** couples like yourselves. But I don't judge! Only the Lord does that.
We're actually with Redlands P.D. on business.
Redlands? My goodness, where on Earth is that?
South Florida. Near Miami.
Oh my, I had a holiday in Miami. Awful place. No one speaks any English there.
If you're going to come over from wherever you come from, the least you can do is learn some English. *"Hola, como estas?"* What even is that? Why should I answer that?
Uh-huh, so sit anywhere, *huh*? Thanks.

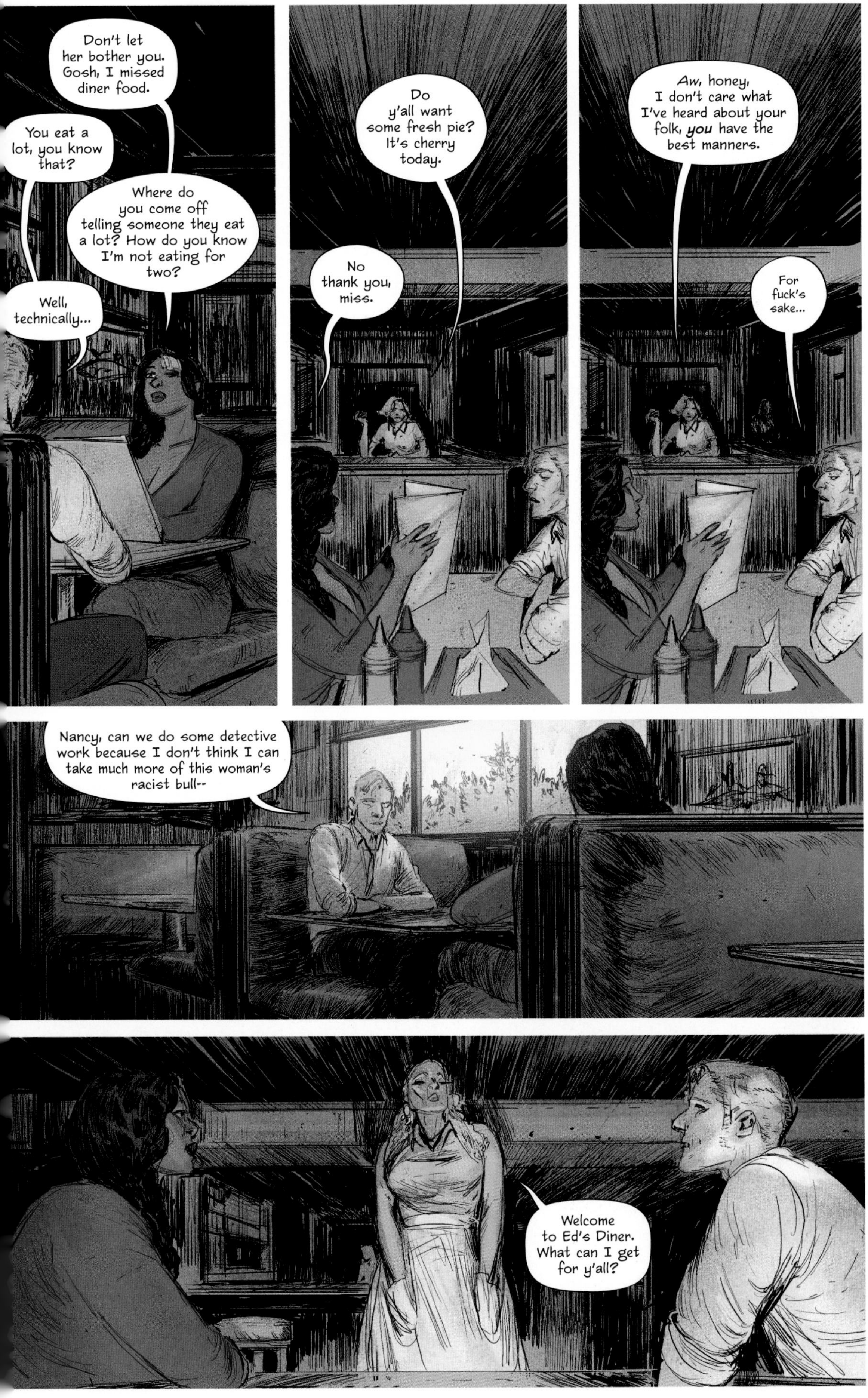
Don't let her bother you. Gosh, I missed diner food.
You eat a lot, you know that?
Where do you come off telling someone they eat a lot? How do you know I'm not eating for two?
Well, technically...
Do y'all want some fresh pie? It's cherry today.
No thank you, miss.
Aw, honey, I don't care what I've heard about your folk, *you* have the best manners.
For fuck's sake...
Nancy, can we do some detective work because I don't think I can take much more of this woman's racist bull--
Welcome to Ed's Diner. What can I get for y'all?

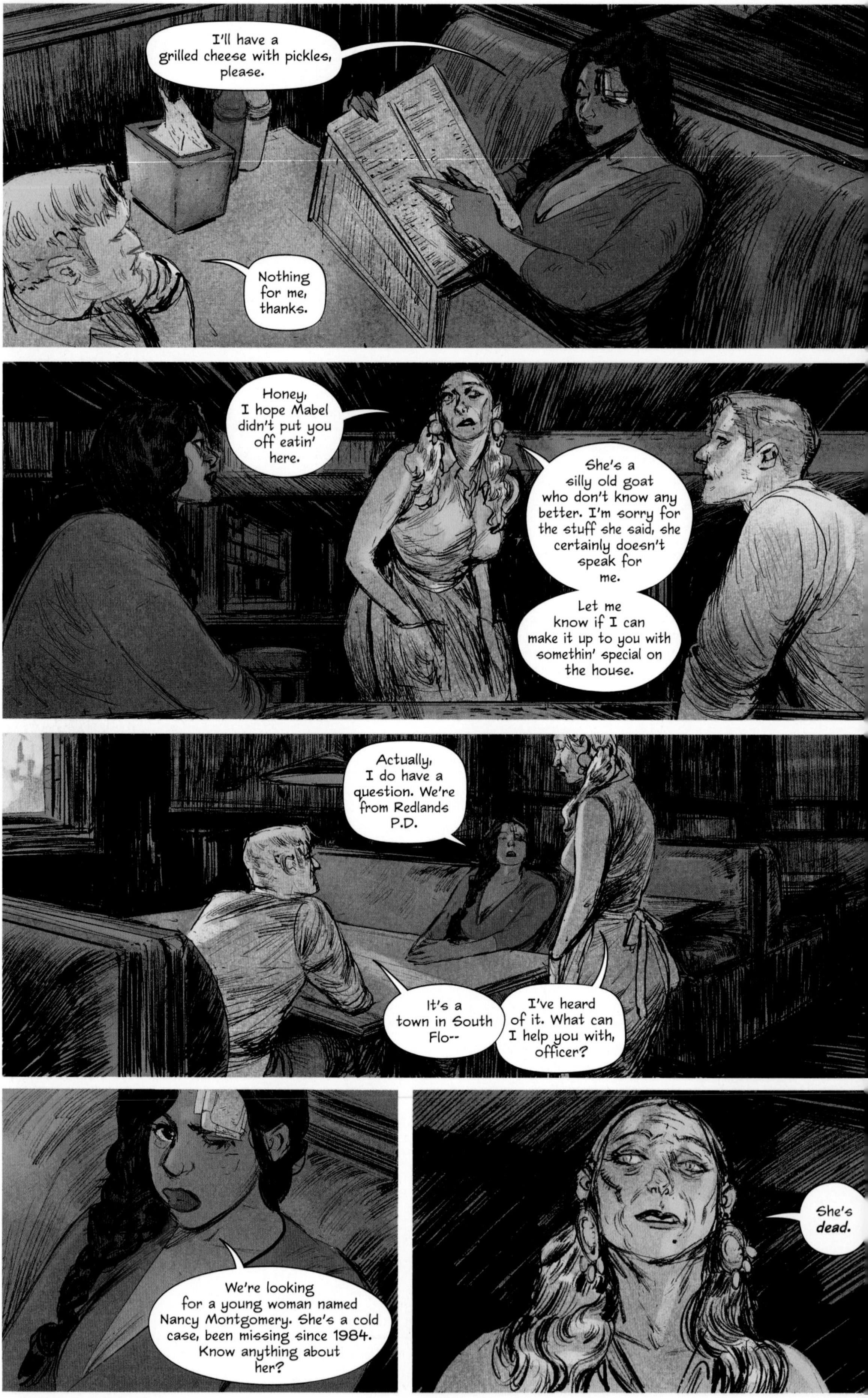
I'll have a grilled cheese with pickles, please.
Nothing for me, thanks.
Honey, I hope Mabel didn't put you off eatin' here.
She's a silly old goat who don't know any better. I'm sorry for the stuff she said, she certainly doesn't speak for me.
Let me know if I can make it up to you with somethin' special on the house.
Actually, I do have a question. We're from Redlands P.D.
It's a town in South Flo--
I've heard of it. What can I help you with, officer?
We're looking for a young woman named Nancy Montgomery. She's a cold case, been missing since 1984. Know anything about her?
She's *dead.*

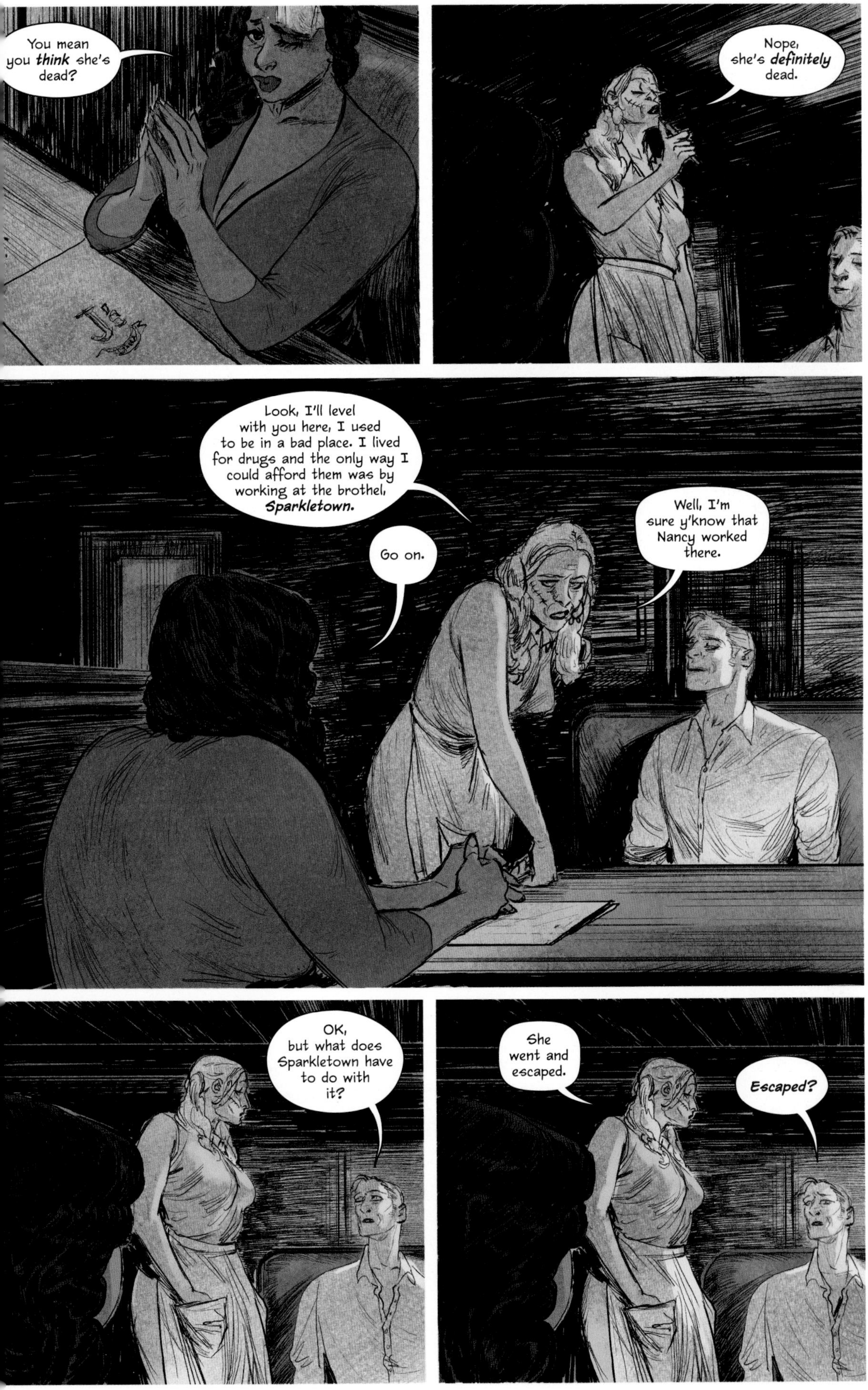
You mean you *think* she's dead?
Nope, she's *definitely* dead.
Look, I'll level with you here, I used to be in a bad place. I lived for drugs and the only way I could afford them was by working at the brothel, **Sparkletown.**
Go on.
Well, I'm sure y'know that Nancy worked there.
OK, but what does Sparkletown have to do with it?
She went and escaped.
Escaped?

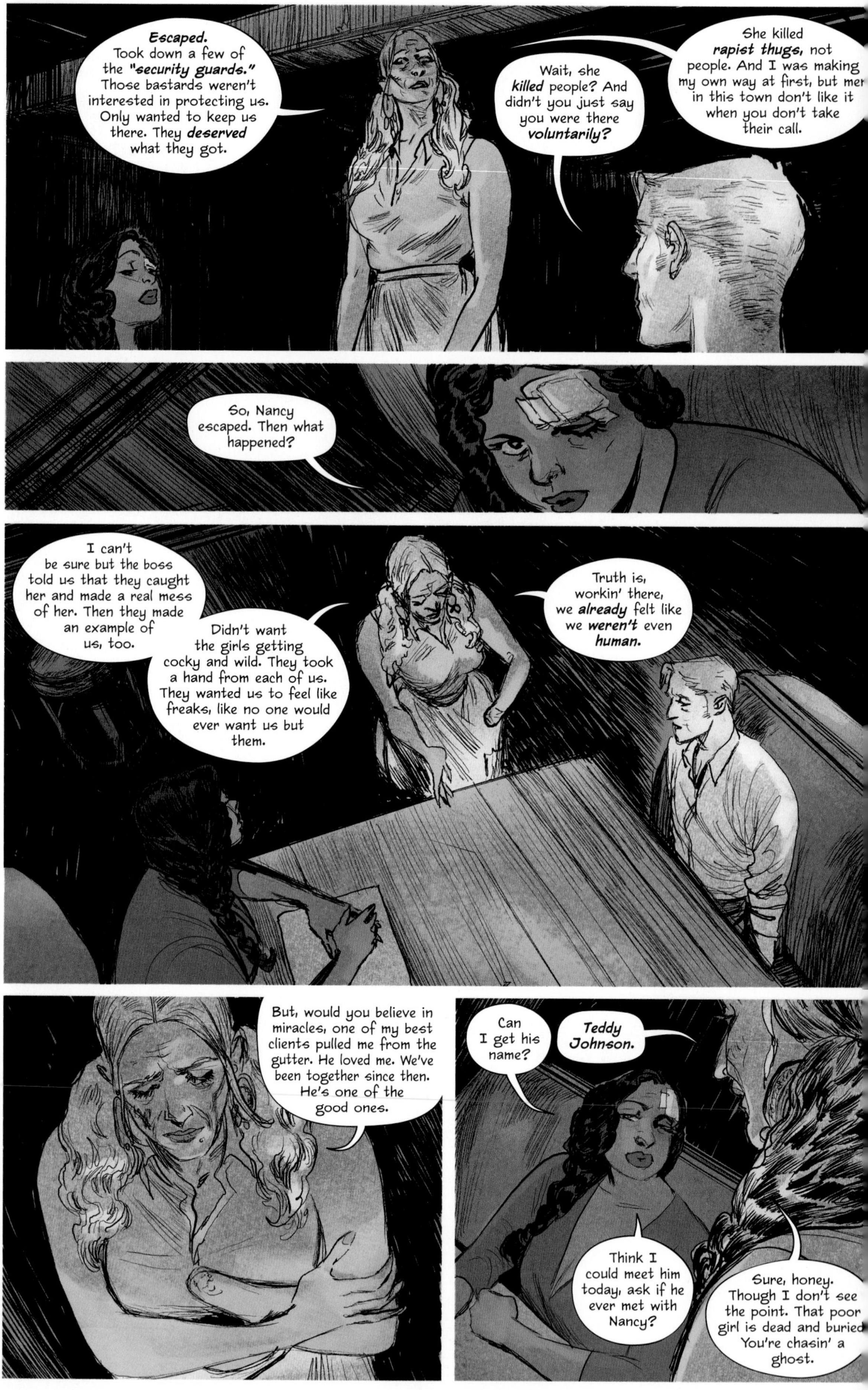
Escaped. Took down a few of the "security guards." Those bastards weren't interested in protecting us. Only wanted to keep us there. They deserved what they got.
Wait, she killed people? And didn't you just say you were there voluntarily?
She killed rapist thugs, not people. And I was making my own way at first, but men in this town don't like it when you don't take their call.
So, Nancy escaped. Then what happened?
I can't be sure but the boss told us that they caught her and made a real mess of her. Then they made an example of us, too.
Didn't want the girls getting cocky and wild. They took a hand from each of us. They wanted us to feel like freaks, like no one would ever want us but them.
Truth is, workin' there, we already felt like we weren't even human.
But, would you believe in miracles, one of my best clients pulled me from the gutter. He loved me. We've been together since then. He's one of the good ones.
Can I get his name?
Teddy Johnson.
Think I could meet him today, ask if he ever met with Nancy?
Sure, honey. Though I don't see the point. That poor girl is dead and buried. You're chasin' a ghost.

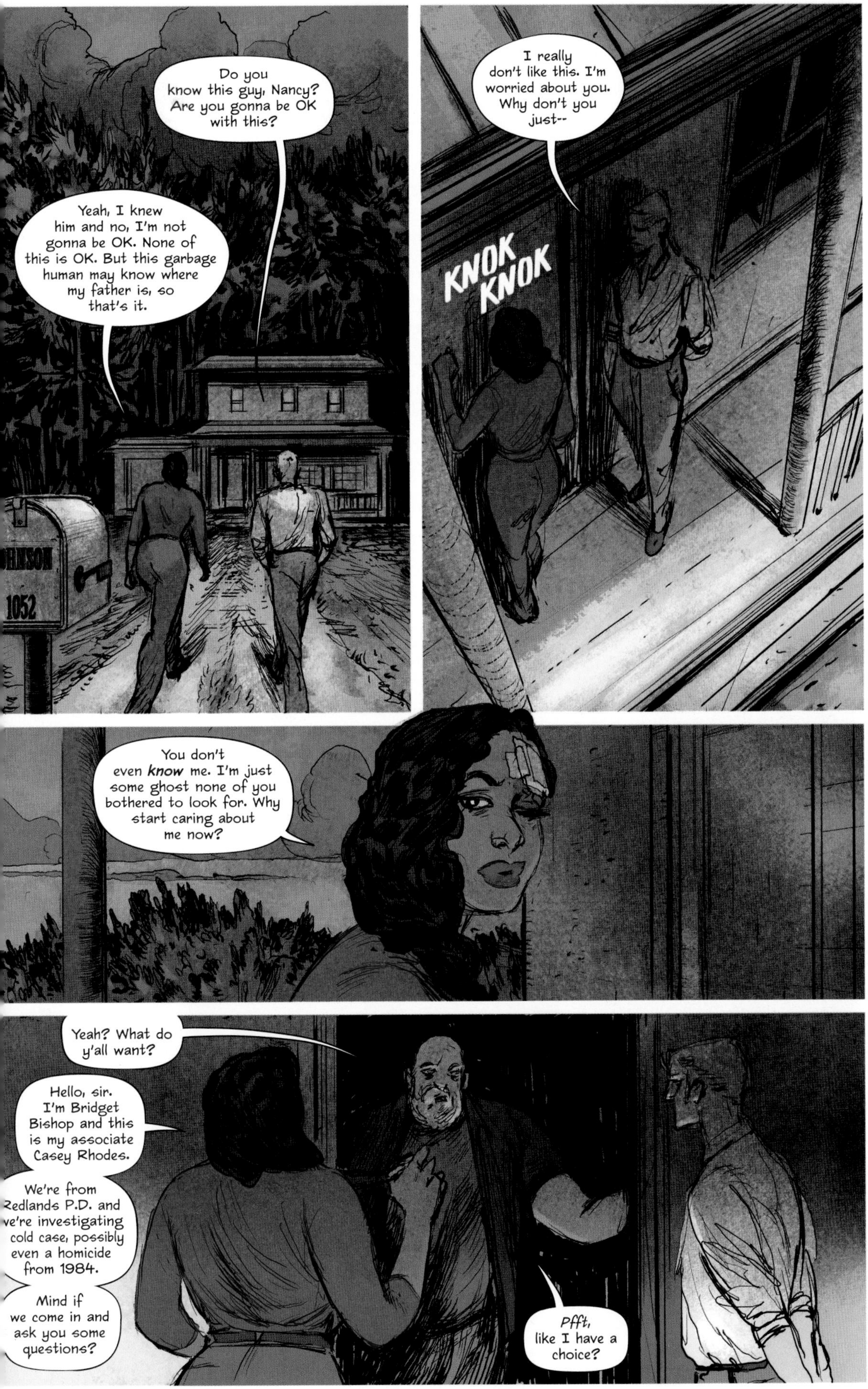
Do you know this guy, Nancy? Are you gonna be OK with this?
Yeah, I knew him and no, I'm not gonna be OK. None of this is OK. But this garbage human may know where my father is, so that's it.
OHNSON
1052
I really don't like this. I'm worried about you. Why don't you just--
KNOK KNOK
You don't even *know* me. I'm just some ghost none of you bothered to look for. Why start caring about me now?
Yeah? What do y'all want?
Hello, sir. I'm Bridget Bishop and this is my associate Casey Rhodes.
We're from edlands P.D. and e're investigating cold case, possibly even a homicide from 1984.
Mind if we come in and ask you some questions?
Pfft, like I have a choice?

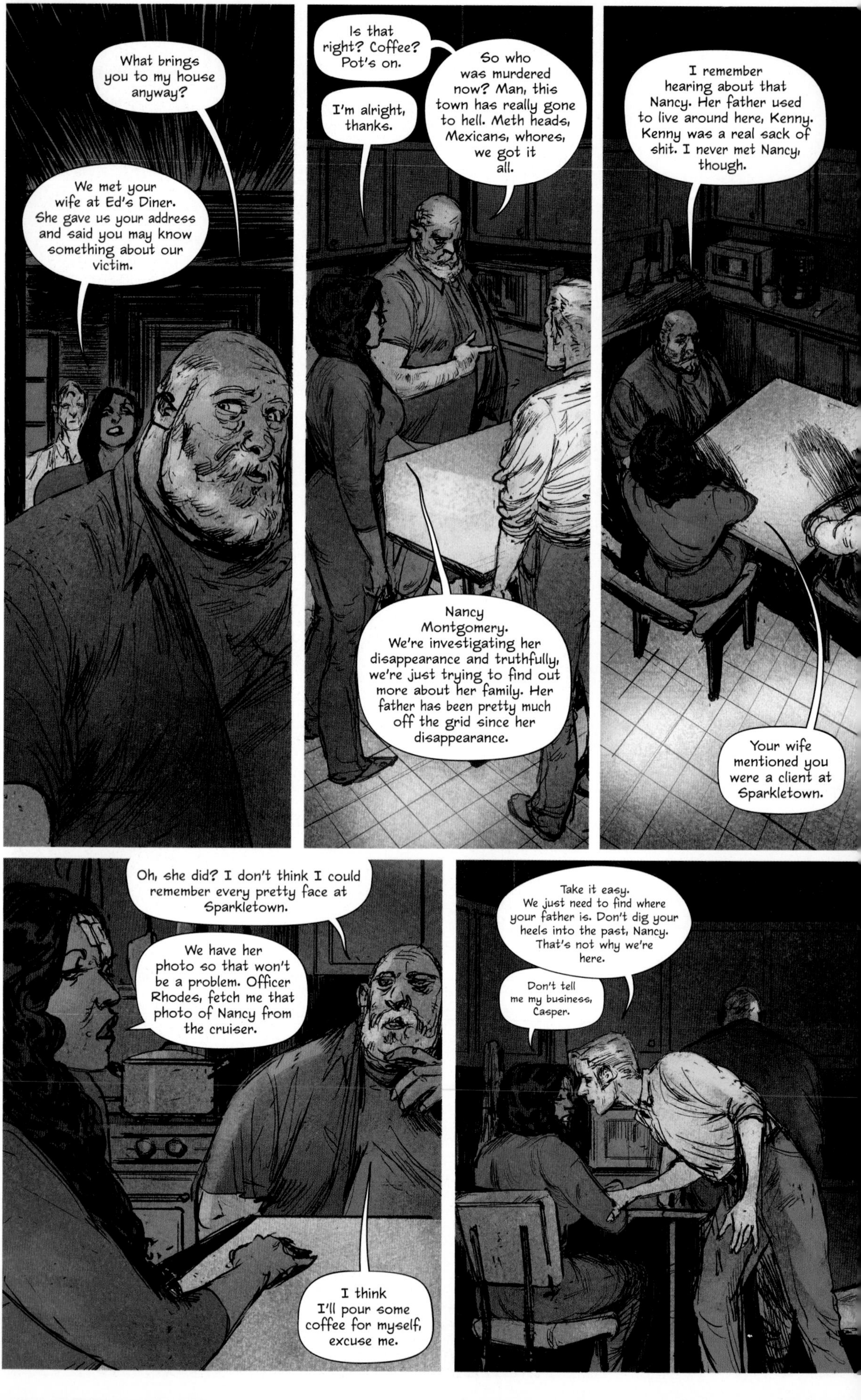
What brings you to my house anyway?
We met your wife at Ed's Diner. She gave us your address and said you may know something about our victim.
Is that right? Coffee? Pot's on.
I'm alright, thanks.
So who was murdered now? Man, this town has really gone to hell. Meth heads, Mexicans, whores, we got it all.
Nancy Montgomery. We're investigating her disappearance and truthfully, we're just trying to find out more about her family. Her father has been pretty much off the grid since her disappearance.
I remember hearing about that Nancy. Her father used to live around here, Kenny. Kenny was a real sack of shit. I never met Nancy, though.
Your wife mentioned you were a client at Sparkletown.
Oh, she did? I don't think I could remember every pretty face at Sparkletown.
We have her photo so that won't be a problem. Officer Rhodes, fetch me that photo of Nancy from the cruiser.
I think I'll pour some coffee for myself, excuse me.
Take it easy. We just need to find where your father is. Don't dig your heels into the past, Nancy. That's not why we're here.
Don't tell me my business, Casper.

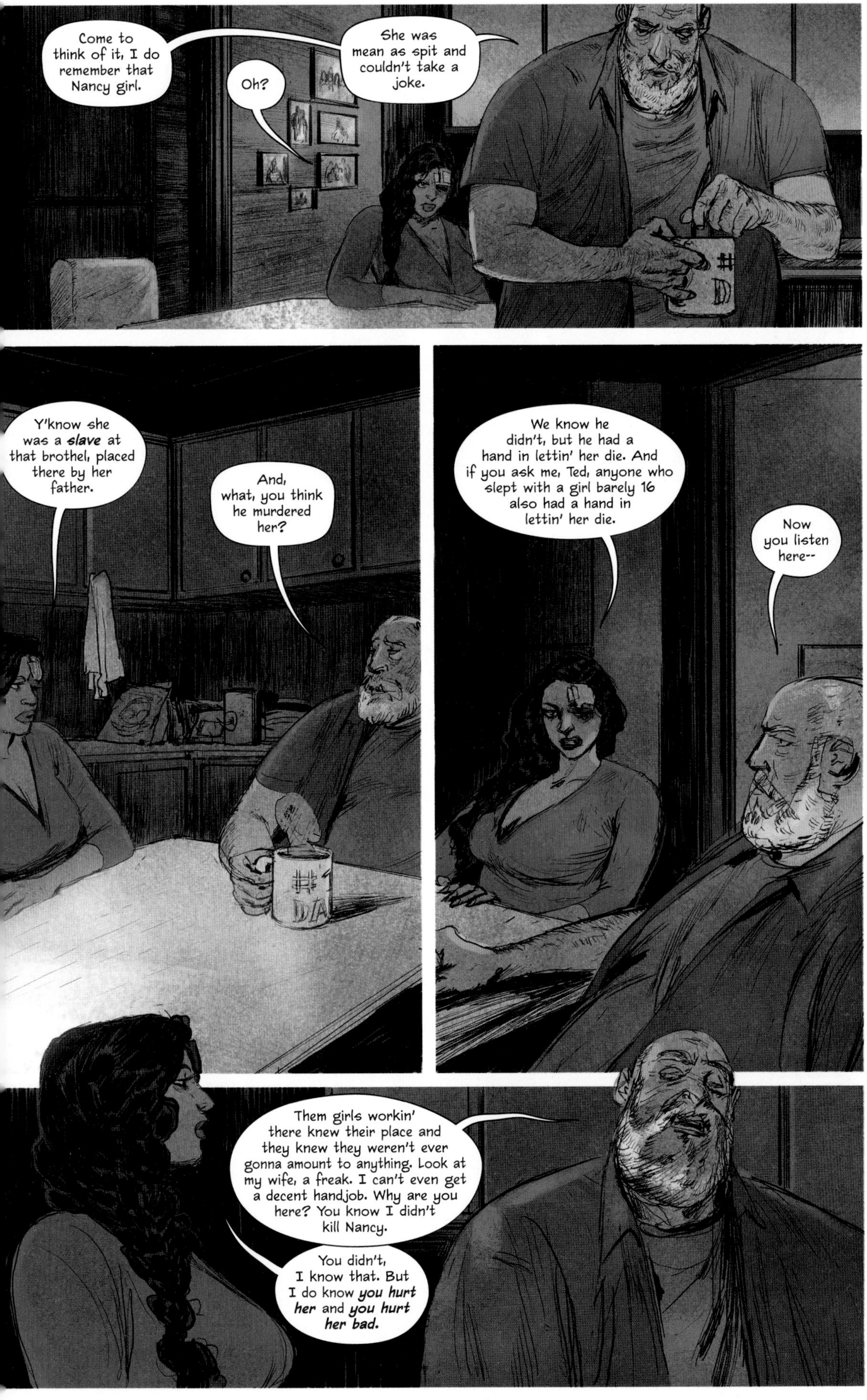
Come to think of it, I do remember that Nancy girl.
Oh?
She was mean as spit and couldn't take a joke.
Y'know she was a ***slave*** at that brothel, placed there by her father.
And, what, you think he murdered her?
We know he didn't, but he had a hand in lettin' her die. And if you ask me, Ted, anyone who slept with a girl barely 16 also had a hand in lettin' her die.
Now you listen here--
Them girls workin' there knew their place and they knew they weren't ever gonna amount to anything. Look at my wife, a freak. I can't even get a decent handjob. Why are you here? You know I didn't kill Nancy.
You didn't, I know that. But I do know ***you hurt her*** and ***you hurt her bad.***

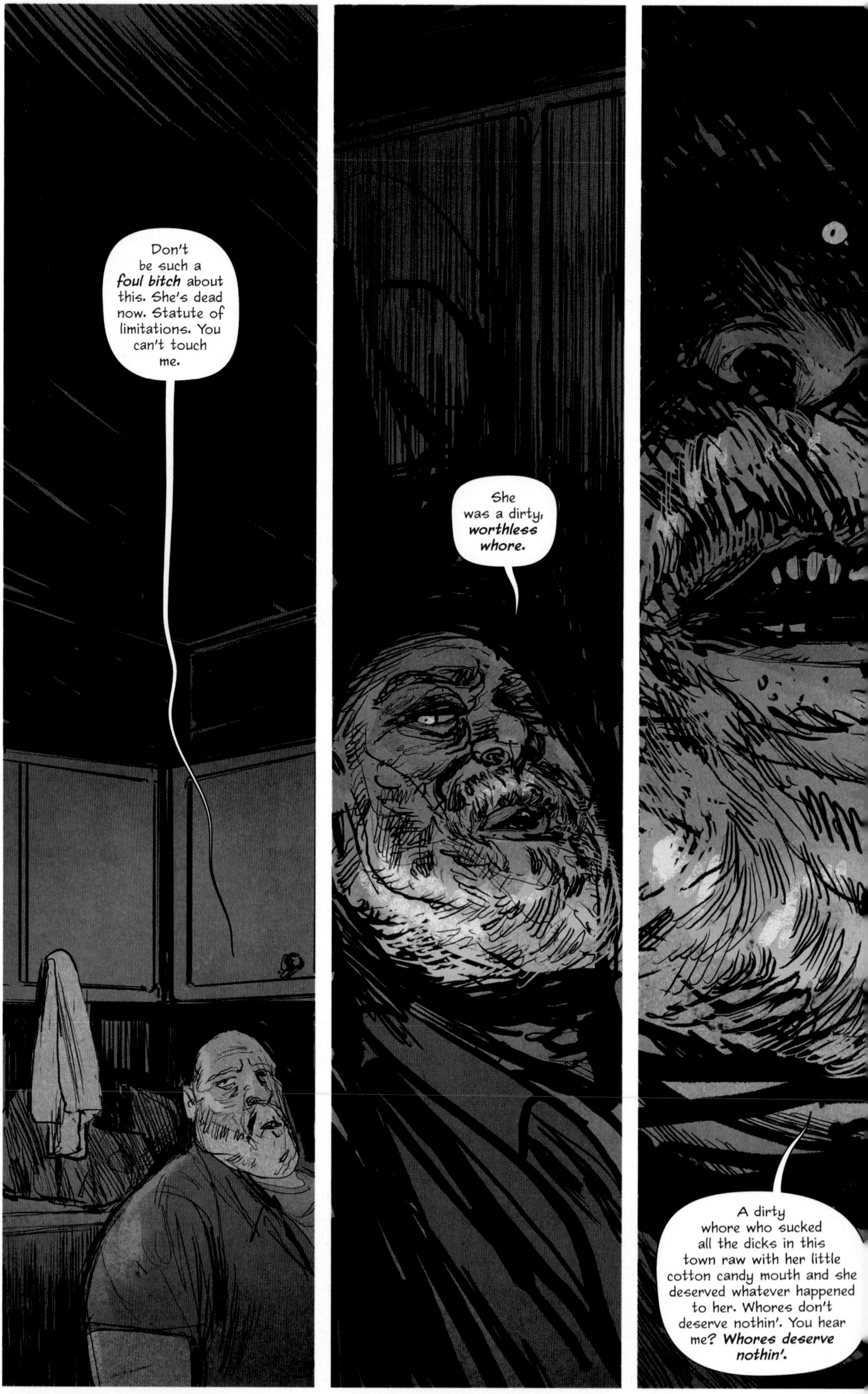
Don't be such a ***foul bitch*** about this. She's dead now. Statute of limitations. You can't touch me.
She was a dirty, ***worthless whore.***
A dirty whore who sucked all the dicks in this town raw with her little cotton candy mouth and she deserved whatever happened to her. Whores don't deserve nothin'. You hear me? ***Whores deserve nothin'.***

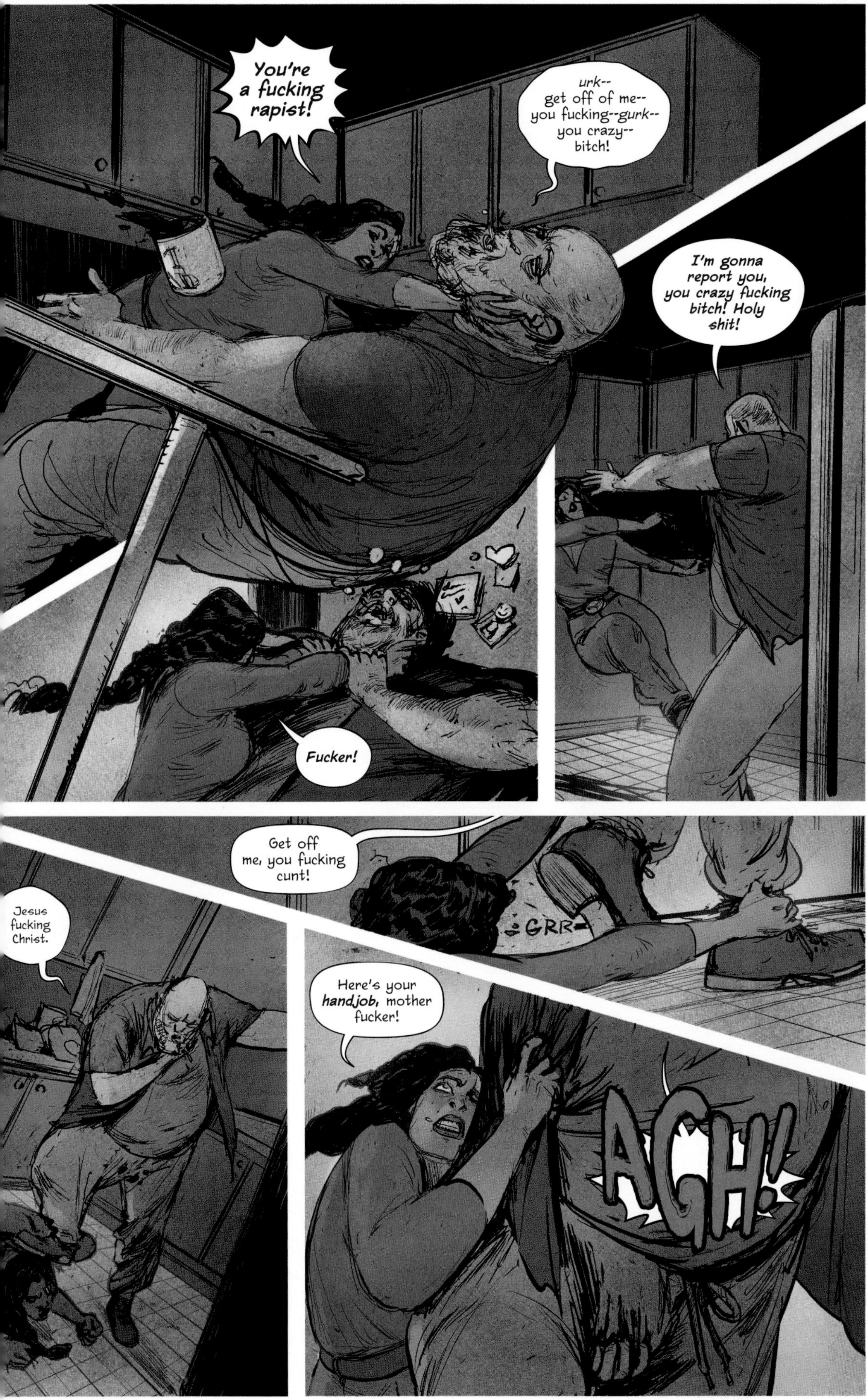
You're a fucking rapist!
urk-- get off of me-- you fucking--gurk-- you crazy-- bitch!
I'm gonna report you, you crazy fucking bitch! Holy shit!
Fucker!
Get off me, you fucking cunt!
GRR
Jesus fucking Christ.
Here's your handjob, mother fucker!
AGH!

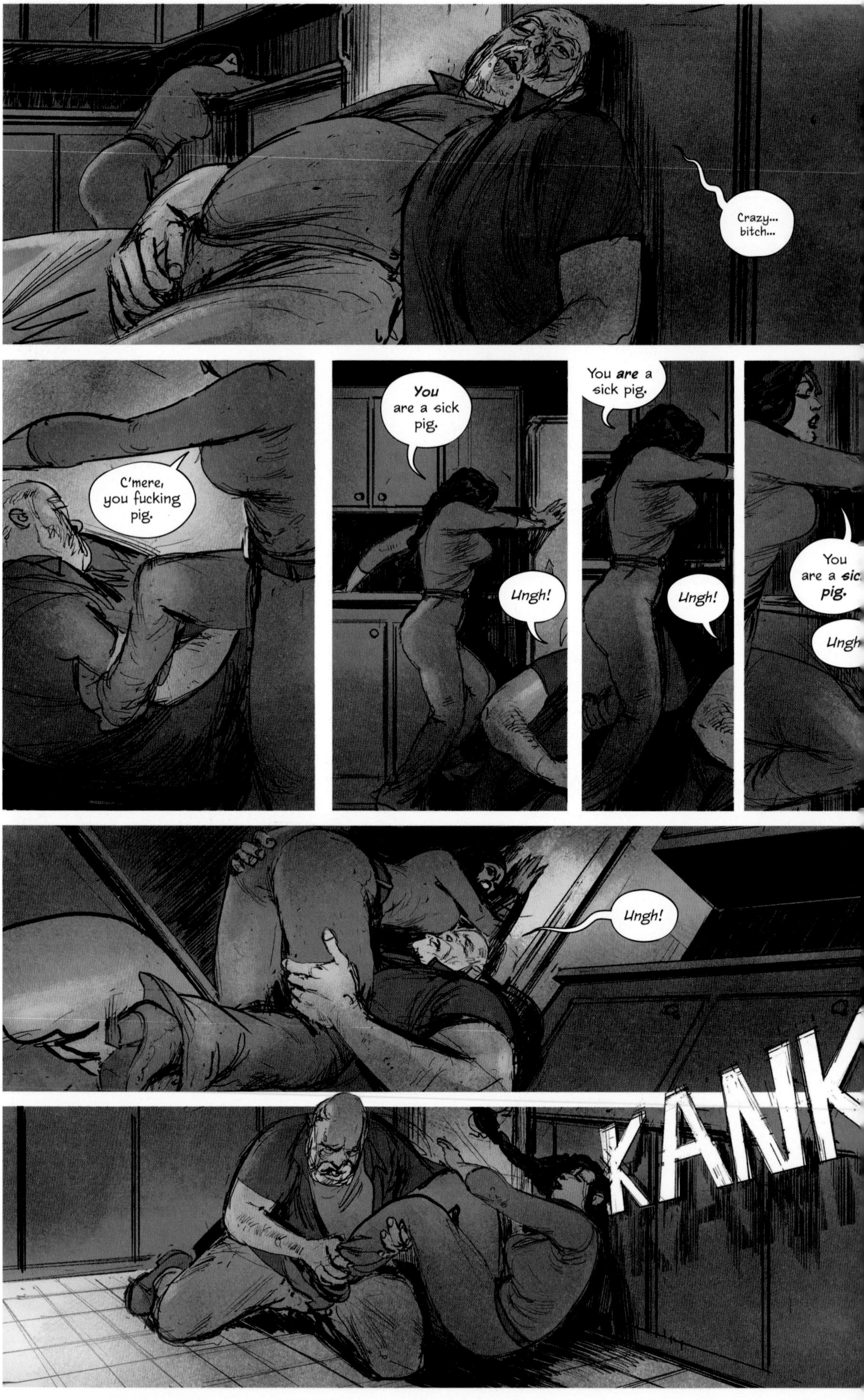

Crazy... bitch...
C'mere, you fucking pig.
You are a sick pig.
Ungh!
You *are* a sick pig.
Ungh!
You are a **sic** **pig.**
Ungh
Ungh!
KANK

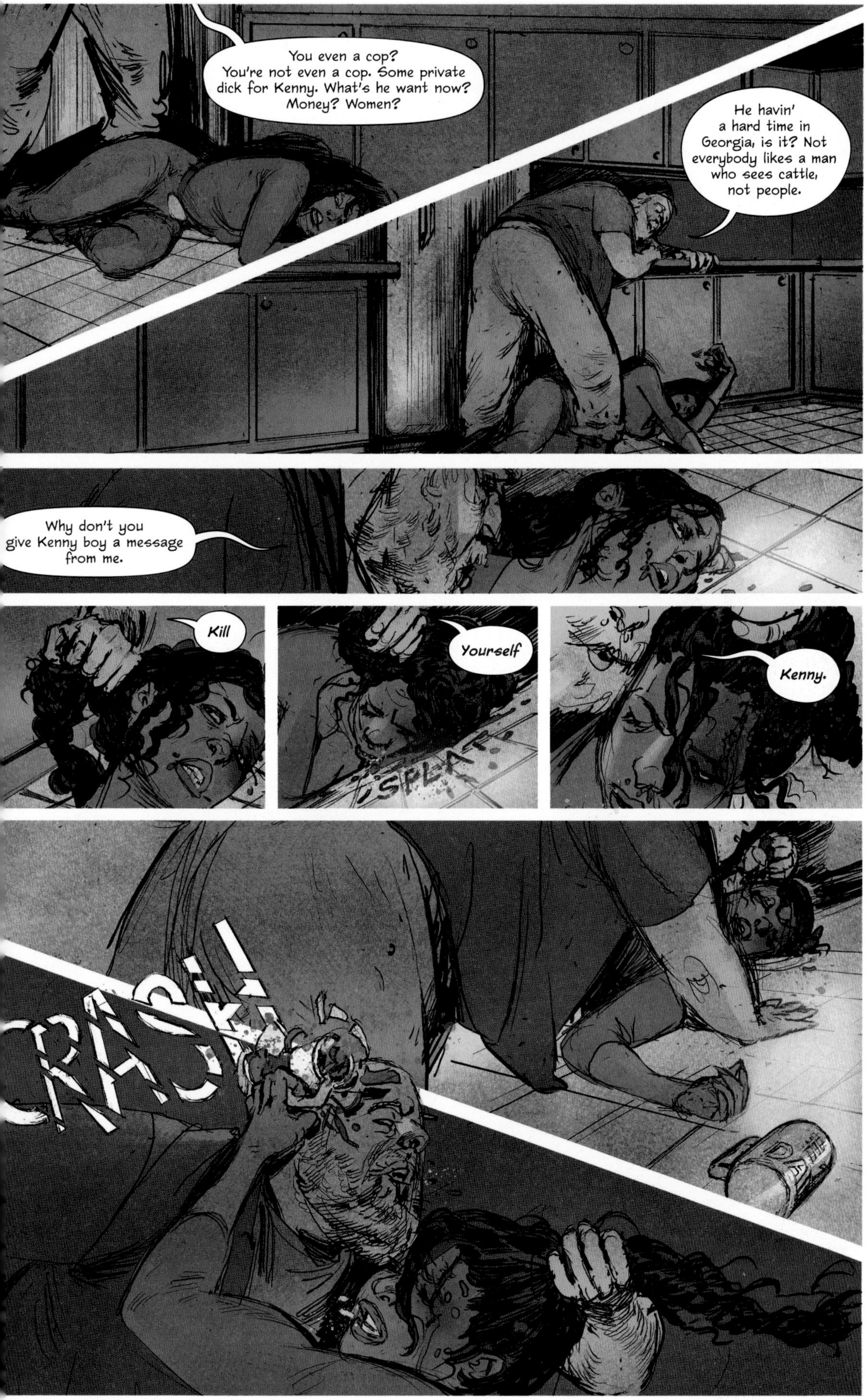

You even a cop? You're not even a cop. Some private dick for Kenny. What's he want now? Money? Women?
He havin' a hard time in Georgia, is it? Not everybody likes a man who sees cattle, not people.
Why don't you give Kenny boy a message from me.
Kill
Yourself
SPLAT
Kenny.
CRASH!!

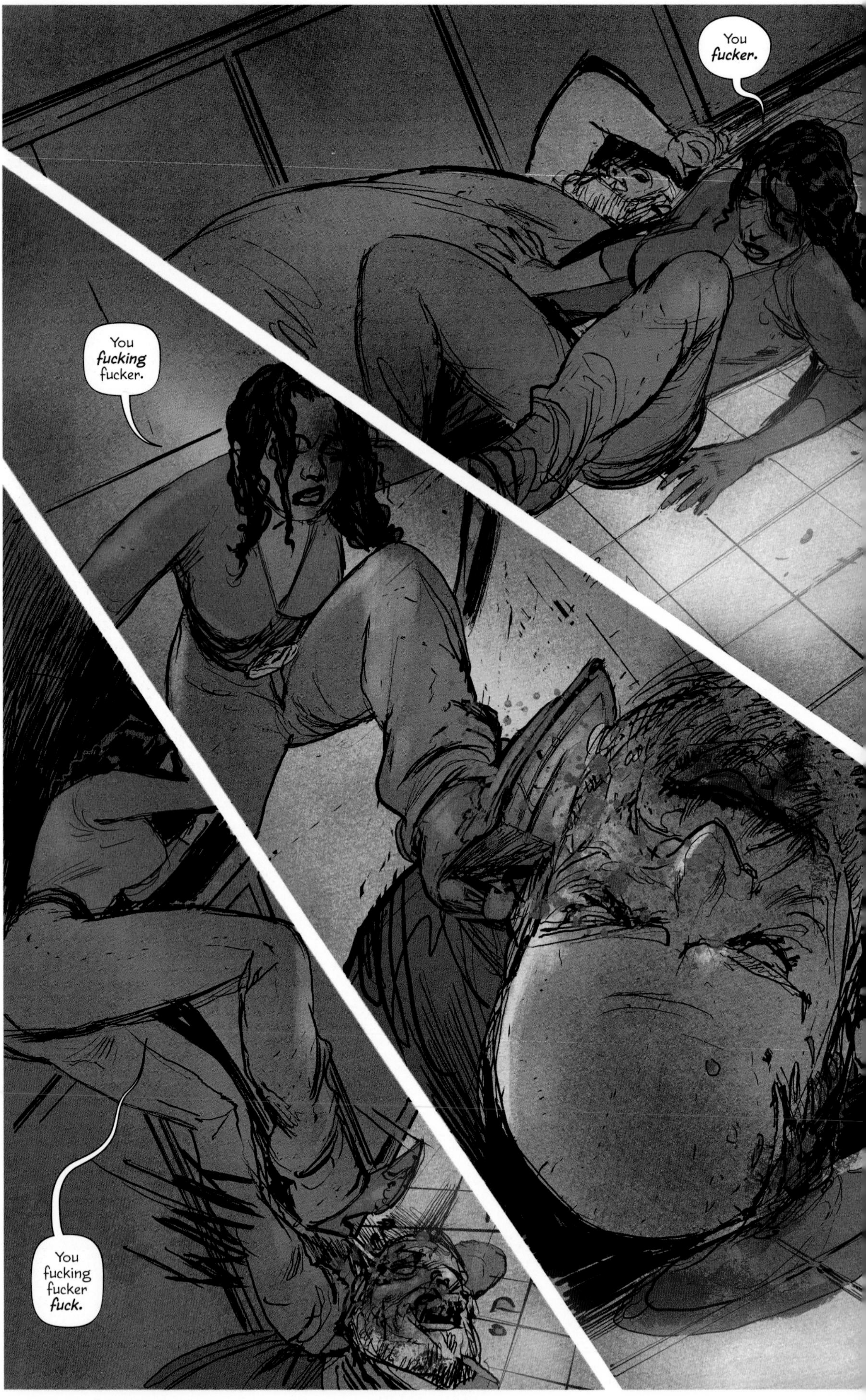
You *fucker.*
You *fucking* fucker.
You fucking fucker *fuck.*

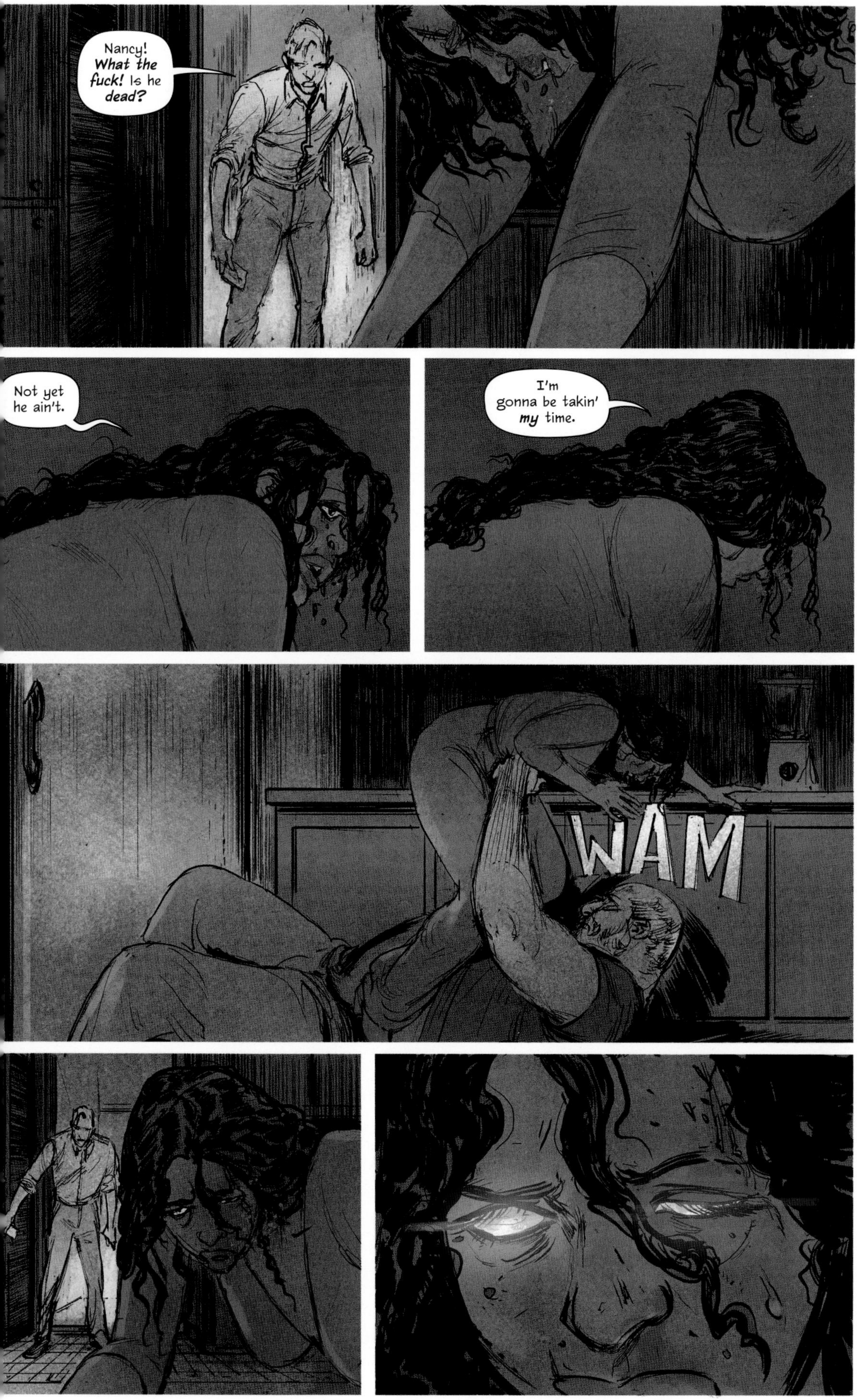
Nancy! What the fuck! Is he dead?
Not yet he ain't.
I'm gonna be takin' my time.
WAM

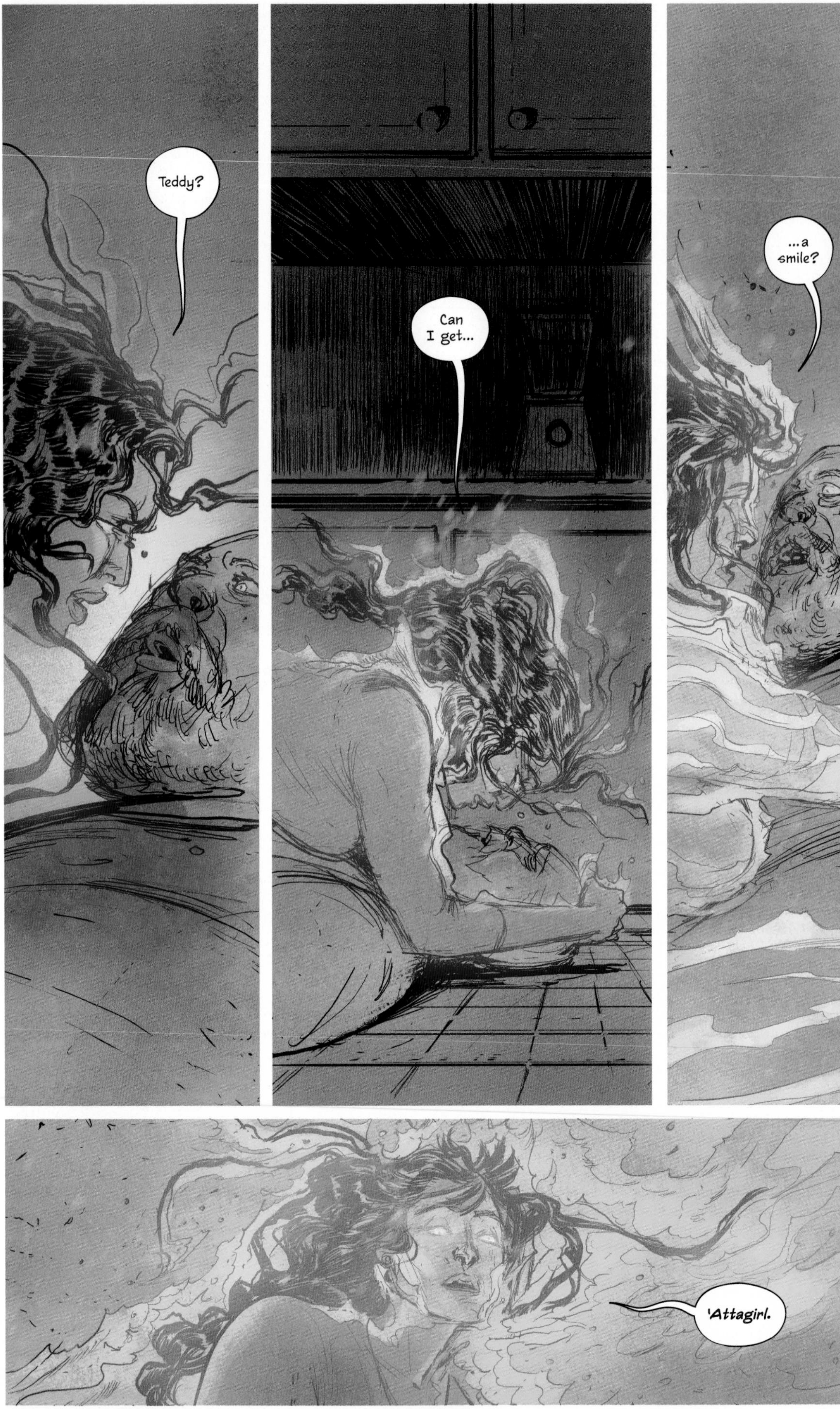
Teddy?
Can I get...
...a smile?
'Attagirl.

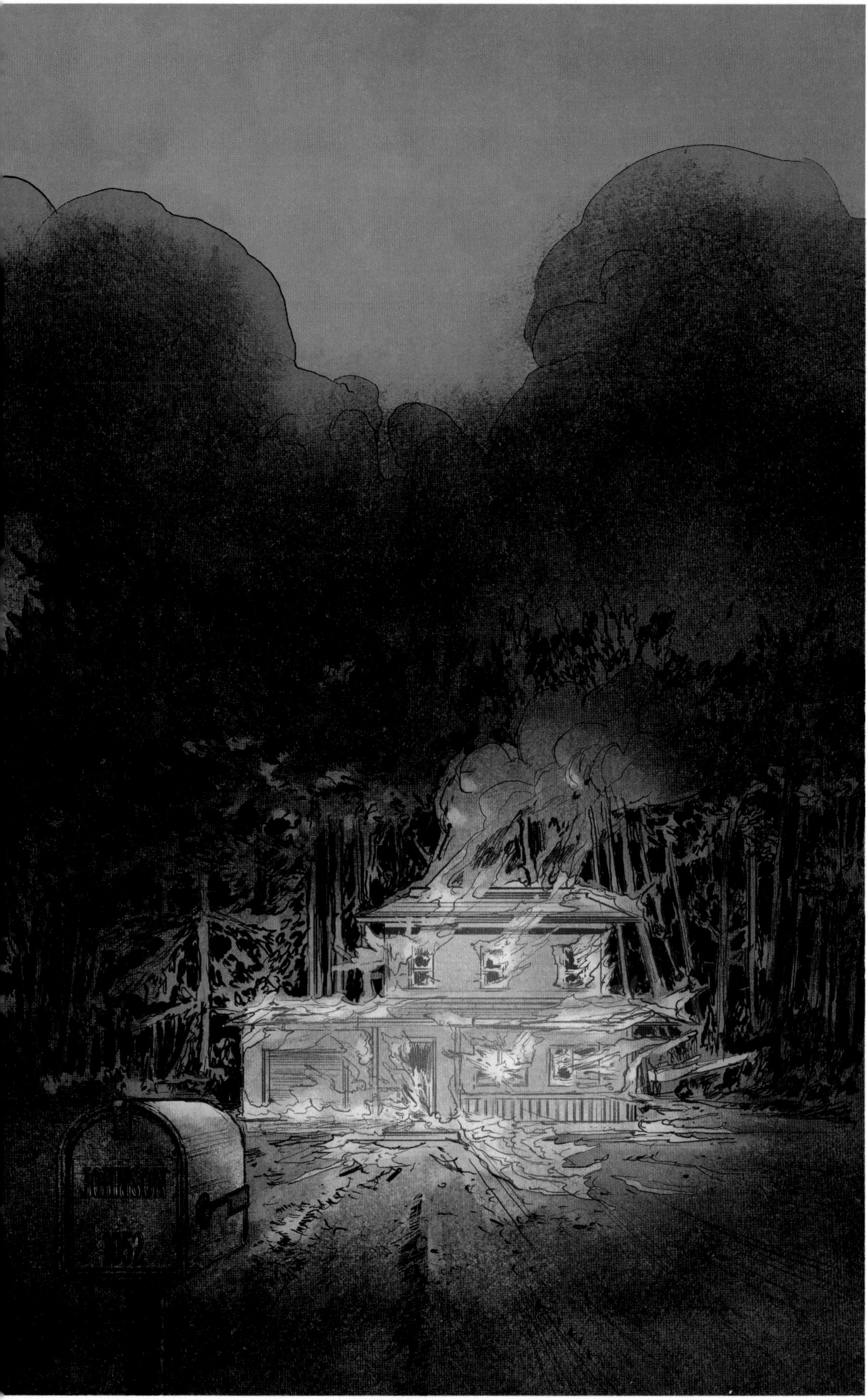
JOHNSON

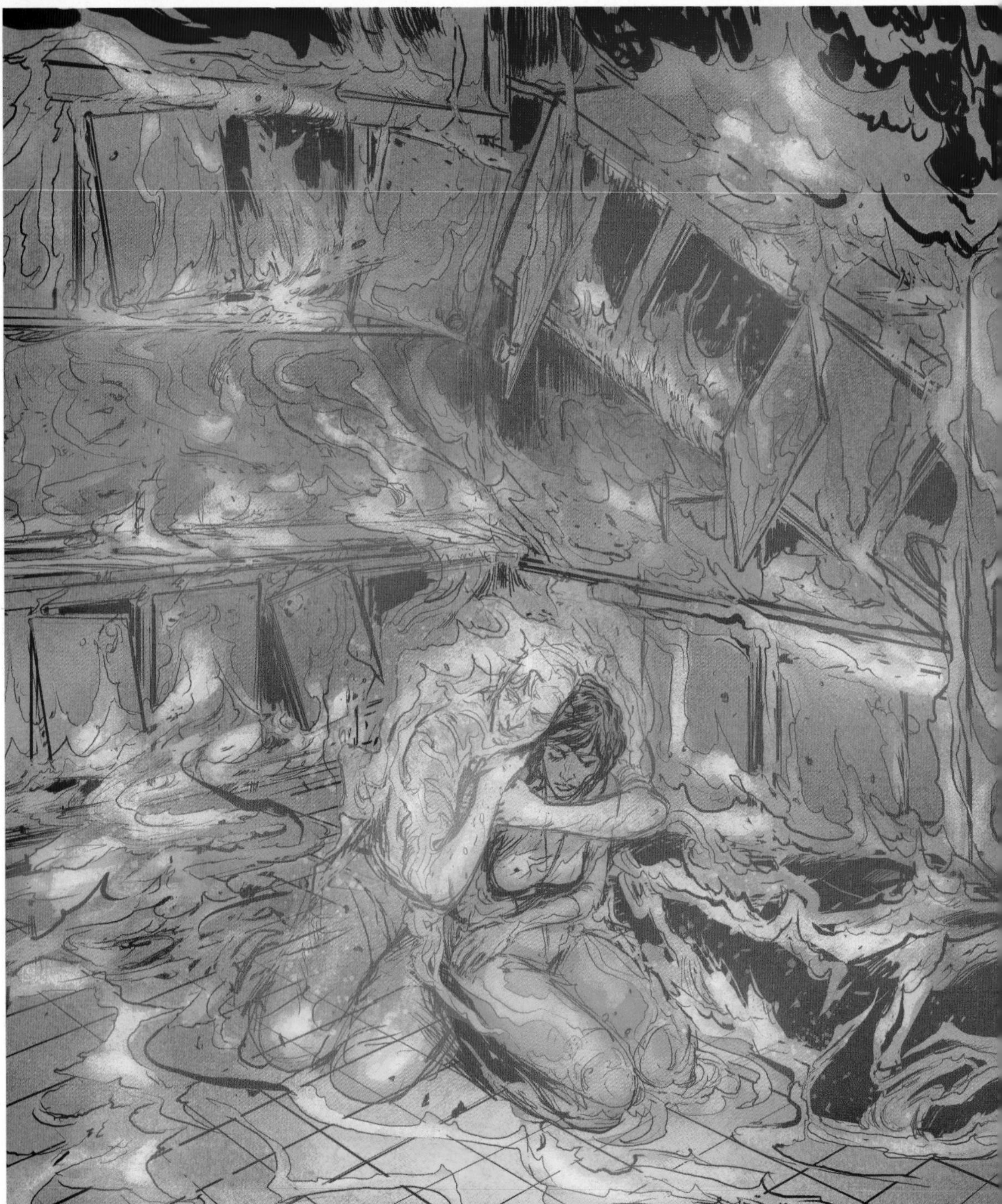
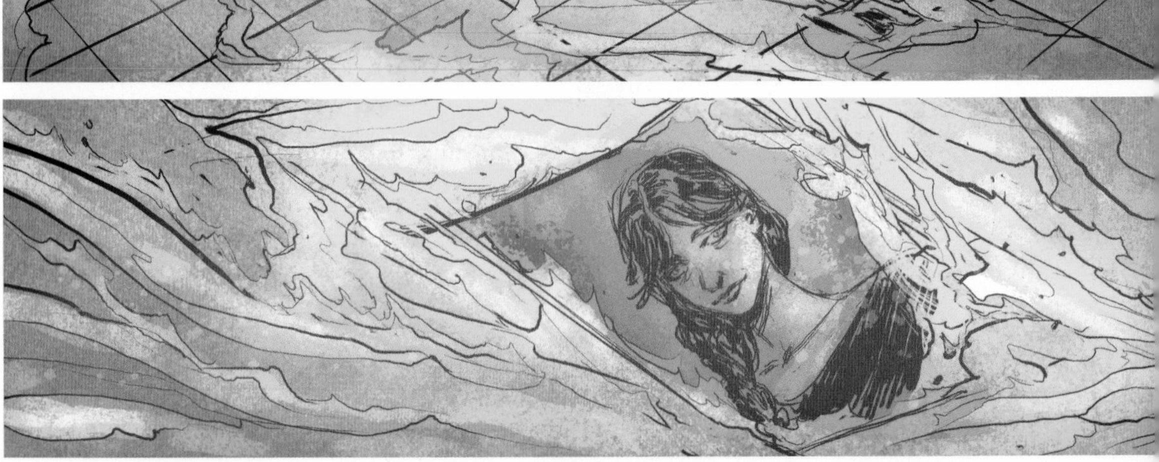

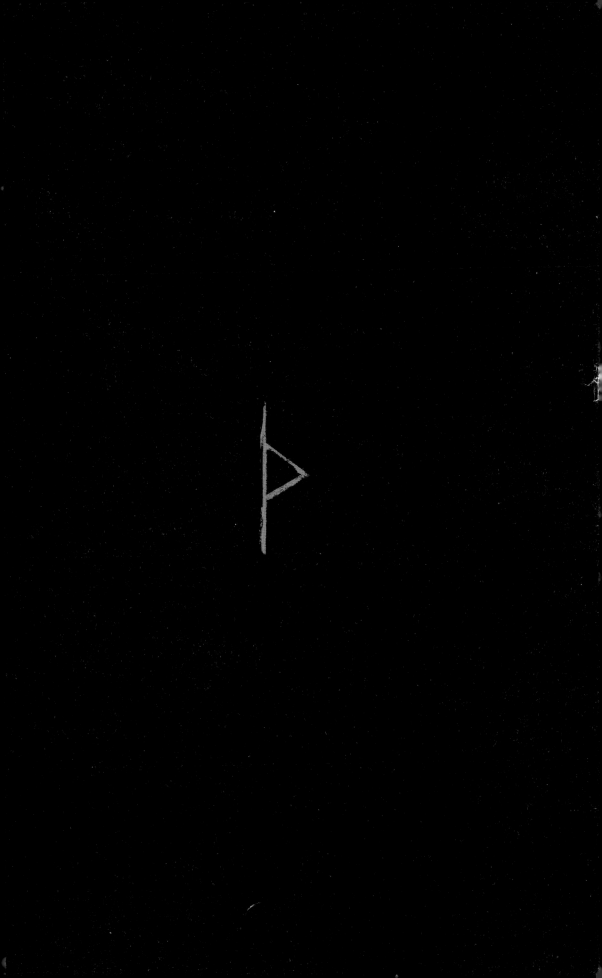

JORDIE BELLAIRE is an Eisner award-winning colorist, coloring projects at Image, Marvel and DC. Her favorite titles include THEY'RE NOT LIKE US, INJECTION and AUTUMNLANDS. REDLANDS is Jordie's debut as a comic book writer and she's still wondering how the heck she got this lucky to do all the things she wanted to do.

Cuban-born creator VANESA R. DEL REY began her career doing concept art for animation. Her first sequential works were THE HIT comic book series and THE EMPTY MAN series published by Boom! Studios. She has illustrated stories for Dark Horse Comics, Marvel Comics and Image Comics. She works and lives on the beach by the tropics.

CLAYTON COWLES graduated from the Joe Kubert School in 2009 and has been lettering comic books ever since. His credits include BATMAN and MISTER MIRACLE for DC, INVINCIBLE IRON MAN, DAREDEVIL, STAR WARS, and THE VISION for Marvel, and BITCH PLANET, PRETTY DEADLY, and THE WICKED + THE DIVINE for Image Comics. He lives in upstate New York with his cats.